ELIAS REBORN

TALES OF IRON AND SMOKE, BOOK 1

JOSEPH TRUITT

Fonts: Crimson Text / Garamond Bold

Illustrations and Cover Art by: Adam Neil Carter

Edited by: Haug Editing

For Holly René, my best friend forever, who, always loved my stories.

CONTENTS

ACKNOWLEDGMENTS

Many thanks, to Chautona Havig for her wisdom and guidance as an author and for not tiring of all my questions. Special thanks to Adam Carter for his fantastic illustrations on the cover art, as well as the chapter headers. Also thanks to my wife Holly and oldest son Joshua for reading the raw unedited copies. Thanks to my beta readers Christian Smith and Noah Truitt for taking the time to read the edited version before publication. Lastly, thanks so much to my editor, Christy Haug for being so kind and helpful throughout the process.

CONNECT WITH THE AUTHOR

My name is Joseph Truitt and I would like to welcome you to the Tales of Iron and Smoke book series. I'm excited to have you join me on this wonderful first tale called Elias Reborn.

For updates on this series you can sign up for my email list at Joseph A Truitt: Tales of Iron and Smoke Facebook page, and I'll send you a free Tales of Iron and Smoke gift. Those who subscribe to the email list will also be notified of giveaways, new releases, and receive updates from behind the scenes.

A simple turn of the page, will get you strapped in to the wild adventurous ride, that is Elias Reborn. I am thrilled you've chosen to journey through this epic fantasy world with me and look forward to having you join me for many more "Tales of Iron and Smoke".

PROLOGUE

THE ALCHEMIST

*S*itting on the park bench, he pinned its left wing to his leg as he admired the beauty and fragility of the butterfly. He smiled as its soft, intricately colored wings reminded him of his mother. The poor creature fluttered and tried to escape as he took hold of its other wing. A pleasantly grotesque thought crept into his mind. Only moments ago he had excused himself from the banquet to calm his anger. It should have been him that was chosen over the others. After all, it was his masterful plan that was presented, but position and pedigree was the law of the land, and he was passed over again.

His pupils grew larger as he watched the poor creature trying to wiggle out an escape. Its soft wings left a powdery residue on him as he held it tight. His heart began to pound harder and faster as he imagined it was one of the many elders of the convocation he held in his hands. He had studied the books of prophecy enough to know them better than their most learned, and yet they had denied him his rightful chance to set his own plan into motion.

He listened carefully as one of its wings began to tear free from its tiny body. He didn't want it to die but only to suffer as he was suffering at this moment. He could almost hear the poor creature's agony as he removed its other wing, but suddenly a sparrow darted in and grabbed its wingless body for a meal. A delightful grin crept up on his face and he decided that night he would flee his people's mountain and prove once and for all that he was the chosen voice of reason. Then they would listen to him. Then they would acknowledge him. Even obey him, and he would rule over them with vengeance. For if he couldn't be the whispering voice of truth; he would be the dark voice of destruction.

At that moment, the darkness took him.

WHAT CAN'T BE CURED
MUST BE ENDURED

*I*t wasn't at all how he expected to die. He'd always thought he would collapse in his father's greenhouse, impaling himself on one of the iron rods used to support some freakishly purple vines. Or fall in the mineral pit, drowning before anyone knew what had happened. He was a bit accident prone, but mostly due to his illness and not out of adolescent clumsiness.

Although, once, he did accidentally hook his jacket on the electric fence surrounding the greenhouse, but he survived with only minor burns. His shoes, however, were blown out at both ends and he lost most of his hair for a few months. For his part, he considered it the most exciting day he'd had all year.

In his weakened condition, there were so many ways he could have died, but mostly his mind wandered into the realm of the unrealistic. Such as one of his father's biogenetically engineered plants suddenly turning into a horrible man-eating beast and devouring him whole. His mother and father watching in horror as it burped up his hat. He managed a small laugh at the thought of it. But what else would you expect from someone whose only friends were plants their entire twelve years of existence.

As he lay in bed contemplating all the ways life could have ended, the muffled voices of his mother and father crept through the half open doorway into his room. They were discussing how to tell him what he already knew.

Elias was dying.

For his mother's part, she had always held out hope her brilliant husband could find a cure in time to save their son, but now, on this last day, she was distraught with grief. All hope was lost. Her son was dying, and there was nothing she could do to save him. Tears blurred Elias' eyes as he listened to her sobbing like a child. Eight long years of watching her son slowly die had finally broken her spirit. For a moment Elias thought he could hear her tear drops splashing on the floor until he noticed some rain beginning to puddle under the open window. A storm was coming.

For a moment his eyes were hypnotized by the curtains dancing in the breeze as they were pushed back and forth into his room. A gust of wind and they would push almost halfway up into the air then fall back down again. Back and forth, up and down. He wasn't sure he could feel the breeze, but the curtain show was more entertaining than staring at the wall waiting to die. Yes, it was true, he once believed his father would find a cure, but he was old enough now to know hope was only a mindset wrapped in a pretty word.

Since that fateful breath of black mist at the age of three, his heart began to die. It left him cold and pale, with an almost grayish color in his face and limbs. His immune system was so weak he'd almost never seen his parents without protective gloves. Try as they might, there was really no good way to hide something like this from him. Also not lost from his view was everything else living with a terminal disease includes. The countless gauntlet of tests, shots, blood work, drugs, herbs, vitamins and anything else that might work. Day after day, week after week, year after year, even a child can sense the abnormality of it.

The wind continued its magical breeze on the curtains, pushing them up and down, back and forth into the room. His room was located in the highest part of their tree house home and was more fitting a fairy tale princess than a young boy. However, this was by design, as his father felt the sunlight aided in his care. He didn't mind the awesome views either. The entire castle-like structure had wooden walkways leaving the complex to the east and west, then down past a coal-fired generator and into his father's greenhouse. The cedar structure creaked in the wind, but its stone foundation provided good stability.

The greenhouse was where Elias spent most of his time. Harvesting plants and replanting dead seeds fascinated him. How something could die and be reborn into the same plant all over again only stoked his imagination all the more. In there he could witness life and death over and over again. It was his own Eden, high above the creeping mold and black mist. High above the world of death and despair; where nightmares lurked in the darkness below.

Back and forth, in and out of the window, the curtains blew. He continued to watch them as he thought of all the stories his father had told him of how the creeping mold had destroyed all the vegetation, triggering a great famine. Those stories made him appreciate his greenhouse oasis all the more. *That's one thing I will definitely miss about life.*

The others living on the mountain mostly kept to themselves, only stopping by for seeds or supplies from the greenhouse. Elias never knew any of them personally because his father always made him stay inside when they came to trade. But one day a big burly man stopped by while Elias was playing in the greenhouse. He overheard the man say things like iron towers, monstrous smoky beasts and grand cities, but his father quickly sent him back inside the house.

On one of his father's many trading journeys, he returned with a dog. - Best day ever. - Sadly though, one night something pulled that dog through the fence. His father never told him exactly what happened, but that was the week they electrified the fence surrounding the property. After that Elias started naming all the plants he was responsible for and speaking to them like friends. Except the ones he ate, of course.

For a moment the wind sucked both of the curtains out the window and held them until a big gust caught one of them and flung it back into the room so high it snapped with a – CRACK – like a wet towel on the ceiling. Startled, his eyes blinked at the sound of it. He managed an ever so tiny grin at the little bit of life it brought back into him.

For his father's part, his hyper focused efforts to save his son were partly out of guilt. As he oft explained to Elias, it was his research team that, thirty years ago, thought they had found the solution to the creeping mold. In their efforts to clean it up, they caused the spores to burst open, releasing a thick layer of black mist into the air. Carried by the wind, the black mist spread the mold beyond containment. It rose 40, 50 and even 60 feet above the ground, and in some heavier, darker places the mist climbed to a staggering 80 feet. Some, such as Elias' father, fled to active volcanic regions, which were more resistant to the mold. Others, too afraid to live there, took to the highest hills in areas where the mold and mist hadn't covered, and when that failed they built cities of iron and steel high above the deadly mist. Still others took to wearing masks and living below ground.

Those who accidentally breathed in the mist were infected. It was a slow, agonizing death that damaged the heart more than anything else. His parents hoped and fought with everything they had. They fought until all options and resources had been exhausted and then they dug down deep and fought harder. They had tried everything to save their boy and he knew it. But in the world of the creeping mold and black mist, no amount of wealth or resources could save you. There was no cure.

The tops of the pine trees were now rubbing so hard outside his bedroom tower, they began to drown out the constant beep of his heart monitor. Pine trees were resistant to the creeping mold as well as the cedar and locust surrounding their mountain fortress. Most animals were never affected by the mold but starved due to a lack of vegetation. The birds and carnivores, however, thrived on what was left, including weak humans still living on the ground. Still there were other things. Things that crept in the darkest parts of the black mist covered land, but most took those for tall tales, dreamed up by fanatics, or hallucinations by those so starved they ate the mold and turned it into dark magic. Those who ate the mold, banded together in cults, and became known as Mist Speakers or Mist Charmers.

The wind had died down for a moment, as if something powerful sucked the energy out of the sky. Both curtains, now hanging limp, vibrated to the distant sounds of thunder. It was in that moment, a flash of lighting so bright it could wake the dead, that something caught his eye. Something small was standing on the window seal behind the curtain.

Could it be true? Had it returned? Another bright flash of lightning proved his eyes were not mistaken. It had been days since he had seen the creature, and now during his last moments it had returned. If only the wind could move the curtains one more time he would know for sure. What a wonderful gift it would be to see it again before his death.

High above the black mist, Elias heard his mother's desperately convincing plea to his father to search for any last second option that might save him. Truth be known he didn't need much convincing. He loved that boy and would have traded places with him if he could have.

Elias lay there watching the window, hoping for some movement or some chance so he might catch one last glimpse. His hopes were quickly dashed when his mother reentered the room. Noticing the rain on the floor, she made her way over to the open window, and after making an effort to close it, she gave up and took her chair beside his bed. She had surely frightened it away now. His heart sank as the wind picked the curtains back up into the air, revealing an empty window seal.

His mother kissed his forehead then picked up a cooled cup and sipped its contents. Even after three days without sleep, she was determined to stay awake. She didn't want to miss a single moment with her boy. Placing her hand on his, she smiled and began humming a familiar tune. The distant thunder and rhythm of the curtains mixed the enchanted tune into a magical-mind-portal, transporting Elias' thoughts back to the days before his collapse. Back to when he first saw the strange little creature.

HIS WEEK BEGAN LIKE ANY NORMAL WEEK SINCE THE DAY HE TOOK his fateful breath of black mist. Soon after waking he would unhook himself from the heart monitor leads connected to his bare chest. Ignoring the rotting smell from his diseased heart, he would stand in front of his window so the sun could warm up the tape on the connection ports. This allowed him to pull them off with less pain. If ever there was a single hair growing on his chest, it never had a chance, but it didn't stop him from checking.

Once the glue warmed, he had two options: pull them off slowly or pull them off fast and deal with it. He started slow with the one on the right and immediately it began to pull on his skin. Better to just get it over with. Taking a deep breath, "Here goes." Gritting his teeth, he pulled down hard on the first one. A short sound of tape ripping from skin and one was done. Standing in his underwear, staring out his tower window, he watched the sun rise above the black mist. It was going to be a good day. *In fact, any day is a good day if I'm still alive,* he mused.

He took hold of the other connection to follow through on his perfect method when, all of a sudden, a small red bird landed on his window seal. It was a common occurrence for a bird to land there during his morning routine, but this bird was new.

"Oh, hey little fella," he said as it bounced around on the ledge. It hopped back and forth and up and down.

"If only you were bigger. I would hop on your back and we could fly around the world. Just think of all the adventures?" That's when he saw it. The bird's eye, it wasn't normal.

A circular metal plate was attached to its right eye, and the eye was spinning like a kaleidoscope. Elias stood motionless as his heartbeat quickened in his chest. He didn't want to spook the little bird, but he wanted a closer look. He had never seen anything like it anywhere on the mountain. What kind of bird was it? Where did it come from? Two quick, blinding flashes from its strange eye and the bird hopped in the opposite direction, revealing a simple normal eye on its left side.

Disappointed, Elias remained frozen, still holding the connection port taped to his chest as he hoped to get another look at its quirky eye, but the bird stayed perfectly still. It was almost as if the little fellow was watching the greenhouse below, but Elias couldn't tell from his viewpoint. He desperately desired another look at its peculiar eye, so he began clicking his tongue on the roof of his mouth to try and entice the little guy to turn again, but he knew that never worked with birds.

His imagination began to run wild with possibilities as he conjured up thoughts of where it might have come from. Did it have an owner? Was there a whole world of little birds with bizarre eyes waiting to be discovered? Maybe the little bird belonged to a mad scientist ruling the world deep beneath the black mist. A frantic knock at his door startled him out of his imagination, causing him to jerk the taped port he was still holding about half way down.

"Elias, is everything okay?"

The little bird darted away like a bullet.

"Y-Yes, Mom, getting ready now." He glanced down at the first layer of skin the half removed port had taken with it. "Crud!" he muttered quietly under his breath. He didn't want her to come in and baby him. Most times her overprotective nurturing was more than he could bear.

"Okay. Breakfast is ready."

"What is it?"

"Scrambled eggs with honey."

"Sure thing, be right down, Mom."

Her calm voice paused for a moment. "Let me know if you need anything."

"I'm fine, Mom." He reassured her to keep her at bay. He definitely didn't want her walking in on him in his underwear. Even if he was slowly dying, he was still growing up and things were changing.

He decided a good quick pull from the bottom up might prevent any more tearing of his skin. Gritting his teeth, he gave it a good yank upwards.

"OW!" It didn't work. He grabbed the first aid kit from the top of his dresser and patched his raw skin. His chest was covered with funny scars from previous patches, and dark veins crawled across its center away from his heart. They were much darker and longer than they were a year ago and seemed to hurt more than before. After rubbing his chest with some plant root cream from his father's lab, he slid on a shirt, pulled on his work pants and laced up his boots. Then he checked his face in the mirror, cleared the crustiness out of his eyes and quickly brushed his faded brown hair.

He started to grab his tooth brush but remembered he still hadn't eaten breakfast. *Should I brush now or after,* he thought. *If I brush now I'll just have to do it again after breakfast. If I wait, I'll probably forget and not brush them at all.* "I'll wait." He hated that tooth paste anyway. Splashing some water on his face, he dried it with his shirt then made his way to a short hallway outside his bedroom.

Directly across from his door was another door leading outside his tower and onto an elevator made of cedar boards. He opened the door and the crisp smell of pine hit him so hard it felt like a pine needle poked him right up the nose. His eyes watered up a bit, then he gave his nose a pinch until the urge to sneeze left him.

In front of him was a wooden platform overlooking two shorter towers. On the platform were three ropes connected to three perfectly weighted bags of stone on the ground, which followed a rope up to a large pulley system above his head. There were also three geared levers on the platform with names carved into the handles. Elias lifted the safety bar and stepped onto the platform, then pulled the lever with his name on it. The structure jolted and creaked as it started to move.

Traveling down on the platform, Elias couldn't get the little bird out of his mind. He gazed out at the pine trees towering beside him and wondered if it might be snuggled deep inside one of them: hiding, watching, spying on him. How did it get that extraordinary flashing eye? His imagination got the best of him as questions sunk into his mind. The bag of rocks rising from the ground dripped droplets of dew as it passed him at the halfway point, then the platform jolted a bit when it finally reached the bottom; stopping right outside the kitchen.

ENTERING THE KITCHEN, HE MOVED MORE LIKE AN OLD MAN THAN a 12-year-old boy. His mother quickly pulled out a chair for him and helped him sit down then she pushed him closer to the table. He gave her a tiny scowl, which she completely ignored. Even though he was slow, he craved his independence from her help. It made him feel weaker than he already was. She loaded up a plate of fresh scrambled eggs and poured some honey over top of them.

"Thanks, Mom."

"You're welcome, dear." She kissed the top of his head and took her place at the table.

Elias quickly dove into his breakfast and took big gulps from his coffee. Milk was a luxury not many had, but thanks to his father's greenhouse, they did have plenty of coffee plants. An almost unheard of luxury for some had become a daily necessity for Elias.

The smoke filled kitchen had its own style of running water coming from rain guttering feeding a large storage tank on the roof then down into the sink on the south wall. A window over the sink allowed his mother to keep an eye on her ailing boy while he worked in the greenhouse. If he was ever out of her sight for even a moment, she came running.

On a coat hook beside an umbrella hung a faded red cap. She forced him to wear it so she could easily spot him moving about the greenhouse. It had faded so much that it was almost pink now. He hated it. Sometimes he hid from her, if only to add some excitement to her otherwise boring life.

The brick fireplace on the west wall seemed as if the bricks were placed together in a hurry, as mortar oozed out of the cracks and drooped over the top of each brick. It looked poorly made but was mostly for rustic decor. A sign hanging on the chimney titled "CASSANDRA'S KITCHEN", and single picture on the mantle seemed to indicate a happy family, despite their current circumstances.

On the north wall was a pantry filled with canned jars of tomatoes, corn, beans, spinach and just about anything else you could grow in a greenhouse. There were netted bags of garlic bulbs and oranges as well as apples and peaches hanging from all sides. The shelves on the east wall held multi-colored bottles filled with all sorts of wonderful spices, herbs, roots, coffee beans, nuts, and even sun dried persimmons. Handmade mugs and plates stocked the cabinets without doors, and several pieces of slate were mortared into place for counter tops. The wood stove in the center blushed red from the morning meal. Glass globes filled with bioluminescent plants added light from the ceiling, making it look more like a wizard's lab than a comfortable setting for family dining.

Seeing his father's empty seat, Elias jerked his head up from his eggs. "Where's Dad?"

"He's in the lab. Started early again this morning," she sipped her green concoction of herbal goo.

"Did something happen?" His thoughts immediately traveled back to the little bird with the wonky eye. "Did he find something?"

"No, dear. He's busy...you know?"

Elias quickly shoveled the eggs into his mouth, adding some more honey halfway through. Then he gulped down the rest of his coffee and squeezed his frail body out from between his chair and the table.

"Thanks, Mom." He moved as fast as possible to get out the door before she made him put on that blasted pink cap.

"Elias."

"Yeah?" his shoulders dropped.

"Your cap, please."

"But, Mom, come on. I'm practically a man now."

"No buts. Put it on."

He grunted, grabbed the cap and secured it to his head, "Yes, Mom."

CLOSING THE DOOR BEHIND HIM, HE PLACED HIS LEFT HAND ON one of the pine posts and his right on the other. Although a few of them were too far apart to grab, he used the ones he could for stability. He followed the wooden walkway until it turned left, past the groaning loose board, up a little climb and then down a steeper one towards the greenhouse. At the bottom he turned left past a large water tower with pipes entering the top of the greenhouse which carried water all the way through it.

Elias went in through the west door and passed by a small bench placed right inside the entryway for him to catch his breath if needed, but today he passed right by it and went straight into the lab located to the right of the entryway.

"Dad, what's up?"

"Elias, good, you're up." His father commented as he turned to pick up a large needle, "I need a sample from one of the veins." Elias removed his shirt without question to reveal the dark veins traveling out from the center of his chest. His father drove the needle in a little ways and pulled out a sample from the vein.

"Anything new? Any updates?"

"I think I might be on to something, if I can just figure out how to isolate the proteins from this....." Looking back up at Elias, he knew his tone wasn't as convincing as he had planned it.

Elias placed his hand on his father's shoulder, "It's okay, Dad. I know you'll find something that works."

"But, your chest... I-It's so scarred. You never flinch anymore. Doesn't it hurt?"

Elias worried the truth would cause him another setback like the one he had a year ago.

"Yeah! Oh yeah, i-it hurts. I wasn't, um; I wasn't paying attention enough to flinch. If you're on to something, then keep at it. I have plenty to keep me busy." His father gave a nod.

"Like you always say, Dad, we learn something new every

day. I know you're going to figure it out soon. I just know it."
His father's face was gaunt and pitifully worn from over work.

He looked down at the needle filled with infected blood,
"Thanks, son."

Still, he tried to pull his father back into a positive mood,
"Do you have anything for me to try today?"

"Oh, um, as a matter of fact I do." He handed Elias a glass full
of greenish liquid. In keeping with the positive vibes, Elias
chugged its gritty contents super-fast, set down the glass and
put his shirt back on. Ten seconds later it all came right back up,
covering his father in vomit.

"Ugh!" Wiping his mouth he mumbled, "Sorry, Dad, I didn't
see that coming."

"Heh, heh, oh dear." His disheveled father managed a
chuckle. "That's okay. I needed a break anyway."

"Probably so." Elias added with a smile, "I'm gonna go ahead
and get started out here and you should probably get a clean
shirt."

"Good idea," his father agreed.

ELIAS GRABBED A QUICK GLASS OF WATER AND HEADED OUT OF THE
lab into the planting area. He swished it back and forth in his
mouth and spit it onto the walkway circling the inside of the
greenhouse. Then he jumped right into his duties, checking
each plant in the garden area outside the lab to the east.

The garden was filled with corn, green beans, tomatoes,
green and red peppers, squash and the like. When he finished
there, he moved to the hydroponics room on the back wall. This
room was lit up day and night and was filled mostly with
spinach and kale. Taking out two trays of spinach and refilling
them with new ones, he checked the mineral bed and then
moved on to the "wall of berries," as he called it, on the back
wall. The eight wooden panels coming up out of the dirt were
covered up and down with blackberries, blueberries, raspber-
ries, strawberries, cloudberries and more. He bagged all the
different berries and placed them in a basket, cleared the bugs

off the cabbages and lettuce on the east wall but left the plants on the south wall alone. The hundreds of strange plants on the south wall were mostly used in his father's research, and some were dangerous.

Then, for the highlight of his day, he checked the mole traps for any dead ones and disposed of those pesky, grub-eating, dirt-diggers. The spiked trap hooked a goodly sized one, so he finished it off with a shovel and wondered if some larger traps might come in handy. He despised the moles and never had forgiven them for twisting his ankle in one of their holes. Why his mountain had to be the one with so many moles was a mystery to him.

In the center of the greenhouse was a pond filled with fish, frogs and eels, which were mostly for eating.

Past the pond was a section of fruit trees perfectly staged to prevent shading of the berries on the back wall. Elias liked to grab an apple or peach from one of the trees and sit down by the pond for a break. Today, he chose a peach.

Sitting there eating his peach, he was admiring the pond when all of a sudden the strange little bird landed right on top of his hat. Elias froze, motionless, like a statue as the creature stared back at his reflection in the water. The little bird seemed to be studying him as much as he was studying it. Ever so carefully, Elias tore off a piece of his peach and placed it on a lily pad shooting up from the water. When a frog jumped in the water it rippled causing him to lose sight of the bird for a few moments. As it cleared he could see the bird was no longer on his hat. He looked around for a moment and realized it was sitting on the lily pad eating the tiny treat. He tore another piece off and slowly placed it in front of his new friend. This bird was no stranger to people. He tried to get a closer look at its curious eye, but it almost seemed as if it were hiding it from him. After the bird tired of the peach treats, it shot straight up to an apple tree and, with two bright flashes, quickly left through a crack in the glass at the far-east corner.

That night, Elias grabbed every bird book his father had and piled them on his bed. He sat there searching, page after page and book after book, trying to find any resemblance to his feathered friend with the strange eye. When the morning sun finally rose, he found his face drool-matted to one of the pages of an open book. Placing his hand on his chest, he realized he had forgotten to hook himself up to the heart monitor last night. His breath left him for a moment as he wondered if he'd forgotten how to breathe, which caused him to sit up so fast he ripped the page right out of the book.

This was the first time since he'd been infected that he had ever slept without the monitor, but as he peeled the page from his face, he thought how nice it was to sleep without those irritating ports stuck to his chest. He smiled and closed his eyes, rubbing his hand all over his chest, enjoying the moment. When he opened his eyes, he was staring down at a half torn picture of his tiny friend. Fitting the torn page back together it read, "Red-Headed Finch," but there was no unusual eye piece on the bird in this picture. It was the right bird but the wrong eye.

He quickly jumped up, leaving his old clothes on and headed down the platform. After dodging questions from his mom about something having to do with wearing the same clothes as yesterday, he grabbed his hat and went right to work. For three straight days, Elias enjoyed the delightful show the little bird put on in the greenhouse. Darting from flower to tree, back and forth, up and down, with flash after flash every time it moved.

On the fourth day, Elias' dad was busy working on another new concoction moments after the little fella came in through his secret crack in the corner. His father must have mixed something wrong in the lab, causing a small explosion that vibrated all the windows, and in a flash the little bird was gone. His mother came bursting through the door with the first aid kit, but the only thing they needed now was something to paint more new eyebrows back on his father's singed face.

Several days passed and the creature never returned. After a short time, Elias took a turn for the worse, and he was so weak he could no longer go down to the greenhouse to check for his little friend. When he asked his mother and father if they had seen the funny bird, they took it as a hallucination due to creeping mold sickness. At that point he figured a full blown wildly-good hallucination would be a welcome change of pace from lying in his bed staring at the ceiling.

One night the light of the moon seemed stuck in the same spot on his ceiling for so long it felt like the night would never end. He decided to use all of his stored up energy from several days in bed to close the curtains, in hopes he could get some sleep. He made his way over to the window, but instead of closing the curtains, he stood there admiring the moon's reflection off the black mist below. Thinking some fresh air might do him good, he decided to open the window about half way. It got stuck at first, but then slid all the way up and made a crack noise at the top. As he stood there breathing in the fresh mountain air, he thought he saw a flash down in the greenhouse. He kept his eyes on it for a few minutes and – POP – it was a flash, then another and another. His little friend had returned and was down in the greenhouse putting on a show without him.

He slipped on his boots without tying them and made his way to the platform as fast as he could. Elias was so excited about seeing the little bird again, he accidentally grabbed the lever for his mother's weight. The platform dropped so quickly, he caught some air time before hitting the ground with a smack, launching him over the railing and right out of the platform. His adrenalin was pumping so hard, he didn't notice he had cut open his hand. No time for a scratch, he might never see the little creature again. He tripped over himself so many times he practically rolled most of the way down the ramp to the greenhouse. By the time he got to the door, he wasn't sure how he got there, but he opened it to an awesome display of flashing light. From one corner to the next, flash after flash, from tree to tree, the little bird flew flashing its magnificent eye. Elias stood there smiling at what he considered to be the greatest moment of his life.

Then, all of a sudden, the tiny flashes started coming from everywhere, until it seemed as if his head was light as a feather and thousands of little birds were blinking and flashing in the greenhouse. Back and forth, up and down—as the world began to spin, Elias began to fall.

A LOUD CRASH OF THUNDER AND ANOTHER SNAP OF THE CURTAIN on the ceiling jolted Elias out of his thoughts. His mother, still holding his hand, had stopped humming her gentle tune and began to wipe his forehead with a cloth. "It's okay, baby boy." Squeezing his hand a little tighter, "I'm still here. I'm never going to leave you." Elias smiled at her as a weird numbing feeling came over his legs. He stared out his bedroom window at the heavy rain clouds. The storm was almost here. He tried to imagine what would happen next. Would he float away on one of the clouds? Or become one and disappear into the sky? Maybe nothing but darkness and silence was waiting for him. *Where do the dead go?* Whatever awaited him on the other side of life was both exciting and terrifying. Of course, he knew none of this mattered now, for all his hopes and dreams were gone. The long awaited time had finally come.

Elias was going to die, and he wasn't ready.

2

WHERE THE DEAD GO

$\mathcal{L}$ anding just inside his open window, the little bird returned. It cocked its head left to right, up then down, as if to communicate a message. Maybe it had returned to take his spirit away, and they would forever soar on its tiny wings to distant lands far beyond the known world. Or what if his feathered messenger was trying to deliver a secret cure, but the message was lost in translation? More than likely, he was the canary in the mine, there to warn Elias of his impending doom. One thing was for certain, it had something small in its mouth, and before he knew it the little trickster had dropped it into his mother's coffee.

"Whuu?" Elias grunted in shock at what happened. He tried to get his mom's attention, but the oxygen mask on his face muffled his voice.

Thinking he was suffering, she tried to comfort him in some small way, "It's okay, you don't have to speak." She dabbed the cool rag on his forehead again.

He raised his arm and pointed at the window, but by the time she turned her head, old strange-eye had flown the coop. What did he drop in her cup, and why? She had never done anything to the little fella to make him angry. In fact, she didn't even know he existed.

Elias tried and tried to tell her something was in her drink, but all his efforts failed. As she picked up the cup and started to drink it, he mustered up some sort of last effort to speak.

"DhOoon, Don'd!" He groaned, as he made an effort to point at the cup.

"Don't worry. I'm not leaving you. Never," she said, wiping his face again.

He dropped his arm and breathed out his frustration as she finished the last of her cup. There was nothing he could do now but wait and see what would happen. Never-the-less he was determined to live long enough to make sure she was going to be okay.

She started to hum her enchanted tune once more, but soon it turned to muffled moans until, finally, her head slumped over next to his. The little peach eater had drugged his mother. Moments later the one-eyed trickster perched back on the window seal, gave two quick flashes from his quirky eye and back out he went. Elias simply didn't have the energy to deal with the sneaky little pest, so he lay there watching his mother, hoping she would be fine.

His breathing slowed. His heart beat faint. Elias started slipping in and out of consciousness. Every time he came to he checked to see if the little bird had returned. He blacked out for a moment but thought he heard something enter his room. He tried desperately to open his eyes all the way but could only get them open enough to see something large perched on the end of his bed. He could make out a shadow of something, possibly a small person. Wait, no, it couldn't be a small person. People don't have CLAWS. Maybe it was the small bird and his mind was playing tricks on him. He was angry with himself for leaving the window open. Why hadn't he closed the window sooner? He could have told his father about it when it broke, but he was too busy thinking about that bird. Now he lay there, powerless to defend his mother from a gang of feathered thugs popping in and out of his room.

Whatever was there, it was definitely gray and had a large head with big, yellow eyes staring straight at him. He closed his eyes super tight, took a deep breath and opened them again as fast as he could. This time he could see much better. He could see it for what it truly was. It was a large, gray owl perched right on the end of his bed. Again his adrenaline pumped up so quick his legs jerked, but the bird didn't flinch in the least bit. *Great! Just what I needed, another bird!*

He blacked out again, but came to once more only to see his bedroom filling with thick smoke. Thinking the black mist had finally reached the top of their mountain, Elias decided he would use every last bit of his dying strength to – close – that – window and save his mother. Closing his eyes and both fists, he psyched himself up with everything he had. With all his force he rolled himself off the bed, knocking his mother out of her chair and onto the floor in the process. He hit the floor much harder than he expected and was sure he heard something crack inside him. No matter, he was resolute, determined, mission driven to save her as he crawled toward the window.

Then it hit him right in the nose. He knew that smell, not black mist, but something else. He was about to put his finger on it when he blacked out again. He must not have blacked out all the way that time, because he was still aware of his surroundings although still unable to move or speak. Whispers filled the air though they seemed to be coming from outside his room and made no intelligible words he could understand.

Then it came to him. The smoke, it smelled like... like coal. Burning coal and something else he couldn't quite pinpoint, but he quickly lost all interest in the smells when he realized he was not alone. Someone was in the room with him, and it wasn't the owl. Not just one person but two, maybe three.

He could hear the heavy drop of their boots hitting the floor as they climbed in through the open window. BUMP! CLUMP! THUD! One after the other the heavy boots hit the floor. He could still hear the whisper in the air as well as some kind of mechanical, whirling noises coming from inside his room. Elias lay there, unable to see who had entered or even ask their names. Whatever was happening to him was beyond anything he'd ever experienced before. He could feel, smell and even taste the nauseating fumes in the air, but he couldn't move or see. He wondered if they were the ones who come for the dead and if he had already died. But wait, he wasn't dead yet! Maybe they were going to stand there and wait for him to die and then they would take him to where the dead go. *Get on with it!*

He could hear them breathing as they stood over him. What did they want, and why did they smell so strange? He didn't mind the grease and oil stench, but the dry, smoke-filled air was so thick he felt as if he might cough or gag on it. If only he could awake from his weird sleep, see their faces and ask what they wanted with him. *That's it! It's a coma!* He didn't black out, he was in a coma. He'd read about people being in a coma and still being aware of their surroundings. What a perfect time to go into a coma, he reasoned. *First time I ever have guests in my room and I fall into a coma.* As terrifying as it was, maybe it was all part of the dying process, but as he lay there helpless, he felt something wet dripping on his face. Wet and grimy and stinky, surely this wasn't part of it.

Then one of the intruders spoke. "Are you sure this is the one the boss wants?" Suddenly someone kicked Elias on the leg. "This guy's almost dead."

In his mind, Elias was angry. "WHAT! You can't go around kicking people while they're dying." If only he could come out of this coma, he would give them a piece of his mind. What kind of sick joke was this? Were these really the ones responsible for taking the dead to the afterlife? Why do they go around kicking the dying? Elias was completely and utterly disturbed by what was taking place.

Then he felt a boot on top of his forehead. It pulled on his hair as it rocked his head back and forth.

"Look at his chest, Gid, He's got the sickness."

Another person with a softer voice spoke, but with an accent he had never heard before, "He's all gray and clammy. He's never going to make it to GFC."

One with a stronger voice spoke up, "Well, he's the one Flit brought us to. He's the one in all the pictures with the greenhouse. It's got to be him."

The one with the softer voice spoke again, "He sure doesn't look like much. I can't understand what the Jackboot wants with an infected creeper, but it's hard to question someone with 27 golden hearts."

A different strong voice spoke up, "Yep, the Jackboot's always working some angle, always got a plan."

Then someone grabbed him by the shoulder and pushed him so he was lying flat on his back. They pushed up and down on him and pinched him on the chest several times. A familiar sharp sticking pain in his chest reminded him of one of his father's blood samples.

"Yea, I can fix him. Buy him at least a few weeks, maybe long enough for the boss to get what he needs. I've never done a gold mod this late in the stage, but sure, why not?"

Elias was stunned. What did they mean fix him? Weren't they there to take him to where the dead go? None of this made any sense. Did they have some cure or some way to make him better? Elias was so mad he wanted scream, but—you can't scream while you're in a coma. You can't move, you can't do anything but lay there and breathe the awful smell of burning coal.

His anger boiled in him so much it forced another burst of adrenaline, and somehow Elias partially awakened from his paralyzed state of mind. At least enough to where he could see again, and what he saw was a line of dirty, black boots on his bedroom floor. They were covered in black coal dust and dripping with rain. One of them certainly liked to kick things, because one of the boots had a circular tear in the leather, about an inch wide, with frayed ends around it revealing a shiny steel plate. Elias imagined maybe it was the boot that had kicked him. He tried to get a look at their faces, but the room was so full of smoke he wasn't able to see them clearly. As if that wasn't enough to make his current situation even more terrifying, he could see was something metal bolted on the face of one of them. At which point he decided maybe it would be better for him to just go back into the coma until this was over and he was finally dead.

A bright flash, a loud crash of thunder and the one they called Gid spoke again, "Let's get him loaded up and get out of here, or we're going to get stuck in this again." Two of them bent down and picked him up handing him through the window to two others. The rain beat down on his face as they loaded him into a strange boat with a large, almost fish-like bubble, on the top of it. He now knew the whispers he heard had not been coming from his captors, but from some kind of propeller spinning off the back of the ship.

As soon as they had him on deck, the ship jarred forward, traveling off into the sky. He thought of how his mother, lying helpless on the floor, and his father, working through the night for a cure, would never know what happened to their boy. He was grief stricken at the thought of never seeing them again. As they traveled off into the sky, he watched the soft glow of light from his window fade into the darkness of the rainy night. Whatever was happening to him now was beyond what he had ever expected.

It truly wasn't at all how he'd expected to die.

HIS COAL CHARRED CAPTORS CARRIED HIM ACROSS THE DECK OF their ship towards an open door as the rain began to pour down on them.

They'd just reached the doorway when the one they call Gid let out a shout, "WYATT! Shut down whisper mode and get us outta here!"

"You got it, Captain!"

"Merlin, save that kid or we'll all end up in the mines."

"I'm on it."

"AVA! I need help. I'm losing him!"

Merlin jumped as someone tapped him on the shoulder, "Right behind you, Victor."

"Don't call me that."

Ava smiled at him, knowing her words would irritate him. "I cleared the table and all your tools are ready."

"I'm not using the table."

"WHAT!" She seemed a bit miffed at all her wasted work.

"I have to work fast. Bogan, Izzy, put him on the floor."

They dropped Elias on the floor next to a table, in what looked like a mad scientist's lab, and Merlin immediately started shouting out all kinds of requests. The others moved quickly to accomplish them, as if they had done this many times before. "Get me eight arch injectors, eight half inch pistons, a full generator pack with gold injection and comm port access, a full gold ring, titanium mount and a glass cover."

Elias couldn't figure out much of what was happening, but for a moment he took Merlin for a little child. He was small and wore goggles with green covered lenses. A metal plate circled the top of his forehead, making it look like his bowler hat was bolted onto his head. He had on big boots that certainly didn't seem to be his size, and thick leather gloves, as did most of the others. They all wore something on their heads, but Merlin's hat seemed to be permanently attached to his. It had two holes with metal rings around them, giving the impression that two green eyes were peering through the hat. Elias couldn't quite make out what was in it. Definitely something bright and green inside the hat, but surely it wasn't what he thought he saw. It would be impossible. None of his father's books ever had anything close to people like this. Surely they were the ones who come for the dead.

Merlin continued his shouting, "Bogan, hand me the sharpest knife in my kit."

"You know mine is always sharper than anything you have."

"Good point. Sterilize it and give it to me."

Bogan dipped a small knife in a container and then handed it to Merlin.

Merlin practically hopped on top of Elias' chest and dug his knee right into the broken rib. Elias wanted to scream, but in his current frozen state all he could do was stare at the ceiling and scream inside his mind. Merlin raised the knife up to Elias' chest, but Ava grabbed his hand.

"Wait! Aren't you going to sedate him first?"

"He looks sedated enough to me. I think he's a vegetable," Bogan quipped.

Merlin didn't pay him any attention as he responded to Ava, "We don't have anything to knock him out, so we'll have to do it cold."

Bogan raised his boot above Elias' head, "Here, I can do it."

"No! We might lose him if we do that," Merlin complained. Then he looked at Elias, "Kid, I don't know if you can hear me, but if you can, I hope this doesn't hurt. If it does, just know, it's nothing personal, but I'm going to cut your chest open now."

Deep within Elias' mind all he could hear was the hollow sound of his own voice yelling, NOOOOO! Please, NO! He might have even cried out for his mother at one point, but he wasn't all-together sure.

A bright flash of lightning shot through the sky as Merlin showed Elias the finely sharpened blade. The glow was so bright, Elias found himself staring through Merlin's goggles at two of the creepiest eyes he had ever seen. Ava looked down over Merlin's weird hat to reassure Elias of their good intentions.

"We're going to save you."

Waves of chills swept through his body as the horror of what they were about to do quickly set in. Merlin brought the sharp blade down onto his chest and, looking back up at the others, he grinned. "Let's get to work."

3

WHISPER IN THE STORM

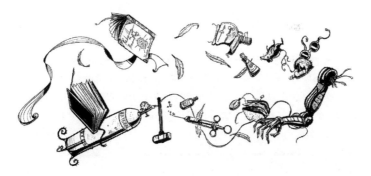

*A*lthough Elias had grown used to the pain of his father's blood draws, skin samples and shots they had done over the years, nothing could have prepared him for the pain he was now suffering at the hands of Merlin. Every flash of lighting gave him a clearer picture of his captor's faces as they stood over him watching this little freak cut his chest open. The fierce and relentless storm did its part effectively to make his nightmare even more terrifying as it pushed the ship left then right, knocking things from the shelves and beating ropes and chains against the outside of the hull. He closed his eyes and tried to imagine himself back in his greenhouse, watering the trees and the wall of berries. It would have worked, too, if not for the sound of crashing thunder all around him and the smell of burning coal and smoke filling the insides of his nostrils.

Several lighting flashes later and Elias was getting used to seeing Merlin's freaky eyes through green goggles. Now if only Merlin would get that knee off his broken rib, maybe he could think through the pain in his chest. Everything seemed to be going exactly the way they wanted until Ava's short blond hair frizzed out like a dandelion before it's blown away in the wind. She stared cross-eyed, looking up at her hair as Izzy and Bogan laughed. It was short lived. Suddenly a tiny prickling wave ran down Elias arms and across the back of his neck. "STATIC DISCHARGE!" Merlin screamed. The air crackled all around them for a moment then let out a crash of thunder that set Elias' ears ringing.

Wyatt called from the front, "GIDEON! Get up here NOW!" The sound of fear was vibrating in Wyatt's voice as the pipes on the ship crawled with tiny green electrical bolts. Gideon hurried out of the room and everyone else checked themselves to see if they were still alive.

Merlin, however, was not fazed one bit by the shocking bolt and continued to work as if he enjoyed the chaotic atmosphere. With one freaky eye squinted, and his tongue sticking out to the left of his upper lip, Merlin picked up a large rubber mallet and began to hammer small pointy things into Elias' chest. "There're eight of these, so hang in there."

Bogan, Izzy and Ava stood over Merlin as best they could with the rocking of the ship, handing him different tools and things as he began mounting his contraptions onto Elias' chest.

"WAIT! STOP," Izzy cried out!

"WHAT NOW?" Merlin complained.

"Tears, there are tears pouring out of his eyes. H-He can feel it," she said.

But Merlin was undeterred, "There's nothing we can do now; we have to finish it or he dies."

Then Izzy knelt down beside him with her soot covered face directly in front of his. Her goggles, now resting on her forehead, left white circles around her eyes, and her dark brown curls hung over each side of his face. She gently caressed his cheek with her hand and looked him in the eyes. For a moment Elias completely forgot all his pain, but then she raised her hand and pulled off her glove, revealing a horribly terrifying mechanical hand. She moved the skeletal like fingers all around and then grabbed both his cheeks and squeezed his lips to a pucker. Planting a big, wet kiss on his lips, she shook her head back and forth.

"Suck it up, cupcake. We're all freaks on this ship." She smacked Merlin on the head.

"Get on with it then."

But something strange began to happen. Immediately after

her kiss, something bitter began dissolving in Elias' mouth, dulling his pain.

Bogan shook his head at her and laughed, "You're so bad, Izzy."

Grabbing more parts, Merlin worked tirelessly hammering them into Elias chest as his goggles steamed with fog. About the time Ava started to wipe them off, the ship jerked hard left, knocking everyone over. Things on tables fell and smashed to the floor, and a large pipe overhead popped and started blasting steam everywhere.

Once again someone shouted from the front of the ship, "FLAME OUT! FLAME OUT! FLAME OUT!" sending Izzy and Bogan running out of the room as the rocking ship beat them into the walls. Merlin seemed more than a little angry as he tried to get his bearings.

"GIDEON! How am I supposed to fix this kid if you can't keep us in the air?"

AS THE SHIP BEGAN FALLING OUT OF THE SKY ELIAS FELT HIS BODY go weightless, but Merlin continued to work on him as they floated up off the floor. He tried to hammer more things into Elias chest, but the ship was dropping so fast he couldn't swing his hammer. They quickly floated apart in the air, and Ava grabbed onto a pipe overhead. She made an effort to hook Elias with her feet, but he rolled over in the air and slipped away to the other side of the ship.

Everything from an oxygen tank to goggles, glass beakers and needles, feathers and a couple of mice as well as several books, a mechanical arm and even a half-eaten sandwich floated around in the air with them. One of the books that passed by Elias' face had a picture of a half man-half machine on the front and was titled *Rebuilding the Human Body* by Hans Kloppenheimer. Another was, *101 Ways to Cook a Bird* by somebody, but it floated away before he could see who wrote it. The only one unaffected by the weightlessness was the great gray owl perched in a deep, dark corner of the room. His beady yellow eyes carefully watching the destructive madness taking place around him, although he may have merely been eyeing the two floating mice for a meal.

AFTER BOGAN AND IZZY'S BATTERED JOURNEY THROUGH THE hallway, they made their way down the ladder to the boiler room. Izzy got down fairly easily, but Bogan tumbled down the ladder and crashed to the floor after the ship rocked sideways.

Crawling her way over to the boiler, Izzy worked fast to restart the flame when suddenly a voice from a large funnel on the end of a pipe bellowed, "IZZY! WE'RE FALLING OUT OF THE SKY!" Bogan pulled himself up off the floor with one of the pipes and pulled a large gun off the wall beside him.

"OUT OF THE WAY, IZZ!"

She'd seen him pull this stunt many times before and secretly loved every bit of it, but she'd never let him know. "BOGAN!"

"MOVE IT, IZZ!"

She managed to grab a pipe overhead and pull her body up flush with the ceiling before he executed his foolish stunt. The boiler door swung wildly with the falling ship, and Bogan waited for his perfect shot. He pulled the trigger, sending an electrical spark through a clear tube on the top of the gun and BOOM! out blasted a big orange ball of fire, igniting the boiler and blowing Bogan off his feet and up against the back wall in a slump. He hit it hard enough to knock a normal person out, but not him.

The shocking blast knocked Izzy to the floor, and she crawled over and closed the boiler doors.

"BOGAN! You lunk!"

"That's how you light the boiler, IZZ! HAHAHA!"

"She's gonna rattle for a month, thanks to you."

"Don't get your goggles all steamed, she's gonna be fine. It's not her first hard start."

BACK AT THE HELM, WYATT WAS NERVOUSLY TAPPING THE pressure gauge with his finger.

"Come on, Come on; Come on!" As soon as the needle started to climb, a big smile cracked across his face, "I've got pressure, Gid! We're back in business." As the ship leveled off and started to climb, Gideon spotted a clearing in the storm.

"Good! Head southeast and get us away from this thing. We'll lose time, but at least we won't die."

"But, Gid..."

"Just do it, Wyatt!"

"Yes, sir."

ELIAS, AVA AND MERLIN CAME CRASHING BACK TO THE FLOOR AS the ship stabilized with a violent jolt. Elias dropped right next to the busted steam pipe blowing over top his open chest, but Ava and Merlin landed on the other side of the room. Before Merlin could reach Elias, a large pipe wrench snapped off its hook above him. The wrench fell right through the cloud of steam towards Elias' open chest. He closed his eyes, thinking it would all be over soon, but the gray owl swooped through the cloud of hot steam and grabbed the wrench in midair.

"CASPER!" Merlin whooped and laughed then went right back to work.

The sweat and steam from Merlin's forehead continued to drip down onto Elias' face as the small man mounted a gold ring to his chest. The sweaty, bug-eyed kid with green goggles hammered away on it, while the blonde girl peered from behind him with a smile. Then she handed him a hose he attached to the cover on Elias' chest and connected it back to a small container. A blast of hot steam blew out of the hose and Elias felt his chest tighten up. Then he blacked out.

CAPTORS OR SAVIORS: ELIAS KEPT HIS EYES CLOSED AS THE

sun came blasting through his window, hitting him right in the face. He took a few deep breaths as he lay in his bed thinking how wonderful it was the horrible nightmare was finally over. He couldn't wait to climb out of bed and do his normal routine in the sun then hurry down to the greenhouse and mentally purge this whole thing from his mind.

Except, his bed felt a little firmer than usual, and the air smelled strange in his nose, not like crisp pine needles, but... but grimy and smoky. Smoky like something burning and something else, something awfully similar to ...COAL! Just the thought of what they did to him sent chills all over his body. It couldn't be, he kept his eyes closed and slowly moved his right hand up toward his chest. He placed it below his ribs and slid it up toward the center as he had done so many times before, but this time his hand stopped.

It hit something hard and metal. It was moving, pumping and pulsing on his chest. Keeping his eyes closed, as if it would somehow make it all go away, he continued to move his hand over his chest. It was round and had small moving devices every inch or so in a circle, with a coil and hose connected to a tiny humming box on his belt. It felt hot and sounded like some kind of motor. He quickly removed his hand and put it back down at his side, then closed his eyes as tight as possible in hopes he was wrong. But a loud clanking sound, followed by a crash and laughter, shot down the hallway. He sat up in bed with his eyes wide open. It was not his bedroom.

Elias burned with anger as he jumped up out of bed in only his pants and headed down the hallway towards the laughter. Gathering his thoughts, he decided he was going to give them the full brunt of his anger, those terrible, horrifying captors who mangled his body.

He rounded the corner of the hallway in full view of an opening where several people were sitting and let blast right out of his mouth, "HOW COULD YOU DO THIS TO ME?"

They all looked over at him for a moment and gawked.

"I SAID, HOW COULD YOU DO THIS TO ME?"

Nothing, no response.

"YOU CAN'T JUST TAKE PEOPLE AWAY FROM THEIR HOME, THEIR PARENTS!"

They were sitting at a table eating breakfast, and one was standing over a broken plate of scrambled eggs and some kind of tiny meat. They hadn't moved or gotten angry or even tried to justify what they did. They simply stared back at him as if they had once stood in the same spot, filled with the same anger and confusion now overflowing from him.

The only response he got was the whispering of the engine outside, which made him even angrier, "Y-YOU'RE KIDDNAP-PERS, THIEVES A-A-And ROBBERS!"

The one with dark red sideburns spoke up, "Saved your life, mate. So we're more like.. life savers, if you ask me."

"Dream makers," said the one who had hammered on his chest.

"Risk takers," said the one standing over the broken plate.

"And heartbreakers," replied the one who'd kissed him on the lips. He didn't forget her so quickly, but that didn't stop his anger in the least bit.

"LOOK WHAT YOU DID, YOU TURNED ME INTO SOME KIND OF FREAK LIKE...LIKE...you people."

The harsh realization of a painful world glared back at him. He hadn't truly been able to see his captors during the smoke and dream like state of his paralysis. But now the fog had cleared and before him in the bright light of the morning, he could see them for what they truly were. Kids, yes strange and freaky, but for the most part young kids, older than him, maybe, but not adults.

As he stared at them, he felt the guilt of his cruel words come back at him like a weight on his shoulders. They were simply products of the harsh world they lived in. A world that chews you up, spits you out and you deal with whatever you can to survive. It was the real world outside of his perfect paradise on the mountain, and now, whether he wanted it to be or not, it was his world. He wanted to hate them but simply couldn't bring himself to it.

The kisser's face exploded with a smile. "Good morning, sunshine!"

"Come get some food, kid." Gideon's invite sounded more like a command than it did an offer, but after standing there for a few minutes he realized how hungry he was, so he sat down in an empty chair next to Gideon.

Bogan pushed out away from the table, "I'll get him a plate. We definitely don't want Wyatt getting it." They all snickered as Wyatt cleaned up the broken plate of scrambled eggs.

Ava covered her mouth quickly, as if it were about to burst open with a secret she simply couldn't hold in, and then she let it out anyway.

"OH, my! Bogan, he looks exactly like Charlie." Bogan turned around and looked at Elias so fast the eggs slid off plate and onto the floor.

Wyatt's revenge was complete as he let out a blaring laugh and pointed at Bogan. "HA!"

The dining room walls were cedar, with three round windows on one side and a table in the center. A small kitchen was located behind a wall of boards staggered like a pallet so you could see from the kitchen to the dining area. Down the center of the boards, a soft blue light traveled inside the wall, over top of the dining table and back down the other side, lighting the whole room. On the other wall was a map, fully detailing their ship with piping, electrical, engine room, boiler room, cabin areas, kitchen and the even the ships command center. On the wall to the right of Gideon were pressure gauges, iron pipes and glass pipes filled with water traveling in all directions, which Ava kept watching. Several times Elias thought he saw something moving through the water pipes, but he was too overwhelmed with everything to be sure.

Then Gideon spoke again. "I'm sure you have a lot of questions, and I'll answer them as best I can, but why don't we start with introductions. My name is Gideon and I'm the captain of the Whisper. That's the name of the ship you're on right now, The Whisper. On the wall over there is a diagram of the entire ship. If you would like to study it at some point feel free to do so."

Gideon's voice now sounded more like an older brother's than a commander's. Elias inspected each of them as Gideon's introductions continued. Gideon was the only one with metal attached to his face, and it covered most of the left side and top of his bald head. His left eye was not human even though it moved like a normal eye, but it was something more mechanical. It made small adjustments as he looked around the room and reminded Elias of the little bird leaving him to wonder where it had gone. There were pipes coming out of different areas, connecting to other parts of his face, and tiny steam bursts would release from the back every so often. He wore a beat-up leather jacket which seemed more for hiding something underneath than for comfort, and a colorful, round ball with glass squares stuck out the sleeve where his left hand should have been.

Gideon pointed at Izzy, "I'll have Izzy give you a full tour of the ship after breakfast. She's our boiler specialist, welder and all around master of metal. She knows the ship well. I think you'll be impressed with the Whisper." Her dark hanging curls bounced a little when she smiled and winked at him. They were hard to see, in fact near invisible, but tiny freckles on her nose shimmered in the blue light of the room. Her mechanical arm and fingers were not covered anymore, and he could see where it was attached, half way above her elbow. She wore leather pants with buckles going up the side, and each one had some kind of small tool in it. Her boots were the dirtiest of anyone, and they went mid-way up to her knees. Not only was she the first young girl he'd ever seen, but also the first girl he'd ever kissed, even if it was unwillingly.

Gideon's voice snapped him out of his Izzy trance, "The guy who got your eggs for you is named Bogan. He is our cook, weapon's specialist and first mate. He comes across a bit brash, but he's good to have in a pinch." Bogan had bristly red hair and thick sideburns. He was stocky but not chubby. Elias looked him up and down for any signs of metal parts, but couldn't find anything.

Bogan grinned as he sat there sharpening his knife, "Wondering where the mods are, huh? Spine and right leg, seven years ago, long story, but hey, at least I'm not as bad as him." He pointed over to Wyatt, who had finished cleaning up the shattered plate.

Bogan was obviously joking, as Gideon seemed fine with Wyatt, "Don't let his looks fool you, Wyatt's the best pilot we've ever had, and he's the one with the most mods."

"Mods?" Elias asked.

"Modifications, everyone has their own stories, but I'll leave it up to them to tell you or not," Gideon explained. For the most part, Wyatt had no arms or legs, at least no human arms or legs to speak of, but his ability to move around was astonishing. Wyatt was small for his age, but his mods made him seem bigger than he otherwise would have been. He wore dark, cutoff shorts that covered where his mod legs connected to his human legs and a shirt that said, "If I'm the pilot, whose flying?" It definitely made Elias wonder. He watched in amazement as Wyatt moved around so confidently with the mods it gave the impression Wyatt would have preferred not to be human at all.

Gideon pointed to his right, "Sitting beside me is Ava. She is also a welder, a chemist and a much better cook than Bogan." They all laughed. "She's the one who detailed the ships map on the wall and also helped Charlie redesign the ship with whisper mode." Ava looked up from her paper she was drawing on with an unusually approachable a smile. She was drawing a picture of someone, but Elias couldn't tell who. Elias didn't see any mods on her and was too afraid to ask out of fear of being embarrassed. Elias decided to divert things so he wouldn't have to know. He picked an easy-out question.

"Who's Charlie?"

Silence hit the room with a heavy blow, and all they could hear was the engine for a full 15 seconds, then Gideon spoke, "He was Bogan's older brother, and the first captain of the Whisper. We lost him more than a year ago to mold sickness."

Eating some kind of food skewered through with a spike coming out of his metal hand, Wyatt blurted out what no one was ready for yet.

"Charlie was the first golden heart-mod Merlin ever did." He pointed the skewered food at Elias, "You're the second one for the mad scientist," he said mumbling while he chewed his food.

Gideon gave him a death stare and Wyatt quickly left the room. The crew tried to laugh off the awkward moment left by Wyatt, who seemed quite skilled at making things uncomfortable. He didn't mean to, but it was merely his nature to be reactionary.

Elias wasn't sure if he truly looked like Charlie or if they were simply trying to keep his memory alive, but Wyatt's statement was puzzling to him.

What did he mean? If Charlie was fixed like me, how did he die? Didn't you cure me?"

"I'll let Merlin fill you in on the details of your mod. I'm sure you remember Merlin." Merlin was sitting at the end of the table twirling a long metal baton in his hand, as if he were a wizard about to cast a terrible spell. "He's our mods expert and doctor, but yes, as Wyatt said, he's more of a mad scientist than anything. Thanks to his father."

Elias nervously looked at Merlin and asked, "So what is my modification?"

Merlin peered through his green glasses at Elias. "We sort of fixed you. Not completely though. It's been known for some time that gold will slow the mold sickness, but there is a limited supply of gold. Not only that, but it won't exactly cure you, but it can buy you more time. The problem is, the mod eventually covers your heart in a fine golden shell, so if the mold doesn't get you, the gold will."

Merlin continued to twirl the metal baton as he explained exactly what he had done to Elias. "Some can live up to a year after the gold mod, but your condition was far too advanced for it. You might have three months or three weeks, it's hard to say. No one's ever gotten a golden mod this far into the sickness."

"So why do this for me? Why not save someone else?"

Gideon explained, "It's not our choice. Only the Jackboot decides who gets a gold mod. You must be extremely important to him. Whatever he wants you for...it's got to be something big to wast...to use this on you."

Elias shrugged off Gideon's stumbling word choice, "Who's the Jackboot?"

"He's our boss. He's also the one who gave us our mods. We were just worthless street kids until he took us in. He calls us his children, but we're really just his spies. Dark things going on in Grand Fortune City these days. I'm surprised your parents never told you about the Jackboot."

"Maybe they didn't know who he was. What does he want with me anyway?"

"We don't know yet. We were only told to bring you to him."

"So where is he?"

Bogan took a break from sharpening his blade to spice things up, "He's the ruler of Grand Fortune City. One of the greatest sky cities ever built. That's where we're headed."

"The city is in the sky?"

"Well it's more like a tower city to be honest," Gideon added.

Merlin tapped the metal baton on the table then handed the baton to Izzy who slid it into her metal arm. "I can't find anything wrong with it. I'm not sure what happened." He looked back at Elias, "You're in for a real treat if you've never seen a sky city. I nearly blow my lid every time I see em."

"Speaking of lids," Izzy said, creeping up behind Merlin and placing her hands on his hat. She gazed directly at Elias, "I'll bet you're wondering what's under this weird little hat of his?" Elias had wanted to hear more about the sky city, but her tone captured him and he was again curious about the green glow he had seen when Merlin worked on him.

She grinned at Elias and slowly lifted Merlin's hat from off his head, revealing a metal band wrapped around a clear glass dome. Inside was Merlin's brain. It was all lit up with a green glow and had blue electrical bolts jumping from four rods tapping down into a center rod with a small ball on top. Izzy wiped her human hand over the glass gently and gave it a big, long kiss. "Isn't it the most amazingly beautiful brain you've ever seen?" Merlin blushed at her admiration, but Elias almost tossed his eggs right back up onto the table. It was unlike anything he could have ever imagined.

Izzy motioned for Elias to come over and see it, but he was reluctant until Merlin said, "Yes, yes come over and see the wonderful brain in a jar." Elias jumped up and went over beside Izzy as she continued her marvel at Merlin's brain, "Look at the lightning shooting back and forth to the center ball. I call the center one the orb of lightning." She crossed her eyes and stuck her tongue out at Elias. He watched speechless at the mesmerizing display of lightning inside Merlin's brain and wondered how such things could ever be.

"You should see his brother if you like this," she said.

When Gideon had had his fill of Izzy's display of affection, he pushed her attention elsewhere. "Izzy, that's enough. Why don't you give the kid a tour of the ship? It'll help to take his mind off everything."

"SURE!" Izzy quickly changed her focus to what she considered to be the true object of her affection, the Whisper."

Ava had finally stopped drawing and jumped back into the conversation. "WAIT! Look, I'm all finished." She held up a very finely detailed picture of Elias from his waist up. "His first mod picture," she said with a smile. "Isn't he great?"

Elias was caught off guard by her kindness and didn't have the heart to tell her he hated what they had done to him. "Oh yeah, th-that's great, really nice, thank you." He reached out to take the picture, thinking she had drawn it for him, but she corrected him.

"Hey! It's not yours. This is for my book of mods."

"Oh, yeah, of course." His confusion fled away as Izzy grabbed him by the arm and pulled him out of the kitchen.

IZZY'S TOUR: "Let's start in my favorite place!" Izzy's dark brown eyes widened as she took a deep glee filled breath.

"Where's that?"

"You'll see," she said as she practically dragged him down the hallway. Pointing to her right she explained, "This is my room," but they continued on down to an open area with stairs. "Here it is." She led him down the stairs into a large room filled with pipes and a large boiler at the end of the room. The heat was unbearable, but she didn't seem to mind at all. "This is our steam boiler. We use pulverized coal hoppers for fuel to give us a better burn. Over there behind the boiler is the rear gunner," she bounced around so fast he could barely keep track of her.

"The Whisper's not a battle ship, but you have to be able to hold your own in a fight. If you know what I mean?"

"Uh, no, what do you mean?" Elias tried not to sound so naïve, but there was no way around his lack of knowledge. She gave him a half-baked look, rolled her eyes and continued to cover every area of the boiler room. While Izzy's information overload increased, he realized something. He wasn't tired anymore. For the first time in years, he felt energized, stronger and alive again.

Elias spotted a half-burnt picture lying next to the boiler. "Hey, is that…?"

"Oh, Merlin likes to burn trash in the boiler. It's probably something from one of his old books." Izzy quickly picked it up, opened the fire door on the boiler and tossed the scrap into the flames.

"Okay, so that's it for the best room on the whole ship. Any questions?"

"Uh, no. I got it I think," Elias wondered if she was hiding something, but her personality was so bubbly he couldn't tell for sure. She was the most alive person he'd ever seen.

"You okay?" she cocked her head.

"Um, yeah, yeah, I'm good."

"Good! Now, on to the whisper room," She took him back up the stairs and down the hall to the back of the ship. On the far back wall, an enormous aquarium allowed a clear view of the propeller spinning behind the ship. There was also a wheel with blades which connected to the aquarium with tubes of water running back into a large tank. The tubes also traveled through the rest of the ship but didn't seem to have much purpose beyond that.

"This is our world famous whisper system. No other ship has anything like it and it's why we get picked for the sneaky jobs," she boasted.

"What makes it so quiet?"

Izzy grabbed a pipe with a funnel on the end and called for Wyatt. "HEY, WYATT! Switch us to whisper mode."

"You got it," a voice echoed back out of the tube.

Elias stood there waiting for something amazing, but the

water was still, no movement, nothing. "Is it supposed to do something?"

"Give it a moment. Don't be so impatient." She looked at him with stern eyes and then quickly changed her mind. "I'm just kidding." She rolled her eyes, "They can be really slow sometimes."

Elias didn't know who she was talking about, "You mean Wyatt?"

"No, silly, those guys."

Suddenly an octopus shot through one of the tubes into the tank and another and another and finally one more. Four of them in total, with helmets mounted on their heads. Clearly something dreamed up by Merlin, and they went right to work swimming out of the tank and through the inside of a glass tube inside a shorter propeller wheel. They shot through the propeller tube back into the tank one after the other, faster and faster, until the wheel started to spin. A tiny bubbling noise could be heard as they passed through the tubes sounding like someone whispering in your ear. Once the ship was in whisper mode, all their prey would hear was a whisper on the wind.

"It's amazing. Do they have names?"

"Those guys? I just call them One, Two, Three and Four, but I think Ava has more personal names for them. She's the one who feeds them the geese that get caught in the propellers. They're kind of her babies."

"I didn't think anything like this was possible."

"And that's exactly the way we want it. You're here-by sworn to secrecy. You can never tell anyone about this, or Merlin will turn you into a toad."

"WHAT!? REALLY? He can do that?"

"No, not really, but Gideon would probably snap your neck if you did."

"Oh, okay, I won't tell, promise."

"Good! So that's the whisper system, and you've seen the boiler room, and you've already seen the kitchen, and I'm guessing you probably don't want to go back in Merlin's lab anytime soon, so that leaves the command and flight control rooms. Oh yeah, and the restroom is right behind you. The one on the other side is mine and Ava's. DON'T EVER USE OUR RESTROOM! GOT IT?"

"No. Never. I-I wouldn't think of it."

She muttered something under her breath about Wyatt and then said, "Good. Let's head up front. You're going to want to see this."

Elias followed her down the hallway and through the control center area.

"This is where we plan all of our jobs and work out the details of whatever task we're given." On the wall were pictures of Elias' greenhouse and the mountain where he lived. There were also pictures of him taking connection ports off his chest and even one of him lying face down on the greenhouse floor. Elias wanted to ask about the red-headed finch with the strange eye, but he was so overwhelmed he kept forgetting.

"As you can see," she pointed out, "you're our project this time." Remorse was in the tone of her voice then she cracked a half smiled and winked at him.

"If I was your project this time, what was your project before me?" he asked.

"The Jackboot had us looking from someone called the Alchemist, but every clue was one dead end after another. He gave up and suddenly sent us here to get you," she seemed uneasy about all his questioning and put an end to it. "Moving on," she said with a smile.

She took him to the next room where Wyatt and Gideon were. The room had two glass window walls going about 20 feet in the air and coming to a point like an arrow. He could see far out over the flight deck in front of the ship, and the view was nothing but sky and clouds in front of them. It was more amazing than all the other areas on the ship from Elias' viewpoint.

Gideon was staring at a map on the back wall and plotting their course back to GFC. Wyatt was sitting in a round glass ball with openings on each side that was connected at the top with a pipe of some sort. There was a circle on the floor below him and one on the ceiling above him, as if the glass ball could travel throughout the ship. Izzy explained some of the different things going on, but Elias' brain was so full at that point he wasn't fully retaining anything anymore. Izzy smacked her hand on the glass ball, "You can shut down whisper mode. We're done back there."

Wyatt pulled a lever, turned a small wheel and moments later the creatures returned to the bridge through the larger clear water tube on the back wall. Directly in front of Wyatt's cockpit was a tubular water tank rising out of the floor with a more traditional ships helm control than what Wyatt had in his pilot's chair. A trapped bubble circled the rounded off tube at the top.

Wyatt was quick to point out how cool the flight center was to Elias. "Best room on the ship huh, kid? I don't have time today, but if you stop in and see me tomorrow I'll show you how this all works. Maybe even let you take the controls."

Izzy was bit unnerved by Wyatt's harebrained idea. "Wyatt! He never even knew what an air ship was until this morning, and you're going to just hand the Whisper over to him. You're cracked!"

"Just cause you named the ship doesn't mean it's yours Izzy." Wyatt scoffed, but Izzy bit down hard on her tongue. She didn't trust Wyatt enough to tell him secrets.

"Whispers." Wyatt's mod finger circled the side of his head while Izzy looked like she was about to rip off his arm and beat him senseless with it.

Wyatt continued his chastising of Izzy, but Elias couldn't seem to take his eyes off the sky. When he spotted the gray owl perched out on the flight deck he asked, "Can we go out there?"

"Sure!" Izzy jumped at the chance to get away from Wyatt.

"The gray owl, is he friendly?"

"Casper? He keeps to himself most of the time, but personally, I think it's kind of creepy how he's always staring out into the distance as if he knows some deep, dark secret."

"Casper, huh? Is he Merlin's bird?" Elias asked.

"HA! No. Casper doesn't belong to anyone. In fact, we don't really know much about him other than he showed up not long after Charlie, and he's been here ever since."

They headed out the side door and walked down the flight deck toward the gray bird.

"Can I thank him for saving my life last night?" Elias was unaware he'd slept for three days.

"Don't you mean a few days ago?"

"Oh."

"Well, you might want to rethink giving him a hand shake or a hug. Maybe a wave would do fine, but even that might be pushing it."

"Why?"

"He's the only bird I know with a bounty on his head."

"What do you mean?" I mean, why?" he changed his wording trying not to sound so clueless.

"He plucked out the Jackboot's left eye with his beak," her eyebrows popped up.

But Elias was unfazed by her warning and seemed determined to acknowledge the bird in some way. So they walked out to the far end of the deck, closer and closer, towards the great gray owl who sat gazing out into the sky, until they were so close they could almost reach out and touch him. Maybe even too close.

- 4 -

THE OWL
AND THE DARKNESS

*I*zzy and Elias stopped dead in their tracks as Casper turned his head all the way around, warning them with his yellow, soul-piercing eyes. Elias thought he was about to have his second mod that evening as Casper raised both wings halfway up, as if to attack, but simply adjusted them and pulled them back down. The sheer size of the bird was now fully evident this close up. His claws gripping the railing were about the size of a dinner plate, and he was every bit as large as Merlin.

"H-He's so big," whispered Elias.

Tilting her head, she whispered back, "Some birds got bigger over the years since the black mist came, but the predator birds grew the biggest."

"Can I say something to him?" Elias quietly asked.

"Sure. Just don't make him angry."

Elias looked at Casper; their eyes met for a moment.

"Thank you for saving me," he gently offered.

The bird did not respond in anyway noticeable that would indicate it understood him. Casper looked down at Elias' heart pumping through the glass cover, watched it for a moment and then turned his head back around at the horizon.

Izzy raised her mod-hand in front of Elias' face, shaped it like a beak and in a high pitched voice said, "You're welcome, Elias!"

Elias grinned slightly, "I guess I deserved that."

"Considering the way he was looking at your heart like a meat snack, you might want to put a shirt on. Speaking of meat, I'm starving, and it smells like Bogan is cooking up some propeller goose."

"Propeller goose?" Elias asked curiously.

A wickedly delicious smile crept across her face as she explained. "The geese always fly into the propellers when we're in whisper mode, so Bogan hooked up a net to catch them after they get thumped. We all took to calling it propeller goose. It's fantastic and really FRESH!"

DINNER THAT NIGHT WAS FILLED WITH LAUGHTER AND INTRIGUE as his captor's told of their most thrilling adventures. They described wonderful cities towering high above the black mist and the most magnificent air ships to ever sail the skies. They told tales of great sky battles and Mod Hero's Elias never could have imagined existed before today, as well as people who built some of the greatest steam powered machines. The bond he felt with his captor's that night was something he had never known. As he watched them toast their successes and laugh at their failures, he decided they were much better friends than plants could ever be.

A sad reminder of the loss of Charlie brought dinner to a close. Merlin and Bogan offered to share a room with Elias, but in the end he chose Bogan. Although he was warned about Bogan talking in his sleep, he preferred that to the ghoulish green glow of Merlin's brain. However, it wasn't too long after Bogan fell asleep that Elias began to regret his decision. Bogan's sleep talking was more like night terrors having something to do with how he lost his leg. They were disturbingly painful to hear, and Elias felt sorry for Bogan from then on. He wondered if the loss of Bogan's leg was what made him so ill-tempered.

Sleep that night was more elusive than ever as the clear night sky passed by through his round window. It wasn't merely the mattress spring poking him in the back, or the hum of his coal generator protecting his heart, or even Bogan's horrible muttering causing his trouble. It was everything. The new reality of his condition was weighing heavy on him. He had only recently accepted his coming death, and now someone brought him back to face it all over again. The only thing keeping him going now was the possibility he could live long enough to see his parents again. Why was he so important to this Jackboot person? What could he ever offer him? Elias didn't know if he should be angry or excited with his new circumstances. Either way he'd had it with laying there listening to Bogan and decided some fresh air would do him some good.

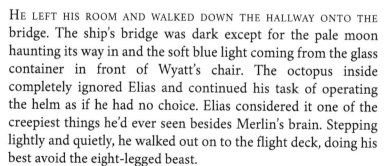

HE LEFT HIS ROOM AND WALKED DOWN THE HALLWAY ONTO THE bridge. The ship's bridge was dark except for the pale moon haunting its way in and the soft blue light coming from the glass container in front of Wyatt's chair. The octopus inside completely ignored Elias and continued his task of operating the helm as if he had no choice. Elias considered it one of the creepiest things he'd ever seen besides Merlin's brain. Stepping lightly and quietly, he walked out on to the flight deck, doing his best avoid the eight-legged beast.

The crisp night air chilled his eyes enough to make them water as he walked to the front of the long spear-shaped deck. His heart generator gave a jolt, forcing him to take a deep breath of cold night air, but it made him feel more alive than ever. Staring out over the world under the stars, he realized this day had been one of the greatest he'd ever experienced. The thought of even one more like it might make the pain of dying all over again a worthwhile venture.

At that moment he felt as if the world itself were created only for him. None of the books in his father's library could have ever prepared him for what he had experienced so far. The world had changed so far beyond the old world that it had become an entirely new one, at least to him, anyway. He'd been given a second chance at life by someone he didn't even know, and for the first time ever he felt he had a purpose. So he made a promise to himself that night as he sailed high above the black mist, that he would live each day to its fullest, even if it was his last.

Standing out on the deck of the Whisper, pondering his life, he hadn't noticed Casper had landed not far from him on the railing. He was facing out away from Elias, staring down into the black mist, so Elias walked towards him slowly, not wanting to startle him. He didn't want to lose an eye this early into his second lease on life.

Once he got close enough, he swallowed hard and called out to the bird, "Casper." The owl gave no response but seemed to be eating something small. Elias moved in for a closer look when Casper suddenly turned and looked directly at Elias. His eyes were no longer bright yellow but were a deep red, as if they were on fire, and he let out an ear piercing - SCREETCH - so loud it echoed through the sky. It startled Elias so much he stepped back onto the bottom railing and almost fell over the side. Then the great bird spread his wings and dove down into the black mist below.

Grabbing the railing, Elias leaned over and peered hard into the mist to see if he could spot the great owl, but the moonlight bouncing off the surface of the mist dulled his view. Then a – SCREETCH – came from the other side of the ship. Elias ran over and spotted Casper above the mist, chasing something through the air. Something with a long tail, maybe another bird carrying something in its mouth, but whatever it was, it was terrified of Casper. It wasn't long before the owl was on top of it and clamped his beak down on its neck. The creature gave a loud – SQUEAL – and a popping, cracking sound echoed on the wind. Casper swooped up onto the deck and began tearing at it for a moment with his claws then swallowed it whole. The bird turned his flaming gaze back toward Elias for merely a second. Spread his wings to the fullest and, with a few flaps, he dove again back down into the black mist.

Elias stood on the deck waiting for some sign of Casper's return when something in the air changed, sending a shivering, hair-lifting chill up his neck. A dark voice rose up through the mist as heavy shadows fell over the ship. The shadows were so dark even the light of the moon fled away. The whispering sounds from the ship were swallowed up by the voice as it grew louder and louder. It said no words he could understand. He only knew that it wanted him to obey. Elias placed his hands over his ears thinking that would stop it, but it seemed to grow stronger until a pain in his heart buckled his knees to the deck. Then, as quickly as the voice began, it abruptly stopped. The whispering from the ship filled the air again, and Elias pulled himself to his feet with the railing.

The experience left him unsettled, and he decided maybe it was time to head back inside. Still no sign of Casper, but as he headed back towards the door he felt a tickle on his neck. He reached back and felt, but nothing was there so he continued toward the door a little faster. Once more he felt the tickle, combined with a scratch this time, but again he reached back and felt nothing. He stopped for a moment and turned around swiftly, but nothing was there. Continuing his path to the door even a bit faster he suddenly felt it again, and this time when he reached back as fast as he could, his hand hit something round and slithering. As he tried to pull it off, it grabbed his hand and coiled around it, then up his arm and around his neck.

Elias pulled as hard as he could, but it only coiled tighter and tighter around his neck, stealing his breath away. Every breath he took the creature took advantage and coiled harder, until Elias grew faint and dizzy. It was the same dizzying sensation from the night in the greenhouse with the little bird, and it dropped him to his knees. Then the creature swung its head around in front of him for the kill. It had a large, serpent-like head and wings like a bat with fangs longer than its mouth could hold. Something clear and slimy dripped from its pale white teeth onto the deck as its mouth opened wide enough to swallow his head whole, and a terrible smell of mold reeked from the pit of its throat. It stared directly at his heart through the glass as if it were an easy start to a meal.

Was this truly how his life would end? This wasn't at all how he expected to die. To be saved by his captors and given a second chance, only to have it stolen away by a flying serpent. Never to know why he was saved or what the Jackboot wanted with him. If only he'd stayed in bed. He was angry at himself for letting his curiosity get him into yet another mess. He punched and pulled at the creature, harder and harder, with everything he could muster, but it was too strong. The serpent grabbed and coiled and tightened every chance it could and wouldn't let him take a single breath. So, again, Elias readied his thoughts for death.

As darkness closed in around his eyes, a familiar sound echoed through the sky. A terrifying – SCREETCH – rang out, so piercing the creature loosened its grip for a second and turned its deadly mouth around. Casper was in full attack mode as he swooped over the railing with blazing eyes of fire, feet first, wings full and talons out for death. Out for blood! The white moonlight flashed off the serpent's dripping fangs as it reared its head back for battle, but it was no match for the great gray. With surgical precision, Casper dug his claws into the serpent's head, sending it limp around Elias' neck. It uncoiled and slid down the front of his chest onto the deck, and Casper dragged it away.

Elias immediately collapsed on his back, holding his neck and gasping for breath. He watched as Casper began tearing the serpent to pieces, but this time he didn't eat it. This time he turned around and kicked it off the side of the deck like a piece of worthless trash. Elias laid there for a moment, watching, as he caught his breath. Then, holding his throat, he got to his feet and with a raspy, "Thank you," limped his way back inside the ship, closed the door and locked it. He looked back out the large windows as the great owl perched back on the railing and stared back into the abyss below.

The creepy, zombified octopus continued his task of flying the ship as if everything he witnessed never happened. Elias walked over and stood in front of the tentacled beast for a moment and waved his hand in front of its face. "Some help you were," he said sarcastically, then headed back down the hallway.

After a quick stop at the restroom, he splashed some water on his face and neck to ease the soreness of the attack. Looking at his chest, he noticed the dark veins from the mold sickness had receded a bit, and his chest looked much better than it had in a long time. The poor lighting made him look even worse than he did before his modification even though he had gained some color back in his skin. He felt fairly good about his new condition until a tiny flash in the mirror revealed his first gold spec had formed on part of his heart. It was a strange sight to see himself in the mirror with the mod on his chest, pumping and heating the gold coil on his heart. It was working, but clearly the cost for his extended life was already self-evident.

Elias returned to his bed. The broken spring creaked as he lay down, and he realized the room was quiet. Bogan was no longer muttering.

"Where you been?" Bogan asked.

Trying not to cause a panic about the winged serpent attack, he kept his words calm. "Just getting some fresh air,"

"Well, don't go outside. That's how people disappear."

"Oh, really? Thanks, I'm glad you told me," he rolled his eyes in the dark.

"Yeah. Okay, good night," Bogan yawned and stretched out his legs.

"Um, do Casper's eyes change color at night?"

"Not that I know of, why?"

"Oh…Um…no reason…good night, Bogan," Realizing there was more to Casper than even his captors knew, Elias decided to keep the matter to himself for the time being.

HE WAS SURPRISED TO WAKE UP THE NEXT MORNING IN MERLIN'S lab with the whole crew standing around him. Bogan was the first to speak with a concerned tone in his voice, "You doing okay, little buddy?"

"Yeah, sure, what's going on?"

"You almost died last night. That's what," Gideon said.

Elias quickly sat up on the table, "WHAT!?"

Merlin's green eyes popped out from behind Izzy, "I probably didn't explain the importance of keeping your generator fueled, but honestly I never thought you would burn through three days' worth that fast. What were you doing last night? Jogging?"

The crew quickly laughed it off, but Elias was shaken that something so simple could have ended his life. He managed a slight grin but said nothing of his encounter with the serpent, for fear being accused of endangering their ship. Although Merlin's guilty tone for his poor communication was evident, his corrective measures were partly to make up for that mistake.

"I took the time to add a few things to your mod. One of them will allow you to plug directly into the ship at night for some peace of mind while sleeping. It also has a reversing switch that will allow you to reverse that action and generate power independently to control some of the ships equipment. It's something new Wyatt has always wanted, but honestly he doesn't have room for it on his system. Oh yeah, I also installed a low fuel alarm in case you forget to refill. It should give you enough time to refill before cardiac arrest," Merlin explained.

Gideon redirected the uncomfortable moment for Merlin by pointing to the coming task at hand and their preparations for docking at GFC. "Ava get him some clothes and have him meet us up front in the command room. We'll be discussing our arrival at GFC today, and I want to make sure the ship is ready for evasive maneuvering."

"WHAT?" Izzy suddenly blurted out as she noticed her metal baton in Elias hand. He had no idea how it got there, but she seemed upset by it. "This is the second time! When I find out who is playing tricks on me they're going to get." She said looking at Bogan, who shrugged his shoulders at her.

"It wasn't me. Honest!" Bogan said as Izzy walked out scoffing at him.

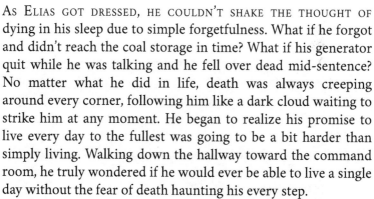

As Elias got dressed, he couldn't shake the thought of dying in his sleep due to simple forgetfulness. What if he forgot and didn't reach the coal storage in time? What if his generator quit while he was talking and he fell over dead mid-sentence? No matter what he did in life, death was always creeping around every corner, following him like a dark cloud waiting to strike him at any moment. He began to realize his promise to live every day to the fullest was going to be a bit harder than simply living. Walking down the hallway toward the command room, he truly wondered if he would ever be able to live a single day without the fear of death haunting his every step.

He didn't say a word as he entered the command room and saw the empty chair. The room was quiet for a moment. No one had sat in that chair since Charlie, but it was the only one left. Ava looked as if she wanted to say something but kept quiet. It was also the first time he'd worn a shirt since his heart-mod was installed, and although it was still noticeable, he felt a sense of normalcy with clothing on. Ava had given him Charlie's leather jacket, and it helped him feel as if he was already part of their close-knit family. Charlie's jacket was unique in that it was made especially for someone with a heart-mod, and it had a convenient option for the generator exhaust port that mounted to his shoulder. With a nod of approval from Gideon, Elias pulled out the chair and sat down.

The meeting began with Gideon removing the round ball from his hand and placing it on the table. It projected a large holographic map above the table as he pointed out their docking options. "The Jackboot wants this to be as discreet as possible, but no matter what we do somehow word always gets out, so we need to be prepared," Gideon said as if he had rehearsed his words. He had been Charlie's second-in-command, and he'd never liked the idea of commanding the ship, even if he did have a reputation for questioning Charlie's leadership decisions. However, from Elias' perspective, Gideon seemed extremely good at it, and it was obvious he knew how to bring the crew together.

Gideon continued, "I don't anticipate any problems, but the Jackboot has many enemies. So, even though his guards will be looking for us, we still need to be vigilant. I want everyone armed except Elias, who can assist Wyatt with docking the ship." Elias got the feeling Wyatt was being forced to babysit him while everyone else watched for real problems. Wyatt's wink and finger snapped guns didn't make him feel any better about it. "Maybe I'll even let you bring her into the dock," Wyatt quipped, and Izzy rolled her eyes at him.

After a few more directions from Gideon about snipers and possible hijackers, Elias began to wonder what was so "grand" about Grand Fortune City. Then Gideon snapped his glass globe back into place and said, "Okay, we're about 30 minutes out, so no mistakes today. Let's keep things tight and right all the way into the docks."

With an, "Oorah!" shout, they all quickly left the room to cover their responsibilities, and Elias followed Wyatt to the bridge.

Wyatt stepped into the large, sphere-shaped cockpit and sat down in the pilot's seat. He disengaged the whisper mode and the octopus quickly released his grip on the helm and dropped back down its watery tube. Almost immediately, Wyatt began to boast of his responsibilities. "This is where all the real action takes place. Watch this." He placed both feet on the floor controls and his hands on the two sticks mounted on the chair. "Climb in. Let me show you what this baby can do," Wyatt smirked.

Elias climbed into the glass sphere, and Wyatt flicked several of the buttons, closing the doors to the sphere and opening a hole in the ceiling above them. "Hold on tight," Wyatt warned. Hot air rushed down through the hole momentarily as the flexible pole quickly pulled the chair up inside the ship's envelope, placing them perfectly inside a clear glass dome. The dome at the top allowed them to see in every direction above the ship, even down on the forward deck below. Wyatt boasted as if he designed this part of the ship, but Elias knew better. "I can maneuver this baby any which way I need to with this set up."

He hit a few more buttons, pulled a different lever and the hole below opened up again, taking them back down to the bridge. "Hold on, I've got one more trick," Wyatt said as he continued his incredible display. He pushed a few more buttons, pulled another lever and the floor below opened up and dropped them down into another glass dome below the ship's hull. From there the black mist traveled like waves below them as they sailed through the sky.

"Closest you'll ever get to flying like a bird!" Wyatt bragged as the wind roared around them.

"It's amazing!" Elias hollered back. Wyatt seemed so proud of his ability to impress that he unbuckled his belt and climbed out of his seat.

"HERE! Jump in and give it a try!"

Elias was instantly caught off guard, "WHAT! No! I-I don't know how to fly."

"Come on. Don't be a chicken! Besides, we'll crash if you don't do it soon."

Horrified by Wyatt's carelessness, he jumped in the seat and took the controls. He flew for a while until Wyatt saw that he was doing exceptionally well and having a bit too much fun. "Okay! Alright there, Maverick, you can get out now. We'll be arriving at GFC soon. We better get back top side." Elias climbed out of the pilot's chair and Wyatt took back the controls. He engaged the levers and the ball headed back up into the ship.

On the way back topside, Wyatt asked with a gleam in his eye, "So what do you think about Ava?"

"Oh, she's nice," Elias said, misunderstanding Wyatt's leading.

"No, dude, what do you think? You know? She's HOT, right?"

"Really? What's wrong? I hope she's okay." Elias grew worried.

"No. Come on, dude. She's, like, the hottest chick in GFC."

"I don't, um. I'm not sure what...." Elias was even more flabbergasted by Wyatt.

"NOT SURE! Dude, you need some serious help." Seeming somewhat angry and confused, Wyatt dropped the topic of Ava as they stopped at the bridge.

Gideon was waiting for them and motioned for Elias to step out onto the forward deck with him. "We're approaching the city. I thought you might want to see if from here since it's your first time." Elias was so filled with anticipation he thought his stomach would flip right out of his mouth and onto the deck. He noticed the sky growing darker and darker the closer they got towards the city and felt it was at least worth asking about. "Is it black mist?"

"No. Coal dust and smoke," Gideon replied. "The coal mine that powers most of GFC is located on the ground. Mining the coal, combined with burning it for power, creates some nasty air. The steam ships and iron weavers contribute to it as well, but the heat helps keep the creeping mold away."

"Iron weavers?" Elias asked confused at how they would weave iron.

"We call them iron weavers here at GFC because they're so good at welding iron."

Suddenly a voice came from the top of the ship. Elias turned around and spotted Wyatt guiding the ship from the upper dome. "GIDEON! Cruiser moving in fast, port side!"

"Is it a Jackboot ship?"

"Can't tell. It's moving too fast, but we'll know soon enough." Wyatt replied.

"This could get ugly, kid," Gideon warned as he flipped a switch on the round globe attached to his arm. A hole opened up on the end of it, and it began to make a low humming sound. "Take cover!"

5

GRAND FORTUNE CITY

*W*ithin seconds the cruiser was right next to them. Shaped like a sideways wheel, it moved much faster and louder than the Whisper, and black smoke trailed behind it. The pilot pulled up next to them, his face staring down the barrel of Gideon's weapon as the cruiser hovered alongside the Whisper. "There's an ambush waiting for you at the docks. The Jackboot himself sent me to bring you through his private entrance," he said as he pulled a gear-shaped emblem out from under his jacket. "I carry his seal as proof." Gideon inspected it for a moment, then motioned for Wyatt to follow the speeder.

The pilot turned hard left and Wyatt followed him. Gideon walked over to Elias, "I'm sorry you won't be able to see the city today, but you will be able to see the coal mine. Let's get back inside and mask up. We're going below."

Gideon called out too Wyatt, "MASKS!" and they followed the speeder down towards the black mist. Elias was still thrilled to see something new. Although, he felt silly putting the mask on, considering he had already been exposed, he figured it was best not to defy Gideon.

Wyatt's movable cockpit dropped back down on the bridge, and the ship descended so fast Elias felt his feet lift up inside his boots. "Hold your lunch!" Wyatt cracked. Even Gideon grabbed a handle on the ship's wall near the glass windows as they followed the speeder into the ocean of mist. Dark gray puffs clouded their view, but Wyatt followed the speeder's every move as if he had done it before.

Suddenly the mist turned black as night, and the sounds of iron clacking and steel banging rang through the air. The mist fully cleared over a giant hole below them, revealing a massive coal mine operation. Yellowish lights speckled the ground and blinked in and out of view as bright blue ones splattered a half-mile-wide tower rising out of the center of the pit. Strange machines with round wheels were grinding, drilling, turning and dumping coal into containers that disappeared into the bottom of the tower. Pockets of steam popped, filling the air with a putrid rotten egg smell that would have choked them without their masks. Every now and then Elias thought he heard a scream, but it was hard to tell with all the noise.

Gideon's mask muffling his voice set a freakish tone to Elias' guided tour of the dark underworld of GFC. "The little yellow lights are miner's hats and the larger ones are mining bots. The heavy, acidic air rusts the tower metal, so the blue lights hanging on the tower are welders doing tower maintenance. Make sure you don't look directly at the welding flash. It's ten times brighter than the sun and could blind you." Elias' heart jumped as he jerked his eyes away from the tower but not before noticing giant spears, longer than the Whisper, mounted on its walls.

"What are the spears for?" Elias asked.

"In case the miners hit a mole tunnel," Gideon explained.

"Aren't those a bit big for moles?"

"They have really big moles."

Elias' mask-covered chuckle sounded sinister as he wondered if Gideon was joking.

"Big enough to eat a man in one bite," Wyatt boasted.

"And claws that could crush the Whisper," Bogan said as he entered the bridge with a large gun slung over his shoulder. Izzy and Ava followed soon after and the Whisper climbed back into the air behind the speeder. A few moments later Merlin entered, nursing a scratch on his arm from locking up Casper.

The speeder came to a stop right under the city's circular base. Bogan tossed a thick rope around an iron hook, and the speeder pilot knocked on the tower. A small square opened and closed then steam shot out from two tiny holes; seemingly out of nowhere, a door opened up in front of them. Then a long telescopic walkway tracked out to the Whisper, and a sharp dressed bald man stepped out. "Come with me," he said.

They followed the man through the door and up a circular iron stair case lit with tubular gas lights. A long pole traveling down the center of the stairs looked like a fast get-a-way to the bottom, and Elias figured that was exactly its purpose. After climbing for several minutes, he imagined the satisfaction of sliding down on the return trip. Quietly hoping in his mind, he might live long enough to return to the Whisper.

They continued their climb to a growing, muffled *boom* sound, until it began to overpower the clacking of their boots up the stairs. They climbed for so long Elias feared he would run out of fuel before they reached the top, so he checked his fuel gage every time Bogan stopped to adjust his mod-leg. The gas lighting gave an eerie feel to the hot, damp climb as everyone's shadow stretched up its circular walls like nightmare creatures about to devour him. His imagination began to fill with dark things as they climbed.

When they reached the top, the bald man pulled a lever and turned a wheel on the wall. He kept turning the wheel until a crack of light grew larger and larger and a wall rumbled open. Elias' palms were already covered in nervous sweat at the prospect of meeting the Jackboot, and the heavy **BOOM** vibrating through the hand rail wasn't helping much either. The stench of their hard climb was evident, and they could see the light of their salvation for fresher air growing larger with every turn of the wheel.

Stepping into the large, bright room, their guide pushed his finger inside a faceless statue's nose, and a well-stocked book-shelf slid closed behind them. It was a marvelous room and looked as if a library had been stolen out of the old world and dropped into a train station. A set of railway tracks appeared from the bottom of one wall and traveled all the way to an enormous glass wall at the other end. There before him on the tracks sat a fantastically monstrous black locomotive with four cars attached to it. The last car was sitting outside an opening in the glass wall, as if it were suspended in mid-air, and the **BOOM** rocked the cars sideways on the tracks.

Someone inside seemed extremely agitated, as their voice echoed throughout the cavernous literary train station. "Yes, I know—I know...yes it is...I know it's a filthy habit, Edgar. I don't need you to tell me that." Their well-groomed librarian kept walking toward the train, but Elias and the crew stood there admiring the iron bull head fixed on the front of the engine. Its two golden horns charging forward as if they were about to spear through the wall and jutting out of its mouth a large harpoon rattled with each **BOOM**. On the side of the engine were red letters, and a red stripe pointed the way to the last car. The letters read, IRON WEAVER.

BOOM! "OH what gloriously nasty habit! Hand me another one, Edgar." The voice shouted as a ting of glass cracking the arch shaped ceiling above them, unfroze their feet from the concrete and they made for the safety of the first car.

Izzy was the only one smiling as she leaned over to whisper in Elias' ear. "The Jack has killed 30 moles with the Weaver's harpoon." Her excitement eased his mind a bit from the troubled faces of everyone else.

At the entrance to the first car the man stopped, turned around and delivered his instructions with a graveled voice. "He's down in the last car, but be mindful, he's in rare form today, so don't touch anything in the cars, and whatever you do don't mention the scuff on his lapel." **BOOM!** The man jumped only small bit, as if he were used to the noise. The voice from the far end of the train bellowed out, "UN....BE... LIEVABLE! I'm a terrible man, Edgar! I know it. I know it. Now hand me another." The bald man closed his eyes and winced at the voice.

The crew looked at each other with eyes wide as cannon balls. Ava's jaw dropped and Merlin snugged his hat down tight. No one wanted to climb into the car, but the anticipation of why the Jackboot wanted him was eating away at Elias, so he figured he might as well be first. He stepped up into the train car and immediately his nostrils filled with vanilla smoke. A collection of hand-carved pipes lined one wall and another - **BOOM** - tilted pictures of a short, chubby man and a tall man with a bushy mustache building all kinds of machines. A haze of smoke floated across pictures of giant steam robots, locomotives, air ships, strange guns, iron buildings and humans with terrifying mods covering their bodies. There was also a beautifully framed picture of a tower city rising from a gear shaped platform that docked air ships between the gear cogs. The smoke continued to slither out from the last train car, as if an angry dragon lay in wait to devour him, but he continued on.

BOOM! The train shook again. "OH! the stench of it! Pitiful, shameful!" Elias couldn't figure out what the voice was complaining about. Mostly all he could smell was a sweet vanilla aroma and maybe something pungent behind it, but the angry voice continued.

BOOM! "I'm a terrible, a terrible man! What a nasty, disgustingly-dreadful habit I have! Now hand me another one—and don't test me, Edgar—What's that? No. I wouldn't do that to you, Edgar. No. I trust you. That's why you're up here and he's down there. Now hand me another one." The words chilled the tiny hairs on the back of Elias' neck, and his legs felt as though he was walking through heavy water as he moved towards the next car.

In the second car, all manner of animal heads were mounted on the walls. Lions, crocodiles, a leopard's head, eagles and a giant black bull's head whose horns made a handy hook for an umbrella. There were even some goodly sized wings hanging above a row of stuffed owls that resembled Casper. Elias was deeply concerned for the safety of his new friend, and the grand display of death sent chills of fear through him unlike anything he'd ever experienced. He was so caught up in it that he didn't notice the Whisper crew had already entered the second car behind him.

BOOM! The train rocked a bit on its tracks.

"I'M SICK! A RUINED MAN! I KNOW IT! DAMAGED!"

BOOM! "OH, what tragedy! How many is that now, Edgar? NINETEEN?!! Oh, my mother would be ashamed, but my father, oh, HAHAHA, oh, he would be ever so proud!"

Elias entered the third car, also filled with smoke, and the smell of vanilla was overpowering, but nothing so far could have prepared him for what was displayed there.

BOOM... "A sullied man, Edgar—polluted!! Hahaha!"

The car shook as if it were possessed with madness, and Elias' eyes beheld a wall full of tongues nailed to a fancifully carved plaque. The plaque read, "TRUTH MATTERS." Beside the plaque of tongues, a plaque full of plucked eyes read, "DARKNESS LIES." His legs froze and his eyes glued to the ones staring back at him—some had looks of horror, others the look of loss—and Elias' hands trembled as fear stole the heat from his body.

BOOM! "HOW mortifying! It disgusts me to my core, dear Edgar!"

BOOM! "THERE IT IS! – Oh, if my mother could see my disgusting habit she would rip out my other eye, but I can't help myself, Edgar. I really can't. It truly is a disease, isn't it?"

A soft trembling voice spoke up. "Y-y-yes, sir, yes it is."

Elias, still staring at the wall of eyes, noticed Izzy had taken hold of his hand to steady its shaking. It made him feel small but also that everything would be okay.

"I am a deep, dark sinner of great despair, and while it is true that I have bloodied my father's anvil in ways even he would never have thought, I have sought cures for my habit, I truly have. You know that I have, right, Edgar?"

"Y-you have indeed, sir." The clattering of a cup on a plate echoed through the train.

"Careful now, you'll spill my drink. Now fetch more tobacco, my pipe is getting cold."

"R-Right away, sir."

A tall, skinny man in a white suit peered into the car with tongues and eyes. "Uh, sir, your appointment is here."

"OH! Good, good. Fantastic! Send them in."

THE CREW STEPPED INTO THE LAST CAR, WHERE A MAN WAS SEATED in the palm of a giant mole paw with claws reaching to the ceiling of the car. His rugged countenance was softened by a fine, buttoned white shirt beneath a heavy black trench coat and custom made dress pants ended at the top of heavy iron boots. His lustrous black hair was complimented by a thick black mustache that kept his finger and thumb quite busy while looking them over. Elias was curious that a black patch covered his missing eye instead of a mod like Gideon's.

"Yes, yes. It's good to see my favorite spies return safely. What took so long?"

"Sir, er we wer..." Gideon started to answer, but was quickly cut off.

"Hold that thought. I have a nasty task to finish here," The Jackboot interrupted as he spun his chair sideways towards an extremely large rifle mounted on a thick iron tripod. It was pointed out a sliding door directly overlooking the mine, and he leaned over and peered through the scope with his right eye then looked back at Elias. "You, boy! Come here."

Gideon gave Elias a push forward and he would have fallen flat on his face, but his right foot caught and he walked over next to the Jackboot.

"Look through the scope and tell me what you see," the Jackboot said. Elias looked through the large glass piece and his sight was instantly teleported down to the mine below. A man was climbing out of the mine and had only reached the top. Elias started to give a description to the Jackboot, but he was pushed away.

"Step back for a moment, son," he mashed his eye back on the scope. "Hold your ears," he warned. The miner quickly dusted off his clothes and looked back up toward the tower as the Jackboot gently placed his hand around the grip, took one breath and squeezed the trigger.

BOOM! The man dropped dead. "OH! there it is again! The dreadful stench of my vengeful habit eats away at my soul," he looked at Elias. "Would that I could vanquish vengeance from my heart, but I simply cannot abide a cheat," he said, grinding his teeth.

Edgar stepped over and handed the Jackboot a beautifully carved pipe, who struck a match off the side of his chair and lit it. "A moment, please," he requested as his puffs filled the air with thick vanilla smoke. Then he stood on his oversized iron boots that were clearly a modification for damaged or missing legs, and walked over next to a wall lined with gold hearts. He lifted a green cloth from a golden bird cage, and inside the little red-headed finch with the strange eye swung on a squeaky swing. The Jackboot took a pinch of feed from Edgar's trembling hand and sprinkled it into the cage, then rubbed the bird's wee little head with his finger.

Taking a long draw on his pipe, he savored it for a moment and released its cloud into the air. "So, Gideon," he paused for a moment as he sat back down into his chair. "Tell me, where is my plant expert?" Gideon jumped at the chance to announce his successful operation.

"Yes, sir. We were delayed by a fierce storm but were able to go around it and safely retrieve the boy. We were unaware of his condition, but we assumed he was the reason you gave us the gold ring for the heart-mod." At this, the Jackboot choked a bit on his pipe smoke but rotated his hand forward for Gideon to continue his report. Gideon seemed a bit unnerved by the choke but worked through it. "Merlin was able to install the mod during the storm, and for now we've at least bought him a few weeks."

THE JACKBOOT CLEARED HIS THROAT, "GIDEON."

"Yes, sir?"

"You used my last gold ring on this dying boy?" smoke poured from his nostrils.

"Y-yes, sir. Merlin wa..."

"Where is my plant expert?" he interrupted gripping the arm of his decapitated mole claw chair.

Gideon grabbed Elias by the arm and pulled him forward. "Right here, sir. We fixed him, and he is ready for you."

"Gideon, my boy—come here, please."

"Yes, sir." Gideon stepped over and the man whispered in his ear.

"The father, Gideon, where's the father?"

"The father, sir?"

"Yes, the father."

"But Izzy ..."

"Let me stop you right there. Now tell me, Gideon. Who is the captain of my spy ship?"

"I am, sir."

"That's right. You're the captain. Now would you like to start over?"

"The boy was the only one in the pictures on Flit's chip. So he's the one we brought."

The Jackboot pulled out a picture of Elias' father working in the greenhouse lab and Elias watering plants. *"Which one of these people do you think is the plant expert?"* the Jackboot's eye twitched.

Gideon focused his mod-eye in on the picture. A small burst of steam popped on his head as it dropped down. *"Th-the one in the lab, sir,"* he winced at Izzy's mistake. He'd never seen pictures of a father working in the lab. How she'd messed up was beyond him, but a good captain takes responsibility for his crew's mistakes.

The man nodded his head and took a draw from his tightly clinched pipe and released it. *"The one in the lab is correct!"*

Gideon quickly and brilliantly improvised. *"Sir, we'll just return and bring the father back here."*

"If only that were possible, but sadly that is no longer an option at this point." The Jackboot leaned in a little closer and bit down hard on his pipe stem, grinding it with his teeth.

Gideon knew all too well the Jackboot's reputation for leaving no loose ends. He'd heard of the Jackboot's struggles with madness, but having the boy's parents killed seemed harsh. Maybe the Jackboot was losing control. Gideon stepped back away from him, seeking the shelter of his crew.

The crew of the Whisper stood frozen as they watched smoke rise from the bull head shaped pipe clinched in the Jackboot's mouth. Sweet vanilla and silence filled the air as he pursed hard, billowing smoke from the beast's head. Elias felt the Jackboot staring at his chest as the pipe glowed hotter and hotter until it turned bright red at the top. Then his eye widened and he looked up at Elias' face.

"Tell me, boy," he began.

Elias sensed a fatherly tone in his voice and instinctively responded. "YES, SIR?" The Jackboot grinned, turned the back of his chair on everyone for a moment and then spun it back around. In his hand he was holding a red flowered plant with three berries on it, and it was growing out of a piece of coal.

"Maybe we can help each other." He smiled. "Do you know anything about this plant?"

Elias looked at it for a moment. "I don't think so."

The Jackboot reached out and handed it to Elias. "Here, take a closer look," he prodded.

Elias took the plant and looked it over carefully. "It smells familiar, but I've never seen anything like it."

"That's too bad. I've given you so much, and yet you have nothing to offer me," he complained as he pointed the stem of his pipe at Elias' chest. Elias had practically forgotten the rest of the crew was with him in the train car until Ava's teeth started to chatter. Looking back at the faces of the only friends he had ever known, he couldn't help but feel he had failed them when they needed him most.

"Wait, I think I've seen that in my dad's lab," he spoke with no little amount of uncertainly hanging on every word.

Taking a breath of fresh air, the Jackboot explained himself. "Look, son. I am a patient man. Am I not, Edgar?" Edgar didn't seem to know if he should answer or not. "And I am aware this might be new to you, so I am willing to give you the benefit of the doubt that maybe, and I highly doubt it, but maybe you didn't see the wall of tongues hanging in the other car. So I want to take a moment and give you a chance to clear your head and tell me the truth."

"Well, I think it was where my dad kept the more dangerous plants, but I was never allowed to go in there. I do remember a flower with three berries, but I don't ever remember seeing it growing out of a piece of coal," Elias said with a more confident tone.

"So, maybe you can help me." The Jackboot replied with glee. "You see, I am a problem solver, young man. That's what I do. I make problems disappear, and if you can help me solve the mystery of this wonderful plant, I will have my personal surgeon replace that nasty heart of yours with a new one." He made his offer in the nicest tone possible, considering the large scar traveling under his left ear and across the lower part of his throat. Elias reasoned that was what caused him some difficulty speaking.

The whole crew looked each at each other with stone-cold, emotionless shock on their faces. Edgar was still frozen over by the bird cage, perhaps hoping he had suddenly gained the power of invisibility.

"You can do that?" Elias asked in a confused tone. "But where would you get a new heart?"

"You see, uh…" He paused for a moment. "I don't believe you told me your name, young man."

"Elias."

"Well, young Elias, I am a man of many resources, and I would have no problem providing you with a healthy, new heart if you could help me with this plant," he proudly boasted.

"But I didn't think it was possible," Elias sputtered in disbelief.

"I believe anything is possible with the right motivation behind it. Take Edgar for example. He has a perfectly healthy heart, don't you, Edgar?" he said with a devilish grin creeping across his face. The cup in Edgar's hand began to chatter on its tiny, white plate. "But I can't give you Edgar's heart because he needs it. Don't you, Edgar?" Edgar seemed unwilling to answer out of fear he had bitten down too hard on his tongue. "And I can't give you mine because I don't have one," he said, laughing. "But if you help me, I give you my word I'll solve your heart problem."

Elias was so overcome with joy he started rambling all of his emotions out in the open. "This is so great! My dad is a brilliant botanist. He'll be so happy to help figure out your plant, and my mom, she's going to be so grateful to you for saving me. Wait 'til you see my dad's greenhouse. It's amazing! You wouldn't believe what kind of pla..."

"STOP right there, my boy!" the Jackboot held up his hand. "I'm not going to go into specifics, but that is no longer an option for me. Gideon's failure to bring your father to me has put me in a bind, and I'm going to need you to – step into your father's shoes – and solve this problem on your own."

"But all we nee...." Elias stopped again as the man raised his hand back up.

The Jackboot sat in his chair in deep contemplation for a moment and then spoke. "Young Elias...let me tell you a story about life and opportunity. About becoming a man and leaving childish things behind." He pursed on his pipe until Elias could barely breathe the smoke filled air. "Once there was a boy who never lived," he pursed some more and then abruptly finished his story, "And then he died, THE END! Is that who you want to be, young man?" he asked, pointing the pipe stem at Elias' chest again.

Silence fell on the train car except for the squeaking of Flit's tiny bird swing moving happily back and forth. The Jackboot stood up, walked over to Edgar and took the cup from his trembling hand. Handing his pipe back to Edgar, he sipped on the cup for a moment and then seemed to have an epiphany. "I believe what we need here is a little time of contemplation. Don't you agree, Edgar?"

"Y-yes, sir, I ble... I believe so, sir." Edgar stammered to get his answer out.

"I'm going to give this young man and my favorite spies a chance to think things through and bring me a more positive outlook on solving my plant problem," he joyfully summarized.

"Bosarus!" he called out, and the bald librarian boarded the train and joined them.

"Yes, Mr. Jackboot," he spoke, his head down in full submission.

"My spies need some time of contemplation," the Jackboot said as he sat back down in his chair and peered through his scope, ignoring the crew.

"Of course, sir, right away, sir." Bosarus agreed.

"Come with me, please." he kindly asked the crew in his gentle voice. They followed him again through the train cars and back out into the library, but to a different bookshelf than what they'd used to enter. Standing next to another faceless statue, Bosarus pushed his finger into its ear, and another bookshelf door opened into an empty room. He motioned with his hand, "Please step into the room for a moment." His demeanor so kind and gentle, so grandfatherly, they all complied obediently, walked in, and stood there feeling as if he would bring them a bag of treats at any moment.

THE MINE: ELIAS WAS STILL HOLDING THE PLANT IN HIS HANDS and wondered if he should hand it back, but Bosarus stepped away and came back holding masks "You're going to need these," he said, tossing them into the room. Before they realized what was happening, the bookshelf door closed and they were all standing there staring at each other confused. Gideon looked down at the masks and seconds later cried out, "GET THEM! GET THEM ON! THE MASKS, NOW!"

Everyone fumbled in the mess of masks on the floor, and when they all looked up everyone was wearing a mask except for Merlin. There weren't enough, and his small hands and short fingers were unable to grasp one as fast as everyone else. No one knew what to say. They all simply stood there staring at him as if he were about to leave them forever, but Elias knew the look on Merlin's face all too well. He had seen it, even felt it, many times in his own mirror. It was the terrifying fear of death.

Elias quickly removed his mask and handed it to Merlin. "Here! Take mine. I don't need it, I'm already infected, and you saved me anyway." Something under their feet began to clack louder and louder as Elias continued. "I'm grateful for the time I've had so far. I want you all to know that I consider you..." Before Elias could finish, the floor rotated into a dark corkscrew tube and down they slid for almost ten minutes, like food down the mouth of a drain.

Darkness veiled their descent, with the exception of bright flashes of metal sparks coming from everyone's mods as they scraped and screeched the sides of the iron slide. Wyatt's was obviously the worst, as all four limbs clacked and screeched down the tube like throwing nails at a chalk board. Merlin used both hands to squeeze his hat down tight over his eerie snow globe of a head, but he eventually lost it, and for a while all Elias could see was a floating green brain above him. Elias was certain Bogan said a few choice words he'd heard his father use in his lab whenever something went wrong, but he couldn't see Gideon or Ava. However, Elias' ride down was somewhat smooth as Izzy had grabbed him and was covering his heart-mod with her hands to protect the glass. He could tell she cared for him in a protective sort of way but nothing more. Nevertheless, her vanilla soaked hair helped calm his fears during the terrible joy ride down.

They reached the bottom and piled out on top of each other into an underworld of laboring coal miners, black coal dust, machines of iron and criminals of an unpleasant sort. White sparks and orange flames burst from hot iron tools, and the clanging and banging of picks and hammers rang in their ears as miners performed their duties. There was no mold in the mine, but the coal dust was so heavy, without a mask you wouldn't last three months. They could feel the grime of the coal covering their arms, and the sulfur from the natural gas pockets seeped through their cheap masks. Before them stood a man with a jaw made of iron, and it clacked when he ordered them to work.

"*GET TO IT, YOU SLAGS!*" He hollered with a wretchedly hoarse voice and tossed shovels and picks at them. Mr. Iron Jaw was his name—and he made sure they didn't forget the Mr.—led them to a spot near a giant mole hole that was overlooked by the Jackboot's tower. The other miners stared at Elias like someone would stare at a corpse as he walked passed them. *"I WANT THIS AREA CLEARED OUT,"* Mr. Iron Jaw barked, pointing at the left side of a large tunnel.

It didn't take long after Mr. Iron Jaw left before Wyatt began to direct his anger towards Elias for their current circumstances. "I thought you were a plant expert. We saw you in all the pictures, taking care of those plants in the greenhouse. We're all going to die because of you" he complained as he pointed at another miner using a pick axe to get his mod-leg to move. "No one survives down here."

Gideon's efforts to diffuse the argument failed as Elias continued to push the idea of returning to get his father. "I don't understand why we can't take the plant to my father. He's the real plant expert, if anyone can figure out what kind of plant it is, he can."

"No! YOU! It's your job to solve it! That's why we wasted the heart-mod on you," Wyatt continued his assault.

"You made your point, Wyatt," Bogan said, getting right to work busting coal off the sides of the wall.

"Gid, why can't we just convince the Jack to let us go back and get the kid's dad so we can get out of this mess?" Izzy's advocating on Elias' behalf fell flat on Gideon's ears, and Bogan shook his head, clearly confused at Gideon's refusal to answer her question. After all, the idea seemed reasonable enough.

"Why not, Gideon?" Bogan asked.

"It's not possible, so let's leave it at that." Gideon continued trying to shut down the topic for Elias' sake, but now even Merlin wondered aloud.

"Gideon, it does seem like the best option, and we could be back in only a week. If Elias can't solve the plant problem, then we need his father's help," Merlin pushed.

"ENOUGH! Okay! We just can't!" Gideon rarely lost his temper with anyone except Wyatt so maybe that's why it was so easy to unload on him now.

"Yeah? What's your beef, Gid?" Wyatt asked.

"BECAUSE THEY'RE DEAD, OKAY!" Gideon blurted out.

"WHAT!?" A sharp wave of adrenaline shot through Elias' back and down his arms.

"GIDEON! Why did you say that?" Izzy asked in shock, reaching over to cover Elias' ears, but it was obviously too late.

Ava grabbed her mouth in shock for the boy. "OH!"

"Who said? How do you know?" Elias asked as everyone watched his heart pounding harder through the glass cover.

"The Jackboot had them killed after we picked you up. He practically admitted it to me." Gideon's head dropped down, not only out of sadness for Elias, but also from his inability to prevent his outburst.

Elias wanted to be angry at them for bringing this on his mother and father, but deep down he knew they were as much a pawn in the Jackboot's game as he was. Izzy and Bogan did their best to comfort him, but Elias wanted to grieve his loss alone.

Elias left the crew and walked across the opening of the large, cavernous hole with rail tracks going through the center, where only a single man was working. He found a good spot and began swinging his pick axe at the wall harder and harder as he punished the stones and rocks for the sadness in his heart. Harder and harder he delivered his blows as tears ran down his quivering cheeks, and the sound of his pick traveled deep into the tunnel. He imagined the Jackboot's face as his pick echoed back out into the mine.

He couldn't hear himself crying over the loud echoing of his pick, but his wailing and punishing blows became so loud the mine workers thought a horrible beast had entered the tunnel. In that moment, his sounds of sadness and heartache gripped the miners with such fear, the entire mine shut down. The white sparks and orange flames disappeared, and the clanging and banging of picks and hammers went silent – all except his. The machines slowed to a grinding halt, and Mr. Iron Jaw was – very, very – unhappy. His tense jaw clacked and clanked as he walked toward Elias to teach him a lesson he would not soon forget. No one stops Mr. Iron Jaw's mine. At least no one that doesn't pay a heavy price.

6

THE DIRTY HUNCHBACK

"*H*EY!" Mr. Iron Jaw called out, but Elias kept wailing and hammering away. "HEY, YOU!" he called again. Izzy desperately wanted to run over to Elias, but Gideon held her back. "HEY, YOU!" Mr. Iron Jaw growled again as the echoing from the tunnel irritated his jaw. "HEY YOU, SLAG!" he clacked.

Finally, the stone Elias had been battering broke and slid off the wall. It was no small stone. Elias turned around and looked at Mr. Iron Jaw, his face was covered in dirt except where the tears had streamed it clean. Gold shimmered through his sweat-soaked shirt as his heart-mod was now fully evident. His chest was heaving up and down from exhaustion as he stood there mask-less, holding his pick ready for another swing.

The man was at a complete loss for words. His mind was utterly bankrupt. He could think of no punishment greater than what the world had already delivered to the boy, and so, in his toughest tone, he let him have it. "Hey, nice work," Mr. Big Bad Iron Jaw said, pointing to the broken stone. He gave a nod and walked away. Elias held his pick with heaving breaths as the other miners gawked at him.

"BACK TO WORK!" Iron Jaw thundered out.

And Elias sat down on his broken rock and rested.

IN THE FURY OF HIS ANGER, ELIAS HAD COMPLETELY FORGOTTEN about the lone miner working beside him until a strange, high-pitched voice spoke up, "Hey, nice work," the dirty miner said, as if to mock old Iron Jaw. The man chuckled a little and Elias started to laugh, and then they both broke into laughter.

"What's your name?" the man asked, still in a strange voice that caught Elias off guard. "Your name? You do have one, right?" he asked again.

"Uh. Yes. It's Elias," he answered.

"They call me the Dirty Hunchback down here," the man said.

He was wearing a large cloak that covered a terribly disfigured hump on his back, and he seemed to have some terrible deformities on his hands, and maybe his feet as well. Elias hadn't noticed before, but the man had no mask, and his clothes were extremely filthy.

"You don't have a mask." Elias said in shock.

"That's what everybody keeps telling me," he said, laughing. His laugh was so infectious Elias couldn't help but to laugh with him, even though it was a serious matter. It was the first time Elias had ever laughed about death.

"But you'll die." Elias said.

"They keep telling me that, too," They both laughed again. "You don't have one either, so I guess were both going to die," he continued laughing in his high tone voice.

"I'd come over there and meet you face to face, but I'm a bit tied down at the moment," he said, lifting a chain clamped to his leg and bolted to a metal plate on a rock.

"Why did they chain you?" Elias asked.

"I guess I'm dangerous," He said with a crooked grin.

"I guess I'm not dangerous enough," Elias said, wiping the grimy tears from his cheeks.

"Strange that you were fortunate enough to get one of those," the hunchback pointed to Elias' chest. "The only people I've ever seen with those are extremely highly valued, and yet somehow you're down here with me," the hunchback curiously wondered.

"I don't think I was ever supposed to have it. The Jackboot wanted my father, but they grabbed me by mistake."

"Your father must be an important man then."

"He was a brilliant botanist," Elias said. Pulling the flower out of his jacket, he held it up.

"The Jackboot wanted him to figure out how to grow more of these, but his spies took me by mistake. I wanted to help him, but I've never seen a flower growing out of coal."

The hunchback's eyes lit up. "Interesting. Do you mind if I have a look at it?" he asked.

"Why not?" Elias said getting up from his rock. He maneuvered his way over the rocky ground toward the hunchback. The closer Elias got, the worse the man smelled. Horrible, putrid odors of urine and feces permeated the air and the man could tell by his face that it was difficult for Elias to approach him.

"I apologize for the smell," said the hunchback. "I know it's terrible, but they won't unchain me from this rock. You wouldn't happen to have the key, would you?" He laughed again.

Elias almost gagged as he reached out and handed the man the flower. He studied it for a moment, but for the hunchback it truly was poor timing, as Elias lost his footing on a rock right as Bogan looked over. Elias fell back hard against the mine wall, and Bogan set off toward the hunchback with his pick axe. The hunchback tried helping Elias to his feet by grabbing his jacket and lifting him, but from Bogan's perspective, it looked more like the dirty creep was roughing him up to steal the plant.

Before the hunchback realized it, Bogan was behind him and punched him as hard as he could in his nasty old hump. "Get off him, you filthy creep!" The hunchback let out a weird howl, and Bogan spun the freak around and slammed him against the wall.

"BOGAN, DON'T!" Elias shouted. Bogan's fist stopped about an inch from the hunchback's face.

"He was trying to help me." Elias explained as Bogan's face turned confused.

"But he knocked you down," Bogan said.

"No! I slipped! He tried to help me up, but his hands are... something's wrong with them," Elias explained. At that moment, Bogan nostrils filled up with the hunchback's rancidness, and he immediately vomited inside his cheap mask. The rest of the crew finally made it over and were ready to pummel the hunchback as well, but they stopped when they caught a whiff of the pungent odor.

"These masks are horrible," Wyatt complained.

"Oh! dear me, uhuag!" Ava wretched.

"NASTY FREAK!" Bogan yelled and punch the hunchback's hump again to punish him for his stench.

"YAUOAL! My poor, poor hump. Why did you do it? It hurts so. Why? Why?" the hunchback cried.

"Don't hurt him," Elias told the others, "he just wanted to see the flower." Getting back to his feet, he dusted himself off as he explained.

The hunchback held the plant up and with a big smile said, "I've seen these before. In fact, I know where you can find a whole field."

"WHAT!?" Izzy's eyes burst wide open, "Gid, he knows where to find the plant?"

"If you can get me out of here, I'll take you to them," the hunchback offered with glee.

Bogan finished wiping the vomit from his mouth and grabbed the man again, slamming him back against the wall. "LIES! I wouldn't take your filthy stink on the Whisper if my life depended on it."

"But, it does, Bogan!" Izzy exclaimed.

"BOGAN! Stop! He's trying to help us." Elias was surprised at Bogan's treatment of the hunchback. "Gideon, please, if he can show us where the plant is, we might be able to figure out what the Jackboot wants with it, or at least get us out of this mess," Elias pleaded.

The hunchback's hooded cloak covered most of his face, but from what Elias could tell he was not the least bit intimidated by Bogan as he winked his funny looking eye at Elias.

"So, where do we find them?" Gideon asked.

"Oh, ha ha ha! I'm afraid I won't be tricked so easily. If I tell you where to find them, you'll leave me here. No. I think not. Take me with you and I promise you, I'll get you more than you can carry." The hunchback's tone was so confident, he was either telling the truth or believing his own lie.

"It all sounds like a grand idea, but we're stuck down here, and the Jackboot's not just going to let us out." Wyatt's pessimistic response killed the mood quickly. At least it was in keeping with his bad mood towards Elias for getting them stuck down there.

"I've had some time to think this through." The best way out is to send someone up in the death baskets. They could retrieve your ship and return for the rest of the crew," the hunchback cheerfully explained in his strange voice.

"HA! You idiot, you're dumber than I thought. It won't work, because someone would have to actually die to get out of here, and they make sure the dead are dead before they send them up." Bogan lifted his chest a little after his brilliant slam of the stinky man's plan.

"I'll do it," Elias said to the shock of everyone. "Turn off my mod and they'll think I'm dead. Merlin can bring me back just like when my fuel ran out."

"ELIAS, NO!" Izzy said in horror.

"Who would turn you back on once you're up there?" Merlin asked in a pondering tone.

Izzy strangely backed off her outrage when she sensed Merlin's confidence in the plan. "He's not doing this unless you go with him," Izzy said warming to the idea. If anyone could make a plan like this work it was Merlin. "You'll go with him, Merlin. You do it!" Her icy cold gaze was frozen with resolve. Merlin nodded his approval.

"I go up with the boy or no deal," the hunchback demanded.

"WHAT!" Bogan roared. "See what I mean! This guy only cares about himself. We can't trust him. Once he gets back up there, he'll leave Elias to die and us down here to rot." Bogan's face was so red now, his freckles had disappeared beneath his anger.

"Bogan's got a point," Gideon agreed. "So the hunchback and Merlin will both go up with him." Bogan shook his head in protest of Gideon's words but said nothing. He knew Charlie would not have approved of the plan.

"They're not just going to let two people go up in a death basket with a dead body. They'll know something's up." Wyatt cleverly ripped up their plan.

Ava, quiet as a mine mouse, finally spoke up. "Tell them Merlin has to take the mod back off and return it to the Jackboot. It's worth a lot. It'll make sense to them." Her simple brilliance always reminded them of why Charlie picked her to help design the whisper mode.

Izzy threw her arms around the girl in a big hug. "AVA! You rock!" she said, squeezing her tightly.

"We won't be able to leave him off for long, so he'll have to play dead right up until old Iron Jaw checks him." Merlin explained. "It's probably best if we get him close to the death baskets before we act, and someone might want to time the ..." Merlin was cut off mid-way through by the hunchback.

"Three minutes, seventeen seconds to the top, give or take a second." The dirty hunchback interjected, pointing to a large clock on the tower.

"Well, I guess you've had time to plan, haven't you?" Wyatt sneered.

"Two hundred and sixty-one days," the hunchback retorted.

"You should be dead!" Merlin's jaw dropped. "No one can survive that long without a mask."

"Don't tell me that now! My body might hear and fall over dead." The hunchback cracked another smile.

The Whisper crew was completely thrown off course by the bizarre man that held their lives in the palm of his gnarled hands. The way Wyatt was gawking at the hunchback's gloves it was clear to Elias that he wanted to remove them so he could see the deformity. Although, from the looks Wyatt was getting from Ava and Izzy, he wouldn't dare go that far.

"Are you sure you want to do this, kid?" Gideon asked. "There is a risk they might not be able to bring you back," he put his hand on Elias' shoulder. "I'm not going to lie to you, if anything goes wrong, you'll die, and this will be the last time we see you."

Elias, in turn, placed his hand on Gideon's shoulder, causing Izzy to pull both her lips in as she tried to hide her smile. "We don't have any other options. We need to find this plant and figure it out, or you'll all die down here, and I don't want to be responsible for that," he said.

"It would help if we could get ahold of a gear cooler. We could hit him with a blast to drop his body temperature. Maybe give us more time to revive him. We'll need one anyway to weaken the chains on this hunchback fellow." Merlin's brain fired bolts of blue and green as his plan quickly formed under his magical-mind-cap.

"I'll get one." Wyatt added a snicker to his maniacal look.

"No funny business, Wyatt," Gideon warned.

"I can't believe we're really going to kill the kid on the word of this deformed freak. I say we turn him over to the Jackboot and maybe cut a deal," Bogan pushed his dissatisfaction.

"If we do that he won't need us anymore, and he surely won't need Elias, which means Elias will die. Are you following this plan well enough now, Bogan?" Gideon's nose gnarled up on his face and his lips pursed together like he just sucked on a lemon.

"Bogan, you guys are the only friends I've ever known, and I don't want to die, but if I do I can't think of a better way than to give my life for you," Elias said, looking at them all with a smile on his face.

"Awww! That's so sweet," Izzy smiled, "But Merlin's not going to let that happen to you. Are you, Merlin?" She messed up Elias' hair on her way behind Merlin. "This magnificent mastermind of a brain won't fail us, will you?" she said, peering from behind the green glowing glob of electrical matter. Merlin blushed. Elias' statement did not go unnoticed by the hunchback.

The rest of the crew went right to work setting up the plan as the hunchback asked Elias to stay with him until they were ready. When the crew was far enough out of ear shot, the hunchback said, "They kidnapped you from your family and put you in this terrible place, and you're ready to die for them?"

"It's true, they did this to me, but I also wouldn't be alive if they hadn't. It's not their fault my parents are dead. The Jackboot is a hard man and might have killed them if they disobeyed his orders. If I can help them, save them, then my short, miserable life might have some meaning." Elias could only hope.

Staring at the flower, the hunchback wondered, "Maybe your heart-mod wasn't a mistake after all."

"Why do you say that?'

"Anyone who can turn enemies into friends so quickly truly is a person of high value," he said with a twinkle in his eye. "Maybe one day you might even call me friend?"

"Maybe so," Elias responded as he tried to keep from breathing in the stench.

The crew returned from their task of securing a gear cooler and hit the hunchback's chain with a freezing cold blast. They waited for the next machine to pass by for cover, and with the swing from his axe Elias shattered the bolts and set him free.

The hunchback started hopping all over the place with mad, crazy joy until Bogan put his foot down. "Hey! Hunchy! Keep bouncing around like that and you're going to ruin this whole plan."

Bogan's slur seemed to stick as Gideon continued it. "Hunchy, get over here. Can we at least move away from that disgusting rock before we all vomit?"

"Yes! Yes! By all means," Hunchy joyfully offered, following them over toward the death baskets.

"They'll have moved the Whisper to the docks by now, so check there once you're top side," Gideon explained. His expression turned to concern. "Are you sure you're ready for this?"

"Yes, but I want to be the one to do it, in case you can't revive me. I don't want anyone to be responsible for my death but me. Dying is all I've ever known, so I can live with it or die with it or whatever," he stumbled around his words as Wyatt lifted the cooling gun.

"You think you look pale now, wait till I hit you with this." A sadistic smile beamed on Wyatt's face.

"Not too close, Wyatt. You'll kill him. Only enough to cool his body," Merlin said, trying to control Wyatt's excitement. Elias started to say something else but was too late. Wyatt blasted him with the cooler spray, knocking him over. Merlin and Hunchy picked him up and immediately carried him toward the death basket. Between Merlin's short fingers and Hunchy's limp from his hump, they almost dropped him three times before they made it.

"We got a dead one here!" Merlin called as they placed Elias into the death basket and a man ran over to Mr. Iron Jaw. Elias' teeth were chattering so loud they were afraid Iron Jaw would hear before they were ready. Looking down at Elias, Hunchy closed his mouth and whispered, "He's almost here."

"I'm ready." Elias mumbled with his shaking cold finger on the switch.

"Do it. Do it now," Merlin whispered through his teeth.

Elias looked into the face of the hunchback and shut down his heart generator. It felt like someone hit him hard in the chest with a hammer. His back arched, eyes rolled back and his legs shook for a moment, then three breaths later darkness filled his gaze.

Elias was dead, and it wasn't at all how he expected to die.

MERLIN CHECKED THE MINER'S TIME CLOCK ON THE TOWER AND made a mental note of it, 3:26:16 pm.

Iron Jaw stepped up and right away caught a whiff of the hunchback's stink. "GREAT CAESAR! Who's the dirty bird?" He grabbed his nose, looking down at Elias. "Oh, a terrible loss, lots of potential, that one." Checking Elias' heart he acknowledged that he was dead. "Definitely smells dead. Send him on up," Iron Jaw commanded.

"We have to go with him so we can remove the gold coil for the Jackboot," Merlin explained.

"No one goes up with the bodies. My mine, my rules," Iron Jaw demanded.

In his strange voice, the hunchback warned Iron Jaw, "Actually it's the Jackboot's mine, and this fellow has a job to do for the Jackboot." He pointed at Merlin's head.

Iron Jaw responded, "I know who he is, but rules are rules. No one goes up with the bodies."

"Time's running out." The hunchback sent a panicked look at Merlin.

"What do you mean, 'times running out'?" Iron Jaw asked.

A small whimper came from Ava's throat, and a tiny rattle came from the shovel in Izzy's mod-hand. Bogan scratched fiercely at his fleshy leg with his pick axe, right above where it connected to his mod, and they all watched from a distance trying to remember how to breathe.

With one eye closed and a small scowl on his face, Merlin's brain fired fast. "What he means is, in a few minutes someone new will be in charge of this mine, because this heart-mod will be useless and the Jackboot will have your jaw hanging on his wall."

Old Iron Jaw stood there mesmerized by the green glowing brain filled with lightning, and something must have sparked in his own brain. "Okay! Take him up," Iron Jaw said as he tried to remove his entranced gaze from the glorious, green glow. He looked up and rotated his finger in the air, then Merlin and Hunchy climbed into the iron tray-shaped basket and its chains jerked, pulling them upwards.

Merlin checked the time on the clock, 3:28:09 pm, then whispered to the hunchback. "Not yet. We have to make sure we're out of Iron Jaw's sight." The basket climbed higher and higher, and about a quarter of the way up Izzy held up three fingers. "Three minutes," Merlin said, "not yet."

Looking at Merlin and then Izzy and then back at Merlin, even the hunchback began to worry. "We can't wait any longer! We have to do it now," he said. Izzy's fingers were no longer visible, but they could make out four raised arms from the crew.

The Hunchback looked back at Merlin. "FOUR, FOUR! We

have to do it now!" he demanded as they reached the halfway mark.

"Okay!" Merlin reached down and turned the heart-mod switch back on. It sparked inside and a flame appeared and then went right back out. "WHAT?!" Merlin restarted it again and still it misfired. His brain fired like mad with bright flashes of blue and green as his frustration grew.

Then he popped open Elias' fuel container. "EMPTY!" He looked at the Hunchback in shock. "Why didn't he check it like I told him?" Merlin started to fracture emotionally. "Okay, okay, uh, we'll get top side and we'll find..."

A blast from a massive air horn cut him off as the mine changed work shifts. They practically fell off the basket as it came to a halt. "WHAT HAPPENED?" Merlin asked, looking at the hunchback.

The hunchback dropped his head, "Shift change. I-I'm sorry. I-I forgot everything stops for shift change. I-I wasn't paying attention to the clock. I-I was so excited to finally be free, I-I'm so sorry. I- don't know wha..." He abruptly stopped his apology. "How many arms are they lifting?" he asked Merlin, but Merlin was so distraught his brain was in a daze. "HOW MANY ARMS?" Hunchy screeched at him.

Merlin looked over the edge of the basket. "Six," he said somberly.

"Don't take your eyes off their arms, and tell me when it changes," the hunchback demanded.

Out of plain shock, Merlin obeyed without question as the hunchback reached into Elias' coat and plucked one of the berries from the flower. He placed the flower back into Elias' jacket then opened the boy's heart-mod cover. He squeezed the berry juice over Elias' heart and closed the lid, then dropped the rest of the berry into the fuel container. "HOW MANY?" he snapped at Merlin.

"Seven... Seven arms," Merlin said, staring at all the raised arms and bowed heads. He had failed her. Failed. The hunchback flipped the switch back on as the basket jerked upward again at the sound of the shift horn blast. It sparked for a second and then again and again, then a crackle, a flame and BOOM! It fired off. Merlin jumped up with surprise and looked at the hunchback. "You did it! You did it!"

"Help me hold him down," the hunchback told him.

"Why?"

"Because I don't know what's going to happen next," Hunchy said as Elias' legs and arms began to shake. Merlin looked at Elias and then back at the hunchback as he held down Elias' legs. The chains on the basket rattled and the basket shook for a moment, then Elias opened his eyes. They were red hot, almost on fire, and his heart was beating strong as it radiated heat from the glass cover. Merlin moved back a bit at the sight of it all, and Elias sat up and took him by the shoulders with both hands.

"What did you do to me?" he asked Merlin with red smoke pouring from his mouth.

"I-I, the hunchback...I didn't ... I don't," Merlin replied in shock.

"What happened? My eyes are burning. My heart hurts. I'm on fire. What did you do to me?" Elias turned and asked the hunchback with sweat pouring from his forehead.

"I'll explain later. We need to get to the ship," he said.

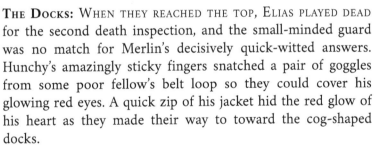

THE DOCKS: WHEN THEY REACHED THE TOP, ELIAS PLAYED DEAD for the second death inspection, and the small-minded guard was no match for Merlin's decisively quick-witted answers. Hunchy's amazingly sticky fingers snatched a pair of goggles from some poor fellow's belt loop so they could cover his glowing red eyes. A quick zip of his jacket hid the red glow of his heart as they made their way to toward the cog-shaped docks.

Lights glittered on steel buildings that scraped the heavens above them as their boots clunked against the iron streets. It was a busy city, and every road had a set of railroad tracks traveling through its center. The rotten eggs smell of the mine vanished behind them and morphed into roasted chicken, fried fish, cooked goose, sweet perfumes and, sadly, the smell of dirty hunchback. Busy street vendors beat away the onslaught of birds from their carts as people filled themselves with delicious treats. On all sides they passed finely dressed gentlemen and ladies in beautiful gowns, pipe smoking gamblers, quick-witted thieves, Jackboot guards and iron workers. A strange, single-wheeled vehicle, with its seat in the center of the wheel, belched black smoke around them and a man hollered, "OUT OF THE WAY!" as he zoomed by. An angry man struggling with a malfunctioning steam bot blasted it off the edge of the docks with a large gun when it dropped one of his supply crates.

Massive air ships groaned and blasted their horns at smaller ones as they passed each other above them. Blue, green, red, orange and yellow lights flickered, blinked and flashed all around from people's mods as well as the strange mod bots performing their daily tasks. They weaved their way through the markets selling everything from carrots, potatoes and deep fried fish; to body-mod parts, work bots, weapons and even eternal life in a bottle. Hunchy laughed at their foolish bottle as he chewed on a piece of fried fish. Merlin looked at him in bewilderment, wondering how he got the fish without ever stopping to purchase it.

Their search was progressing fairly smoothly until some crazy cultist without any mods stopped them. He was carrying a sign that said, "THE END IS NEAR," and yelling, "THE DESTROYER COMES! HE WIELDS HIS HAMMER OF DESTRUCTION! BEWARE ALL YE EVIL DOERS!" He stopped them in the middle of a crowded area and said, "Friends, prepare thy-selves, do ye not know the Destroyer comes? He wields his weaver's rod with great wrath. Many will perish."

Elias could tell Merlin was incensed with the crazed man, but Hunchy was worried they would be discovered in the crowd of people beginning to gather. "Back away!" Merlin warned, but the man was relentless with his kooky doomsday warnings.

He grabbed Elias, "The Alchemist has warned: the Destroyer comes. I tell ye, he comes, he wields his iron rod with the fierce wrath of vengeance, ye shall surely perish," The crazed kook shook him so hard the oversized goggles popped off his head.

"FOOL!" Merlin scoffed. The crowded faces instantly changed from smug to frightened, eye-popping glares at Elias.

His eyes still glowing red, he asked the crazed man, "Who's the Destroyer?" When the people saw the red mist pouring from his mouth, they fled, screaming. The crazed man dropped his sign and ran uncontrollably through the docks until he ran right off the edge of Grand Fortune City.

"Well," Hunchy said, standing a little straighter, "solves that problem." He gave Elias a pat on the back. "What do you say we find that ship, huh?" Even though Merlin seemed more than a little unnerved by the whole ordeal, he pushed the goggles back over Elias eyes and agreed.

They didn't have to travel much further until they spotted the Whisper docked with no one in sight. "Can you believe it?" Merlin wondered. "They left it unguarded."

"I'm not so sure about that," Hunchy responded. "Would you by chance employ a giant owl on your crew?" He pointed at Casper, perched on the far side of the ship, blocking the door.

"He got out!" Merlin said with a guilty look on his face.

"He certainly doesn't seem pleased. There's no small amount of blood on the deck, and I do believe he is holding someone's fingers in his claw," Hunchy revealed.

"That's not good," Merlin said. Elias remained silent, listening as they discussed the problem.

"What sort of predicament are we in?" Hunchy asked.

"I had to hide him from the Jackboot."

"And what exactly did that entail?"

"I locked him up," Merlin said, unhitching the ship's rope from the dock.

"A poorly calculated move on your part, but it looks as if he handled the guards rather well. So what's the plan?" Hunchy asked.

Merlin looked down at the scratch on his hand. "I'm not sure. Maybe he'll let us on the ship, but be ready in case he's still angry."

"Does he like fried fish?" Hunchy asked.

"What?" Merlin looked at him befuddled. "How should I know, and why does that even matter?"

Hunchy reached into his pocket, looking greatly disappointed. "I guess he can have my last piece of fish," he said, pulling the fish out. He sniffed it for a second, and it instantly caught Casper's eye. Hunchy held it up, waving it and Casper raised his chest. "Oh, I think he does like fried fish. Don't you, Mr. uh…What's his name?"

"Casper," Elias said, but with only a tiny bit of red mist floating out of his mouth this time.

Hunchy shook the piece of fish around in the air for a moment, "Casper, would you like some tasty fried fish?" He pitched the fish away from the door and onto the deck, and Casper quickly dove down on it. It was gone in seconds, but it was enough time for them to sneak past the angry bird and onto the bridge.

Once inside, Merlin looked to Elias and said, "I'll check the boiler, you get this thing moving."

Removing his poorly-sized goggles he squeaked out, "W-What do you mean?"

"You know, fly. Let's go pick up the crew," Merlin looked at him strangely.

"I can't fly this thing."

"What? Wyatt showed you how, right?" Merlin was beginning to wonder if Elias had forgotten his training.

"Wyatt only let me fly for 10 minutes, and never close to other ships like this."

"WYATT!" Merlin slammed his head on the side of Wyatt's pilot capsule.

"Why don't you fly it?" Hunchy asked Merlin.

"I don't fly. It's not my…I-I had a bad experience once." Merlin explained.

"Why can't we put it in Whisper mode and have the octopus fly it?" Elias asked him.

"They can only fly to preprogrammed destinations with few evasive maneuvers. They can't pilot the Whisper out of the docks and down to the mine. That takes a pilot," Merlin placed both his hands on top of his globe. "Ugh! We didn't think this through very well." He paced, trying to get his brain to fire off some sort of plan. He looked at the hunchback and wondered if he could fly, but the hump was obviously too big to fit into Wyatt's chair. So he looked back at Elias, "Do your best, kid. If we crash, we'll blame it on Wyatt. He was told to train you," he shook his head.

"Okay. I'll give it a try." Elias said as he climbed into Wyatt's chair, strapped himself in and looked up at Hunchy. "You might want to hold on to something."

"I'll be fine. Don't you worry about me, I'm sure you're better than you think. Have some confidence in your skills," the hunchback said with a nod of encouragement.

Elias stared directly into Hunchy's eyes and said, "I don't have any skills. I've only done this once."

Keeping his gaze on Elias, the hunchback raised his gnarled hand to a supporting beam and gave a nervous chuckle. "Okay. Now I'm ready."

Merlin returned from the boiler room, "There's not much fuel, but the boiler's loaded. Let's roll!"

Elias placed his hands on the Whisper's controls, flicked a few buttons and pulled the lever like he'd seen Wyatt do, and the Whisper began to move backward out of the dock. Everything was progressing well until the Whisper's forward spear-shaped deck began to scrape the side of a larger, more elegant ship called the Bradley Dunbar. The richly-finished wood popped, cracked and split, sending chills down Merlin's back as Elias tried to adjust his bearings, but then he hooked the ship's dock rope and ripped it off. A large beefy man stepped out on its deck and began yelling and shaking his fist at them.

Hunchy gritted his teeth as he cocked his head over and over in the opposite direction, as if that would somehow help straighten the ship. The beautifully-crafted air vessel, now horribly marred on one side, began to drift slightly toward the starboard side until it hit another ship of similar design. Slowly, ship after ship started to collide with another, until chaos quickly seized the dock area.

7

TUNNEL TERROR

"Get us out of here, now!" Merlin ordered with a stressed cringe distorting his face.

"That's what I'm trying to do!" Elias explained in frustration.

"Maybe if you could simply move it over this way a bit," Hunchy prodded as he continued to tilt his head.

"I'M DOING THE BEST I CAN! IF YOU CAN DO BETTER, THEN TAKE IT!" Elias burst out.

"Nope, nope, I...fantastic...y-you're doing excellent. Good job." Hunchy said, nervously rubbing the back of his gnarled hump.

Finally, they were away from the dock far enough, and Elias started his decent downward into the mine, but they couldn't see the crew anywhere. Then Hunchy realized what the problem was.

"Bungled!" he said, "We're on the wrong side of the mine! We need to go around to the west." So, Elias carefully guided the Whisper around the circular mine.

Fortunately, the mine was so wide Elias had no trouble navigating through the work area, but none of them realized the Whisper's anchor rope had dropped off the edge of the ship and was dragging on the mine floor. It hooked several small mining cars, pulling them off the tracks and one by one knocked more cars off. They couldn't hear the angry miners hollering and trying to get their attention to stop. By the time they spotted the crew, the rope had broken free from the cars, and their path of destruction was complete. Mr. Iron Jaw was unaware of the mine car disaster because he had run the opposite direction when someone alerted him to the possibility of an air ship falling toward the mine.

Merlin ran out and dropped a rope ladder down to the crew. Gideon and Bogan climbed the ladder, but Izzy aimed her mod-arm at the ship and her cabled hand launched off her arm and grabbed the Whisper's railing. She rose off the mine floor quickly, straight to the ship's deck. Wyatt launched a cabled hand at the railing as well and grabbed Ava, pulling both of them to the top before Gideon and Bogan ever made it up the ladder.

"Why's the anchor rope hanging down?" Izzy asked Merlin.

"What? How did that happen?" Merlin looked down and pulled the rope back to the ship, still not knowing the destruction it had brought to the other side of the mine.

Once Gideon and Bogan made it topside, they asked Merlin who was piloting the ship. Merlin explained that Elias was and that he had done a fantastic job getting out of the docks. Izzy, Ava and Bogan immediately ran to the bridge to see Elias when they heard he had made it.

"Good work, Merlin," Gideon said, patting Merlin on the back.

"It wasn't me, Gideon. I tried everything I could, but he was dead. Real dead! I couldn't get him back. It was the hunchback that saved him."

"Really? Well, I guess he proved useful after all," Gideon said with a pleased tone in his voice.

"Gideon," Merlin took him quietly by the arm. "I don't know what he did, but he did something to the boy that I've never seen. Red mist poured out of his mouth... red mist, Gideon."

Gideon gave Merlin's statement some thought and told him, "Keep this between us for now."

"I understand," Merlin nodded.

Gideon and Merlin entered the bridge where everyone was lavishing praise on Elias. "Nice work, plant expert, but I'll take it from here," Wyatt raised his shoulders. No sooner had Wyatt taken his place back in the pilot seat than a small, flaming air ship came crashing down in front of them. Heavy booms above them, like the sound of crashing thunder, vibrated the Whisper. Flaming boards and ship parts started floating down from the sky all around them.

"Elias – what did you do?" Wyatt asked, looking at Elias. Wyatt wasn't sure what happened, but he only looked for a chance to kill Elias moment of praise.

"I did the best I could, okay," Elias pushed back at his statement.

"Wyatt! Get us out of here!" Gideon ordered.

"HOW? WHERE? I'm not taking the Whisper through that mess," Wyatt said defiantly.

Gideon stepped out onto the deck and looked up toward GFC. Directly above them a large air ship was being devoured by monstrous flames and drifting downward toward the Whisper. Behind them, the mine guards had started firing their weapons, and in front of them, flaming debris from another air ship littered the tunnel entrances. In that moment, Gideon froze.

He preferred to take his time and weigh all the possibilities, unlike Charlie. Gideon had always questioned Charlie's reactionary and impulsive leadership as something that put the crew at unnecessary risk. Charlie's impulsiveness was why he was exposed to the black mist in the first place and died, but it was also what saved everyone on the Whisper. Deafening silence filled Gideon's ears as the whole crew cried out at him, but he was hypnotized by the flames surrounding them and wondered what would Charlie do?

Izzy shrieked at him, "GIDEON, WE'RE ALL GOING TO DIE!" but the loss of Charlie had finally caught up with him.

Then Elias spoke, "No, we're not! Wyatt, into the tunnel!" Wyatt hesitated for a second, still looking to Gideon, until Elias looked at him and again demanded, "INTO THE TUNNEL!" Maybe it was the small amount of red mist still in Elias' eyes, or Wyatt's own need for direction, but he instinctively obeyed and pushed the Whisper full throttle through the burning debris and into the dark, cavernous hole.

MERLIN SWITCHED ALL THE WHISPER'S LIGHTS TO FULL POWER, while Ava and Izzy pulled Gideon back in and took him to the command room. The mine tunnel was large enough for Wyatt to maneuver the Whisper through, but the areas where the walls had collapsed required some skillful piloting even for him. Elias and Hunchy remained on the bridge with Wyatt while Bogan went down to the rear gunner position to watch for trouble.

They all knew at some point the Jackboot would send his speeders after them, so when Bogan hollered out, "WE'VE GOT COMPANY!" no one was the least bit surprised.

The speeder started blasting away immediately, but its aim was terrible, hitting the sides of the tunnel and missing the Whisper every single time. Bogan took a shot at the ceiling in front of the speeder, knocking some debris down on top of it and sending it spiraling out of control.

"I got it!" he yelled back to the crew. "Just can't find good help these days," Bogan muttered to himself as he wondered why it was so easy. He waited for a while, and when no other speeder showed up he joined the rest of the crew.

The escapees traveled only a short way before they came upon a fork in the tunnel. Wyatt stopped the Whisper while they debated which way would be best.

"I think Karl's Labyrinth is this way," Bogan said, pointing to the right tunnel.

Karl's Labyrinth was a vast series of tunnels that linked together to form a giant, underground city. They were purveyors of whisky and tobacco, but thievery and swindling was what they loved the most. Genetic modification was typically preferred over metal mods and they forced their prisoners to fight in the Arena of Heroes for a chance at freedom. The labyrinth rulers did have a code, but it was fairly loose in practice and always involved money.

"Their tolls will rob us of all our fuel funds. I don't trust them," Merlin argued.

"And they won't let you out until they've robed you of everything but your boots," Izzy claimed.

"They'd just hand us back to the Jack for a fee and strip the Whisper of everything of value," Wyatt said, nodding his head in agreement.

"Okay! So we take the other tunnel," Elias said acknowledging their reasoning. "We either go left or right. We can't sit here all day waiting for the Jackboot to catch up with us."

Loose dirt was falling from the left tunnel as they discussed their options and seemed to grow more noticeable as they hammered out their differences. Casper startled all of them when he landed on the deck and started pecking wildly at the door, wanting in. Izzy ran over and opened the door, and he quickly flew in, landing right in front of Wyatt's cockpit. She started to close the door and then stopped and leaned her head outside.

"Do you hear that?" she asked.

More dirt fell from the top of the left mine tunnel.

"Hear what?" Elias wondered, leaning his ear over in her direction.

"Quiet!" she said, holding up her hand. "That noise. I've heard it before." She leaned out a little more.

"Wait, I hear it now," Ava confirmed.

"It sounds like screaming," Hunchy said, breaking his silence. It was clear he was uncomfortable being in the tunnel, as he spent most of his time looking at the ceiling in hopes it wouldn't fall in on them.

"I hear it," Elias agreed, "it does sound like screaming or wailing of some sort." More dirt collapsed from the left tunnel ceiling, and rock crumbs started sprinkling the deck of the

Whisper. It grew louder and closer and sounded more and more like the howling of a banshee, followed by clacking and chugging.

Then Gideon stepped out of the command room with his faculties seemingly intact, "It's the Iron Weaver! Wyatt, left tunnel, full throttle, NOW!"

Wyatt responded to Gideon's command with amazing speed and agility, forcing the Whisper through the rain of dirt and into tunnel. Bogan, Elias and Izzy ran down to the rear gunner's bubble at the back of the boiler room and Hunchy followed. Peering through the glass bubble, they gazed upon the terrifyingly fearless weaver of iron and steel standing on the Weaver's bull horns. The Jackboot was coming.

The train's wheels threw bright orange sparks from both sides and billowed black smoke with balls of fire from every new load of coal fed into its boiler. The Jackboot straddled the bull's horns with arms crossed and nothing but his magnetic boots to hold him down. A stern, confident look covered his face as smoke rolled off his pipe and over his thick black hair which was being driven back by the fierce wind. Bright white lights shot out of the bull's eyes, illuminating his way to the Whisper as speeders passed on both sides.

Bogan jumped in the gunner seat and started firing, but the speeders bobbed and weaved out of the way, never firing back. "Why aren't they shooting?" grumbled Bogan as if he were disappointed.

"He makes me so mad sometimes," Izzy said, glaring awestruck at the Jackboot, "but when he does stuff like this – he can be so... AWESOME!"

Bogan peered up at her with a wonky look in his eye, "Are you daft, Izz? He's trying to kill us."

Hunchy chimed in to point out the obvious, "To be certain, he's not actually shooting directly at us."

Not that Bogan wanted to hear his viewpoint, and he made it perfectly clear he had not warmed up to him. "What are you doing down here, Humpy? Better get back up top before we all catch the hump."

Elias deflected Bogan's comment to keep from having another fight, "Yeah, why isn't he shooting at us?"

Instantly, both speeders shot past the Whisper and out of sight. The four of them sat in the gunner's bubble wondering what was going on until Bogan had a revelation. "They're gonna cable us. Get up top and tell Gideon. Quick!" Bogan warned.

By the time Elias, Izzy and Hunchy made it back up top, one speeder had already locked its cable on to the Whisper.

"They're going to..." Elias tried to warn him, but Gideon finished his sentence, giving the surprise away.

"Cable us! I know. They already landed one," Gideon explained. Wyatt dodged the speeders the best he could, but he didn't have many options in the tunnel.

Then Bogan's voice rang over the bridge, "I don't mean to alarm you, but we're about to be hooked to the Iron Weaver."

"We need options!" Gideon said as the crew wondered if he was going to freeze up again.

"LOOK! Up head, it's another tunnel!" Elias shouted.

Wyatt jogged the Whisper hard left and right, scrapping the sides of the tunnel into a heavy cloud of dust until the speeders disappeared. Then he turned left into the tunnel, stopped the ship and killed the lights.

When the speeders shot past them, they assumed the Jack-boot would be next, but when he never showed Gideon sensed a trap. "Maybe he turned toward Karl's Labyrinth?" Elias said, taking his best guess at stealthy tactics.

"There's still too much dust to be sure. No, we wait," Gideon answered, hoping to regain the confidence of his crew. Wyatt switched the ship into whisper mode to prevent the larger blades from throwing more dust out into the passing tunnel and dropped the pilot's bubble to the lower level to watch from behind.

All they could hear, for the most part, was the bubbling of the Whisper and their own breathing, of which the hunchback's was the loudest. "Are you alright, Hunchy?" Ava asked as she watched him shaking. The rest of the crew turned and watched him as he braced his gnarled hands on his knees.

"Come on, Hunchy," Bogan quipped, "you're fogging up the windows."

Gasping as if he were out of breath from a hard run Hunchy stuttered out, "I...um...don't do so well...uh, in tunnels. Especially...underground."

Elias wiped his hand across the window, but nothing came off. "I don't think it coming from Hunchy's heavy breathing," he said, checking his hand to be certain. "I think it's on the outside of the window."

Elias walked out onto the main deck and wiped his hand on the windows and the moisture cleared "Yeah, it's definitely coming from out here. The air is wet— like my father's greenhouse—but it smells foul, like wet socks," he said, wiping more of the fog from the windows.

Bogan, Izzy and Merlin stepped outside with Elias to check. "You seeing this, Gid?" Bogan asked. Gideon nodded as he continued to listen for any word from Wyatt as to whether they were in the clear yet.

"Ugh," Izzy pinched her nose, "it does stink out here."

"Yeah, smells like Izzy after a long day in the boiler room." Bogan chuckled. Izzy turned and slugged him in the shoulder with her mod-hand. "OW!" Bogan bit his lip and pretended like it didn't hurt, but anyone could tell she left him a good bruise to remember his mistake.

Wyatt's round cockpit popped back up through the floor of the bridge, returning from his lookout duty in the rear dome. "Nothing. It's all quiet. I mean, there's still some dust, so I can't be totally sure, but I think we can head back."

Gideon stared at the floor, considering his options for a moment, and then made his decision. "This tunnel won't be much different from the others. I don't think it's wise to turn back and risk it. Let's continue with this tunnel. Only one light and we go slow." Wyatt confirmed Gideon's orders by flicking on a single light to lead them through the darkness, and to everyone's surprise they had pulled into a dead-end tunnel.

"HEY, GID, IT'S BLOCKED!" Bogan shouted what everyone had already figured out. Gideon stepped out from the bridge and walked down to the end of the forward deck with Elias, Bogan, Izzy and Merlin.

"Do you think it's a cave in?" Elias asked, scanning the sides of the tunnel walls.

"Maybe they hadn't completed this part of the mine yet," Izzy said, still holding her nose.

"Bogan, did you notice any tracks when we entered?" Gideon wondered.

"I don't remember, Gid, we came in here so fast and I was lookin' for speeders. What are you getting at?" Bogan asked, still rubbing his arm a bit.

"That's not going to make it heal any faster." Izzy giggled.

"Shhhh!" Gideon warned as he pushed a few buttons on his globe hand and a light beamed out from the end. He scanned the wall in front of them several times, up and down, and then shut the light off.

"Um, I have a question," Elias said nervously.

"What's up?" Bogan replied.

"It's probably nothing, but the other tunnel didn't have lumpy walls, so why are the walls all lumpy in this one?" he asked.

"What do mean lumpy?" Izzy's nasally voice squeaked.

Gideon flipped his light back on and scanned the side walls. At first he didn't notice anything, but Elias pointed to one of the lumps. "Right there!" he said. Gideon shined it on the lump as they investigated the strange anomaly. Then Gideon started to breathe as heavy and as hard as Hunchy, who was still slumped over on the bridge.

"What's wrong, Gideon?" Izzy asked. Gideon tried to speak, but something had stolen his voice away and all that came out was a cracking noise.

"C-aaac."

"Come on! Spit it out, Gid," Bogan prodded.

Gideon tried again and almost had it this time. "B-B-B, Mmm," he muttered.

"Oh, good grief, Gideon! Suck it up and say it!" Merlin blurted out his frustration at Gideon, but it wasn't a fair assessment of the situation. No one had ever seen anything like this before. Nothing could have prepared Gideon or any of them for what lay before them. Sure there were stories, but that's all they were, stories. Nightmares, in fact, but there it was staring Gideon in the face, and he was doing his best to get it out. He took a deep breath and scrunched his face a bit as he mustered his spine and forced out his words just above a whisper. "M-Mole. B-Big mole." Their eyes grew big when he pointed to the lump on the tunnel wall. "C-C-Claaaawwww!" he said with a whispered grunt and raising his finger to his lips.

This was no "small claw" like what Elias had seen the Jackboot sitting on. This was a monster claw, every bit the whole length of the Whisper and maybe longer, and that was only the claw. The rest of the paw was buried somewhere in the mass of dirt behind it. There were five claws on each side of the tunnel and they were dug into the dirt at the ends.

"Shhh, back to the bridge," Gideon said, pointing their way back. The four of them looked at him and nodded their heads in agreement as they all stepped carefully backwards.

It started as a twitch, just a small one, then a tickle. She didn't mean for it to happen, but she had been holding her nose too long. She squeezed harder, hoping it would go away, but it was already a full blown sneeze. "AACHOO!" Izzy grabbed her mouth with both hands and opened her eyes wide with shock. They all stopped dead in their tracks.

No one moved. Not a single sound. The mole was silent. Everyone breathed a sigh of relief and carefully continued stepping their way back toward the bridge. Then some dirt slid off the sides of the wall and everyone stopped again. Tiny crumbs, nothing more. They stood quietly again and waited for Gideon's all clear to start their walk. And then it happened.

It wasn't completely his fault. Besides, it was a new feature. He had only had it for one day, and it had been an exceedingly long day at that. In all the commotion of flying the Whisper down to save everyone and being chased by speeders and the Jackboot, even Merlin and Hunchy had forgotten. The new low-fuel alarm that Merlin had installed on Elias' heart-mod went into full alarm. They had forgotten to refill his coal hopper when they returned to the Whisper. Merlin had simply thrown him in the pilot's seat and sent him on a one way ticket back into the mine. For the last two hours he had been operating on the one berry Hunchy had put in the hopper, and now it was gone. Elias looked down at the flashing red light, then back at the crew. Izzy's mod-hand was covering her mouth, Bogan and Gideon were staring at each other, and Merlin eyes were mashed closed in shame. The alarm kept blaring and wouldn't stop until they filled the hopper. So they ran. They ran hard, and the beast awoke from its slumber.

Bogan grabbed Elias in mid-run as he worried the boy would fall over dead before making it back to the bridge. Izzy knew she had to get coal for his fuel hopper and passed everyone up. Merlin could only think of his failure and didn't want to see the beast rip the Whisper apart, so he kept his eyes closed and ran blindly in shame. But Gideon couldn't help but want to see it. He turned, right as the leviathan's snout rose up and blasted them with a dirty snort. Izzy blew right off the edge of the Whisper, but half a second later her mod-hand snapped hold of the railing, and she leaped back up on the deck in front of the door. Bogan's mod-leg kept him up straight as he met Izzy at the door with Elias.

Merlin was blown over and rolled all the way to the glass window, and Gideon's face was mashed into the window so he could barely slobber out his command. "WYATT! GET US OUT OF HERE!"

Wyatt was munching on some kind of crunchy treat he had scavenged from the kitchen and couldn't see the giant beast in front of them with only one light. He stopped mid-crunch with a mouth full of food and muffled out his question. "Whut?"

"LIGHTS!" Gideon demanded. "LIGHTS!"

Wyatt snapped on the lights, revealing a massive snout directly in front of the Whisper. With lightning speed, Wyatt flicked switches, moved levers and turned and pulled others. The Whisper went full reverse at its fastest speed, and Wyatt forced the dry snack down with a hard swallow.

Gideon and Merlin crawled their way into the door as Izzy returned from the boiler room with Elias' fuel right when Wyatt barked out, "HARD TURN!" but no one was really ready for it.

Wyatt flipped the Whisper around in a hard swinging motion, turning it around and toward the other end of the tunnel. Everyone was tossed against the walls like rag dolls from his hot rod move, and Izzy dropped Elias' refueling container. Wyatt slammed the ship into full throttle, knocking everyone around again. It was hardest for Hunchy, as his hump prevented him from rolling as well as everyone else. He yelped and hollered in pain as he tumbled around the bridge.

The dust at the other end had settled, but the cloud behind them was so thick they couldn't see the mole. They were almost back to the tunnel crossover when the two speeders popped out of nowhere, blocking their path. The tunnel continued behind the speeders, but Wyatt was worried the Whisper wouldn't fit between them, so he started to throttle back until Gideon blasted out, "BLOW THROUGH! BLOW THROUGH! FULL THROTTLE!" And that's exactly what Wyatt did. He squeezed right between the two speeders and disappeared into the opposite tunnel, leaving the speeders to the terror inside the dust cloud.

THE JACKBOOT'S LOYAL MEN THOUGHT THEY WERE GETTING THE drop on the crew of the Whisper, but nothing could have prepared them for the ten claws of terror that appeared out of the thick, nasty cloud. Their speeders, like specks of dust on a single claw, were flung against the tunnel and instantly crushed.

It wasn't the Iron Weaver's horn or lights that redirected the beast's attention away from the Whisper, but more so the vibration of the train tracks the beast landed on. The Jackboot, still pursing on his pipe when the beast came into view, practically dropped it right out of his mouth. "BOSARUS!" he roared. "FULL STOP!" Bosarus responded quickly, with the brakes scattering hot sparks and flames from the rails as it slowed and blasted steam from both sides, nearly covering the Jackboot's view. He didn't need to see it anyway. He could hear its grunting and ferocious digging, and he knew it was coming. The Jackboot placed his hand on a large lever and waited.

He knew the rumors had gotten out of control, but he figured they only helped to strengthen his hard reputation and keep his city safe. Had he truly killed giant moles? Yes, but most certainly not 30, and definitely nothing like what was headed for him now. How that number ever got to 30, he didn't have a clue. It was more like three, and he'd killed the beasts by crushing them against the tunnel wall with the front end of the Weaver. He added the harpoon after those kills, and specifically for a day like today. Had he tested it? Yes. Hope was a battle plan for fools, he oft said to himself. Had he tried it on a giant mole? Soon, very soon that question would be answered.

He pursed and puffed on his pipe, harder as the snorting and grunting from the beast turned the air foul, like rotten food in a hot dumpster. The Weaver's lights were no use in the massive dust wall created by the oncoming beast. He'd have to rely on instinct and a good bit of luck. He gripped the lever harder.

"BOSARUS!" the Jackboot hollered.

"YES, SIR!"

"BRACE YOURSELF!" He pulled hard on the lever, releasing the pressurized weapon as the beast's claws emerged through the heavy cloud of dirt.

AFTER GETTING THEIR BEARINGS AND FINALLY REFILLING ELIAS' fuel, they continued through the tunnel at a more cautious pace. The Whisper crew only had to travel a short distance before they came upon a large opening in the tunnel created by a mole breaching through. Gideon called for masks and everyone but Hunchy put one on.

"Why start now?" he reasoned. But it was just another thing Bogan added to his list of reasons why the hunchback shouldn't be trusted.

It was around midnight by the time Wyatt guided the ship up through the opening, and it only took a few minutes to climb 300 feet above the black mist. Wyatt had some concerns about the Whisper's steering, so he switched to octopi-auto pilot and used his mod-hands to climb around the side of the ship to check the rear rudder.

Elias helped the stinky hunchback out to the forward deck so he could recover from his claustrophobia, but even more so to keep the nasty smell out of the ship. Hunchy began to recover almost instantly once the cool night air filled his lungs. If the timing had been better, Elias would have offloaded the nagging question about what the hunchback did to him, but the boy thought it best to wait until he had fully recovered from his tunnel terror. When Casper waddled out onto the deck and hopped up on the railing next to them, Elias wondered if it was time for another night of hunting. Elias convinced the hunchback that he probably shouldn't stay out much longer, and it might be best for everyone if he cleaned up. Hunchy's eyes lit up at the thought of washing the smell of captivity off his body, and so Elias showed him to the men's' washroom.

Wyatt returned from investigating the rudder problem to find Bogan, Merlin, Elias and Gideon in the dining room, recovering with a snack and questioning why the giant mole was waiting outside GFC. Elias wondered if he was reliving some sort of sick karma for all the moles he'd killed in his father's greenhouse, and they had finally come to punish him for his transgressions, but again he decided to keep his thoughts to himself. He felt a little better when Gideon started to explain how the moles usually go straight for the attack and how strange it was to find it quietly resting not far from GFC.

Wyatt abruptly interrupted him to give his damage report on the rudder, but when Izzy, returning from the boiler room, ran in, she tried to beat him to the punch. "We've got a problem!" Izzy and Wyatt said at the same time, then pointed at one another trying to beat each other to the word, "JINX!"

- 8 -

TRUTH MATTERS

*T*he **Hunchback:** Standing alone in the washroom, he knew it had been more than a year since he had seen his own face. He locked the door and checked it twice, then prepared himself for the truth in the mirror. He removed the gloves from his strange hands and pulled off his hooded cloak, letting it drop to the floor. What was once considered a beautiful garment of great value was now ragged, filthy and unworthy of even the lowest of beggars on his mountain. He filled the sink with water from a container and rested his hands on edge of it. He knew what he was about to see would be difficult, but after the mine and many other hardships, he felt he could handle anything. He strengthened his emotional resolve, took a deep breath and raised his head to the strange man in the scuffed mirror. At first he wondered if the mirror had disappeared and he was truly staring out a window at a horrible creature clinging to the outside of the ship. Was that really his face?

How could life have gone so horribly wrong? He was disgusted and repulsed with himself.

But it wasn't the repulsive smell that he had grown used to, or the shame in his eyes, or even the disappointment in his failure that caused the tears to slip down his face. It was self-pity that weighed heavy on him. He wept so hard he feared someone would hear him, bust through the door and see him for what he truly was. The pathetic sight before him was more than he could bear, and it buckled his knees under him as he clung to the sink weeping.

If the king saw him now would he run to him and embrace him with forgiveness and love, or scoff at his failure and remind him of how wrong he truly was? The king loved his son dearly, but he could not let his disobedience stand. Mocking his authority in front of the leaders was a new low for the prince. The most difficult thought of all was that his father had been right and he would have to admit his failure and shame in front of the convocation. Not lost on his thoughts were the others that went with him. How could he return without them? Were they even alive? What if they had made it back and blamed everything on him? Prison or worse might be waiting for him. But the leaders were heartless and his father too weak to stand up to them. They were all content to live on their mountain, above everyone else, while the world below them slowly died. Only Sunago the Great, who had gone on many years ago, was brave enough to defy them. Someone had to do something and who better than the king's son? He had always been the voice according to his people. He was the one with vision, hope, and direction and if anyone could fulfill the prophecy it was him. Even if it wasn't him, he would force the prophecy, because results are more important that prophecies. Only now he was nothing but a mere jester of his own ideas.

Whoever it was looking back at him in the mirror, one thing was certain to him now; a failure was standing before him. Even his father's servants were better cared for than him. Better fed, better clothed and better smelling. In that moment he decided he would finish the task of helping those who'd freed him, then return to his father's mountain and beg for forgiveness. He would not be so bold as to ask for the rights of a prince, but if he returned with several bags of fire berries, the leaders might be convinced to allow him to take a humble servant's position. A slight smile snuck up on his face as he began to wash the filth and stench from his body.

Even though the truth mattered to him, he couldn't reveal the whole truth to his deliverers. He worried they might be overcome with fear and try to harm him. Especially the one named Bogan. So he cleaned his cloak and gloves until there was no soap or water left. Leaving the once tidy washroom now splattered with grimy blotches of coal dust and the stench of soiled, moldy towels, he stepped out feeling clean, upbeat and focused. Nothing was going to stop him from making it back home, because now he finally had a plan.

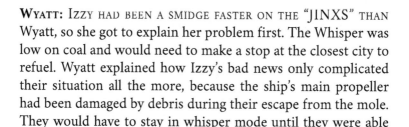

WYATT: Izzy had been a smidge faster on the "JINXS" than Wyatt, so she got to explain her problem first. The Whisper was low on coal and would need to make a stop at the closest city to refuel. Wyatt explained how Izzy's bad news only complicated their situation all the more, because the ship's main propeller had been damaged by debris during their escape from the mole. They would have to stay in whisper mode until they were able to repair it.

Wyatt tapped his right hand on his left shoulder as a signal to Gideon that he was having pain at his mod connections and needed to remove them to rest his limbs. He'd set up the secret signal after he explained his feelings for Ava and that he didn't want her to think he was less of a man for showing his pain. He made every effort to prevent Ava from seeing him without his mods because he couldn't bear the thought of her seeing him in such a helpless state. He wasn't even sure she liked him, but he had hope that one day things might work out in his favor. He made sure only Merlin or Gideon would come into his room when his mods were off and that he was always covered up before the door opened.

Once his mods were removed, he rubbed salve on his limbs

to help them heal. Then he slid his right stump through a looped rope attached to a call bell in case he needed help. He never slept well when his mods were off and it was even worse if the ship was in whisper mode because the whispers turned into her lies.

Of all those on the Whisper, none had lived the nightmare that Wyatt experienced at the hands of his mother, who had sold his arms and legs to the mold cults for their magic. As he lay there without his mods, he felt like that little boy again. The little boy who trusted her, who believed the lies she whispered in his ear every time she asked for another limb. The mother who smiled at him with eyes of love, but behind them deep darkness had made its home.

Some nights, like this one, he remembered the day that shiny black monster of a train stopped in front of his mother who was pushing him in his shopping cart. There were 12 of them with her when that heartless man stepped off his train and slaughtered all except him and his mother. Wyatt never forgot the burning anger in his eyes as he looked at his mother. When the man lifted him out of the cart by the back of his coat, Wyatt wiggled his tiny limbs as hard as he could to get away, but he had no mods to save him. The man left him on the train, stepped back outside and chained her hands to the shopping cart. Wyatt screamed and cried and wanted desperately to hurt the man, because the only truth that mattered to him was she was his mother, no matter how cruel she had been. He hated her and he loved her.

ELIAS: THAT NIGHT HIS MIND RACED THROUGH SO MANY questions as he lay in bed trying to process the events of the past few days. Aside from his secret desire to live long enough to drive a pickaxe into the Jackboot's head, he'd begun to like these strange freaks that had kidnapped him. They had become fellow prisoners that he'd given his own life to save from the murderer of his parents. That all would have been far more than he would have ever expected to witness in his short life, but what he couldn't get out of his mind was what the hunchback did to him.

Whatever happened, all he could remember was the voice calling him. He thought about the voice on the ship that night with Casper, but this voice was different. He felt fire in his mouth, in his heart and in his hands, and he heard it calling his name. Why did the red mist come out of his mouth when he spoke? Why did the people of GFC run away from him? He wanted desperately to ask Hunchy these questions, but the hunchback had been cleaning up in the washroom most of the night and that was a good thing for everyone. Finally, his lack of sleep caught up with him, and not even Bogan's night terrors could keep him awake.

That next morning everyone grabbed a quick bite to eat, then Izzy, Gideon and Merlin went right to work repairing the main propeller. Ava worked to repair the weld on a metal plate mounted at the front of the envelope, while Bogan and Elias handed parts up to her. Hunchy was practically useless with that gnarled hump of his, so he stood out on the front of the ship daydreaming. This really grinded at Bogan, who simply couldn't stop complaining about how useless Hunchy was during the whole repair. Elias finally grew tired of Bogan's attitude and used it to convince Bogan to let him talk Hunchy into helping, but truthfully, he merely wanted a chance to ask those burning questions that kept gnawing at him.

Hunchy was much cleaner than before, and most of the smell was gone. There even seemed to be some shine to his cloak as he hunched over the railing muttering or whispering something. Elias thought a gentle touch on his back would keep from startling him. He placed his hand on the hump, but when something spongy moved inside, the hunchback swung around fast and practically knocked him over. The hunchback was much faster than Elias realized and caught him mid-fall with those gnarled hands. Fortunately for Hunchy, the ship kept passing through thick, patchy clouds that hid the incident from Bogan's view this time.

"I'm sorry. You startled me," his face quickly turned from disturbed to that familiar smile Elias had seen back in the mine.

"That's okay. I should have said something." He could have kicked himself right there.

"What can I do for my deliverer?" Hunchy happily asked.

"I want to know what you did to me in the mine," Elias said.

"Yes, of course. I told you I would explain, didn't I?"

"That's right. You did."

Hunchy paused for a moment, seeming to gather his thoughts. "What I did with the berries shouldn't have worked. In fact, it's never been done before. I only did it because you were already dead. What did we have to lose?"

"Berries?"

"Oh that's right," Hunchy laughed, "you were dead, weren't you?" He cleared his throat. "I placed the berry juice in your fuel container to restart your generator, and then I put the rest on your heart and hoped for the best," his hooded cloak covered most of his smile.

"So why did it work?"

"I don't know. It should have destroyed your heart. Even now I don't understand how you are still alive. I was always told the berries were too dangerous for hu…" He paused for a moment as if to hold his tongue from something. "Only now I know that was a lie. If they hadn't put that mod in your chest I might have been able to save you." Hunchy explained.

"I'M SICK OF BEING TOLD I'M GOING TO DIE!" Elias realized he was yelling and toned it down to keep Bogan from coming over. "I've been hearing that my whole life, and I'm tired of it. Look at me! My parents always told me I was going to die, but I've already outlived them. When you brought me back from the dead I never felt so strong in all my life. My whole body was burning like it was on fire, and all I could see was red, the heat was so intense and I felt so alive and the voice kept…"

"WHAT!" A dark look came over the hunchback's face as he responded in shock.

"Well, I'm not sure it was a voice. Maybe it was my ears ringing." Elias doubted his own words.

The friendly demeanor and kind smile were gone now as the hunchback grabbed Elias by his shoulders. "What did you hear? What did it say? Tell me now! Tell me!" he demanded.

"I-I don't know. It sounded like it was saying something, but I could barely hear it." Fear gripped Elias as hunchback's powerful hands dug deep into his arms and that unveiled eye pierced through him.

"Tell me the truth!"

"I-I think it whispered my name. Yeah, it was calling my name. I think," Elias said.

The hunchback's mouth dropped open and the strength went out of his hands, but it was too late. Bogan was already on his way.

"HEY, LUMPY! Let go of him before I snap that ugly hump off your back. Kid, go help Ava. I need to set something straight for a moment." Bogan seemed determined enough, and Elias was so startled by the hunchback that it seemed best to leave him to Bogan's scolding. Elias watched as Bogan moved in so close to the freaks face that his sour breath seemed punishment enough to Hunchy. Nevertheless Bogan demanded his satisfaction as he snapped out his sharp blade and pressed it against the sneaky hunchback's chest. "I kid you not, lumpy, you touch him like that again and I'll cut out your heart and feed it to Casper." He pointed to the giant owl perched on the rails. Still in shock the hunchback nodded his understanding, then Bogan walked back towards Ava with a nice, big, happy grin.

Ava: Charlie had taught her all the tricks to running a good weld bead, and although Izzy was faster, Ava was an artist with the welder. Gideon always gave her the welding jobs that were visible, so the ship looked professionally crafted by the Jackboot himself. To tell the truth, Ava's perfectionism was mostly due to the fact she always felt like Charlie was watching over her, and her need to please him was greater than anyone else's opinion. No one loved her like Charlie did, and she had never dreamed someone so kind and gentle could have ever existed in this cruel world.

Several months before his death, Charlie decided it would be easier on everyone if he left, so they wouldn't have the memory of watching him die a slow, horrible death. When he was sneaking out late at night, Gideon caught him, but Charlie made him promise not to tell Ava. Gideon eventually told anyway, hoping it would help ease her pain, but it only worked to drive a wedge between them. Unbeknownst to Gideon, it did help Ava, who now lived with the idea that Charlie had somehow survived and was secretly watching over her. When her welding helmet was down and it was only her looking through that little dark window, at that tiny blue light melting the metal, she felt his presence right there with her. Nothing else mattered to her but his wonderful smile whenever she lifted off her mask. Charlie gave his life for the crew of the Whisper, but in truth she knew he had done it for her.

The last metal plate to repair was out on the edge of the Whisper's envelope and helped protect the soft cloth at the front from damage. It had been hit by a piece of debris that fell from one of the burning airships at the mine.

She used a safety cord to hang off the side of the ship while she attached the plate with an anchor, then welded it in place. Bogan had been using a reaching pole to get supplies up to her while she worked, but now he was too busy giving Hunchy his scolding, so she asked Elias for help. Elias stood on the forward deck in front of the glass windows and reached a new welding rod up to her with the pole. The clouds were so thick that day that it was hard enough to see her up there, but he managed it well. Bogan, who was quite pleased with his strong arming of Hunchy, returned and gave Elias a pat on the back for his good work. The clouds swept around her as she welded the plate down, but what happened next was no one's fault. These things happen sometimes no matter how good you are or how many times you've done the job. Accidents just happen.

BOGAN: THE BRACKET SLIPPED ON THE ANCHOR BEFORE AVA HAD it secured with the weld and swung off the anchor bolt, slicing her safety cord from the ship. The bracket fell to the deck in front of Elias and Bogan, and her cord flipped down against the window. Bogan caught something falling out the corner of his eye and off the side of the ship and immediately looked down over the railing to see Ava falling through the clouds.

"AVA!" He placed his hands on his head and screamed. "GIDEON! No, no, no, no, no.

GIDEON!" His hands trembled at the thought of losing his friend and the love of his brother's life.

Elias and Bogan looked down into the passing clouds as the rest of the crew came running. "Gideon, she—she's gone. Merlin, I can't—I can't believe it." Bogan stammered.

"What? Who's gone?" Gideon begged.

"Ava. Ava. She's... Ava's gone," Bogan's eyes welled up. "She was welding the bracket—it fell and her cord snapped. I-I watched her drop through the clouds."

"No, it couldn't have been. Maybe you're mistaken. AVA! Maybe she's..." then Gideon stopped and noticed Elias shaking his head.

They were destroyed with grief when Izzy finally made it to the forward deck. "What's all the yelling? What's wrong?" Izzy asked. Their crushing anguish was evident. "Where's Ava? Bogan, where's Ava?" When she saw the tears streaming down Bogan's face she ran and looked over the edge. Bogan shook his head slowing then dropped it.

"NO! It can't be true, it just can't be true. WHY? What happened? NO, Bogan!" Izzy beat him on the chest with both fists. Even though it hurt, he never flinched. He felt he deserved it. They stood there looking over the railing, wishing Ava could have grabbed it as tight as they held it now, but no one said a word. They simply let their tears fall into the passing clouds below. Everyone knew she was gone. If the fall didn't kill her instantly, the black mist would eventually.

A voice behind them broke their moment of grief. "Can I get a little help over here?" Hunchy asked, but they were too frozen to answer him.

"Pardon me, but I could use a little help here," he asked again.

Bogan was starting to get annoyed with the hunchback for his disrespect of the moment. Still gazing over the edge with the rest of them, Bogan mutter through his teeth, "He's got to be the stupidest—of all the—can't he see we just lost Ava?"

"Please, I need some help here…"

Bogan lifted his head, "I'm going throw him over the edge." He turned around, "Listen here, Hunchy, I'm…AVA!" Bogan cried out in disbelief and they all turned around to see the hunchback holding an unconscious Ava.

"I need some help here. She must have hit her head, but she's breathing," Hunchy said.

"HOW?" Gideon asked in wonder at the hunchback's amazing feat.

Hunchy pointed to his belt, "I saw her fall and I clipped this springy cord on and jumped after her."

Izzy ran over to him and hugged him while he was still holding Ava in his arms.

"Thank you so much. How can we ever repay you for this?" Gideon said as he and Merlin relieved the hunchback of her.

"It's a good thing this springy cord was here. Funny thing bounced me right back up on the ship," Hunchy said, unclipping the cord from under his cloak and dropping it on the deck.

"Let's get her inside and check out that bump," Merlin said as Ava began to regain consciousness.

Hunchy followed them all inside as they continued to shower him with praise. Wyatt, however, had only heard that something had happened to Ava and crawled out on all four stumps into the hallway, frantically asking if she was okay. Elias started to run in and help him up, but Bogan caught him by the arm.

"Hold up," Bogan said, pointing to the strap on the deck beside another strap that wasn't tied down. "Which one of those did Hunchy use?"

"That one, I guess. It's the only one tied down."

Bogan gave Elias a smug look, "I'm sure it was the other one. I watched him drop it."

"That's impossible, Bogan. It was obviously the one hooked to the ship." Though he tried to hide it, Bogan was still harboring bad feelings towards Hunchy, and judging by the expression on Elias' face, he wasn't doing a good job.

"What's it matter anyway? She's safe, right? We need to be in there helping out." After a bit of prompting Bogan let Elias convince him to drop it and go inside with everyone else.

Ava recovered quickly after an injection from Merlin and no small injection of loving care from everyone else. Izzy and Gideon made short work of the propeller repair, but Gideon chose to leave the ship in whisper mode to conserve fuel until they got to Gabriel's Harbor. He also felt like everyone needed to mentally recover from the trauma of almost losing Ava, so he wanted everyone to report to the mess hall for an early dinner. Once everyone was seated, Gideon stood up and gave a humble apology about letting them down or something, but no one remembered any of it after he pulled out a bag of coffee he had been saving. Merlin's brain almost exploded with lightning, and Izzy jumped up and grabbed the bag out of his hand. A few moments later they were sipping joy in a cup and laughing. When Elias explained how he had coffee every day back on his parents' mountain, they all playfully threw their napkins at him. Wyatt joked about how they should have left Elias and took the coffee, but no one laughed. He had become their friend.

Their dinner quickly took a downward turn when Bogan asked Gideon a question. "How many of these flowers do you think it's going to take to cover all the damage to GFC?"

It sucked the energy right out of the room and they sat there silently pondering the weight of destruction they'd left behind. The sounds of whispering filled their ears as the ship cruised for Gabriel's Harbor into the setting sun. The silence was broken when Bogan finished his cup, set it down hard and glared at the hunchback.

"How did you do it?" Bogan asked.

Hunchy smiled at him, "Do what?"

Everyone looked up at Bogan, worried he was about to start another confrontation with Hunchy, so Gideon moved to stop it. "Enough, Bogan!"

"No, really. How did you do it?" Bogan asked again.

"I'm afraid I haven't the slightest idea what you're talking about." The hunchback looked baffled.

"You said you used the cord to save Ava, but the one you

used wasn't hooked to the ship. So what I'm asking is—how did you do it?" Bogan took a harsher tone this time.

"Bogan! He saved my life," Ava chimed in to scold. "Leave him alone."

"Bogan," Gideon tried again.

"It's an obvious misunderstanding. You see, there were two cables, and you must have gotten them confused," Hunchy explained.

Izzy had been in the process of putting her cup back down on the table but stopped about an inch above it and held it there for what seemed like an eternity as the tension built. Bogan looked over at Elias sitting there sipping his cup, hoping no one noticed that it was already empty.

"I know what I saw. I followed the one that you unclipped from your belt all the way back to the end, and it wasn't hooked to the ship." Bogan was so sure of himself he was starting to convince Wyatt. Hunchy was about to speak again when Bogan blurted out, "I bet you're one of the smoke charmers the Jackboot talks about, aren't you? That's why you were chained to the rock in the mine."

At this point it was difficult to tell if Hunchy was shaking from too much coffee, or if Bogan had revealed the truth about him in front of everyone, but he smacked the table and stood up, clinching his gnarled fists.

"I saved your friend. Would your smoke charmers do that?" His voice was sharper, even menacing.

"He hasn't even told us where he's taking us, Gideon! How are you okay with this?" Bogan snapped.

"Bogan! You're confined to quarters until we reach the harbor," Gideon ordered.

Bogan stood up and smacked the table, startling an octopus in the water tube behind Gideon. "The truth matters, Gideon. Charlie always said it, the truth matters." Pointing at Hunchy's face, he repeated, "It matters." He huffed and then stormed off to his quarters. Behind him he heard Gideon apologized to Hunchy who quickly accepted, and then seemed to decide some fresh air would do him good, so he walked out onto the forward deck as the sun was dropping in the sky.

Izzy: A few moments later, Izzy got up and followed the hunchback outside. If there was anyone on the Whisper who knew firsthand how to deal with difficult people like Bogan, it was Izzy. She was skilled in the art of maneuvering difficult people into working together in a way that only an expert hypnotist could do, but all she needed were her charming eyes and the seductive voice of her mother. Most everything else she got from her father, who was driven mad after her mother was killed by mist charmers when she was about four years old. But her father's continued insanity came from something much deeper. Something only she could solve when the time was right.

It was a difficult time for her father, who was employed by Angus Grand as a welder or iron weavers as some called them. Angus Grand was the man who built Grand Fortune City, or funded its construction— depending on your viewpoint. When her father killed Eddie, the son of Angus Grand, the city was thrown into chaos. Her father fled to Gabriel's Harbor, as Angus wanted him dead, so he left his daughter with a man named Big Bobby Kitchen, who became a sort of surrogate father to her. After a time, her father remarried a woman from the harbor named Vanessa, in hopes of giving his daughter more of a woman's touch, but she had already grown to love the world of iron, thanks to Big Bobby.

The marriage didn't help her much anyway because, the truth was, her father and step mother mixed like gasoline and fire and she knew it, but she was always able to bring them together. When her stepmother couldn't take the man any longer, she ran away, but many in others said her father was the one that sent her away. Whatever their last fight was about, Izzy knew her father's anger towards Vanessa was unlike anything she had ever seen before. However, when Izzy learned of Vanessa's connection to the mold cults, she wished he'd gotten rid of her sooner. Izzy already despised the mold cults for what they did to her mother, but now that her stepmother had joined them, her distain for them grew even deeper.

As Izzy approached the hunchback, she built up her confidence by thinking of all those fights and arguments she had helped them work through, in hopes it would prepare her for this one. She announced herself as she got closer, "Hunchy, it's Izzy." He was whispering something, but stopped when she arrived. He turned his head slightly back toward her but said nothing. The big orange sun behind his head made him almost seem saint like as it continued to drop toward the horizon. At least it made the strange man seem more approachable than his usual creepy demeanor. She crossed her arms and leaned them on the railing the same way Hunchy was leaning and looked out at the orange ball.

He smelled much better than before, and what she could see of his face looked clean, but the other half was always covered with his cloak. She thought it would be best to start with a kind gesture. "We're all grateful for what you did for Ava, including Bogan. I know it seems like he doesn't like you, but since Charlie's death he's been short with everyone. I know if you give him some time he'll come around."

The hunchback looked over at her, and the light from the setting sun revealed strange markings on the hooded part of his face. They caught her off her game and she lost her train of thought when he countered with a strong, commanding voice. "No, he won't. I've known his kind my whole life, and they never change. They see someone like me and they want to harm me, even kill me. Speak no more of him to me," and he turned his head back toward the sun.

His words sent a familiar numbing feeling through her chest. She wondered if the hunchback was as hard a man as her father, who'd never gotten over the loss of her mother. He was an impressive man, who had accomplished much for GFC and made a great name for himself, but he was also a cruel man with a nasty reputation for vengeance. That didn't matter to her because she admired his skill, strength and achievements over those nasty rumors. Lies, she called them.

He truly would have never done those things people accused

him of. No matter how many times she heard wretched brute, malcontent, mobster, murderer, scoundrel or butcher, he was still her father, and that truth was what mattered to her. Their terrible lies were just that, lies. She loved him and deep down truly believed his motives were good. She knew somewhere within that tortured man they all called villain lay the heart of an overprotective father, but what she didn't know, was at that exact moment he was slowly being crushed under the carcass of a giant tunnel mole.

THE ALCHEMIST: THE PRICE HE PAID FOR HER LOVE WAS STEEP, but she gave him so much more in return. She taught him how to speak smoke into form until he became more powerful than her and so the pupil became the master. Because of what she'd done for him and what she meant to him, he was willing to forgive her failure and allow her another chance to bring the boy to him before the prophecy awakened. If she continued to fail, he would take control. After all, it was his destiny at risk.

BOGAN AND CASPER: AS THE LIGHTS FROM GABRIEL'S HARBOR came into view, Ava, Gideon, Merlin and Elias joined Izzy and the hunchback on the forward deck. It was a wondrous sight for Elias, who had never seen city lights at night. The harbor was much older than Grand Fortune City and was far more impressive with its triple platform design. Each city platform had its own tower, and from a distance they looked like magical toad stools speckled with glitter, rising from the black mist.

Harbor I, the first and oldest tower platform, was the lowest of the three and was built by an extremely wealthy man named Gabriel Rand III. When the black mist began spreading the creeping mold throughout the world, Gabriel assembled as many scientists, doctors, engineers and all manner of intellect to build a safe haven for mankind. Gabriel's Harbor was everyone's dream city, but only those who were truly gifted were allowed in. As the city grew, it fell far from whence it came, and it no longer mattered if your intellect was that of a gnat. As long as you had a sponsor from the council, you were granted citizenship. Those who tried to change things back to the glory days of Gabriel Rand would disappear, never to be heard from again, but there were quiet pockets of resistance still thriving in the city.

As they stood on the deck of the Whisper admiring the city lights, Bogan left his quarters and joined Wyatt on the bridge. However, Bogan's eyes did not fall on the beautiful lights of the harbor as they had so many times before. No, Bogan's eyes went directly to something he had never seen before. Casper had landed right next to Hunchy out on the deck, and Hunchy was petting him on the head. That bird had never let anyone touch him freely without taking at least a piece of flesh from them, but there he was, letting the hunchback stroke his feathers. Bogan wanted to say something to Wyatt, but he didn't want to cause a collision with any of the other airships coming into the docks.

When the hunchback reached into his cloak and started feeding the gray owl, Bogan wondered if maybe Casper was merely being nice for the tasty snack, but when Casper turned his head all the way around, Bogan's arms went prickly with chills. Casper's eyes were glowing bright red like fire. Bogan wanted to scream for Wyatt to look or call out to the others so they could see, but he couldn't move. All he could do was stare at the bird with his mouth open. Then Casper swooped off the railing directly at the window Bogan watched from and turned hard left and down into the black mist below. Bogan pointed where Casper had flown and stammered to get his words out, "But...he..."

"Yes, Bogan, it's the harbor. Sheeesh! We've seen it a hundred times. Now sit back and leave the flying to me, would you?" Wyatt said.

- 9 -

GABRIEL'S HARBOR

*W*yatt docked the Whisper at the original lower level of the harbor because it was cheaper than the other levels. Cheaper mainly because the black mist had risen so high you could practically spit in it and watch it plop through like a rock into wicked pudding. A security guard stepped up beside their ship as they were docking and asked them where they were from and the nature of their visit to the harbor.

"We need to refuel and pick up supplies," Gideon explained, hoping the guard wouldn't realize he'd failed to mention where they'd come from.

"How long do you plan on staying at the harbor?" the guard asked.

"Just long enough to get what we need and we'll be on our

way." The uncomfortable look on the guard's face made Gideon uneasy as he worried news from the Jackboot may have already reached the harbor ahead of them.

"And where did you say you were from?" the guard asked, looking down at the GFC dock tag still on the side of the Whisper.

"We're passing through on our way to Sullivan's Coast. Good fishing there this time of year." It sounded believable enough to Elias, who wondered if that's where they were truly headed. Being the spy ship that it was, the Whisper had no identifying marks or name on the side like other ships, so when the guard kept looking Gideon spoke up.

"She's called the Charlie," he said.

"Oh, thank you, I couldn't find a name anywhere." The guard thought for a moment. "Are you certain? I believe I've seen this ship here before." He gave Gideon the old squinty eye, so Gideon figured a show of force might buy him a little confidence with the nosey man.

"I think I would know the name of my own ship, wouldn't I? Now are you going to let us dock or not?"

"All right, all right, don't get in a tizzy. I'm only doing my due diligence here." The guard backed off his pushy questions and stamped their docking papers. "Enjoy your time here at the harbor," he grumbled.

When the guard finally released them, they locked down the Whisper and walked towards the main focal point at the entrance, called Captain's Courtyard. It was quite the busy place, even at night fall, as ships unloaded supplies and people bustled about the docks with their robot mods, who were busy unloading all manner of crates and goods from their ships. The cool air felt nice on Elias' skin, which seemed to have never fully cooled from the events of Hunchy's berry revival. He had a slight moment of panic regarding his fuel that cleared his head, and he quickly looked down to make sure he had filled his hopper to the max. The overpowering smell from freshly built pine crates reminded him of home, and he wondered if a city like the harbor could ever take its place.

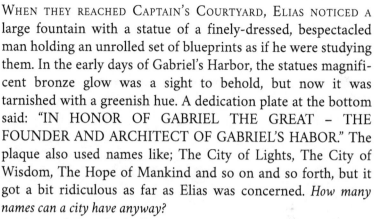

When they reached Captain's Courtyard, Elias noticed a large fountain with a statue of a finely-dressed, bespectacled man holding an unrolled set of blueprints as if he were studying them. In the early days of Gabriel's Harbor, the statues magnificent bronze glow was a sight to behold, but now it was tarnished with a greenish hue. A dedication plate at the bottom said: "IN HONOR OF GABRIEL THE GREAT – THE FOUNDER AND ARCHITECT OF GABRIEL'S HABOR." The plaque also used names like; The City of Lights, The City of Wisdom, The Hope of Mankind and so on and so forth, but it got a bit ridiculous as far as Elias was concerned. *How many names can a city have anyway?*

Ava and Izzy both flipped coins into the fountain, as was their tradition whenever they came to the harbor, but the guys had already seen it enough times to be as unimpressed as they could be at this point.

While they were still standing there admiring the fountain, two well-dressed men in trench coats and top hats approached them as third person in a long black dress, carrying an umbrella, stopped and waited a good distance behind them. All three of them had nicely woven G&B crests on the left side of their garments that clearly indicated they were people of importance in the harbor, but Elias guessed the woman to be of greater importance. Her long, dark hair poured down over her right shoulder and she held the umbrella in an almost sinister way, so no one could see her face. Elias wondered if she was carrying the umbrella for just that reason, since there wasn't any rain, and she must have been smoking as, every so often, a tiny black puff would roll out from under the umbrella.

Gideon quickly stepped out in front of the crew and prepared himself for whatever they might ask him.

"Don't be alarmed. We are representatives of the Harbor Council," they spoke quickly when they noticed Gideon's unsettled stance.

"We know who you are."

And with that one statement, Bogan pulled the biggest hand

cannon out from who knew where and pointed it right at them. Elias kept trying to figure out where Bogan had pulled it from, but one thing was for sure, Bogan was not playing games.

"Please, there is no need for violence. If we wanted you dead," the one speaking pointed to the armed guard towers surrounding them, "we would have done it when you arrived."

Gideon placed his hand on the top of Bogan's gun and lowered it. "Put it away," he said.

Elias watched as the back of Bogan's mod-leg opened and he placed the gun back inside. The leg closed and he slapped the strap on his pants, locking it back in place. Elias began to wonder what other secrets his friends had stored in their mods as the man from the harbor council explained their reason for meeting them.

"My name is Councilman Forsythe and this is Councilman Cillian. We at the Harbor Council have received word of your exploits at Grand Fortune City and are thrilled at the opportunity this might bring. The Harbor has never been comfortable with the Jackboot's harsh methods, and we believe this provides an excellent opportunity to bring about a healthy change for everyone," he cleared his throat, looking for a positive response from Gideon. But when he got nothing he continued on, "We believe you and your crew have helped put things into motion for a more positive relationship with those in GFC more aligned to...um...our way of thinking," the representatives smiled, and Izzy cracked a smug look herself.

"We're listening," Gideon replied.

Forsythe mopped his forehead directly under his large hat with a white handkerchief and cleared his throat again, "We were fascinated with your escape from the Jackboot's mine, unharmed even, and since you seem so skilled at such things, we would like to entertain an opportunity for you to solve a problem of ours,"

Elias wondered why councilman Forsythe didn't introduce the lady council member standing in the distance. Every so often she would tilt her umbrella so he could almost see her face then hide it again when she caught his gaze. His eyes were quickly diverted away from her when Cillian vigorously began rubbing something inside his coat pocket. Councilman Cillian's nervous demeanor was making Elias just as uncomfortable, and he wished Bogan hadn't put that hand cannon away so soon.

"We at the council would like to offer to cover your expenses for a full load of fuel, food and supplies in return for help with a simple task at one of our mines," Forsythe went on to explain.

Gideon didn't like where this was heading but continued listening anyway. "What's the job?" he asked.

"Two recently repaired steam bots have, um...malfunctioned, if you will, and we would like for you to simply shut them down," Forsythe said with a gentle expression on his face.

"Shut them down? All you want us to do is shut them down?" Gideon skeptically asked. "

"Yes. We are not concerned with how you accomplish it, as you seem to be good at damaging the Jackboot's property well enough. So their condition at the end is of no concern to us. As you will see, they have caused us a great deal of trouble. These bots have damaged our mine and equipment, and with no small loss of productivity, which has severely impacted our coal supplies. Not to mention the deaths of four valuable miners," Councilman Forsythe explained as he continued clearing the sweat from his brow. He didn't much seem like a sweaty man, so Elias wondered what exactly was stressing him.

"Four miners dead? No thanks! We'll pass." Gideon answered. Elias watched as Councilman Cillian immediately stopped his incessant rubbing and looked at Forsythe.

"Well, then I guess that leaves us no choice. Councilman Cillian, let them have it!" Forsythe said.

Cillian quickly removed his hand from his cloak.

"BOGAN!" Gideon burst out as everyone jumped back, but before Bogan could draw his hand cannon again, they noticed that Cillian had pulled out a key and was dangling it from a chain.

Confusion descended on the crew as they wondered what kind of trick these men were trying to pull.

"We'll merely have to up the ante then, won't we? How about a night's stay at our finest hotel: the Argyle," Forsythe and Cillian grinned.

Izzy and Ava gasped in surprise at the prospect of their childhood dream coming true.

"Wait just a moment. You're going to let us," he pointed to his roughly dressed crew and their mods, "with all these modifications, stay in your finest hotel? I thought the harbor didn't allow moddies anywhere near the Argyle, let alone sleep in it." Gideon still wasn't sure he trusted them. Normally he would have taken a day to decide on something so far out of the norm, but his crew was instantly overjoyed.

"Whoa! Gideon, come on, it's worth it. Think of all the jobs we would have to pull to be able to afford one night at the Argyle. We'll probably never get a chance like this again." Wyatt was so stoked.

"The Harbor Council has made an exception for you and your crew. Sort of a thank you for what you did at GFC," Forsythe explained. "Think of it as the beginning of a new and beneficial relationship."

"We've probably had harder jobs. A few steam bot malfunctions and we don't even have to save the bots. I mean, come on, they're harvesting bots. It's not like they're fully armored war bots. I like the sound of it, Gideon," Merlin said, quickly calculating the job's benefits and risks.

"It truly is a chance of a lifetime for your small crew," Forsythe eagerly encouraged.

"I don't know, Gideon," Bogan said with a skeptical tone. Hunchy maneuvered himself behind the crew, doing his best to not draw anyone's attention as he seemed to be hiding from the Councilmen.

"Well, it sounds like my crew has already agreed to the job, so I guess I better get on board," Gideon answered as the rest of them started shouting excitedly about the hotel's lavish buffet.

"Excellent," Forsythe said, placing his handkerchief back in his pocket. "I'll have Councilman Cillian provide you with the manufacturer's specification for the bots in the morning, as well as details for your payment. One of our envoy ships with be going with you to ensure the task is completed to our satisfaction, and then you can be on your way with your payment. Now, if you wish to come with us, we'll get you settled into the

Argyle for the evening. Dinner is on us." Councilman Forsythe motioned for them to follow him to a small airship landing outside the courtyard entrance.

The Argyle Hotel was located on Harbor III, the largest of the three platforms that towered over the other two and separated the extremely wealthy from the average and the poor. Large glass elevators took riders back and forth from each level, and each level had its own dock for airships. The levels were simply titled Harbor I, II and III, with Harbor I being the lowest and poorest level in the harbor.

They started to follow the councilman to the airship but Elias noticed Hunchy was still standing over by the fountain, almost acting as if he wasn't even part of their group. Elias returned and asked him what the problem was, and Hunchy explained that he simply couldn't ride in a ship that small and that his hump was hurting him badly. Elias called Gideon over and explained the problem, who seemed none too happy about the prospect of walking through Harbor I and II at 7 o'clock in the evening.

"Elias, that's at least a two hour walk to the Argyle," Gideon complained.

"Well, I'm not leaving him. He helped us escape and he saved Ava, so I'm walking with him," Elias gave Gideon a firm glare. Gideon let out a sigh and turned back toward the crew.

"We're walking," he said.

"WHAT!" exclaimed Wyatt, whose mods were still bothering him from not resting enough, but he dared not show any signs of weakness in front of Ava, so he gave his arm a hard pat and looked pointedly at Gideon.

"You've got to be kidding me," Merlin agreed.

"Come on, guys! Where's your sense of adventure?" Izzy said, slapping Bogan on the back as she ran over toward the fountain. "Besides, Elias never got to see much of GFC, and Harbor III's even better than that," she prodded.

Councilman Forsythe and the robed council member climbed into another smaller vessel and shot up to the third platform while Councilman Cillian grew frustrated with their indecision, "What's it going to be? Are you walking or riding?"

As Ava began to walk toward the fountain, Gideon answered him, "I guess we're walking." Merlin, Wyatt and Bogan seemed perturbed by Gideon siding with the hunchback but agreed to stick together.

"I will be waiting for your crew in the lobby of the Argyle once you arrive," Cillian explained. "Do you have any special requests as far as dinner is concerned? I can have it prepared and ready for you by the time you finish your walk," the councilman offered.

Elias wasn't sure exactly what everyone blurted out, but he was certain he heard lobster mentioned at least three times and maybe even beef, but that couldn't be right. He had always been told there were no cows anymore. Cillian quickly shot off to Harbor III as Gideon pushed for a quick trip through the two lower cities.

"We better get moving if we're going get to the Argyle in time to enjoy it," he said looking at Hunchy, who dropped his head down a bit.

"Thank you all so much," he rubbed his hump. "I do appreciate your thoughtfulness."

HARBOR I: Once they left the courtyard, Elias immediately bombarded the crew with so many questions he didn't notice he was overlapping their answers with new ones. He asked so many questions he even began to annoy himself, but the culture shock was too great not to. Gideon explained that sometimes the black mist would mix with fog, lifting it above the mile-wide platform, and that's why everyone in Harbor I carried their masks. He kept the crew on the outskirts of the city as much as possible, as it looked like a large area was without power. He said it was possibly due to a lack of coal, caused by low production since their steam bot malfunction, and it seemed to make him feel better about the councilman's offer.

The putrid stench from the powerless areas of Harbor I swept the people to the outskirts and packed the small walkways with all manner of strange folk. Most didn't have any mods, but those that did had lower quality mods than that of the Whisper crew. Metal doors creaked loudly on rusted hinges, and the street lights struggled to keep their path lit. If not for the blessing of twilight and a full moon, they might have had to use Gideon's light for safety. People bumped into other people as they stepped over those resting on the sides of the tight walkways. The glorious days of Harbor I's high-class apartments had passed, as now they flecked droplets of water down their necks from rows of hanging laundry towering ten stories high on each side of them. Elias wished he had an umbrella like the council woman's as they passed under the laundered garments. Elias also kept a watchful eye on Hunchy for any signs of another claustrophobic attack.

He also wished his nasal passages hadn't cleared back at the docks after they passed an unusually obese man with yellow stains covering his shirt. When the man let out a nasty belch, Elias could almost see the particles floating towards his face. He retched in his throat and covered his mouth, then looked at Izzy and Ava to see if they were holding their noses, only to find them wearing their masks. Izzy rolled her eyes at him and winked as if she had walked these streets enough to know better. Elias was so distracted by all of the strange sights filling his eyes, he was almost deluged by an old lady tossing out a rancid bucket of mop water filled with fish and bird guts, but Izzy quickly pulled back on his jacket just in time.

Their path almost seemed to come to a dead end in front of another high rise metal apartment as it turned sharp to the left. A small boy kicking a ball against the wall of the building was coughing severely, and Elias knew right away it was creeping mold sickness. He looked everywhere for another path, alley or walkway they could turn on to avoid the boy, but there simply wasn't any other options, so he tried to hide behind Bogan as they passed.

The little boy's condition was so advanced that black veins practically drew the shape of his heart on his bare chest, and dark snot oozed from the nose on his ghostly pale face. Elias froze in place when the little boy stepped out in front of him and looked into his glass heart-mod. The little boy placed his hand on the glass and felt Elias' heart beating as he stood breathing raspy breaths of death. Bogan seemed to want to end the uncomfortable moment, by pushing the boy away, but Elias stopped him. Elias simply couldn't get past the idea they were about to stay in the plushest hotel this side of hell and there before them stood the harsh reminder of their tragic world.

With black mucus dripping down his nose and onto his chest, he looked at Elias and with labored words said, "The Destroyer comes," then removed his hand and went back to kicking his ball.

Hunchy broke the bitter moment quickly by stating the obvious, "Well, now, that was a bit awkward, wasn't it?"

Ava and Izzy didn't seem pleased with his callous assessment, but said nothing, probably out of respect for Hunchy saving Ava.

HARBOR II: Once they reached the glass elevators, they took the 140 foot ride up to Harbor II, which was more of an industrial city with its steel mills, iron factories, train, airship, and carriage manufacturing, as well as all manner of other vehicle construction.

It was a quiet ride as they looked over the slums of Harbor I, until Elias asked that burning question, "Why do people keep saying the Destroyer is coming?"

Wyatt busted out a snort and coughed, trying to hide his laughter, but after some dead silence and the slow moving elevator, Gideon decided to explain. "It all depends on who you ask," he paused, "some say the Destroyer will set the world right again. Others say he is coming to destroy the smoke charmers and their mold cults; and still some believe he will lay waste to the mountains and tunnel labyrinths with fire and crush the tower cities with his mighty hammer of vengeance. It began as a rumor of false hope that grew into a twisted prophecy for anyone looking to cash in on the weak minded. Some have even tried to force it into reality."

"That's enough, Gideon," Izzy gave him a stinky eye and rocked her head towards Ava.

The whole thing was just getting good and Izzy had to go and ruin it. It irritated Elias that Izzy always shut down anything that might upset Ava.

The back of the elevator opened and Harbor II was right behind them. A man stepped up and said, "Councilman Cillian thought you might want a taxi to speed up your trip to Harbor III and asked me to offer my services at the council's expense." The man pointed to four fancy wooden chariots pulled by rambunctious ostriches. Each chariot seated two people and had one driver, but, yet again, Hunchy declined and asked to walk, protesting of cruelty to animals. Gideon wasn't having it this time, as he watched Wyatt fiercely tapping his shoulder, and ordered Hunchy to get in. Then Hunchy complained he was too big and his hump wouldn't fit into the seat. It seemed that Gideon wanted to strangle Hunchy for a moment, but instead he had the man call for another chariot so he could ride alone. Gideon held his ground, and eventually Hunchy chose the chariot with a cruel driver who was constantly whipping the bird to get it under control. Elias watched as Hunchy walked up to the bird and whispered something to it as he gently rubbed its neck. A strange calm came over the creature then Hunchy boarded the chariot. Ava could see that Bogan was about to explode on Hunchy, so she doused his fire with a smile and pat on his back.

With the crack of a whip, their chariots shot off into the busy streets. Elias ended up in a chariot with Merlin, who didn't seem all that eager to ride them either and gripped the bar in front of them even though he was well strapped in. Elias tried to make a mental note of their ride in keeping with his promise to himself that he would embrace everything to the fullest, but the sprightly birds were simply too fast. The two-legged fowl darted in, out and around other carriages and chariots pulled by ostriches, emus and cassowary. The chariot bells clanged as warnings to people swiftly slipping across the road in front of them.

Merlin even removed his hat out of fear he would lose it to

the gusting wind created by the bird's spirited motivation at the driver's whip. They passed by shops so rapidly, the only one Elias could remember was the eye glasses shop called The Great Spectacle, but mainly because a monocled fellow stepped out and double checked his vision due to Merlin's green, glowing brain. The hopping and vibrating of the chariot distorted Elias' view so much he felt like someone was shaking his brain. He even checked to see if Merlin's brain was jiggling inside his glass globe. One of the chariots in front on them hit a goodly sized puddle on the edge of the street, dousing a man lighting his stogie. He tossed a few choice words back at them, as well as the ruined cigar, but they were moving too fast for either to make contact.

Their drivers took a shortcut through the steel mill, where men hammered out iron into tools, repair parts, belt buckles, boilers and weapons. The smell of smoke filled the air, and the warm sparks were a welcome change from the biting wind of the previous street. Elias closed his eyes as they passed through and listened to the industrious sounds of clanging hammers forging hot iron into shapes, and he felt a strange comfort from it.

The dizzying trip through Harbor II was quick and exciting and ended abruptly with a jerk that opened his eyes to flashes of light from the glass elevators leading up to the next level. They hopped the elevators to Harbor III, which would be a first for everyone since the crew of the Whisper had never been offered the privilege of entrance to that level before today. They had only seen it when the Whisper would pass by. Harbor III was the largest of the levels and was supported by four massive outer towers and a large center tower. The city platform was two miles across, with buildings towering 40 and 50 stories high. The Argyle itself was 46 stories, with a massive, bronze statue of Atlas holding a letter A on his shoulders.

HARBOR III: They stepped off the elevator to hot steam blowing everywhere, and a man wearing a hard hat was standing in front of a street barricade. "Folks, you can't go this way. We had a steam valve blow about 20 minutes ago, and we won't have it fixed for at least another hour. Which way you headed?" he asked as steam rolled down the streets behind him. They could see the Argyle Hotel through the clouds of steam only four blocks away, but the steam completely blocked their path. People in the distance popped umbrellas everywhere as the steam fell back on them like a fine dew.

"We're headed to the Argyle," Gideon said.

The man looked them up and down and laughed, "Right, you are, and I suppose you're the guests of honor as well, then," he mocked.

"Yes, we are!" Elias blurted out with a spiteful snap as he stared the man down. When the man noticed the gold heart-mod on Elias' chest, he figured maybe they were telling the truth.

"Alright then, take Gallery Street," the man pointed to the road next to them, "about two blocks and turn left on Evergreen for about four blocks, then another left on Argyle Boulevard and you'll be there in about 20 minutes." The man turned around and went back to setting up more barriers while the crew started their trek down Gallery Street.

"This is your fault, Hunchy," Wyatt complained as he rubbed his sore mod connections, all while carefully making sure Ava wasn't watching. "We could have been feasting at the Argyle already, but you and your poor hump had to walk," he mocked.

"I'm with you," Bogan said in agreement, but stopped at that so as to not draw Gideon's ire again.

"It's only 8:15pm and we're making good time, thanks to the chariots, so cut the complaining and let's get going. Besides, none of us have ever been here before and may never get another chance in our life time. Let's enjoy it," Gideon rubbed his neck and moved it side to side with a crack.

They'd only traveled one block when Merlin noticed a back alley called Raven Alley. "Why not cut our trip in half? It looks like this alley goes the whole four blocks down," he looked at Gideon and gave a nod towards Wyatt who was tapping his shoulder like mad. Wyatt was hurting and needed rest, so Gideon agreed.

ABNER'S APOTHECARY: THE ALLEY WAS FAIRLY BARE EXCEPT for a dumpster every so often, and they were making good time until they came to a half-lit sign that said Apothecary. Another small sign said vitamins, antibiotics, bandages, medicinal salve and specialty cures. Wyatt was quick to pull Gideon aside and explain how he could use some salve since he had forgotten his, and Gideon agreed it was a good enough reason to check it out.

Wyatt, Merlin and Hunchy went right in and Elias naturally followed, assuming everyone was going inside the store, but Ava, Izzy and Gideon remained outside talking about food options. A bell at the top of the door dinged when they entered, and the air had a funky, noxious smell like someone had spilled garlic, alcohol and vinegar. The shelves were lined with glass containers filled with herbs of all sorts, dried roots, tea leaves and spices and glass bottles lined a wall with red, green, black, yellow and many other multi-colored liquids. A small, spectacled man in a white coat was standing behind the counter and introduced himself.

"Welcome, welcome, my name is Abner. How may I be of service to you fine gentleman?" he asked.

"I noticed your sign said medicinal salve," Wyatt said.

The man adjusted his glasses, taking a sharp look at Wyatt. "Ah yes, indeed, mods giving you fits are they? I have just the thing for you." He went over to the shelf and pulled down a bottle filled with yellow cream. Wyatt paid the man while Merlin looked at every shelf like a kid in a candy store.

"Would you like a bag, sir?" Abner asked.

"Uh, no thanks," Wyatt answered, shoving it into his pocket and exiting the store as if he'd never made the purchase. The bell dinged as Wyatt left, but Merlin was still entranced when the store clerk noticed Elias.

"Young man, I see you have come down with a bit of the sickness," as if it were merely a simple cold.

"I guess you could say that," Elias said, looking at the multi-colored bottles that reminded him of his mother's pantry.

"If you're looking for something to help with that I do carry some products for the more culturally sophisticated customers," he said, quietly leaning over his counter, but Elias was still too mesmerized by the wall of colorful bottles to pay much attention to him. The man walked to a back room and returned with a glass bottle filled with a thick, red liquid. He placed the bottle on the counter and tried to get Elias' attention, but when that didn't work he gave a little silver bell a good DING! Elias, Merlin and Hunchy quickly turned their heads toward the counter.

"As I said, young man, I have something here that would greatly benefit someone like yourself, if you're interested," he said, tapping the top of the bottle cork with his finger. They all walked over to the counter to see why the man was being so mysterious.

"What I have in this bottle is practically the CURE for black mold sickness," Abner said, overemphasizing the word cure with his salesman-like demeanor.

"Oh, here we go," Merlin taunted, "this should be good." He laughed, "No, no really, really, I'm sorry, please continue," he said barely able to contain himself.

"Plenty of skeptics, like your friend here, have walked back to me with more than a humble tone in their voice after seeing how well this elixir works. There are some right here in the harbor that have lived more than four years in advanced stages, thanks to this medicine," Abner said, sneering at Merlin.

"And what is this wonderful elixir," Merlin asked, motioning with finger quotes around the word elixir, "only you happened to have found?"

Abner straightened up a bit and adjusted his white lab coat, "As I stated earlier, this is for the more discerning customer, who is not afraid to cross a few—um—broken moral boundaries to save their, or even a loved one's, life. But I can see that you're another nonbeliever willing to let your good friend die a horrible death." Abner started to say something else, but Merlin grabbed the bottle and popped the cork lickity split. He put a drop on his finger, tasted it and quickly spit it back on the man's lab coat. Elias stepped back, thinking there was about to be an altercation, when he noticed Merlin's anger.

"Blood! You're selling blood as a cure for mold sickness? I should report you," Merlin chided.

"Not just any blood," Abner lifted his finger, "but fresh blood of an immune," he boasted, wiping the splattered blood off his white coat, but he didn't seem worried at all about Merlin's threat to report him.

"HUMAN BLOOD! You're sick! There are no immunes, so stop giving him false hope," Merlin shook his head and grabbed Elias by the arm. "Come on, kid, let's get out of here. There's a sucker born every minute."

They stepped to the door, but while Elias was waiting for Merlin to get through the doorway he heard Hunchy whisper to Abner, "I'll take all you have."

Abner almost fell over. "Well t-that's impossible, sir, the subject is still alive."

"That's exactly what I was hoping you would say. The fresher the better," the hunchback said with a devilishly evil grin. "I prefer my prey alive and kicking."

Abner snickered like a giddy little school boy, "Oh, oh, oh you truly are a peculiar connoisseur of eccentric tastes. The Great Alchemist would very much approve of you," he adjusted his spectacles. "It will be quite costly, but if you're staying at the Argyle I'm going to assume you're a person of some means."

"Indeed. I am quite the wealthy man; eccentric, but wealthy," the hunchback boasted.

Abner jotted down something on a piece of paper and handed it to the hunchback, but the door closed behind Elias, and the dinging bell blocked most of what was said. All he heard was, "Harbor I, tonight."

Elias wanted to tell the crew what he'd just heard, but the slithering cold chill down his neck froze his tongue to his teeth, and by the time he was ready to speak Hunchy stepped out and joined them. He was grinning from ear to ear as he wiped his mouth. Elias wondered if he had already drunk the bottle of blood Abner put on the counter, and Elias couldn't stomach even looking at him.

DINNER AT THE ARGYLE: Once they'd arrived at the Argyle they were promptly taken to a great dining hall and given the most lavishly filled smorgasbord of a table they had ever seen. The extravagant, candle-lit table was piled high with lobster, fish, shrimp and no small assortment of fried foods and desserts, and the crew swiftly went to work on its contents. They cleared plate after plate, and with each finished course Bogan would tap his fork on a fancy glass and call for their tuxedoed waiter with the pointy goatee and nasally voice. That was, until Wyatt showed him the little brass bell he was supposed to be using, and then he practically drove everyone else mad with his incessant ringing. A live band kept the room hopping and its drums vibrated the beautiful, gas-lit chandeliers whose lights shimmered like orange ghosts against the black marble floors.

Elias sat directly across their circular feast from the hunchback, who seemed to be stuffing himself quite well for someone who was about to guzzle eight pints of human blood. Elias tried to eat, but he was so repulsed by the fish juices slurping, sopping, slushing, and dripping off the hunchback's chin like—like—blood onto his still-hooded cloak and gloves. And that was another thing. Why did he still have those nasty gloves and filthy hood on? He was among friends, so why not remove them? What was he hiding? Some hideously embarrassing birth mark or scar perhaps, but no one would judge him now, especially after he saved Ava and promised to take them to the location of the Jackboot's flowers. What if they had made a terrible mistake in trusting him? What if he was merely waiting for them to fall asleep so he could devour them into his gullet for nutrients to increase the size of his squishy hump? His imagination got the best of him when he thought Hunchy was gnawing on a human leg bone as blood poured from his mouth onto the table, but he was knocked back to reality by Bogan.

"Hey, little buddy," Bogan started, "aren't you hungry?" Elias hadn't noticed Bogan trying to get his attention until Izzy tapped his shoulder, giving him a startle.

Elias looked down at his empty plate, "Huh? Oh, uh, yeah. I just—I guess I just got caught up in everything."

"Well, that's understandable," Gideon said, chewing and popping a crab leg in half. "We've never done anything like this either."

"And this room," Ava sloshed her drink all over the table as she pointed at the ceiling with her glass.

"This is fantasstunct," Izzy muttered out poorly while washing down her lobster tail with her bucket-sized coffee mug.

"Tell me about it," Bogan said as he leaned over with his own knife to cut a turkey leg off a finely roasted bird in the middle of the table. Wyatt was eating some kind of lobster bisque soup that seemed to have no bottom to the bowl, thanks to his ringing bell that kept refilling it. "I could eat this stuff right out of the Whispers toilet bowl," he bragged, bringing everyone to a raucous laughter.

However, Merlin's sweet tooth could not be sated as he polished off his third slice of caramel coated cheesecake and started working on some kind of cobbler with strawberry sauce. He drew looks from every table in the hall as his brain fired multiple bolts of blue lightning with every sugary bite, but he added nothing to the conversation. By the time Merlin's brain had practically turned into a disco ball, everyone but Hunchy had finished.

Hunchy's awkward sounds of snorting, grunting and crunching sent many people on their way as the crew watched in awe of his ability to eat large, whole chunks without a single chew. When he finally pushed away from the table and stretched his gut a bit, he let out a high pitched screech of a belch that tossed a small shrimp back onto his plate. It even stopped the band momentarily. "Pardon me," he chuckled nervously, then tossed the shrimp back into his mouth.

Merlin's energetic attitude toward the cheesecake convinced Elias to try some, even with his nauseous thoughts, and eventually he scarfed three pieces of his own and several cups of coffee, as he had big plans not to let the hunchback out of his sight. At half past 11 o'clock, when everyone was preoccupied with the band's sprightful tune, for good measure, Elias slipped a sharp steak knife into his belt in case things took a dark turn that night.

Just as Bogan was about to give the little brass bell another ring, Ava snatched it away from him and gave it a long ring. "Box, please," she said with a tiny burp.

-10-

UNLEASHED

*T*hey were so stuffed by the time their sharp-dressed, legless bellhop arrived, they could barely waddle their way behind his unicycle-mod. "My name is Dudley, and I'll be taking you to your room this evening," he said with a high-toned, throaty voice as he straightened his bowtie. He was a bald man with beefy arms, half a man by figure, but a whole man by presence and he moved around on his single-wheeled-mod faster than most people with legs.

Dudley divided them two to a room on the 45th floor, and Elias boasted openly of Dudley's fantastic bellhop skills, which made his request for a room with the hunchback a sure thing. Although Gideon seemed none too pleased about having to tip Dudley double his normal percentage due to Elias' showering praise.

By the time they settled into their beds, the night had buried its stars in darkness, and a fine mist of rain pushed the city smog back down into the streets. An ominous, murky moon bounced dark shadows off the hunchback's face as he gazed out into the dreary night, and Elias desperately wanted to spark the murderer's scheme into motion.

"Aren't you going to sleep?" Elias asked as he turned out the lights and darted quickly back to bed.

"Sleep?—Oh, yes...I was...just thinking." His hooded eyes were glossed, wet, like black pearls that seemed to gleam of death itself, but he continued standing by the window, never climbing into bed. Elias gripped his stolen steak knife tight under the covers and squinted his eyes, pretending to sleep, but the hunchback never moved.

After some time, Elias heard the hunchback ask if he was still awake, but when he never responded, the large, humped, blood drinker walked over to his bed and sniffed the air above him. Elias lay motionless, almost dead, as he griped the sweaty handle of his knife hard enough to permanently imprint his fingers into it. Again, fearful thoughts raced through his mind as he lay there wondering if he had come all this way only to be killed by a monster he foolishly set free. He closed his eyes tighter as the hunchback leaned his head closer to Elias' face and sniffed twice. Then the room went quiet for a long time— too long, and Elias feared the hunchback was up to no good. Elias waited until he simply couldn't take it anymore and decided he had to know what the hunchback was doing, but when he opened his eyes, the room was empty. Gone! But how, he wondered.

Then he noticed the wind pushing, blowing, lifting the curtains through the open window. Back and forth, up and down, so he ran to the window and scanned the cloudy street below. The mist blurred the street lamps, but not completely, and he wondered how the hunchback could have gotten 45 floors down so quickly. Right then, out of the corner of his eye, through a wisp of cloud, he caught something moving, climbing, clawing its way down the building on the other side of the street. It was him! The murderer! The blood drinker! The hunchback—and he was hopping from floor to floor, light as a feather, two and three floors at a time, using only the iron window ledges to hold on to.

Elias was frozen as he watched the creature scale down the

building like a child in a playground. Then it hit him. The elevator! GO NOW! He ran out of the room and down the hall. Dudley was at the elevator and Elias shouted for him to hold it, but he was a bit slow on the take so Elias jumped through the closing door, almost ripping his heart generator right off his belt.

He tumbled into the boxy-people-mover to Dudley's formal greeting, "Good evening, Master Elias. Going down, I presume?"

"Yes, yes, down," he tried to catch his breath.

The journey down 45 floors seemed like an eternity but in reality was only a little over a minute. When the bell dinged, the door slid open and Elias bolted out, through the lobby and into the gloomy streets of Harbor III. He regretted not bringing his jacket as he scoured streets, alleys and buildings for the hunchback, but there was no sign of the crafty killer.

He considered asking one of the night watchmen, who were practically on every street corner, if they had seen anything, until he heard someone yelling. "HEY! HEY, YOU! DOWN FROM THERE!" one of the watchmen ordered as he pointed his light at something grappling on some rafters. Elias glanced over toward the excitement and spotted the hunchback swinging from a monorail track traveling above the streets.

The hunchback leapt from rafter to rafter without ever losing his grip, but now four night watchmen were hot on his tail. He took a giant leap into an alley and all four of them followed him in with their guns at the ready, but what Elias heard next was not the sound of a cowering hunchback surrendering to the law. No. Not in the least bit. What Elias heard next were the sounds of terrified men pleading for their lives.

"No! No! Please! W-W-What are you?" one of them cried out, but his scream ended abruptly with a loud pop, crack and snapping that echoed out of the blackness and into the street. The horrible screams of the others were silenced quickly as each one was mysteriously dispatched deep in the hollow darkness of the alley. Elias was grieved at what he had unleashed on the people of Gabriel's Harbor.

A SLOW MOVING CARRIAGE MADE FOR GOOD COVER, AND ELIAS peered from behind it as the hunchback reappeared at the top of the alley building. He scaled his way back to the rafters with great haste, then went straight for the glass elevators at the end of the harbor. Elias quickly checked his fuel reserves and realized he would need to find a better way to follow the culprit. When he spotted a swift moving carriage slowing he grabbed on to the back, riding it all the way to the end of Harbor III. By the time he squeezed into the crowded elevator, he figured the hunchback was already on Harbor II and he knew he needed to get to Harbor I ahead of the traitor since he had no clue of his final destination. He glanced around at the other passengers, surely someone would have a better means of transportation than running.

"Does anyone know a faster way to get to Harbor I?" Elias boldly and loudly asked.

A tall gentleman with a finely groomed beard and mustache looked down at his heart-mod and spoke up, "You in a hurry to die, are you, boy?"

"Not anymore, once this week is enough, thank you very much," Elias quipped back as the people gasped and stepped back against the elevator walls, afraid they might catch the creeping sickness. Some even slipped on their masks, even though they knew he wasn't contagious. Their comfortably safe lives at the harbor had filled their heads with all manner of lies regarding the sickness, and they ignorantly swallowed them up and fed them back to their children.

Another chubbier man, cleaning his monocle, spoke up, "What you need is an Ever-Wheel."

"What's that?" he asked as the riders leaned in a bit to see if he had suddenly grown a third eye, then they burst into a demented laughter at his question.

As the elevator rumbled to a stop, an overly-perfumed old lady holding an umbrella and a cat squeaked out her wisdom like a mouse, "Young man, just look for the big wheel with the seat in the middle."

He wondered if she was talking about the large wheel that almost ran him down at GFC but was too embarrassed to ask any more questions. He smiled back at her. "Thanks, ma'am!"

THE ELEVATOR DOORS OPENED TO A THICK HAZE OF FOG THAT left haunted halos around the street lamps in Harbor II, and he started to worry about the conditions he might face in Harbor I. Elias checked the streets in front of him, but there were no signs of an Ever-Wheel. Then he scanned the tops of buildings for the hunchback, but the fog was so thick it was almost impossible to see anything above three stories high. He nearly lost his breath when someone behind him tapped him on the shoulder. It was the tall man with the nicely groomed beard. He was putting on a leather jacket and goggles and pointed to the far end of the elevators where the old cat lady's description of an Ever-Wheel appeared before his eyes.

"Sorry about those folks back there, kid. This place used to be a place where people helped one another. Maybe one day it will be again. Until then, I'll do my part to make it better," he gritted his teeth in frustration. "Come with me, son. I'll get you there in no time. Just don't tell your parents," he said, stretching on his leather gloves and striking a partial grin.

"GREAT! Thank you, sir, that shouldn't be a problem." Elias felt like a toddler as the man picked him up, sat him on the back seat and then shook his hand.

"My name's Tom. I own the steel mill here in Harbor II, so we'll run a short cut through my mill without any problems. It'll save you lots of time." Tom fired up his Ever-Wheel with the kick of a lever, and black smoke rolled out the fat exhaust pipes with a violent shake. It was loud but beautiful, Elias thought, and he couldn't stop grinning from ear to ear as his teeth chattered from its fierce vibrating.

"HANG ON!" Tom hollered, and they were off like a bullet as the force threw his head against the cushiony leather seat.

The Ever-Wheel spit water, mist and black coal dust everywhere, and Elias thought a better name would have been an

Ever-Dirty. Tom's hands gripped the handle bars tight as they barreled down the empty street. They turned so hard and sharp, Tom's knee almost touched the road, and then another hard turn back to the right and all of a sudden they were traveling through the steel mill. The workers raised their hammers to Tom as he passed, then went right back to smashing their red hot iron. Blasts of fire balls roared out of machines, and bright blue welding flashes popped spark-filled smoke around them from both sides as they passed through the mill. Then Tom pushed a green button and the vehicle increased its speed by almost double. They came up on the elevators so fast because of the fog, and Tom had to squeeze the brakes hard enough that they slid right to the edge of the platform.

"Here's your stop, kid. I'm not going down there tonight, and you probably shouldn't either," Tom warned.

"I'm already infected, sir, so it won't make much difference either way. Thanks for the ride though," Elias said with a smile.

"Point taken. Good travels, kid," Tom pulled away with a blast of smoke that disappeared instantly into the hanging fog, and Elias quickly hopped the elevator down to Harbor I.

The Ever-Wheel ride was one for the books for sure, but with Merlin's last estimation of two weeks left on his heart-mod, he wished he could do it again before everything ended. He was too active; not resting enough and burning up the gold-mod faster than most people because of his advanced condition. The cruel, foreboding hand of death would once again tighten its grip around him and end it all. But he had no time to think about that now; he had a hunchback to catch.

IT WAS A DARK, LONELY RIDE DOWN TO HARBOR I, AND HE wondered whether he had beaten the hunchback down or missed him. Gone were the brightly lit streets of Harbor III, and he would have even settled for the haunting lights of Harbor II, but there were no comforting glows in Harbor I. Nothing but black mist-filled-fog slithering, crawling, weaving; biting its way around his coatless body. Other than a pack of wild dogs disappearing into the mist, the streets appeared void of life, but it was difficult to determine with such low visibility. He took a position around a corner and watched the elevators for any signs of his target.

The deadly fog crept silently over him, like a phantom reaching for its prey, as he waited for the hunchback. Suddenly the sound of flapping wings drove the fog away, and a familiar friend landed in front of the elevators. Casper was back from his late-night hunt. For a brief moment Elias felt a sense of comfort and safety, until he noticed the bird's glowing red eyes. Casper was in war mode again and that meant danger.

Then, like a bomb dropping through the clouds, the hunchback broke through the foggy ceiling and landed feet first beside Casper. Casper didn't even flinch. The hunchback reached into his pocket and checked the paper Abner had given him, then crumpled it up and dropped it on the ground. A strange noise came from his mouth, and Casper hopped up on the back of his nasty hump as if he had been commanded by the monster. *Did they know each other? Why would Charlie's bird obey an evil hunchback? Elias was going to get answers tonight, even if— even if it killed him.*

He tracked the mysterious pair as close as he could through the murky, misty walls of fog in Harbor I. Every so often the hunchback would stop, turn around and sniff the air before continuing on with the great gray on his back. They turned down a street where four rough-looking men were standing with metal helmets and armor. These night watchmen were military grade, unlike anything Elias had ever seen. They challenged the sinister bird-carrier as to his business, and the hunchback clicked his tongue, sending Casper up to a large sign pole hanging over them.

The hunchback warned the men, "Let me pass, or this very night you will suffer." Elias was chilled in his bones at how callous he was with them. How could this be the friendly man that sympathized with him in the mine and saved Ava from death? Guilt weighed heavy on Elias, and he couldn't seem to shake the responsibility he felt for unleashing the hunchback's night of terror.

The watchmen laughed and pulled out large shocksticks with bright green balls of lightning at the end and pointed them at him. The first man sent a bolt from his stick directly at the hunchback, but he missed and his shockstick was quickly removed from his hand and directed at his fellow watchman. The hunchback's speed seemed humanly impossible as he targeted his opponents with ease. With a whirlwind of cracking, leaping, splattering, grabbing, pouncing and flinging, the hunchback dispatched the four of them like a seasoned, fearless warrior. Elias envied his fearlessness and wished it was his own, but the hunchback's cruelty was unlike anything he had ever witnessed.

When he had finished his bloody handiwork, he pointed to Casper and gave a command that must have meant to stay, because the gray owl didn't move a feather. Then, two doors down, the hunchback entered a green door into a building. Elias ran down the street right under Casper, who didn't give him even a, "How's the weather?" look, but simply watched the green door with those flaming eyes. The windows were completely painted over, but there was a small, broken wedge in one of them where Elias was able to see Abner and the hunchback talking. The room didn't look anything like the apothecary Abner had on Harbor III but more like a rundown warehouse filled with crates, boxes and mechanical parts. Water dripped from the ceiling inside, and Abner seemed extremely uncomfortable that the hunchback was there, even nervous, as if something had already gone wrong with his plan.

The hunchback moved in close to Abner, but Elias couldn't make out what they were saying until the hunchback asked loudly, "Were those men for me?"

"No, no, no. I-I promise I have n-no idea what they were doing there," Abner trembled out with an air of guilt in his voice.

"LIAR!" The hunchback grabbed Abner by his white lab coat with both hands and lifted him off the floor.

"Okay, okay they—they were. I-I'm sorry. I-I just thought..."

"Thought what? That you would capture me as well and drain my blood for money? I know your kind." His voice deepened with anger. What did he mean Abner wanted to drain his blood? It didn't make any sense. Didn't he come here to eat the man Abner had captured? Elias was confused.

"I-I'm sorry, I just," Abner's legs dangled like broken limbs as the hunchback held him higher.

"WHERE IS HE?" the hunchback demanded.

"H-He, He…"

"DON'T TOY WITH ME! WHERE IS HE?"

"H-H-He's in the back," Abner said.

"Take me to him now!" the hunchback demanded with a sense of authority in his voice, as if he were someone used to commanding others.

The hunchback let Abner down, and he took a key from around his neck that he used to unlock a door at the end of the room. When the door opened, Elias could see a window at the far end of the room but located on the other side of the ware-house. He ran back down the alley, underneath Casper, around the front of the building and down the other side to the window. Before he even got there, he could hear the hunch-back's angry voice echoing in the hollow alley. Elias found the window and peaked around the edge, where he could see a strange man with horrible scars locked in a cage. The man looked pale and weak. His body was severely mangled and his ears seemed to have been removed leaving only holes remain-ing. His face was covered with some kind of matted scales or fur and was unlike anything Elias had ever seen before. His nose was a bit oversized and his eyes were sharp with a piercing gaze. Adding to the strangeness of the man, his feet and hands looked more like claws than fleshy human digits. The man was lying against the bars in the cage, and the hunchback faced the man with his back to Elias.

"WHY? WHY?" the hunchback screamed. Elias wondered if the hunchback was displeased with Abner because there was no sport in killing a half-dead man. Then one of his nasty gloves dropped to the floor. Elias couldn't see what the hunchback was doing, but by Abner's comment he knew something dark and deadly was about to happen.

"Now, now w-w-wait just a minute here, I-I wasn't the one

who took his..." Abner tried to explain something, but the hunchback whipped around with violent speed and grabbed Abner by the throat, ripping his windpipe out with one swipe. Elias rubbed his eyes in disbelief. How could someone kill another so quickly? He wanted to call out for help but worried he would be next. He at the least had to live long enough to warn Gideon and the others.

Abner's body dropped to the floor, and for the first time Elias caught a glimpse of the hunchback's ungloved hand. Not a hand at all. Not even an embarrassingly deformed hand under his sneaky glove, and most certainly not a human hand, but a claw. A claw with sharp talons for fingers, talons more like the creature in the cage, and each the size of railroad spikes. Elias prepared himself for the terrible gore and bloodshed he was about to see, but what happened next sent a chill through Elias' heart. The hunchback knelt down beside the creature in the cage, and through the iron bars he embraced him.

Then Hunchy wept bitterly, with great sobs, and the creature in the cage wept with him.

"Mellontas," Hunchy groaned out his name and the creature looked at him. His face lit up with joy, "Sire, is it truly you?"

"It is, my brother. It is," Hunchy said, but as quickly as the man's face had brightened, it then turned to shame and he tried to move away from Hunchy.

"Sire, please don't look at me. I-I am grotesque. Defiled! Look what they did to me. I can't believe it myself," the man cried, but Hunchy grabbed him, cradling his chin as he lifted his face back up.

"I am not here to punish you, my friend."

"I'm sorry, sire. I failed."

"No, Mellontas," Hunchy took the edge of his cloak and wiped the blood from Mellontas' face. "I failed you," he dejectedly bowed his head.

"Then we all failed, sire."

"Maybe not, my friend. I think I have found the one who hears the voice," Hunchy said.

"Sire, we have thought that so many times and been wrong. It was more of a dream than a prophecy anyway, my lord,"

Mellontas seemed put off by Hunchy's statement. Then Hunchy moved in close to him.

"Mellontas, he is here, I tell you, with me in this city. The one who heard the voice is here, but there is something I don't understand," Hunchy shook his head.

"What?" Mellontas breathed out an exhausted breath.

"The boy is dying. It doesn't make any sense to me. Why would he be dying if he is the one spoken of in the book of prophecy?" Hunchy seemed confused, and Elias wondered what boy Hunchy was talking about as he practically shoved his ear all the way through the wall of the building.

"Prophecies never do, my prince," Mellontas managed a smile through his blood-dried cheeks.

"It has to be him. This day I give you my solemn word that I will find out," Hunchy cut his palm with his own claw and wiped the blood on Mellontas' forehead.

WHAT! Elias couldn't believe what he was hearing. *Prince?* The murderous beast unleashing terror on Gabriel's Harbor this exact night, and this guy was calling him a prince? Elias wanted to burst through the door and demand an answer, but all he could do was stand in disbelief. What dying boy? The only dying boy Elias could think of was—was HIM!

"I'm taking you with me," Hunchy said as he ran over and grabbed the bloody key from around Abner's torn neck. He tried it in the lock on the cage, but when it didn't work he tried smashing it with his boot. Mellontas kept trying to get his attention, but he wasn't listening.

"No. Please, my lord. It's useless anyway. He doesn't keep the key here. Please, sire! I beg you. I am ashamed and a hideous sight to behold. I won't make it anyway, and if I did I would be an outcast, for they have stolen my glory," he pleaded grabbing the bars on the cage.

"NO! NO! I won't allow it. I brought this on you. It was my plan that failed," Hunchy fell on his knees in front of Mellontas and they both wept again, but Mellontas' shallow breathing caught Hunchy's attention.

"You won't live if I don't get you help soon."

Mellontas spoke weakly and almost too softly for Elias to

hear, repeating his plea, "I won't survive the journey, my lord, and even if I did, I would be cast out from the convocation because of my shame."

"No, my friend. Never an outcast, never," Hunchy tearfully vowed.

"Leave me, sire, but you must take something with you. Please, I beg you. She's being held in the back of the shop. He had not started carving on her yet. She is unharmed. I made sure of it. Please take her from this terrible place," Mellontas begged. "The door is locked and I don't know which key opens it."

"Mellontas, why did you bring her?" Hunchy said with a displeased tone in his voice.

"We didn't think they would be this cruel, my lord," Mellontas shook his head at his own poor decision.

Hunchy stood and placed himself in front of the door beside the cage, lurched back with a raised boot, then smashed the door in two pieces. The breached room was dark, and Elias couldn't see who was in it. He tried to reposition himself several ways, but it was impossible to get a good look.

"Come on out," Hunchy called, then someone appeared halfway through the door's entrance, and Elias desperately tried to get a glimpse.

The person was partially shrouded in darkness, but with a glimmer of light across their face, spoke with gentle voice, "Sire," the figure made a slight bow. Hunchy grabbed a large burlap tarp that was covering a wooden crate, sliced a hole in the center with his claw, then draped it over the person.

"You're coming with me," Hunchy ordered.

"Yes, my lord."

Elias raised himself up on the window ledge, trying his best to get a better look, but slipped on the misty, wet edge and fell to the ground. It was loud enough for anyone to hear and he knew it, but he lay motionless hoping he was wrong.

"Someone's coming," Mellontas said. "You must go now!"

Elias winced, but got to his feet and quickly wiggled himself back up on the ledge.

"I'll hide her on their ship for the night and place the gray warrior on guard. Goodbye, Mellontas, my dear servant," Hunchy said with regret in his voice.

"Father, please, no. Come with us," the softer voice pleaded.

"There is no time, dear one, go with your prince. He will take care of you now. GO!" Mellontas demanded as Hunchy pulled the girl away from the cage and they crept their way out of the warehouse. Hunchy clicked his tongue and Casper followed. Elias knew he had to move fast if he was going to beat the hunchback to the Argyle Hotel or he might bring suspicion upon himself and incur the wrath of the monster.

ELIAS WAITED UNTIL THEY WERE OUT OF SIGHT AND THEN FLED the alleyway back into the unconscious streets of Harbor I. The light from the street lamps had been swallowed up in the darkness of the black mist, and there were no night watchmen anywhere to be seen. No bustling of people or hammering of workers, no grinding of machinery, no scouring of dogs or sneaking of cats and no scratching, clawing or biting of rats. Harbor I was void of life this night, but Elias couldn't shake the feeling that someone or something was following him. Whether alive or dead, he did not know. His pace seemed to slow as he continued looking over his shoulder for any signs, but no one was ever there. He paused at the corner of a building when he noticed the black mist in front of the elevators had taken the shape of a hand. For good measure, and partly due to the creepiness, he decided to wait until the shape moved on, or at the least maybe changed into a happy puppy.

Once the dark, ghostly hand passed he walked out slowly, checking everywhere, and then made a run for it. His boots splashed through grimy puddles that smelled of mold, and he could feel the sliminess of the mist wetting his arms as he ran. The elevator door opened as soon as he pushed the button, but when it closed an alarm blasted his ears, flashing a red – CONTAMINATION – sign, and instantly tiny nozzles in the ceiling burst hot water down on him that smelled of cleanser and rubbing alcohol. After a blast of hot air, he felt his hair frizz up like Ava's after the static shock back on the Whisper. He matted it down as best he could and then the elevator door opened behind him.

Harbor II was almost as dead as Harbor I, and he decided to take the fastest route—through the mill. By now the fires of industry had died out, and only a few glowing embers remained as evidence of the men's hard work that day. Elias was thrilled to find a small pile of pulverized coal and decided to refill his heart generator. After he locked down the lid on the hopper, he took a deep breath and ran, something he hadn't done in a very long time, and the crisp night air in his lungs felt good. About half way through Harbor II, he hopped on the back of a carriage to save time and conserve his newly refueled generator, but about a quarter of a mile from the elevators he noticed a strange apparition coming up fast on the carriage.

It couldn't be possible. Maybe it was lack of sleep, or maybe he had coal dust in his eyes, but he was sure that same ghostly hand of black mist was chasing him; reaching to pull him off the back of the carriage. He gripped the rails tighter and wanted to tell the driver to hurry up but was afraid of being caught. The hand moved faster and closer until Elias could see there was no way it could be his imagination or his mind playing tricks on him. It had well-defined finger shapes and even finger nails and was reaching for him. The fingers came so close they could almost scrape him with the nails, when suddenly the carriage turned hard left down another street and the hand shot past him.

He hopped off the carriage when it slowed but still managed to tumble and skin up his elbow a good bit. He ran down the last block and didn't stop until he'd boarded the elevator, which doused him with another round of decontamination suds. When the doors opened on Harbor III, he noticed the workers still cleaning up from the steam line break and decided to avoid them so he wouldn't have to explain why he was wandering the streets at night. He took the same short cut route back down Raven Alley, past Abner's Apothecary, but stopped dead in his tracks when he noticed a boy with an umbrella standing before him, wearing a shiny, teal-colored cloak with silver stitching and a fine crest on the lapel. He was carrying a staff with a glass ball at the top, and it was filled with a dark-greenish—almost black-like—fluid that glowed in the misty alley.

The boy began to speak strange words that almost seemed to come alive in his mouth as they formed a black, smoky hand that reached out for Elias. The glass ball glowing atop his staff swirled blackish ink-like streams within the green liquid faster and faster as he spoke his dark words. From behind the boy, on each side, appeared two flying serpents like Elias had seen that night with Casper, but there was no great gray to save him this night as Elias felt a sharp pain in his heart and a voice in his mind. Unlike that night on the Whisper, this night the voice was darker and its motives terrifyingly clear. And as Elias tried to cover his ears, he could hear in his mind the words, "Bow, submit; obey your master." Black mist poured from the boy's devilishly crafted words, and with every strike of his staff on the ground, sharp pains gripped Elias' heart. The serpents flicked their wickedly forked tongues and tails in unison with the boy's chanting, as their bat-like wings beat the misty hand closer and closer toward him. They were much larger than the serpent he'd encountered on the Whisper, with larger fangs dripping white puss and every bit the size of their green-eyed master of death.

The pain was so great, Elias looked down at his heart through the glass horror stricken that it had turned black as coal and his gold was melting faster and faster. He collapsed to his knees and a feeling of dread filled his mind and body, but the boy suddenly stopped his dark incantations of death and looked up. His coiled minions stopped their intimidating dance and also looked up. Elias noticed something was falling from the roof awfully fast; something big, like an uncontrollable sack of garbage someone had tossed down from the roof top. The boy stepped back as if he were preparing to run, but it was too late. It dropped directly on him, fast and hard, with such explosive force it instantly crushed him to death. That's when Elias noticed the "sack of garbage" had arms that had reached out and grabbed the two serpents. It flung one of them against the side of the building, where it collided with a splat, and the other it grabbed with both hands and tore in half. When the creature turned around, Elias' breath was almost stolen away from him.

"*HUNCHY?*" Elias said in shock. His vision was a little blurry and he struggled to catch his breath. Why would the boy want him dead? Why did Hunchy kill him so fast? Why didn't he first trying to reason with the boy? Maybe it was a simple misunderstanding. Elias certainly hadn't been at the Harbor long enough to make enemies. So many questions raced through his mind as he tried to piece together a plausible explanation, but nothing seemed to fit.

"Are you okay?" Hunchy asked.

"You just killed that boy!" Elias said still catching his breath.

"And he would have done the same to you," he picked up the glass ball and smashed it against the building. "What are you doing out of the room?"

"I-I was just getting some fresh air." Elias thought quickly, "And what were you doing out of the room?"

"I was, um, I—I was getting some fresh air as well," Hunchy replied. "Listen. We need to get back to the room right away before someone notices we're gone."

"And why is that?" Elias asked, trying to see if the hunchback would be honest with him, but was immediately taken aback by his response.

"You don't know what you've gotten yourself into. Your nightmares are only just beginning. You should have never toyed with the darkness. Now let's get back to the Argyle." Hunchy grabbed the dead boy's body and tossed it into a dumpster sitting beside Abner's store, as well as the lifeless serpents and his staff. Then they made their way to the Argyle.

"We can't go in the front of the building. I'm covered in blood and they'll ask questions. We'll do this my way," Hunchy explained.

"And what way is that?" Elias asked as if he didn't already have a fairly good idea of what it would be.

They snuck around to a taller building beside the Argyle and Hunchy said, "Hold on to my back." Elias didn't want to do it, but after what he had seen the hunchback do to the watchmen, Abner, his thugs and the dark boy, he decided it was best not to argue with a murderer. So he grabbed the strange, squishy hump and held on as best he could. The hunchback leapt two floors with astonishing force as they scaled, grasped and hopped up the side of the building with breathtaking speed until they were finally towering over the Argyle.

"Hold on tight," Hunchy said and he jumped off the side of the building, over the street, and landed on top of the Atlas statue of the Argyle. Then he scaled down the side and into their open window. Even though he was still somewhat shaken from his ordeal in the alley, Elias practically bit his lip off to prevent himself from smiling. At this point in life he couldn't imagine anything would be able to top the terrifyingly wonderful climb on Hunchy's back.

"HOW DID YOU DO THAT? Who are you?" Elias demanded.

"This is not the time to discuss it." Hunchy said sternly. "I need to get cleaned up and we both need some rest. When the time is right I'll explain everything. I promise." Then Hunchy went right into the restroom. Elias figured since he'd showered twice already he didn't need to clean up, so he climbed into bed. He listened to the sounds of Hunchy almost beating the walls to death as he cleaned up and then the door shook open. His hump seemed a bit lopsided and got caught on the door frame. After no small struggle, and some angry grunting, he managed to work free of the restroom doorway then he climbed into bed.

"Good night, Elias," Hunchy said, but the room was quiet for a moment before Elias spoke.

"I know you hid someone on the Whisper—My Prince." Hunchy jumped up and would have responded, but all of a sudden their door burst open.

"Time to get up, sleepy heads," Izzy enthusiastically pounced into the room and flicked on the lights, then hopped onto Elias' bed. "I don't know about you guys, but I slept like a baby in those feathered beds."

"Yeah, same here." Elias said looking at Hunchy.

"Come on, you two can't sleep all day. Councilman Forsythe is downstairs waiting on us."

Elias and Hunchy stared each other down for a moment. A

thick cloud of tension hung over the room until Elias stretched his arms in the air as if he'd been sleeping all night, "What time is it?"

"It's 6:00am! The sun will be up any minute now," Izzy said with a smile. Even though he was exhausted from his night of terror, it was hard to resist her joyful charms and those big brown eyes.

"Oh, wow, I guess we did sleep in, right, Hunchy?" Elias prodded.

"I'm quite rested, thank you," Hunchy pushed back.

"Well, alright then. Councilman Forsythe is waiting on us. He's got several guards with him, and he looks like someone just spit in his coffee." Izzy wrinkled her nose.

She jumped up and walked out, pausing right at the open door when Elias asked, "Why is he on edge?"

"I guess something happened in the harbor last night. Oh well, see you two downstairs," she bolted out of the room, leaving Elias and Hunchy with frozen stares. Hunchy gave a slight, nervous chuckle.

Immediately they both jumped out of their beds and started to question one other, but Hunchy quickly relented and agreed to tell Elias everything once they made it safely out of Gabriel's Harbor. If not for the way Hunchy treated Mellontas, Elias would have already turned him in, but he agreed to give the hunchback a chance to explain himself before handing him over to the authorities.

AWAKENING

*S*unlight brightened the sidewalk in front of the Argyle as it spotlighted a scruffy newspaper boy calling out his headline for the morning, "EXTRA! EXTRA! READ ALL ABOUT IT! MONSTER TERRORIZES HARBOR!" The people practically shredded their pockets for money as they pummeled the boy with coins for his copies of black and white mayhem that Hunchy had delivered for free.

Wyatt slipped in fast and grabbed a copy while bragging about the wonderful salve he had gotten from Abner's Apothecary. The salve must have worked fantastically, because he was overtly loud without realizing Ava was standing right next to him. "I can't believe it. That old guy sold the best mod-salve ever. I feel like a well-oiled machine in this stuff. It's like moving in butter," he boasted.

"Maybe it is butter," Merlin quipped, insulting the dead charlatan's product.

"I hope they catch the creep that did this and throw him off the harbor," Wyatt said in obvious disappointment that he might never be able find salve as good or as slick as Abner's. Elias glanced over at Hunchy, and the hunchback gave the tiniest shake of his head, clearly hoping Elias would stay quiet.

They made their way to Councilman Forsythe, who was waiting by two clunky iron airships prepared to take them to the Whisper. Several guards stood on each side of him, and from the look on his face Elias feared they were about to be arrested. The rest of the crew were oblivious to the fact that they were standing next to the terrorist of Gabriel's Harbor and thought nothing of the extra security measures.

Forsythe handed Gideon the manufacturers specifications on the steam bots and explained, "Everything you need for your job is in this packet. The council representatives will accompany you in an emissary ship to Mine Five, where you'll shut down the bots. Once you've completed the task, our representatives will make sure you're paid in full, and you can be on your way."

"Wait, did you say Mine Five?" Gideon asked.

"Yes, that's correct," Forsythe answered.

"The same Mine Five that's only three miles from Grand Fortune City? That Mine Five?"

"Yes, I do believe that's the one," Forsythe grumbled out.

"No! No way! You've got to be kidding me," Gideon said as he threw the packet back at Forsythe. "You're sending us right back toward GFC," he bellowed as he checked his crew's faces for their reactions.

"Well, if that's going to be a problem, we'll just have you settle your hotel bill, and you can be on your way," Forsythe said with a sly look in his eyes, knowing they could never afford to pay the bill.

"You set us up." Gideon's aggressive posture brought readied looks from the council guards, but Forsythe halted their action as he encouraged Gideon.

"I'm certain you can accomplish the task and be gone long before the Jackboot is any the wiser. Your team truly is quite talented at eliminating things," Forsythe said, looking directly at Hunchy.

"Look, we don't have time for this, we're supposed to find..." Gideon almost blurted out the purpose of their quest and why they were on the run from the Jackboot, but caught himself midsentence. Forsythe had obviously thrown him off course with the new information.

"Find what? Is there something we can assist you with?" Forsythe offered.

Gideon sensed his back was against a wall and figured he'd better decide quickly. "Never mind, just give me the packet. We'll do it," he bit his lip as if to punish himself for his own poor judgment of the situation. Surely Charlie would never have made a mistake like this, but he resolved himself to getting his team out of it so they could get on with their task of finding the flowers before the Jackboot caught them.

THE WHISPER CREW LOADED INTO THE AIR TAXI AND IT BLASTED thick smoke all the way back down to Harbor I. A funeral procession filled the streets below them near Captain's Courtyard, but it was not that of the wicked apothecary owner. Looking down from the sky, Elias could see the little boy from Harbor I lying in an open casket. The sounds of mourning filled the courtyard as their ride landed and Elias stepped off the ship and walked out towards the crowd of mourners. He couldn't hear Izzy and Gideon calling him back to the Whisper. Thoughts swirled in his head. It shouldn't be this way. Why had no one found a cure for this terrible sickness? How many more would die before the world could heal? Anger filled his thoughts and his damaged heart ached with sorrow for the boy that he might soon join. A gloved claw wrapped around his right shoulder and Hunchy spoke.

"It can be stopped," he said quietly, "Trust me." Elias' eyes grew big as the smile he had seen from the mine returned to Hunchy's face.

"I'll tell you everything you must do," Hunchy gripped his shoulder tighter. "Now come, we need to help our friends out of this problem so we can get about our business of saving the world." Elias gave a hopeful nod and followed him back to the Whisper.

Gideon tried to convince the emissaries to give them enough

fuel to get to the mine, but they refused any payment until the job was complete. "Councilman Forsythe's orders," they said. The crew waited until the supply ship was filled with their payment and prepared for another long journey stuck in whisper mode. Ava made certain their hard-working octopi were well fed with the bucket of leftovers from their Argyle dinner and went through her standard whisper mode check list. Elias and Hunchy, however, fell asleep on the deck while everyone else prepared for the journey and would have slept the whole time if Izzy hadn't teased them so often about being sleepy heads. She was relentlessly annoying to the point of almost angering Elias. It didn't seem to bother Hunchy, who boasted that only half of his brain needed sleep.

By the time the supply ship was loaded, it was already late in the afternoon, but the shifty representatives refused to leave and said they were waiting on someone. Gideon grew extremely frustrated, and about the time he demanded to see Forsythe, they pointed to a small airship landing in the courtyard.

"Now we can leave," they said as the council member with the dark umbrella stepped off the ship. Elias watched as a light breeze swept her long black coat across the dock making it appear as if she had no feet. Her umbrella was still hiding her face while she boarded the emissary ship and disappeared somewhere to a back room. Then they finally unhooked the Whisper from Gabriel's Harbor and set off into the sinking sun.

THE CREW OF THE WHISPER WAS EXTREMELY DISAPPOINTED TO BE traveling through the night stuck in whisper mode again, but none as much as Gideon who, immediately after leaving, walked into the command center and kicked over a chair. Everyone stood silent, waiting to make sure he was finished with his tantrum and then finally he said, "Izzy?"

"Yes, Gid," she always called him Gid when she knew he was stressing about something.

"Find Hunchy a place to sleep tonight, would you?" Then he

interrupted himself and turned to address the hunchback, "You know, it doesn't seem right that we keep calling you that. What's your name, anyway?"

"Hunchy or Hunchback is fine by me, and I'll sleep out on the deck if that's fine by you."

Wyatt chuckled, "Outside?"

"That's correct," the hunchback said with a sly look in his eye. No one had ever seen the other eye, what with his hooded cloak always hiding it. Elias was beginning to wonder if he even had one.

"Well, I'm most certainly not sleeping outside," Merlin said as he headed back to his quarters. Ava offered to bunk with Izzy and let Hunchy have her room for the night, but he refused and said he'd grown used to the cool night air while being chained in the mine. Everyone headed off to bed, including Elias, who only intended to pretend to sleep long enough for everyone else to fall asleep.

But Elias was more exhausted than he thought from his long night of tracking the hunchback through Gabriel's Harbor, and his heavy eyes got the best of him. Three hours later he jolted awake from a dream having something to do with checking mole traps in his father's greenhouse. It was a horrible, nightmarish dream filled with moles pulling him down into their holes and eating his legs.

He listened to Bogan's usual muttering from his night terrors about his leg, which made his dream seem petty, then suddenly it hit him. The hunchback was supposed to tell him about Mellontas and the stowaway and why he'd killed Abner.

He jumped out of bed and slid into Charlie's jacket shirtless, hoping that Hunchy hadn't fled with the stowaway. Then he ran out to the main deck to wake up the sleeping beast, but he wasn't sleeping at all. Hunchy was petting Casper, who was perched on the railing. The sight of the two reminded him of another nagging question. Why was Casper so nice to Hunchy, and why did he obey him? Answers, he was going to demand answers or turn the hunchback over to the Whisper crew that night. His mind raced with every question possible as he walked out towards the hunchback.

The cool night air from back at the harbor had now turned frigid and pushed away every cloud from the sky as they sailed below the star-speckled heavens. Elias was not slow in his stride and hoped his full steam approach would be intimidating enough to pluck out the answers he needed. He stopped next to the hunchback and with a raised finger started to speak, but was caught off guard by the hunchback's interruption.

"Where have you been?" Hunchy asked. Elias started to respond but was cut off again. "I've been waiting on you for some time now. No matter, it's a beautiful night anyway," he looked up at the sky and took a long deep breath. Elias raised his finger higher and managed a small throat noise before he was again cut off. "Yes. Yes, I remember. I promised you answers, and you shall have them all and then some. More than you could ever imagine or even want, but know this; you'll never be able to go back once I tell you," Hunchy looked at him with a kind smile. "Are you prepared for that?"

Elias was stunned that his demands were being fulfilled so easily, "Well, um, yes. Yes I am." In keeping with his strong tone and firm backbone he continued resolutely, "Let's start with the stowaway. Where did you hide the stowaway?"

"She's behind you," Hunchy said, pointing to the top of the Whisper. Elias turned around to see the hunchback girl standing on top of the Whisper's envelope. He was about to scold Hunchy for putting her up there when he was interrupted again.

"Before I answer any more of your questions, there's something I need to do," the hunchback said.

"Wait just a minute, you told me you would answer my questions." Elias face flushed red with anger and his fists tightened so hard his knuckles cracked. "I knew it. I knew you wouldn't keep your word. I never should have trusted you. I never should have freed you. I should have left you chained to that rock forever." Elias realized belatedly that he must have really crossed the line with Hunchy, because what he did next was beyond anything Elias could have ever imagined in his worst nightmares. The hunchback grabbed Elias and lifted him off his feet.

"Remember when I said your nightmares were only beginning?" he asked. "I'm about to show you what I meant. Now say goodbye to the world you've always known." Then that dirty hunchback threw him over the side of the Whisper, down to earth below, down into the black mist, down to toward the dark death.

Elias watched as the ships sailed the clear black sky without his falling body. He regretted his trust in the hunchback as he fell towards the earth, towards his old enemy the black mist and wondered if he would soon see his parents. Fear of his impending death would have taken hold of him, but he had grown numb to it. He closed his eyes and decided it was time to finally embrace his long awaited death. It would not be slow this time but fast. In the blink of an eye it would be over. Through the top of the deadly mist he sunk, through darkness, through moldy stench, through silence, until something hit him hard. He couldn't tell what it was, but he knew this much, he didn't hit the ground and he wasn't falling anymore. Something was holding him, carrying him, cradling him. Something big; something with wings had caught him midair.

As he cleared the black mist, the creature landed on the mold-covered earth below, stood him up and turned him around. It was the hunchback, but he was no hunchback at all. Gone was the nasty cloak that covered his hump, and gone was the hump itself, replaced by enormous, reddish-brown wings. His face was not old looking, but youthful and strong, and he had no visible ears. Large talons replaced his gloved hands, and his face was strangely marked and amazingly different from anything Elias had ever seen, whether in books or reality. His eyes were sharp, with a soul-piercing gaze, and he smiled that gentle smile Elias had seen back in the mine.

Then he reached out his claw like hand, "My name is Enupnion." He waited for a response from Elias, but nothing would come out, he was – speechless, gob smacked; astonished. The hunchback of old was no man at all but something beyond Elias' understanding. When he didn't respond, Hunchy extended his claw closer and said his name slowly, "En – oop' – nee – on," but Elias was frozen in shock.

Suddenly the girl dropped through the black mist and landed on a pile of creeping mold, sending its deadly cloud into the air around them with no concern or fear of the pestilence. She was winged as well, but her wings and hair were a deep, bright red with black tips on each feather. Both of their clothes were uniquely different, with round buckles clasping the center of their chest, and in the center of the buckle was an emblem of the red flower they were looking for. Half of her face was white and the other half marked with a hot, red blotch around her eye, as if it had exploded with red and black ink, and her eyes were black as the night sky. She knelt down in front of Hunchy on one knee and lifted his dirty cloak and gloves.

"Your covering, my prince," she said bowing her head.

"No need of formalities down here, Epekneia. Please stand," he commanded.

If that wasn't enough for one day, Casper dropped down through the clouds and landed beside them, rubbing up against Hunchy, or now Enupnion, as if he were a pet. Elias must have concerned Enupnion, because the creature reached out and shook him to make sure he hadn't died standing up.

"I realize this is a lot to take in. That's why our people, the Petinon people, remain in hiding to this very day. For thousands of years it has been our responsibility to keep the mold at bay by planting the fire berry seeds throughout the earth, but our people became apathetic to their task," his disappointment was clear as he explained. "When our people saw how quickly the mold covered the earth they cowered in fear, and our leaders decided it was best to stay on the safety of our mountain instead of fulfilling our responsibilities of old." Enupnion spoke with authority and no longer pretended to hunch his body over. The sides of his face had tiny feathers that drew back on his head and slightly moved when he spoke.

It was dark under the cover of the black mist, but on this clear night even the black mist couldn't prevent the full, powerful ambition of the moon's glorious, white glow. They began walking in the direction the ships were traveling as they had already been on the ground for several minutes. Elias stumbled over a set of railway tracks buried beneath the creeping mold, but the winged girl caught him. She said nothing but continued following behind them as the prince presented his case to Elias. Casper hopped from place to place and every now and then would flap into the air and back down on the ground in front of them. He seemed happy and pleased to be with his winged friends.

Enupnion continued his story, but with a more regretful tone, "I grew frustrated with my father and the convocation of elders and thought I could replant on my own. Inspired by Sunago the Great, who set out alone many years ago to plant seeds throughout the world, I, too, set out with a large bag of seeds. As I was soaring over a mountain, someone shot me out of the sky, thinking I would make a good meal, I suppose. It was Charlie, the former captain of the Whisper. He'd found a fairly-inhabitable mountain where he'd planned to die, away from his beloved Ava. I thought he was going to roast me, as stories from long ago had warned, but instead he had compassion on me. Charlie helped heal me then took me back to our people. Our plan to convince them to begin replanting went terribly wrong when the people saw Charlie's heart-mod. They thought mankind had become monsters of metal and decided to put Charlie to death. My father's generals even wanted to destroy mankind, until Charlie's kindness towards them changed their minds. So they stayed their course of hiding on our mountain and allowed Charlie to live out his days with them. It's a long story. Maybe Charlie can explain it to you if he's well enough."

"WAIT! CHARLIE'S ALIVE?" Elias shook with excitement. "We have to tell Ava, Gideon; Bogan. We have to tell Bogan!"

"I don't know if Charlie's alive or not; I've been gone so long," the prince said. "He was when I left, but he was not well then, and the heart-mod had already damaged him badly," his head dropped a little before he continued. "When my father and the convocation put a stop to all efforts to replant, Charlie helped several of us devise a plan to contact those he trusted. He became a loyal friend and told me what had become of the world. How he worked for the Jackboot and that I might be able to convince him to help replant the seeds and end the mold."

"The Jackboot...a friend? HA! Why would Charlie ever think

a murderer like the Jackboot would help you replant?" Elias' condescending tone was disrespectful because he'd let his heart be filled with hatred for the Jackboot, but the prince was no stranger to mockery and continued unfazed.

"At first the Jackboot was extremely interested in the seeds, but I made the mistake of showing him who I was. He was more than little surprised, to say the least, and saw me as threat. Somehow he already knew about the seeds and our flower. He chained me to the rock in the mine and accused me of being a mist speaker or someone called the Alchemist. I've gone through it in my head many times, and I can't figure out what he wants the seeds for. How would he even know what to do with them? Charlie said his last mission for the Jackboot was to find the Alchemist, but he said they were never able to complete the mission. I honestly don't know anything about the Alchemist, but the Jackboot must have figured out something with the flowers and searched out a plant expert to help. Although, I can't understand why he had your parents killed. Why didn't he just release me and ask for my help? I would have gladly helped him plant thousands, even millions, across the earth. For some reason he didn't trust me."

"You said mist speaker, what's that?" Elias asked as he noticed the winged girl staring at his beating heart through the glass. She quickly looked away when she thought he caught her gaze.

"Your people call them smoke charmers, but we have always called them mist or smoke speakers."

"The boy in the alley at Gabriel's Harbor," Elias blurted out. "He was a mist speaker or smoke speaker or whatever they're called."

"Yes, that's right, and he would have killed you...or worse. He might have turned you into one of them, and considering whom you might be, that would be bad for everyone," Enupnion seemed uneasy about his own words, and Elias wondered what he meant. He preferred to be Elias and nothing more, except to maybe live a little longer than a few days and have some sort of enjoyable existence in this cruel world.

As they continued their walk over the moldy railway tracks,

they passed by what looked like an old dumping ground from some of the tower cities. It was large pile of putrid waste that smelled of mold, rotten eggs and sour meat. It was crawling with bugs, and mangy rats darted in and out of holes and pipes. Casper made short work of a goodly sized rat with a quick down the hatch method similar to what Hunchy had used himself back at the Argyle. The dump was filled with rotted timbers, old clothes and boiler parts, shopping carts, old train parts, chains, iron bars and even a skeletal human hand.

"Was Mellontas one of those who went with you?" Elias asked.

"Yes, he was," Enupnion explained.

"But where were his wings?" Elias asked.

The winged girl named Epekneia spoke up with a tremble in her voice, "They cleaved them for the healing blood." Then, fearing she spoke out of turn in front of the prince, "I'm sorry, my lord, I…" her wings dropped in a cowering motion.

"No need for apologies. You have lost someone dear to you, as well as I. Speak freely as you chose," the prince said, brushing the top of her wing. Elias thought it weird that someone would call the dirty hunchback "my lord" and struggled with the drastic change he was witnessing.

They continued following the railway tracks as the winged prince kept his promise to answer Elias' questions. "I picked those I trusted most, and we put Charlie's plan into action. We split up to cover more ground, with the intention of hitting the mold hardest in the areas that were most populated. Mellontas took Gabriel's Harbor, but I didn't know he had brought Epekneia with him. Hexpteroox went to the coastal cities, as he was our strongest flyer, and the only one who could make the flight. Deethenton went to the Labyrinths, Hekastos, Anakrino and Thumacheo went to the mountain fortresses, and I went to Grand Fortune City to meet with the Jackboot. I know not if my other companions were successful, or if they met the same fate as dear Mellontas. But one thing I do know. If I return to my father with sacks of fire berry seeds, he will be pleased and maybe he can be convinced the world can still be saved. There's only one more thing I need to know."

"What's that?" Elias asked.

Enupnion stopped where a dead oak tree had grown in the middle of the tracks and said, "What I truly need to know now is, who you are?"

"I don't understand what you mean. I'm Elias," a confused look overtook his face as Enupnion reached into a small pouch and pulled out a handful of seeds.

"Listen carefully. My entire life I was told of a prophecy that one day someone would come. Someone who, when they ate the seeds, would hear the whispering voice. This person would lead our people back to their rightful task of replanting the earth. Our people always thought it had to be from among our own, but all the prophecy said was that it would be the one who hears the voice when they eat the seeds. It never said who, or where they would come from. Of course, there were other prophecies about a wingless friend of the bear and the heart of a prince. Have you ever befriended a bear?" he asked inquisitively, as though it were silly nonsense anyway.

"I've never even seen a bear before."

"What about a heart of a prince? You wouldn't be a prince like me, by chance, would you?"

"No, I just lived on the mountain with my parents until the Jackboot killed them and took me." Elias felt rather confused by all this talk of prophecy.

"No matter, but like I was saying, our people live and breathe by these prophecy books, and some of them even tried to force the prophecy of the planter by feeding their children too many seeds, at the cost of their lives. But, as I learned, you can't force prophecies. When you told me you heard the voice, I knew it had to be you, because no one's ever heard the voice. What I don't understand is why you're dying. But this much I do know, you're going to eat one of these seeds, and we are going to find out the truth."

"I don't want to be a prophecy or a world saver/destroyer person or anything like that. I just want to be me and live," he tried to hold himself together in front of the winged girl, but he knew at least one tear slipped out. "I'm sick of dying every day of my life. I want to live. Really live," then another one slipped out of the other eye.

"We hate death as much as you," Enupnion said, "and that's why we want you to eat these seeds. As you once said, you want your life to mean something," he held the seeds out closer towards Elias and smiled.

Elias still hadn't gotten used to the culture shock of witnessing two winged creatures standing before him, or their strange piercing eyes, but Hunchy had kept his word. That dirty hunchback that had been chained to the rock in the mine for nearly a year had saved his life at GFC, and from the smoke charmer in the alley and now only wanted to save others. A prince who didn't mind eating with someone who had nothing or bringing joy to a boy who needed the comfort of a friend when his parents died, but now he was asking Elias to trust him and risk it all on the chance that he truly heard a voice.

Elias reached out and took a handful of seeds, "What if I was wrong? What if I only thought I heard a voice? What will happen?"

"Humans aren't supposed to eat these seeds, and many have terrible allergic reactions to them. The ones I carry in my pouch are dried and ready to eat, so they're somewhat safe, but never, and I mean "NEVER", eat a whole fresh berry. Birds can, but not humans. So to answer your question, if we're wrong about you, you might explode into a horrible fireball of bone-melting flames," Hunchy said straight faced. But Elias surprised him.

"That's what everyone keeps telling me," he said with a grin, and they both laughed together, but the winged girl seemed to think maybe they had been down in the black mist for too long and had finally lost their minds. Death was no laughing matter to her, but she had never stared it in the face as they had and lived to mock it.

With a single motion Elias placed the seeds into his mouth, chewed them up and swallowed them. He stood there for a few minutes, wondering if something was going to happen. "Maybe they don't work, or maybe it only works on your people," he said, but the prince and the girl simply stood there waiting. He leaned back on the dead oak tree for a moment, then abruptly said, "Do you hear that?"

"Hear what?" they both asked.

Suddenly everything disappeared in front of him, and his sight was teleported into a vision. The prince and the girl had no idea what was happening as Elias stood there with his eyes burning red like fire. His heart generator churned harder as the mod burned through the lifesaving gold faster and faster, until he let out a red, smoke-filled scream. Casper flew off to somewhere, anywhere, to get away from the bothersome screaming. Then Elias bent over, placing his hands on the tree for support and Enupnion reached out to touch him, but hesitated and pulled back. Red smoke covered the ground and everything around it, then Elias vomited all over the tree and part of it caught fire. After which, he collapsed and awoke moments later with Enupnion and the winged girl standing over him.

"Are you okay?" Enupnion asked.

"I-I think so," Elias said.

"What happened? Did you hear the voice?"

"I saw something," Elias said.

"A vision?" the winged girl asked.

"I guess so."

"Yes, of course! Tell us what you saw," Enupnion demanded.

Elias gathered himself together with several breaths before explaining, "I was standing by a river flowing with creeping mold, and people came from everywhere to gather at the water's edge. They were drinking from the river and some had even died and fallen into the moldy water, but people kept drinking it even with the rotting corpses in it. Then I opened the door to my heart-mod, tore out my heart and cast it into the water." The winged girl and the prince softly gasped as Elias continued, "The water turned red, and some continued to drink it and were healed. Others were angry the mold was gone and picked up large stones to stone me to death, but an iron man rose from the water, caught fire and the people fled in terror." He continued with fire burning in his eyes and sweat pouring from his face. "After that, a strange gaunt-looking man reached into the water, stole my bad heart and struck me down. Moments later I realized I was walking the streets of Gabriel's Harbor with the little boy from Harbor I, the one who died. His heart was missing and he was whispering something, but I couldn't hear it. Then suddenly I was taken to many cities, plains, mountains and dark valleys with him until he disappeared and I was left standing alone on a lush, green mountain covered in fire flowers. Then I woke up."

"What was the boy saying?" Enupnion begged.

"It sounded like he was whispering the word "speak," but I'm not sure. I'm sorry," Elias said.

"The voice, did you hear the voice?" asked the prince, who was kneeling down next to him.

"Yes, I did," Elias said, still breathing heavily from his ordeal.

"Did it tell you to save them? Did it say to replant the seeds and heal the land? What did it say? What did it say?" the prince demanded.

"It said one word loud and clear."

"What? What was it?"

"Destroy," Elias said and the prince nearly fell over backwards in shock.

"WHAT? That can't be. Are you sure?"

"It was extremely clear. Every place the boy took me it said loudly, one word, DESTROY," Elias said, feeling as if he had disappointed his friend.

"And the boy? Was he also telling you to destroy?"

"No, it sounded more like he was whispering a word, but his voice was so quiet all I could hear was the loud voice yelling, DESTROY. If it makes you feel any better, I don't want to destroy anything. I only recently learned there was a destroyer. I for sure didn't know it was me, and I don't even know what to destroy anyway," Elias tried to calm the devastated prince.

"I don't understand. Our books said the one who hears the voice would lead us to replant. Something is terribly wrong." The prince seemed destroyed himself with the news Elias had delivered to him, but they could stay there no longer as the Whisper had already traveled far, and they would have to fly hard to catch up with the ship. The winged girl helped Elias and her prince back to their feet, as both seemed emotionally stunned from the traumatic vision.

"I'll carry your cloak and gloves, my prince," Epekneia offered. The prince cradled Elias in his arms, and they all lifted off the ground and above the black mist. They had only flown for about 30 minutes when they realized the ships had stopped midflight and all the lights were beaming. They glanced at each other, worried someone had noticed they were gone, so they approached with caution, and when the moment was right they landed softly on top of the Whisper's envelope. They checked Elias' eyes to make sure no red smoke was left and made sure their stories matched in case they were questioned. Then the prince slipped on his cloak and he and Elias climbed down the left side carefully and walked around to the forward deck, leaving Epekneia on top of the ship. After such a long time in captivity, she was pleased to be left alone, resting below the open sky. After all, she had been through a traumatic experience of her own that she wasn't prepared to speak of. When Elias and Hunchy saw all the lights on in the command center, they walked in as if they had been on a simple evening stroll around the deck of the Whisper.

However, the crew seemed extremely unsettled, and even the air on the Whisper had a dark, eerie scent about it. "Where you guys been?" Bogan asked, seeming a bit miffed that Elias would be hanging out with the hunchback.

"We were resting on top of the envelope, enjoying the beautiful, clear night," Hunchy said quickly to avert a mistaken statement from Elias.

"WHAT!" Izzy barked out, "you could have fallen off and been killed." She threw a deadly glare at them from her beautifully angry eyes, "Don't ever do that again. We almost lost Ava that way."

"Yes, please don't ever do that," Ava agreed.

"Well, if you guys were up there, you certainly must have heard all the screaming," Gideon prodded.

Fearing the crew may have had heard Elias, they both denied any notion of such a thing.

"Screaming?" Elias pretended.

"You've got to be kidding me. You two better get your ears checked," Wyatt sneered.

"What happened?" Elias asked.

Then Gideon explained, "The council woman on the emissary ship must have had some sort of uncontrollable seizure. I guess she's okay now, but she was screaming so loud, one of the windows on the Whisper's bridge cracked," Gideon pointed at the window.

"As soon as she recovers, we'll be on our way to Mine Five, but this job can't end soon enough in my opinion." Gideon looked pale and queasy, and Ava was sitting in a chair holding a picture of Charlie close to her heart.

Merlin kept looking out the window and saying to himself, "Where is it? I'm not going crazy. I know what I saw."

Bogan's shaky hands could barely sharpen his knife. The only one that didn't seem shaken was Izzy, who had a small drop of blood coming from her ear. She gave Elias the impression she was about to lay waste to some horrible creature of darkness, and her presence alone made him believe she could do just that.

THE ALCHEMIST: Something terrible had occurred. He could feel her pain and wondered if somehow the Destroyer had awaked. Things were happening faster than he anticipated, and he would need to step up his efforts, even if it was a delicate situation for her. True he need the boy alive, but only long enough to complete the task. Then he could take the heart and his rightful place among his people.

-12-

DARKNESS LIES

*B*osarus was unsettled as he approached the enormous beast lying in front of the Iron Weaver. No one had ever heard of a mole this large, let alone seen or killed one, but the Jackboot had done just that. Although, he was nowhere to be found, and Bosarus grew fearful that he might be lying dead under the body of the great beast. "Mr. Jackboot, sir," he called with a shaky tone in his voice. He was mostly more terrified of what the Jackboot's enemies would do to him than he was the death of the hard man he called sir.

A few years ago he had chosen to make an enemy out of the Jackboot, and after the Jack had laid waste to his city, he was forced into a lifetime of service. Bosarus knew he never should have raised the price of goods so high to purposefully crush GFC's economy, thereby causing many in GFC to starve to death. He had listened to the advice of some crafty advisors and brought down the Jackboot's wrath on his own head, but now he had come to respect the man and realized only men like the Jackboot survived this harsh world. The Jackboot had spared his own life and the life of his family, and for that he was loyal to the end, which might be soon if the Jackboot was dead.

Standing next to the creature, he noticed it started to move, so he quickly ran and grabbed a long blade from inside the train. Returning he drove it deep into the beast. "Good, now it's dead," he muttered to himself. But the beast moved again so he stabbed and he stabbed, but it kept heaving up and down. The beast looked dead enough so why did it keep moving? Bosarus went mad with bloodlust as he hacked and plunged the sharp blade into the relentless beast. Suddenly the top of the creature's back burst open, and the Jackboot climbed out covered in its blood. Much to the Jackboot's surprise so was Bosarus, who had been hacking at the dead creature for some time now.

"Dear me, Bosarus, I think you've finally killed it," mocking his efforts to slay the dead beast. The Jackboot climbed down out of the mole with his blood covered face smiling.

"NOW THAT'S A MOLE, BOSARUS!" he said proudly as he slapped the man on the back.

A SPEEDER SHOT DOWN THE TUNNEL AND SLOWED TO A HOVER over top the foul, dead beast. "MR. JACKBOOT, SIR!" the pilot squalled.

"What is it?"

"There is an uprising in the city, sir."

He had grown used to hearing these things, but knew instinctively this time it was different, "Who's leading it?"

"Bobby Kitchen, s-sir," the speeder pilot stuttered.

The Jackboot dropped his head and shook it in great disappointment. Big Bobby Kitchen, as he was sometimes called, had always been loyal to him and was one of his seven best men. Bobby Kitchen had helped him take GFC from Angus Grand and put down several uprisings since, but truth be told, his last name wasn't really Kitchen, but Mahoney. Big Bobby was given that title because everyone said he was as big as a kitchen. Those who had survived fights with him had even said his punches had felt like he had hit them with the whole kitchen sink, and thus began the tales of the Jackboot "dropping the Kitchen" on someone. Even though the Jack was no stranger to hard fights, what truly bothered him was that Bobby had been a loyal friend and was greatly respected throughout all of GFC.

It was Big Bobby Kitchen who cared for his dear Isabella after Angus Grand cut off his feet. However, four-year-old Isabella didn't like calling him the Kitchen and dubbed Bobby with her own secret term of endearment she felt more befitting a large, bearded bear of a man. It was also Bobby that helped hide him in Gabriel's Harbor, where Tom Rand and Hans Kloppenheimer crafted his iron boots. Even more so, it was Bobby who sent word to him that his ex-wife might have been pregnant with his child. The events that transpired sent him into horrible, tormenting madness that lasted for years, and Grand Fortune City almost fell to Bosarus' mountain kingdom. But again Bobby came to his aid and helped lead the charge against Bosarus to set the city right again.

There wasn't going to be an easy solution to this problem. Even if he won he would still lose. If he killed the Kitchen with his rifle, he would lose a great deal of respect from the people for not giving him a fair fight. If he fought the Kitchen, his chances of beating him were slim to none. He hoped his big kill would work in his favor, or at least provide him with a substantial intimidation factor.

Considering all the damage the boy had caused to the city, it must have been easy for Bobby to build enough support to overthrow him. The Jack wasn't sad that the people had turned against him, those were everyday problems for a leader, but he was truly hurt that his faithful friend and fellow soldier had betrayed him. He would have to deal with Big Bobby Kitchen the hard way. He would have to deal with him the Jackboot way, and that bothered him.

He told the speeder pilot not to speak a word to anyone in

the city of the giant mole but to tell them he would be returning soon. After the speeder left, he instructed Bosarus as to the plan.

"Get the ropes and the winches, we're taking this beast with us," he said, examining his blood-covered hands.

"Shall I get you a wash cloth, sir?" Bosarus asked.

"No. They'll see me as I am. It's good theatrics, Bosarus. Now where's my pipe?"

"Right away, sir! EDGAR! Find the Jackboot's pipe," Bosarus ordered, and Edgar came running out of the train immediately, scouring the ground for the pipe.

"And find my beautiful harpoon!" he snapped with a twinkle in his eye.

Once they had finished strapping the beast down to the top of the Weaver's boiler, Bosarus put the train in reverse and headed back out of the tunnel. A half hour later, the Iron Weaver exited the tunnel backwards into the mine and they were welcomed by a gauntlet of miners hurling everything from insults, chunks of coal and stones, to pieces of destroyed airships that had fallen into the mine. They busted out windows and scuffed the sides of the train cars until the steam engine finally appeared and they saw what was strapped to the top of it.

Those holding stones and chunks of coal dropped them about as fast as their own jaws dropped. The Jackboot stood beside the monster mole, still covered in its blood, and held his rifle across his right shoulder.

"Next one who hits my train with a rock or some other childish projectile, I'll blow a hole in him the size of this mole," he threatened. Most of them stood there in shock, largely out of disbelief in the size of the enormous dead beast strapped to the Iron Weaver.

When they finished exiting the tunnel, Bosarus switched the track points and the train lurched forward, traveling back inside Grand Fortune City's tower. The train climbed the circular tracks that crawled up the sides of the tower as the supply train passed by on the other side, on its way back down to the mine. The supply train took coal from the mine up to the city and supplies for the miners on the return trip. However, the other set of tracks was made specifically for the Iron

Weaver to travel to and from the mine anytime the Jackboot pleased.

At the top, the Weaver exited the tower into a large warehouse that allowed the Jackboot to keep unsavory characters from sabotaging his tracks. Two rough-looking men with guns opened the door, let them out into the city and closed it behind them with an iron beam. They circled the edge of GFC's platform until they came to the tracks that ran down the center of Main Street and all the way to Monument Circle at the center of the city. The city branched out in a circular pattern from there, moving away from the great monument. At the top of the monument stood a statue of a small girl holding a torch that, by order of the Jackboot, was always lit, even when coal supplies ran low. At the base of the statue was a plaque titled, "Isabella's Light."

"Theatrics, Bosarus! Theatrics," he thundered, stomping his iron boot on top of the train. Bosarus knew exactly what he meant and pulled the steam release on the boiler, blasting out white steam from the bull's nostrils. The white smoke filled the air surrounding the train so much so that not even the Jackboot could see the road in front of him. He couldn't see them, but he could hear the people standing on the sidewalks, cursing him and shouting cheers for the Kitchen.

Bosarus stopped the train in front of the monument and let a good, long blast of steam out for about five minutes, covering everyone's vision and stoking their anger all the more.

But he cut the theatrics when he heard the Kitchen's voice, "Enough with the games, Bosarus! Send him out!" The seven foot, nine and three-quarter inches tall man was standing on the platform waiting for the Jackboot.

The people's shouting and complaining died out instantly when the Jackboot's blood-covered face cleared through the white cloud, but when the steam dropped below the giant mole strapped to the boiler, even Big Bobby Kitchen's breath was caught away. The women pulled their children closer as their angered voices turned to gasps of shock, and men placed their hands on theirs guns and moved in front of them. The moist air from the Weaver's boiler only contributed to the dead beast's putrid odor that now covered their clothes and filled their mouths. Some even put on masks, and others tried to cover their faces with handkerchiefs, but the stench was too potent.

"I understand there are some unhappy citizens in my beautiful city today," he said as he climbed up on top of the beast, puffing his pipe. Blood oozed out of the mole and down its matted, bristly hair dripping on the Iron Weaver's wheels and following the rails back into the city streets.

A fancy-dressed, little man carrying a black umbrella who stood beside Bobby Kitchen spoke up. "We're sick of all the destruction you bring to Grand Fortune City, and we've chosen our new leader and challenger," he patted Bobby Kitchen on the arm.

The Jack tossed his pipe down to Bosarus, who was leaning out the conductor's window, then brushed his dried, bloody mustache and adjusted his eye patch, "What are my odds?"

A young boy stepped up and in a squeaky voice said, "A hundred to one in favor of Mr. Kitchen, sir."

"Wow, that's fairly steep, don't you think? I should be able to hold my own better than that."

"Oh no, Mr. Jackboot, sir, those aren't the odds of the fight, sir. Those are the odds you'll run away."

"WHAT?" The Jackboot was extremely incensed that someone would even set such odds. "Who's calculated that?" he asked.

"That man right there, sir," he pointed to the little umbrella man standing next to Bobby Kitchen.

Immediately, the Jackboot dropped his rifle from his shoulder and blew a six-inch hole in the man's chest, splattering blood all over Bobby. The crowd jumped back in horror at how quickly the Jackboot dispatched the unfair trickster.

"While I'm out saving our city from the monsters that terrify your children at night, you're up here plotting and scheming to kill me. I must say I am extremely disappointed in all of you. Have you all forgotten how I freed this city from the grip of Angus Grand? And Bobby, we fought together. Your betrayal hurts more than all of these lemmings standing here. If they'll betray me so quickly, how long do you think you'll last?" He jumped down off the beast, onto the ground, vibrating the rails in the middle of the street with his heavy, iron boots. "This doesn't have to go any future than that dead guy lying beside you. Just tell me he was the one that talked you into this mess and all is forgiven. No one else needs to die today."

Big Bobby took off his bloodied shirt and threw it to the ground.

"We're past that now, Owen."

The Jackboot never liked it when anyone used his real name, and the Kitchen was clearly using it to dig at him. He was also disappointed that his massive kill and bloodied figure didn't intimidate Bobby in the least, but the Kitchen knew all too well his love for theatrics and had prepared himself for anything.

"You're putting me in a tight spot here, Bobby. If I hurt you, that girl is never going to forgive me, and if I have to kill you, well, she'll never speak to me again. She's probably already mad at me for throwing her in the coal pit."

The whole crowd gasped with shock.

"WHAT? Come on, I wouldn't have left her down there for more than a few days."

The crowd gasped again.

"Wow, you people have gone soft."

The Kitchen began to warm up his 486 lb. physique as two men dragged the body of the smart-mouthed man off the edge of the platform. Bobby's hands were twice the size of the Jackboot's, and he was almost two feet taller. He had no mods to speak of and was generally a quiet man with a gentle approach. With good advisors, he might even make a better ruler, the Jackboot acknowledged. But now wasn't the time for speculation, now was the time for two men to settle matters the way real men do; with blood and bones. This hard world had made them the hard men they were today, battle seasoned and no stranger to war, death or famine. They had fought side by side and even comforted one another when loved ones had died, but now, in this time of prosperity, things had changed. There hadn't been a war in four years, and now Grand Fortune City wanted a different kind of ruler; a gentler ruler that didn't blow holes in men who insulted them. The city agreed now was the time for Big Bob Kitchen to take the seat of power.

The Jackboot hadn't seen his old friend in quite some time, and when he stepped up on the platform he was instantly reminded of how big the Kitchen was. He knew right away he would have to use Bobby's kindheartedness against him, and so he thought it through and asked, "Friendly handshake to start with, what do you say, Bob?" Reaching out his hand, it felt child-like as the Kitchen took hold of it, and as he looked up at Big Bobby, he knew that pain was coming soon. Typically, the Jackboot would shake hands as a means of disarming his opponents and then crush their shin bones with his iron boots, but Bobby knew this move too well. When he noticed something under the Kitchen's pant leg, he figured Bobby had installed some sort of leg protection to guard against his classic move. Was it even possible to bring down someone as big as the Kitchen? He would have to be crafty or he would soon be dead.

Then he saw it. Something that could work to his advantage, "Good luck, Bobby," he said with a smile. The Kitchen nodded back at him with a blank stare in his eyes.

They were still shaking hands when the Jackboot did his classic shin breaking move, and as he suspected, Bobby had been ready. His boot hit with a – CLANK – and the Kitchen smiled.

"Ha, not today, Owen. I was ready for…." While the Kitchen was still bragging, the Jack, still holding that large hand, reached in and grabbed Bobby's loose belt and gave it a hard yank, pulling the belt all the way off. Before Big Bobby knew it, his pants had dropped completely off and down around his ankles. The crowd let out a blistering laugh as Big Bobby's bottom glared in the light of the setting sun. When Bobby reached down to pull up his drawers, the Jackboot stepped back and punted him with a blow to the head from his iron boot. Big Bobby dropped to his knees in a daze. It was enough for the Jackboot to make his next move. He ran around behind the Kitchen and slipped the belt around that large neck, cutting off his air supply. The Kitchen's face turned deep red and then blue as he started to lose consciousness. The Jackboot figured he could talk some sense into his old friend after he came to, but what happened next shocked everyone, including the Jackboot.

BOOM! A shot rang out and missed the Jackboot by inches. He loosened his grip on the Kitchen's neck and turned around to see Edgar holding his rifle. "You're supposed to die," Edgar hissed as he reloaded the weapon, "You're supposed to die!"

Some in the crowd fled in terror, and others were too afraid to move. Big Bobby slumped over, gasping for breath, while the Jackboot tried to talk some sense into Edgar. "Edgar, what are you doing with my rifle? Put that down before you get hurt."

"You're supposed to die. They said you would lose. They said you would die," Edgar complained as he raised the rifle again, pointing it at the Jackboot.

BOOM! Edgar fired off another round, nicking him in the shoulder.

"Edgar, I demand that you put that rifle down before I ..."

BOOM, another round ricocheted off his boot.

"DIE! DIE!"

BOOM!

"Missed again, Edgar, You should have learned to handle a real man's gun," the Jackboot laughed. Owen looked back at Big Bobby still catching his breath when he noticed something wet all over his chest. "Owen?" Bobby said holding up a bloodied hand.

"BOBBY!" he answered in shock as Big Bobby Kitchen slumped over. Edgar had missed the Jackboot and shot the Kitchen square in the chest.

The Jackboot was furious with rage and with his hands clinched tight ran straight at Edgar, who was loading another round into the chamber. Edgar raised the rifle again, but it was too late. The Jack kicked the barrel with his boot, causing the rifle to fire off into the sky, then he grabbed it away from Edgar, who fell to his knees weeping.

"You're supposed to die. They said you would die." The Jackboot knelt down in front of Edgar, grabbing his white suit jacket with dried bloody hands.

"Who said I'm supposed to die?"

"The voices, the voices said you would die," Edgar stared off into nothingness with vacant eyes. "They promised."

The Jackboot took Edgar by the chin and raised his head up to look him in the eyes. "Didn't anyone ever tell you, Edgar?"

"Tell me what?" he asked with a glossy look in his eyes.

"Darkness lies." The Jackboot lifted him up by his nice, white suit and addressed the crowd. "Today this man has murdered our friend and robbed him of his right to a fair fight. Today justice will be delivered."

"JACKBOOT JUSTICE!" The crowd parroted back.

Edgar died that day at the hands of the Jackboot.

A sense of dread instantly fell over the Jackboot as he began to piece together horrible thoughts in his mind, "Izzy, my dear Isabella," he said quietly to himself, then bellowed out, "Bosarus!"

"Yes, sir."

"Find my spies; my daughter. They're in danger. Send the bird! Get Hans…"

"SIR! Mr. Kitchen is alive!" Bosarus called out in disbelief.

"WHAT?!" The Jackboot ran over to Bobby, knelt down beside him and lifted his head up. The Kitchen coughed blood all over his friend's face as he tried to get his words out.

"O-Owen, I'm sorry."

"Forget it. I'm going to save you, brother—BOSARUS! Get my physician now!"

"No, Owen. I'm sorry." he said, reaching into his pocket. The Kitchen pulled out a piece of paper and handed it to his old friend. "I'm sorry they got to me. I wasn't faithful enough….to be your friend."

"At least your wounds were," he smiled.

"Truer words were…" and death took the Kitchen away.

The note had only two words written on it, but it was all he needed. "BOSARUS!"

"Yes, sir!"

"Ready the Iron Weaver!"

"Right away, sir."

-13-

MAJOR MALFUNCTION

"There it is again!" Merlin exclaimed looking out the window, but no one else on the bridge knew what he was talking about. "I knew it. I knew I saw something," he seemed determined to prove he'd not gone mad, but by the time he was so certain of himself the emissary ship pulled up alongside the Whisper and one of the representatives climbed on board.

"She's feeling much better now. I'll remain here on your ship until we arrive at the mine. This way the guards feel less threatened by your crew," he said, but Hunchy sensed something strange about the man and began sniffing him. The man stepped back away from the hunchback, but Hunchy came closer and looked the man right in the eyes with that one uncloaked eye of his. Elias knew how frightening it could be looking into that deep, dark pearl of mystery and sympathized with the awkwardness of the moment.

"Good grief, Hunchy, are we going to have put you on a leash?" Bogan appeared pleased with his new insult of Hunchy, and even Izzy let out a tiny snicker that forced the secret prince to back away from the man. After adjusting his long coat and brushing off his lapel in disgust, the man strangely reminded them of their agreement to destroy the bots and then stepped away from the crew. Sleep eluded everyone that night as the haunted screams of the council woman filled their thoughts, but for Elias it was mostly due to his wild vision of tearing out his heart and being stoned to death by crazed mold eaters. Hunchy, however, couldn't seem to take his eye off even the slightest movement of the council representative.

They sailed on for a few hours towards the eastern light cresting over the horizon that soon revealed the mine in the distance. Towers of thick, black smoke climbed into the sky and mushroomed together above the rising sun, and it was obviously not part of the normal mining operations. As the Whisper closed in on Mine Five, they began to notice pieces of mining equipment scattered everywhere, as if they had been violently hurled out of the mine. Mine Five was a strip mine with five large bench walls circling a massive one mile hole in the ground. Unlike Grand Fortune City, there was not enough heat to keep the black mist completely away from the area. Gideon called for masks, at least until they were close enough to the mine to breathe safely, then they walked out onto the deck for a better look at the devastation.

Black smoke rolled from every direction, and they could hear the malfunctioning bot bending and crushing the iron of a harvesting bot it was in the process of dismantling. Another bot's arm had been torn off and was throwing sparks all around some mashed up train cars piled onto a tower of spilled coal. Some miners were cowering on the ground behind the train cars, and others had taken cover in one of the five secure towers overlooking the mine. One of the towers was vigorously waving a bright orange cloth to get their attention, so Wyatt switched out of whisper mode and made a hard turn directly towards the tower. His timing was impeccable, because their job began sooner than they expected when they received a warning from somewhere above them. No one knew who said it, but Hunchy and Elias had a fairly good hunch as to whom the strange voice belonged to that rang out over the sounds of destruction coming from the mine, "WATCH OUT!"

Everyone on the deck of the Whisper looked up as a large mining bot's decapitated head was sailing through the air towards them. Wyatt caught it out of the corner of his eye and made another hard banking maneuver to the left, sending everyone on deck tumbling into the railing and each other. Merlin practically went over the side, but Elias grabbed him by the arm and Izzy grabbed Elias by the leg and all three of them held on to their faculties until Wyatt righted the ship. Then he promptly aimed the Whisper for the safety of the mining tower. That's when the crew noticed the supply and emissary ships had stopped following a good distance away.

"Would you look at that? Wouldn't want anyone to damage their umbrella, now would we?" Bogan sarcastically scoffed at their lack of bravery.

Gideon gave the harbor rep a revolting look that sent him back inside the Whisper. It was obviously a much harder job than Councilman Forsythe was willing to admit, and Gideon couldn't help but feel like they had been set up.

Wyatt pulled in as close as he could to the mining tower to keep the Whisper out of harm's way, and one of the miners stepped out onto the tower balcony.

"Are you the elite soldiers Councilman Forsythe said were coming?" the man asked. The crew looked at one other and wondered what they had gotten themselves into, and then Merlin answered him in classic fashion.

"No, sir," he smirked, "we're Dream Makers."

"Heart Breakers, to you fellas," Izzy twisted her big, brown curls with her mod-hand.

"And Risk Takers," Elias finished it off, much to Izzy's surprise, so she gave his hair a good messing up.

The man hadn't a clue what they meant, and after shrugging off their odd introduction, he asked, "Well, who are you then?"

Gideon stepped in to clear up the confusion, "We were sent by the Harbor Council to shut down the malfunctioning bots. Is there any information you can give us that might help solve this?"

"Yes. Did you happen to bring any high explosives?" he asked.

"No," Gideon responded.

"Well, then you might as well turn around and go home, because these things are unstoppable."

"It's only a harvesting bot, how hard can it be to shut it down?" Bogan asked.

"About six weeks ago we sent a few bots off for repair. One or two, I think, but when they returned we couldn't get them back online. Our lead bot, the one slumped over there," he pointed down into the mine at one of the bots, "finally started up and then started sending out all kinds of crazy commands to the other bots. We were able to shut it down, but by the time we did the other bot started attacking and smashing the whole mine and the other harvesting bots. It was a total disaster. We lost eight miners in the process," the man explained.

"EIGHT!" Ava said in shock.

"You say you sent them off for repair. Where did you send them?" Gideon asked the man.

"Well, we sent them to GFC like we always do. It's the closest city, and they have the best bot repair shop. We for sure wouldn't use Karl's Labyrinth anymore. Dirty thieves," he muttered under his breath.

Gideon took a deep breath and rubbed his hand over his bald head, scratching it hard where his mod connected at the top. He hadn't noticed the harbor representative had stepped back out onto the deck and was standing directly behind him.

"You're still required to finished the job or forfeit your ship as payment to cover your bill to the Argyle," he said in an arrogant tone.

Gideon didn't like the man in the first place, and he for sure didn't like being snuck up on. It caught him off guard enough to light up his temper in front of the crew. He swung around fast and popped the man right in the face, knocking him to the deck, "GET BACK INSIDE," he bellowed out. Then he brought his voice down to a more teeth-grinding resolve, "Or I promise I'll throw you into the mine with that mad bot," he said, sending several blinking lights on his head into overdrive. Elias was taken aback to see Gideon's calm and collected demeanor turn dark and unhinged.

After the man gathered himself together, mostly by scurrying across the deck on all fours back into the Whisper, Gideon looked at his crew and, for the first time ever, he pulled a Charlie out of his hat. "I'm open to suggestions here, if anyone has any?" he asked. Bogan almost fell backwards over the rail to his doom, but Ava gently smiled at him.

"Well, it's about time," Izzy said, crossing her arms.

"What's about time?" Wyatt asked as he joined the crew, swinging his nicely salved mod connections, but everyone was too busy thinking up options to fill him in on their progress. Wyatt knew the drill anyway; late comer always loses out.

"If we can get someone inside the lead bot's cockpit, maybe we can upload new commands to the malfunctioning bot," Merlin suggested.

"That's a great plan. Why didn't we think of that?" the mine worker scoffed. "Oh yeah, that's right, we did, and that man right there," he pointed to a dead man lying on one of the bench walls, "has the control module in his hand. We might just be miners to you people, but we're not stupid, you know," he seemed more than a little offended by the theft of his credibility, even though that was not their intent. "Anything you do with that lead bot will have to be done in manual mode, so I hope you know how to operate a manual cockpit," he went on to explain.

"Why not send someone down to operate it manually and smash the other bot like it's smashing everything else?" Wyatt said as if he were trying to convince everyone he was the man for the job.

"Works for me," Izzy agreed.

"Umm, about that," the mine worker cleared his throat. "That might be a bit of a problem as well. You see, when we shut the lead bot down, we cut the power supply to the controls. You'll need to rewire the power before you can operate it manually," he scrunched his face in disappointment.

"No problem. I'll just slide down there, rewire it, fire that bad boy up and give that bot a good, old fashioned whooping," Wyatt bragged.

"What about my generator?" Elias asked. "I thought you said it could operate equipment on the ship. So can it operate that bot?" he asked, looking at Merlin.

"Well, yeah, it could, but something that size would run your tiny generator out in about 30 seconds, and then your heart would stop and that mad bot would bury you permanently inside the other one," Merlin explained.

"No problem, short stuff. I'll take it from here," Wyatt had no intention of being upstaged by anyone now that he was fully recovered.

"That's the best plan I've heard so far," Gideon said. "Let's get the gear together and get Wyatt down there as fast as possible. Izzy, Merlin set up a diversion for the bot while we get Wyatt down there," he added.

The plan was sound and Wyatt, though a bit cocky, was good at those types of jobs. They chose to use the same springy cord that Hunchy had used to save Ava, since Merlin considered it good luck, but in truth only Elias and Hunchy knew how Ava had truly been saved.

Izzy and Merlin decided to use Casper for the diversion, mostly due to Hunchy's prodding. The secret prince winked at Elias when he made the suggestion, and Elias cracked an ever so tiny grin back at him, but their sly, inside body language did not go unnoticed by Bogan, whose mental notebook was rapidly filling up.

Once Wyatt was in place, Hunchy sent Casper off toward the malfunctioning bot with two clicks of his tongue, and they all watched in awe as the great bird toyed with the iron beast. As far as the crew was concerned Casper had never done anything like this before, but he seemed to know exactly what he was doing. Casper would skillfully dive down into the smoky destruction of the lower mine, pick up a piece of scrap metal and drop it on top of the mad-mechanical-machine, but this bot's malfunctioning program was also allowing it to learn, and fast.

Gideon realized Wyatt was still standing there beside the rest of the mesmerized crew and feared their diversion wouldn't last long if they didn't get on with the plan.

"Wyatt, get moving!"

"Huh? Oh, right," and with that Wyatt hopped over the side of the Whisper and shot down to the lower part of the mine with a snap. When he touched down on the second bench wall, he let go of the springy cord which shot back up toward the Whisper and flung something shiny back up over the railing. It passed right over their heads and landed hard on the deck behind them with a loud, clanking thud. They all simultaneously turned around to the jaw-dropping revelation of Wyatt's left mod-arm lying on the deck. The whole crew was totally flabbergasted at the lifeless, metal limb lying before them and words failed them. Merlin, however, was suddenly sent into an uncontrollable fit of gut-busting laughter. He fell to his knees in tears he was laughing so hard, but the rest of the crew thought he'd lost his mind with his insensitive response to Wyatt's mechanical mishap. Even Gideon, who respected Merlin a great deal, was more than a little unsettled by his mockery. After a time, Merlin managed to wheeze out an explanation for his behavior.

"B-butter," Merlin said, catching his breath during his raucous laughter, "butter." The crew was at a loss as they tried to piece together his explanation.

"Did he say butter?" Bogan asked.

"Abner's—butter," Merlin continued. Then Elias spoke up and explained what he thought had caused Merlin's glass egg of a brain to finally crack.

"You mean Abner's mod-salve?" Elias asked. Merlin raised his finger and pointed at Elias, nodding his head up and down. Elias began to laugh as well and explained to the crew, "Wyatt kept saying it was the best salve ever; slick as butter."

"Y-y-yes! Oh dear, I'm going to die. I-I can't, I can't breathe," Merlin said, holding his stomach. "That old coot sold him BUTTER. HA HA HA." Merlin wept with laughter a little longer.

Then a voice from below called up, "Is my arm up there?"

Everyone instantly rolled into hysterical laughter for several moments that ended abruptly with a shockwave of chills down their arms from a blood-chilling scream. "GIDEON!"

The mad bot had determined Wyatt a threat and was standing over him. Wyatt tried to hide behind a large rock on the bench wall, but Abner's slick salve was causing him all kinds of trouble, and he kept stumbling as he ran around the rock. Everyone was in complete hysterics trying to think of some way to help him, but by that time the bot had picked Wyatt up by the legs and was shaking him upside down. Both Merlin's hands were on top of his glass dome, and his face had gone numb with fear as his friend was tossed around like a wee, metal doll in the giant's grip. It didn't last long, though, because Wyatt slipped right out of his buttery mod-legs and fell to the ground. He hit so hard the other mod-arm was knocked completely off, leaving him mod-less, staring straight up at the crew and Ava. Normally, Gideon would have been swift to block Ava's view and keep his word to Wyatt, but he was frozen at the sight of his friend lying on the ground helpless. Wyatt himself was mortified as he stared up at them, trying to tap his left shoulder until he fully realized the other mod-arm had come off.

"G-G-Gideon," Wyatt bellowed out a sorrowful cry, "A-Ava! Oh, why? Why? Why? I hate you mother! I hate you!"

Maybe it was the vision by the oak tree, or the voice of destruction. Or maybe it was the sight of his broken and defenseless friend crying out the heartache of his shattered emotions, laid bare before the girl he loved. Or maybe he just wanted to eat more seeds and see what else might happen, but something switched on inside of Elias and he spun around, slipped the seed pouch out of Hunchy's cloak, grabbed the cord and dove over the edge of the ship. Hunchy knew what he had done, but didn't stop him, mainly out of a desire to know if Elias would hear the voice again. Izzy, however, practically lost her mind as she watched Elias dropping into the pit.

Gideon knew Elias had no clue how to get the bot up and running, even if his generator could power it for a few minutes. So, as soon as the cord flipped back up on the deck, Merlin grabbed it, looked at everyone, and with Gideon's nod, dove over the railing after Elias.

Izzy's knuckles washed white on the railing as she watched Elias run towards the slumped over lead bot with Merlin not far behind him. Bogan seemed to be preoccupied, as he couldn't take his eyes off of Hunchy, who was somehow sending commands to Casper with a clicking sound in his throat.

Elias finally made it to the lead bot but had no clue how to open the access door to the cockpit. Much to his surprise, Merlin arrived seconds behind him and pulled the override lever, opening the door. They both climbed in, and Elias was instantly confused by the controls. There were no seats or sticks or anything like it. Only two large boots connected to the floor and two large gloves connected to cables and hoses resembling a sort of complex puppeteer system by which the bots were manually controlled.

"Where's the seat?" he asked Merlin.

"These things don't work that way. I'm kind of surprised these advanced bots even have manual controls. Most are fully automated now, but I know this design well," Merlin said, looking at the setup.

Wyatt's screaming suddenly brought them back to their task. "You'll only have a few moments to kill that bot before your fuel runs out and your heart stops, so you have to be quick," Merlin explained.

"Okay, so what do I do? How do I control it?"

"Put your hands into the gloves and feet into the boots, and everything you do it will do. If you want to run or walk, hit the treadmill button. It's not hard, trust me. I'll connect your generator, but whatever you do, don't hit that thruster button," Merlin said, switching several levers to put the bot into full manual mode. Then he plugged Elias' generator port into the bot, "I can't stay in here. I hate these things. Don't ask. But as soon as this thing powers up, stand it up and take several swings at that thing until it's out of commission. Be quick about it," Merlin said with a firm look.

"Okay," Elias said, slipping into the boots and gloves. Merlin stepped to the access door and climbed out.

"As soon as the bot's down I'll have some fuel ready for your generator. Let's hope you don't power down before I get to you."

"Okay. I'm ready."

"Good luck, my friend," and Merlin shut the door behind him.

It was lifelessly hollow inside the cold, iron beast, and looking out the round window of its chest, he felt as if he had become the beast's own infected heart. The sounds of Wyatt's broken, desperate cries were mostly muffled by the thick walls and a beeping red light in front of him flashing – MANUAL MODE. He slipped his hand out of the control glove and into Hunchy's seed pouch. He didn't measure it. He didn't even know how many Hunchy had given him the last time, but he filled his generator hopper to the brim. Then he placed another handful of dried seeds into his mouth, slipped his hand back into the control glove and waited for the green power light to come on. It didn't take long.

All of a sudden, every light in the bot started beeping like mad, and several of them exploded, sending colorful glass everywhere inside the beast. The green power light flashed rapidly, then popped as the beast made a loud, metal groaning sound, and Elias felt the control gloves and boots vacuum tight around his hands and feet. Something felt strange about the bot. His skin even felt pleasantly comfortable inside the machine, as if it were made for him. He jumped up and the beast hopped into the air and landed on its feet with a loud BOOM!

Elias turned and looked around for the other bot, only to see Merlin jumping up and down, yelling something and pointing behind him. Elias turned around to a giant, flying fist hurling towards his bot and SMASH— he fell to the ground, but much to his shock, his hands and feet stayed in the controls. He smiled with a bright red, smoking grin as he felt the seeds jolt his mind into action, and he hopped back up on his feet. The malfunctioning bot took another swing, but he made a crouching move with the controls and it missed him. "If this is my last day, my only day left, it's going to be the most fun I've ever had." He said to himself.

He noticed Merlin waving his arms again and pointing to something over on the ground. It was a large coal-harvesting hammer with a pick on one end and a square, spiked striking end on the other. He made a run for it as the maniacal-metal-man chased after its new target, and with a rolling-ground-flip he grabbed the hammer and raised it with both arms, blocking the bot's fist. As he stood there holding the mad bot's arm up with the hammer, he noticed something opening on its head. Next thing he knew, a big Gatling gun rose up out of the top and let loose a barrage of lead against the front of his bot. Elias was curious how it withstood the heavy artillery, as he remembered what Merlin had said about harvesting bots not being armored. Why would someone turn a harvesting bot into a weapon? Realizing he was daydreaming while holding a killer robot's arm in the air, he shook his head of those thoughts.

Then the bot hit him hard with the other arm, sending him into the air and knocking a heavy cloud of red smoke out of his mouth. He'd just gotten his bot back on its feet and saw the other bot charging when he heard the voice loud and clear again, "DESTROY!" Louder than ever, it was. "DESTROY!" it kept saying, but this time a giant, murderous monster of iron and smoke was charging at him, and he was completely in agreement with the voice. He raised the harvesting hammer like a ball bat and waited for the oncoming steam machine to reach him. His eyes were burning from the seeds, but his vision was never clearer as the bot entered the sweet zone for contact, and Elias swung his hammer with a fierce blow.

SMASH!

He crushed the mad bot's left arm, then he flipped his hammer over to the spiked end and caved in the bot's Gatling gun head. The headless bot turned in circles as it smashed itself with its right arm, trying to figure out where the enemy had gone. So Elias capitalized on his lead and laid waste to the beast with blow after blow, throwing chunks of iron into the sky until his enemy was a pile of mangled, steaming junk. He turned around to the sight of his friends jumping joyously up and down on the Whisper for his conquering victory over the beast. It felt good to win.

But Elias paid no attention to the dawning expression on Merlin's face, because his eyes were focused on Ava, but it was Ava's face that concerned him the most. She looked terrified, but at what? Then Izzy pointed about the time he could feel the earth vibrating beneath his bot's iron legs. Gideon was right not to trust Councilman Forsythe's information, but there was not time for I told you so now.

Elias closed his eyes knowing there was another bot coming, and he could tell that it was bigger by how hard the ground was shaking. He didn't understand how or if it even made sense in his own mind, but he could feel the metal as it came closer. A rear view screen showed the bot right behind him, bringing both its fists down toward him, so he ran, and he ran hard. Then he climbed up one of the bench walls and ran across it. If not for the window in front of him, he wouldn't have believed he was going anywhere as he ran across the treadmill underneath his feet, but he was moving much faster than he thought. The other beast was bigger and had a larger stride than his bot, so it was closing in on him fast. He jumped off the next two lower bench walls deeper into the mine and hid behind some train cars that had been piled on top of each other during the bot's rampage.

Most of the lower mine was clear of smoke, but some areas still lacked good visibility. Elias waited for the bot to drop down off the next bench wall and soon enough it did just that with a heavy thud. It scanned the area around him and even where the train cars were, but it didn't spot him. Suddenly, he was startled by someone knocking at the back hatch of his bot, and it abruptly opened. It was Epekneia. She walked over and faced him as he was still hooked into his controls.

"There's a large machine over on the far shelf. I can lead the creature under it if you can drop the machine on top of it," she nodded her head. "Good plan?"

"Y-yeah, good plan," Elias agreed, and she climbed out the door, darted up into the smoke and back down in front of the bot. Elias snuck out as stealthily as he could for being in a giant, creaking, metal bucket and made his way over to the next shelf. Epekneia made good on her plan to get the creature under the large mining drill, nearly at the expense of her own life as the bot almost shot her down twice. Elias was astounded by her ability to dive, swoop, spin and rocket into the sky away from it. He was simply in awe of her skill and was happy to have witnessed something so amazing with what little life he had left. By the time he made it over to the large drill, the seeds had almost worn off, so he refilled his hopper and himself as she kept the bot busy.

The bot almost got her, and, if not for Casper, it would have knocked her out of the sky, but it was also Casper that caused the bot to move away from the drill before Elias could drop it on the beast. Once it had locked onto Casper, it went after him full speed back toward the Whisper, back towards his friends. Epekneia had disappeared into the clouds and he hoped she was okay, but he couldn't think about that right then. He had to stop the bot before it attacked his friends.

There was no possible way Elias could catch up with the bot by chasing it, and if there was any time he needed some thrust, it was now. He reached down with the bot arm and picked up his hammer, steadied himself and hit the thruster button. His bot launched up into the air a good ways and moved him closer to the other bot, but not close enough. He needed more thrust— more power, so he dumped the rest of the seeds from Hunchy's pouch into his generator, shutting the hopper door with some effort and mashed down on the thruster button.

He lifted up into the air so fast he almost dropped his harvesting hammer. Then he shot through the thick, black smoke of destruction all the way above the mine until he was overlooking his friends who were standing on the deck the Whisper. That's when he spotted Epekneia pulling Wyatt out of the way of the charging bot, but there was so much smoke the crew had no idea what was going on below or what was headed their way. Gideon pointed up to the sky at Elias as he started his descent back down toward them with his hammer raised high.

"He's overdoing a bit, if you ask me," Bogan said, scrunching one side of his face. Merlin had almost made it back to the cord drop when the bot appeared through the smoke with terrifying sounds of clanging, banging, creaking and groaning and headed right towards him. The monster was about fifty feet away from them all when Elias' hammer came down on it with a single, crushing blow. He hit is so hard with the spiked end he split the bot clean in half. Better if it would have been the Jackboot's head a part of him considered.

His friends were as stunned as was he for a short time, but his mind was instantly captivated by the sound of the voice again, "DESTROY!" At first he didn't understand. It said it again and again as he looked at his friends, and he knew what it wanted. The voice wanted him to destroy them. His heart was gripped with that same pain he felt in Raven Alley and that night with Casper. Why would it want him to destroy his friends? It didn't make any sense. What kind of prophecy was he to fulfill anyway? He felt as if he would collapse if he didn't obey soon, and so he raised his hammer to the shock and fright of his friends.

"DESTROY! DESTROY!" It said again and again. He fought it as hard as he could until he noticed the secret prince had uncovered his face. He was pointing toward the emissary ship and whispering.

Elias closed his eyes and tried to block out the intensity of the mind-melting voice, and that's when he heard a whisper. He couldn't tell what it was saying, but it was enough to help him focus long enough to block out the increasing volume of the voice of destruction, and he made a choice that day to trust his friend Enupnion. Elias swung his hammer down and released it sideways toward the emissary ship. His hammer traveled at breakneck speed through the sky and smashed the supply ship with a violent explosion.

The secret prince swiftly covered his head and turned his gaze to the crew's horrified reactions at the loss of their payment. The emissary ship had made a hard turn and was out of their view in mere seconds as Elias' metal warrior collapsed to the earth.

ELIAS WOKE UP IN MERLIN'S LAB NEXT TO WYATT, WHO WAS mumbling something about a beautiful angel pulling him to safety, but the rest of the crew chalked it up to an emotional breakdown. A few groans from Elias brought Izzy over next to his bed.

"You know, you're going to have to tell me your secret at some point." Izzy said with sly look in her eye."

Elias feared that she somehow learned Hunchy's secret. "What do you mean?" he asked.

Izzy reached down and took her baton from his hand. "How you keep stealing my baton every time you end up in here."

Elias was nearly speechless as Izzy eagle eyed him waiting for a response. He wasn't sure what to say, so he whispered. "I think Bogan's doing it."

Izzy wrinkled her nose. "I knew it!"

But Elias felt bad for blaming Bogan. He truly had no idea how her baton kept getting into his hand every time he was injured. Elias didn't want to be accused of being a thief, but now he felt guilty for blaming Bogan. One thing he knew, the baton made him feel safe and strong. It was the same strange feeling he had back in the bot. Almost like Izzy's baton was made for him, but how could that be?

"HEY, DAYDREAMER!" Izzy shouted.

"Oh sorry." Elias said, realizing his mind had spaced out for a moment thinking of the baton.

"Are you feeling okay?" she asked.

"Yeah, I guess, but my chest hurts," Elias said.

"Merlin said your bot must have malfunctioned after the landing. Makes perfect sense to me," Gideon said voicing their conclusion as they all tried to understand why Elias would have threatened them and destroyed the supply ship.

"I guess we won't be getting any more jobs from Gabriel's Harbor," Wyatt let out a laugh, holding his broken ribs. "Thanks for saving me, kid," he said humbly.

"You're welcome. I just wish I hadn't messed things up and lost the supplies. What are we going to do now? How will we find the flowers?" Elias asked.

"Calm down. We worked it out. We're headed there now," Izzy explained. "The miners didn't care what happened. They were just happy you saved their lives and their jobs. They let us load up with as much coal as we could, and we let them keep the harbor representative," she added with a nefarious twinkle in her eye. "Ava is piloting the ship full speed now, and we're headed toward the Valley of Bones."

"Valley of Bones?" Elias asked.

Merlin stepped over towards him, "Not that we want to go there." He added, "It's a place where dark sorcerers used to practice terrible mold magic, if you believe in that sort of thing. But that's where Hunchy says we'll find the flowers, so that's where we're headed. He calls it the Glorious Valley, but I don't think he's been there in a while. We've been on the way now for about four hours, so you and Wyatt rest up and heal, okay? We should be there by early morning."

Bogan was standing silently in the corner, sharpening his blade, and Izzy noticed the concern on Elias' face. She chimed in to reassure him, "Don't worry about him. He's in a bad mood. He'll get over it soon enough." But now, more than ever, Elias sensed that Bogan was determined to prove Hunchy was not what he seemed.

14

VALLEY OF BONES

erlin was awake, wide awake. Full on, green, glowing brain illuminating the ceiling with invisible thoughts, awake. Everyone else happily collapsed at the chance for some shut eye before reaching the Valley of Bones. Even Elias was down for the count, still sleeping in the lab with Wyatt, but not Merlin. He couldn't stop thinking about what he saw before they reached Mine Five, although he didn't even know what he had seen. His blue brain bolts had finally almost slowed to a nice, rhythmic sleeping pace when he heard Wyatt mumbling in the lab across the hall. His chance for sleep was at last stolen away by pity.

When he entered the lab he noticed Wyatt was sitting up without his mods, not an easy feat, mind you, but pulling the covers up to his face with his stumps was even harder. Merlin had always been inspired by Wyatt's ability to overcome his handicap, but he also took pride in the fact that Wyatt was the first quad-moddie he'd ever constructed. Although, his father, Hans Kloppenheimer crafted the limbs, they were Merlin's design. Wyatt was more than just a friend to Merlin, he was a masterpiece of man and metal. Standing next to Wyatt's bed, Merlin could tell he'd had another night terror about his mother. Wyatt was sweating profusely, with his glazed eyes stuck to the lab wall. Merlin dipped a rag in some water and wiped his friend's face carefully so as not to startle him. If Wyatt came out of his state too fast, he would wake everyone with his screaming, and after the day they'd had, sleep was too precious to lose.

Merlin poured a glass of water and pulled a chair next to Wyatt. He grimaced as the chair screeched across the floor. Casper's yellow eyes stared him down and he whispered. "Sorry." Then he helped Wyatt sip the water, until he slowly came out of his catatonic state. However, unbeknownst to Merlin, his chair moving had vibrated the floor loud enough to wake Elias.

"Oh, hi, Merlin, how long you been there?" Wyatt asked.

"Not long—couldn't sleep."

"Me either," Wyatt said, taking another sip of water. "Merlin…I don't know if I can go into the valley…what if she's still there?"

"She's gone, Wyatt. You know that. She's dead."

"But what if she's not? I mean, how has Hunchy survived so long without a mask. Even you said he should be dead by now."

"I know. I can't explain it. It doesn't make any sense to me. He doesn't even seem to care about the mist. But trust me, Gideon is fully aware and watching him closely," Merlin continued wiping the sweat from his friend's face.

ELIAS ACCIDENTALLY LET OUT A SQUELCHED THROAT NOISE BUT was able to quickly turn it into a fake snore, salvaging his pretense of sleep. However, he was more awake now than ever. What did Merlin mean Gideon was watching Hunchy? What if they were on to the prince? They might hand him over to the Jackboot, or worse, they might turn him into propeller goose stew. He wanted to get word to Hunchy, but if he moved Merlin might suspect something. He decided it would be best to lay still and see if he could learn more details from their conversation.

WYATT SPOKE AGAIN. "YOU KNOW, MERLIN, IT'S LIKE THE LAST few days all we've done is run and hide, and I can't even figure out what this mission is about. I know Gideon trusts the Jackboot, but what if he really did kill the kid's parents?" Wyatt was starting to get himself worked up again and began shaking.

"Calm down, okay? You're going to get all stressed out and wake everyone." The moonlight shining on Wyatt's pale face made him look even more disheveled as Merlin tried to reassure him. "I know we aren't always given all the information, but I trust Gideon, and he's done right by us since Charlie left."

"Merlin—do you think the Jackboot's really my father?" Wyatt asked.

"I don't know if we'll ever know the truth. If he is, then why doesn't he just say so? If he isn't, then why doesn't he put an end to the rumors and tell you? Anyway, now is not the time to discuss that, Wyatt," Merlin wiped a heavy drop of sweat from Wyatt's pale face.

At first he thought it was the rag that caused the shadow, but he stopped and held it to his side while Wyatt continued to talk. He wondered if maybe it was one of the octopi passing through the water tube in the outer hallway but remembered they were in whisper mode so everyone could rest. While in whisper mode, one octopus would pilot the ship and the other three would operate the propeller. So it couldn't have been one of them. Merlin tuned Wyatt out, waiting, watching his pale face, wondering if the shadow would cross it again, and it did.

Whatever it was, he didn't want Wyatt to see it. The last thing his distraught friend needed right then was some great big nothing of a myth he'd conjured up in his exhausted mind to terrify Wyatt even more. Merlin kept Wyatt talking with the classics of, "Yes, I understand, and I totally agree with you," while not retaining a single word Wyatt uttered. He blocked

Wyatt's view of the window across the hall by walking backward to the lab door and closing it.

"THERE'S SOMETHING I FORGOT TO DO, OKAY? I'LL BE RIGHT BACK, so just hang in there for a minute," Merlin explained as he walked out the other door and down to the bridge. He snuck down behind octopus number four, who was quite submerged in his work of piloting the Whisper, and carefully waited for proof.

It didn't take long before the shadow passed over top the Whisper's deck again. Whatever it was, it was big. He knew it couldn't have been Casper, who was perched at his usual spot on the forward deck and didn't seem bothered in the least by the shadow. When he spotted Hunchy sitting on one of the supply crates they had received from Mine Five, he decided to go ask the hunchback if he'd seen the shadow as well. He kept watch overhead while he approached the hunchback, in case it reappeared, then quietly called out to the crouched figure. "Hunchy?" but he didn't answer. Again he called out under his breath, "Hunchy!" Still there was no response. He walked the rest of the way over and placed his hand on the hunchback's shoulder, then spun him around.

To Merlin's astonishment, it wasn't Hunchy at all but yet another hunchback with a strange, red face.

"WHAT!" He stepped back and checked all around, worried the Whisper would soon be crawling with hunchbacks. "WHO ARE YOU?" he asked. But the smaller hunchback slowly stepped away toward the railing as if it were about to jump over the edge. "WHO ARE YOU?" Merlin was about to grab ahold of the imposter when Hunchy appeared behind him.

"It's okay," Hunchy said.

"No it's not," Merlin snapped.

"I wasn't talking to you, Merlin. I was talking to her," Hunchy explained.

"HER? You mean there are two of you? How did she get on the ship? A STOWAWAY! I want answers now, Hunchy!"

Merlin demanded, but the hunchback didn't like his tone and grabbed him by the shirt. Biggest mistake Hunchy ever made. Merlin pushed one of the round bolts mounted to his glass dome, sending a shock wave through Hunchy's hands and knocking him to the ground. Then Merlin raised the alarm. He ran over to a bell next to the door and rang it hard. The clanging was so loud it echoed all around them, and everyone but Wyatt ran out to the deck. They were only wearing night clothes, but everyone was armed for danger. Their tongues instantly forgot how to speak at the sight of two hunchbacks standing before them.

"It's okay, there's no problem. It's only a misunderstanding," Hunchy explained.

Bogan was the first to free his frozen tongue, "See, I told you, Gideon. Now there's two of 'em."

"What's going on here, Hunchy?" Gideon asked as, BUT, just about everyone was surprised at the sight of two hunchbacks STANDING before them. Hunchy got back to his feet and gathered his bearings after Merlin's mind jolting blast.

"A stowaway, Gideon, he's been hiding a stowaway on the Whisper," Merlin explained. "Another hunchback just like him."

"I'm sorry. I should have told you. I found her at the harbor, and she had no place else to go. I should have spoken with you, Gideon, and for that I apologize, but I," Hunchy paused as Bogan began walking around behind him, looking him up and down.

"Did you say her?" Ava asked curiously. "I didn't know there were hunchback girls." Ava felt sorry for the winged girl, thinking she was diseased like their friend Hunchy.

"I promise I will cover her expenses. Whatever I need to do to make this right, but she has no place to go. As soon as we get the flowers we'll be on our way," Hunchy explained.

"And just how are you going to cover her expenses?" Bogan sneered. "You've been living off of us since we saved you from the mine." Bogan walked over toward the girl hunchback and began poking her hump.

"Whatcha got under there, huh? Another squishy, puss-oozing hump, I bet."

"STOP IT! She's friendly Bogan." Elias shouted at him before realizing he was giving himself away.

"Wait, you knew about this?" Izzy drew back.

"No…well…y-yes, but they don't deserve to be treated like that," Elias said. Hunchy shook his head at Elias to make sure he didn't reveal them.

WITH A DEVIOUS LOOK IN HIS EYE, BOGAN WALKED OVER TOWARD Hunchy and began poking his hump to escalate the situation. This was his time to prove he was right. To prove the hunchback was a dirty rotten scoundrel that couldn't be trusted.

"Does this bother you, too?" Bogan prodded Elias.

Ava didn't like Bogan's cruelty towards the hunchbacks in the least bit, "ENOUGH, BOGAN!"

But he was undeterred by her anger.

"I bet it's a nasty, old, gnarly hump, oozing with green puss!" Bogan exclaimed.

Gideon seemed unusually silent about the whole deal as he tried to think the problem through carefully. They still needed Hunchy to lead them to the flowers, but a stowaway was not a good sign. On the other hand, they could use the extra help to carry more plants.

"Always hiding. So secretive, aren't you hunchbacks? Don't you all want to know what's under their cloaks? I know I do. How about you, Merlin? Izzy? Come on, Gideon, don't you think it's time to stop all the secrets and start treating this freak like the Smoke Speaker he is?" Bogan jerked on Hunchy's cloak.

"STOP IT," Elias demanded, but went too far this time. Not that it was totally his fault. He didn't know the processes of royal protocol when speaking to or about a Petinon Prince, but Epekneia knew it well enough to not dare break it. "He's not a freak! His name is Prince Enupnion of the Petinon people," Elias blurted out.

And with that, Epekneia dropped to her knees in front of the prince. The confused crew stepped back in clueless bewilderment at what she was doing, and Gideon finally couldn't stay quiet any longer.

"What do you mean prince? Who? Hunchy?"

"Prince of the hunchbacks," Bogan laughed. "I can't wait to see the princess. I bet she's a real looker."

Hunchy dropped his head and looked down at the girl. "Rise, dear Epekneia. The time for hiding is over."

"Finally, something we can both agree on," Bogan said, grabbing the back of Hunchy's cloak. He was so excited to finally shame the hunchback in front of everyone and prove just how wrong they'd been. The feeling of justification filled his chest like a giant balloon when he lifted the cloak off that deceitful huckster of a hunchback, but his pride was instantly deflated by the unfurling of glorious wings. It would have been nice to have had the chance to take it all in and fully understand what happened, but the moment of awestruck wonder was ruined by Izzy.

She instantly pulled out a sharp metal baton and jumped in front of Elias. "GET BACK," she warned, "they're dangerous! They'll kill us all!"

"IZZY," Ava reprimanded, embarrassed at Izzy's behavior.

"Hold on a moment, Izzy. Let them speak," Gideon tried to calm her, but fear filled her eyes. The secret prince had seen that look before in the eyes of others.

"You've seen one of us before, haven't you?" Enupnion asked. "Where? Who?"

But Izzy held her ground with her weapon in front of her, a simple baton with deadly points at both ends. Charlie had told Bogan stories of Izzy and her baton. Those stories sent chills down his mod-spine as he stared into her vacant eyes. Izzy was in warrior mode, and whenever she held her baton she was capable of the most inexplicably miraculous feats. Words were to be chosen carefully now, and Bogan knew it for his own safety.

"No one move!" Bogan warned. "Izzy, it's okay, just let them speak. We'll get to the bottom of it, I promise you." But his words had no effect on her.

She pointed the baton at him, then everyone else, as if they were about to turn on her. Elias stepped around from behind her and placed his hand on the baton. "Izzy," he lowered it until it was pointing directly at his heart. "They're not enemies," he said. She seemed numb, and her gaze was lost for a moment, then she lowered the weapon.

"I've heard rumors my whole life about bird people, but I never thought it was true," Gideon said as he was as awestruck, as Ava.

But Merlin was having a crisis of scientific proportions. He sat down on the deck with his back against the supply crate trying to calculate the possibilities and blurted out, "Wait—so Bogan was right? I mean, about the cord, about when you saved Ava?"

"Yes. Yes he was, and for that, Bogan, I sincerely apologize," Enupnion gave a tiny bow towards Bogan, who was stupefied by a prince bowing to him.

"Uh, well, yeah, y-you should. I-I was right, wasn't I?" Bogan reiterated.

"Yes, you were, Bogan," Enupnion admitted.

Bogan smiled at Hunchy for the first time ever. What else could he do? His whole concept of an evil hunchback with a wicked, magical hump was instantly ruined by Hunchy's own prestigious act of the appearing bird trick. Not by choice, mind you, but it was a magnificent trick and the bird was spectacular.

"Sire, may I remove my cloak?" Epekneia asked.

"Yes, by all means. Our secret is out. These are our friends, and they can be trusted," he said.

And so Epekneia removed her cloak and boots as the prince had done. She was so much different from the prince, whose feathers still seemed worn from GFC's coal mine. Enamored by them both, Ava moved closer. "I hope I'm not being offensive, but may I touch your wings?" she asked Epekneia. But Epekneia stepped back, uncomfortable with the idea. She had only experienced cruelty from the hands of her captors in Gabriel's Harbor and was reluctant to embrace the crew so soon.

"Oh, I-I'm sorry," Ava said, realizing she had been overly forward. Then the prince gave Epekneia a look which caused her to drop her wings behind her, where they disappeared almost completely from view.

"It's okay," Epekneia said, "you can touch them." It had been a long time since the crew of the Whisper had seen Ava so happy, although it was clear to Elias that Epekneia was extremely uncomfortable.

"I think that might be enough, Ava," Elias said. After which he noticed the crew was suddenly goggling him with funny looks, "What? What? I was just...you know...I mean it's probably uncomfortable for her."

"Why are your wings so red?" Ava asked her.

"My parents fed me too many fire berry seeds. They thought I was chosen, but they were wrong and it almost killed me. The berries turned my wings dark red and marked my face," Epekneia explained.

Ava was determined to make a friend out of Epekneia and with a bright smile she said, "You're very beautiful!" Her kind words were a delightful contrast to the words used to describe Epekneia by some at Gabriel's Harbor, and a smile sprang up on her face. Her wings even rose back up, but the explosion of red on the one side of her face made it impossible to tell if she was blushing. The crew was so awestruck by them both, they didn't notice the ship had already entered the Valley of Bones.

"What do you mean fire berry seeds?" Gideon asked.

"The flower we're taking you to is called the fire berry flower. It is the flower of our people," Enupnion gave Elias another intimidating look to make sure nothing more would be revealed to his friends until they were ready. He worried they would get angry and blame him and Epekneia for the mold covered world. Even though his people had failed and truly were at fault, they themselves were not, for they had tried to plant the seeds and set things right.

"Do you know why the Jackboot wants it?" Merlin asked.

"I do not. I can only guess that he has seen it before, even as Izzy has seen one of us before," Enupnion said, pushing the conversation back towards Izzy, but Merlin had more questions.

"Before what?" Merlin's craftiness caught the prince off guard.

"Before I brought it to him and he responded by chaining me to a rock in the mine. But now I might know why," Enupnion said, looking at Izzy. "If you've seen one of us before, then maybe the Jackboot has also."

"Oh, yeah, that's another thing," Bogan said, "Why don't you have to wear a mask?"

"Birds are immune to the black mist, Bogan," Merlin said as he was beginning to come to grips with a more reasonable understanding of their situation. At least this was a problem he could wrap his mind around, unlike all that foolishness of a destroyer, false cures and sorcery baloney. A good, scientific explanation was always behind the mysterious.

"Sort of, but not quite," Enupnion said. "We're not like Casper, who simply grew larger because of the creeping mold. Although that happens naturally because the birds that helped scatter the seed with us GREW from eating them.

"With you?" Izzy asked.

"Yes. Casper belongs to me. He is my pet but also my friend. I sent him to watch over your crew at the request of my friend Charlie," the prince explained.

"CHARLIE!" Ava screamed. "WHAT DO YOU MEAN CHARLIE?"

"Oh, yeah, that's right," Elias added, wanting desperately to jump into the conversation with his new information, but Enupnion fiercely shook his head no. He didn't want Elias to explain the situation incorrectly, as they didn't know if Charlie was alive or not, but the boy's excitement got the best of him.

"Charlie's alive!" Elias said jubilantly! Ava started to hyperventilate and then stopped breathing all together.

"AVA! AVA! Breathe, honey. Breathe, girl!" Izzy hollered. But Ava was turning pale fast and her eyes rolled back in her head. "GRAB HER!" Izzy cried out. Enupnion stepped up fast and caught her in his arms. "Elias! Why would you say that to her?" Izzy snapped.

For the first time ever, Izzy was upset with him, and he lowered his head for not heeding the advice of the prince to keep his big mouth shut. He was thankfully saved by Epekneia's weird noise she suddenly made with her mouth that startled everyone. Then Enupnion, who was still holding Ava, made the same noise and they both flared out their wings. Izzy took this as an aggressive sign and pulled her baton to ready a preemptive strike, but seconds later their ship stopped with a hard jerk, sending them all tumbling into each other.

It was a jumbled pile of iron and feathers when they all stopped at the end of the forward deck. Ava was still unconscious, but the rest were tangled in confusion. Izzy blew a feather out of her mouth, and Bogan pulled one of her mod-fingers out of his left nostril. Enupnion was on the verge of another claustrophobic attack with so many people piled on top of him, and Epekneia's horrified face was smashed up against Merlin's glowing green brain. Thankfully, no one was injured by Izzy's baton, which had somehow ended up in Elias' hand. Casper, who was still perched in his favorite spot directly over top of them, glanced down on their awkward mess with a wonky-eyed look of bewilderment.

"Easy for you," Bogan said, looking up at Casper, "you were already hanging on."

Gideon was usually very composed during awkward moments like this, but Epekneia's glove had come off her hand and her left claw was gripping his face like he was dinner. He let out an embarrassing howl that Elias figured would not soon be forgotten by the others during future dinner conversations. They should have smiled for the camera though, because Flit landed right on top of Casper's shoulder, snapped three pics and darted back off into the mist. No one said anything, but they knew they were running out of time.

They gathered themselves together and got to their feet, confused about what had happened. Bogan wanted to investigate the problem right away, but Gideon thought it best to check on Wyatt and have Ava looked at before they checked the ship. Gideon and Enupnion carried Ava back to Merlin's lab, but it didn't cross their minds that Wyatt had not seen the new winged Hunchy nor did he know there was a stowaway. Merlin was the first to walk into the room and notice Wyatt's bed was turned over on its side, and Wyatt was nowhere in sight. Then a voice came from around the corner.

"Merlin," Wyatt whispered. Merlin turned and spotted Wyatt cowering in the corner shaking.

"Oh, there you are," Merlin said. "Are you okay?" Everyone else was waiting to get into the lab with Ava, but Merlin wouldn't get out of the way.

Wyatt shook his head at Merlin, "Something's out there." He motioned toward the door that had popped open again, and that's when Merlin realized they hadn't told him about Hunchy and the stowaway.

"Oh, it's okay, I figured it out. You see, Hunchy..." but Wyatt interrupted him.

"Look at the window, Merlin," Wyatt trembled. Merlin looked over, and something was blocking the window. It was round and large enough to cover most of it. It instantly captivated Merlin, who walked the rest of the way into the room to check it out, forgetting to tell the already terrified Wyatt about Hunchy.

Gideon and Enupnion carried Ava the rest of the way in and Izzy straightened one of the beds for her, but all Wyatt saw was Ava being carried by a monster with enormous wings and claws. He screamed in horror and tried his best to get out of the room but fell on his back and couldn't get away. For several minutes he was totally unhinged, until Gideon was able to explain the situation and sort of calm him.

About the time Ava came to, Merlin, who was still standing by the window, muttered something and Gideon walked over. Maybe they were too busy gawking at the prince and the winged girl to notice anything, but somehow the Whisper had gotten tangled in a mass of thorny vines. After trying to figure out why no one had spotted the vines, they formed a plan to continue on without the Whisper. Bogan preferred to have Prince Hunchy and the stowaway fly off, get the flowers and bring them back, but Gideon was more leery of that plan in light of new developments. When Bogan suggested the prince carry the crew one at time, even Enupnion and Epekneia didn't like that plan.

It was finally agreed that Wyatt and Ava would stay back and work on cutting the Whisper loose from the vines while the rest continued on foot into the valley. Wyatt, of course, agreed instantly to the plan as it was his chance to be alone with Ava, and tell her how he truly felt as well as avoid reliving his own personal nightmare. The Valley of Bones was where the mold cults took their children and did unspeakable things. Even though he couldn't remember much of what had happened at such a young age, he'd retained enough to construct nightmares for a lifetime.

Enupnion grabbed Elias, Epekneia took Merlin, and the others watched as they dropped to the valley floor with graceful ease. However, Izzy wanted no part of the winged ride and used her mod-hand to get down. Bogan and Gideon took the rope ladder, and Casper did his own version of hopping, hunting and soaring above them.

The valley was about 300 feet wide and had sharp rocks shooting up from both sides at an angle that almost brought them towering together at the top. The once magnificent valley was now a terrifying wasteland as they stumbled over the mass of bones, before almost tripping over the railway tracks running down the valley's center. It smelled of mold, but they only knew that because Elias and Enupnion told them. Elias had decided he no longer wanted to wear a mask as his heart was already changing from the gold-mod. The two Petinon's walked the valley traumatized by what had become of their childhood dreams. They had both been told what a magnificent place it was and how their flowers grew by the millions, but now it was utterly trashed.

"You can thank Angus Grand for the all the iron and garbage left here, and the mold cults for all the bones," Gideon explained. "Angus used this as a dumping ground for Grand Fortune City in the early days, and when he was done the mold cults took it over, at least until the Jackboot wiped them out."

"Why did he wipe them out?" Elias asked. The Jackboot seemed even crueler than Elias had first imagined.

"To be honest, I don't know for sure, but there are rumors, you know. You hear things and you piece them together. Whether it's true or not, but some say the mold charmers took his son. I'm not saying I know this for sure, but some in GFC say Wyatt is his son," Gideon seemed skeptical of his own words but delivered them anyway. Izzy immediately scoffed at his statement loud enough to get a look from everyone else.

"Now, Izzy, you know he caught Vanessa bringing Wyatt here. He even stole that floating umbrella of hers." Izzy's breathing grew rapid as both her lips disappeared into her mouth, but Gideon continued.

"Well, it's hanging on the bull's horn in the Weaver's trophy room," Gideon said, but neither he nor any other member of the Whisper, except Merlin, knew the Jackboot was her father. Merlin knew, because his father worked with the Jackboot during the great tunnel war. The other Whisper spies had come from Gabriel's Harbor. They assumed the whole reason why Izzy hated those rumors was because she and Wyatt didn't get along, but there was a deeper reason. She knew the Jackboot wasn't his father. Vanessa wasn't even his mother, but Merlin wouldn't let her tell Wyatt for fear it would break him emotionally. Several times she'd almost told him out of anger, but she kept her promise to Merlin that she wouldn't do it.

"WAIT!" Elias was suddenly horrified and stopped dead in his tracks. "Are you saying we might be stepping on Wyatt's arms and legs?"

"Uh? Oh, no, these are the bones from the great battle of vengeance the Jack unleashed on the mold cultists when he thought they had his son. Some in GFC call this the Valley of Vengeance. An angry father is kind of like a mad bear, so don't poke him," Izzy said with a twinkle in her eye.

"After the battle he burned the entire valley," Gideon added.

"HE BURNT IT ALL?" The prince was mortified. "But the flowers, the berries! They would have been destroyed. How long ago did he do this?"

"It was sometime after the war for GFC." Merlin chimed in.

"Wait, are you saying the flowers were supposed to be here? Actually in the valley?" Gideon asked.

"YES! YES! This was the last place where Sunago the Great planted millions of seeds. It was in his letters to us. He said he'd found the perfect place to begin replanting. I-I don't know..." the prince collapsed onto a pile of old bones, unable to stand.

"HA! I wish you would have told us this was the place instead of being so secretive. We could have told you this is nothing but a graveyard for the wicked now," Merlin laughed. "What a waste!"

"I don't understand," Elias said. "The flower the Jackboot showed us was growing out of a piece of coal. I thought that's how these flowers grew. Are you saying they grow in soil like any other flower?" he asked.

Enupnion was devastated and held his face in his hands. "What do you mean?" he asked. "I thought the flower in the coal was a joke. Like maybe you people didn't know how to plant. Are you saying the flower was truly growing out of coal?" the prince asked.

"Yes! Yes, it was!" Elias shouted.

"How is that even possible?" Gideon asked.

"I don't know, but my father would have known. He was a brilliant biogenetical engineer. He could work wonders with plants," Elias clinched his jaw and bit his tongue hard to prevent himself from tearing up.

"Can we get out of here?" Merlin asked. "This place gives me the creeps, and since the flowers aren't here we're sitting ducks, no offense, Prince Bird-Man. But people disappear when they come here. I know the stories and I don't care what the Jackboot did, I'm not going sit around here sulking until some mythical beast eats me for dinner."

They turned and headed back toward the Whisper but stopped when Casper landed on a sharp rock across the other side of the valley.

"What the devil!" Gideon shouted. "Look at Casper's eyes!" Enupnion jumped to his feet. Bogan was as surprised as Gideon, but Izzy had a big smile growing on her face as if she were holding in a secret she could barely contain.

"There are berries here," Elias said.

"How do you know?" Gideon asked.

"That's what happens when you eat them. Your eyes glow red, or at least mine do," Elias blurted out.

"That's right! That's what happened after Hunchy—I mean—sorry—the prince, that's how he brought Elias back from the dead in the mine," Merlin explained.

"Oh, yeah, I'm the Destroyer," Elias said with a smile.

"WHAT!" The stunned crew shouted.

"No you're not! You're…" Izzy stopped short of finishing her thought and bit down hard on her lip.

"No more secrets, right, Hunchy?" Elias winked.

"It's true," Enupnion confirmed.

"I'll explain later, but right now we need to follow Casper to where he found the berries," Elias said, pointing at the great gray owl taking flight over top of them. Elias knew Enupnion was unhappy with him for blurting out their secret, but at least it was finally out in the open and the prince would no longer have to shoulder the burden of the Destroyer's identity. Besides, why keep secrets when you only have days to live.

15

CHARMING WEATHER

*W*yatt was beaming as Ava wrapped his chest to keep his broken ribs tight. He was bruised good and in pain but only physically. Emotionally he was soaring. Ava was also quite chipper as she happily hummed a tune while helping him, but the room was stale with silence as she helped him reconnect his mods. It was something he'd never imagined letting her do a week ago, but now that she had seen him helplessly crying out at Mine Five, the worst part was over. Ava finished helping him get ready, then they grabbed some tools for cutting and went port side to begin removing the vines. All he had to do now was block out his mother's voice so he could open his heart to Ava, but her voice only grew louder.

Wyatt couldn't take his eyes off of Ava as she continued humming her joyous tune. It was so infectious he even found himself humming along with her, even smiling with her, all good signs the timing was right. They snipped, sliced, cut and hacked away at the vines as Wyatt carefully looked for the perfect opportunity to reveal his heart. For some reason, and maybe it was only bad timing on his part, but every time he started to say something, Ava's tune got louder than normal.

Not a problem, though, he'd waited this long and the crew probably wouldn't be back for several hours, so he kept his eagerness in check. By the time they'd finished cutting the port side, he realized they hadn't spoken a word yet, and he was getting the distinct impression she simply didn't want to talk.

They headed over to the starboard side and began chopping, stabbing, carving and breaking the vines off that side of the ship, but he simply couldn't find the right words. When Ava went back inside to replace her glove with the hole, he dug down deep within himself and mustered the courage to get it done. As soon as she stepped back out the starboard door he would tell her. He took some deep breaths and cracked his neck for good measure. He could hear her coming down the hallway fast, so it was ready or not here goes everything.

Ava shot right out the door and shouted, "WYATT!"

"Ava there's something…" but he couldn't get it out before she blurted his name out again. Even if he did like the sound of it, he needed to tell her now.

"WYATT! Come here quick," she said, bolting around the front of the ship and back around to the port side. He did a short jog to catch up and saw her standing looking down the port side of the ship.

"Ava, I just wanted to tell you that I …" he was cut off.

"Wyatt, look," she pointed down at the vines crawling all over it again.

"WHAT!" Wyatt was stunned. "How?"

"I don't know," Ava said.

Wyatt quickly ran back over to the starboard side with Ava close behind, and likewise the vines had already started wrapping back around the Whisper again.

"What kind of vines are these, anyway?" Ava asked.

"I don't know. Maybe Hunchy or Merlin will know, but we're wasting our time trying to cut them if they're just going to grow back. Maybe we should just take a break and have some coffee." Wyatt was never more pleased to see the Whisper caught in a trap. The opportunity had finally presented itself now that he didn't have to waste time with the vines.

"But, Wyatt, the coffee is only for special occasions, and

Gideon and the others aren't here to enjoy it with us." Ava was disturbed by Wyatt's strange timing for celebration, especially while the rest of the crew was trekking through the valley and the Whisper was still caught in the vines. She knew just what he needed to help cheer him up until the crew returned.

"Oh, Wyatt, I almost forgot to tell you," she beamed.

"Forgot what?"

"Charlie's alive! Or at least that's what the prince said."

"WHAT! HOW?" Wyatt clinched his jaw in anger.

"Wyatt! What's wrong with you? I thought you would be happy about that," Wyatt's anger caught her off balance. Their long lost friend, whom they thought was dead, might be alive, and all of a sudden he acted like he hated Charlie. For Wyatt's part, he felt like she had removed his heart with her cutting shears and cast it into the valley with his arms and legs. He wanted to collapse into her arms and beg for her love, but a strange, glaring, green light behind the Whisper caught his eye. It looked like some kind of train with passenger cars sitting on tracks below them, but it wasn't like any kind of train he'd seen before. Not to mention, his mother's voice was ringing so loud in his head now, he was starting to believe she was right next to him.

"Ava, I think we need to get inside the Whisper and lock it down," Wyatt had just finished his warning when someone spoke behind them.

"*Wyatt, I'm disappointed in you.*" The dreadful voice of death chilled the air around them as it echoed from all directions. Wyatt knew that voice well. It was the unmistakable voice of his nightmares. It was the voice of evil that haunted even his good dreams. He wanted to protect Ava, but he was frozen at the sound of it. He was so numb even his metal mods felt numb. He knew that terrible voice of darkness behind him as they both turned around. Floating down from the mist-filled sky, six dark figures descended onto the Whisper with black umbrellas. Their faces were concealed by the umbrellas as they landed with ease on the forward deck. They were all dressed in long, black coats that seem impossibly darker than black, except for one dressed in a dark green robe. Their hands were sheathed with dark gray gloves and their eyes beneath their umbrellas were freakishly gold. The frigid, hollow voice spoke again, only this time it meant to wound.

"Just look at you, boy, he turned you into one of his metal monsters. If only he hadn't taken you from me, you might have become a powerful Umbrella Charmer. You wouldn't have needed arms or legs, and you might have even become the fulfillment of prophecy, but now you're nothing but a useless, iron slug," the voice was soft, but ruined.

"M-M-MOOOOMMMM!" Wyatt cried out.

Wherever Casper found the fire berry he ate was a mystery to everyone. He led them from one rock to another and then back down into the valley. They even dug through the bones, thinking maybe they might find soil rich enough for something to take root, but only bones were planted in the Valley of Bones. The deeper they dug, the more bones they found, until the horror of it all finally got to them.

"I'm never going to sleep again after this," Bogan grumbled.

"I agree," Gideon said. "Maybe we should check the rocks again, or at least a spot with less death."

"I don't understand. His eyes are red, so he had to have found one somewhere," Elias complained.

Casper landed on a large, knife-shaped rock that shot out of the ground at an angle. At its base was a mound of dirt with mossy grass patches, and he was pecking at the base where the rock emerged. Elias ran up the mound but couldn't see around Casper, who was busy scratching at the ground. Elias gave him a few shoves, and he finally flew out of the way. A single flower was growing at the base, with only one berry left on it.

"I FOUND ONE!" he yelled, plucking it up and showing it to the crew.

"One flower," Merlin said, "all this for one stinkin' flower!"

Elias pocketed the single berry anyway, for good measure. He never knew when his fuel container might run low. He turned around and spotted Casper, who had flown to the other side, rooting around on a similar rock formation.

"LOOK! He's found another one," Elias called out and ran into the valley, almost tripping over Angus Grand's train tracks as he passed by Enupnion.

"Give it up, my friend," Enupnion said, "All is lost."

But Elias paid no attention to him as he ran back up the other side to Casper. He tried pushing the bird away, but Casper was having none of it from Elias this time. He simply wouldn't move.

"But what if the berries are scattered all over the valley and we just have to find them?" Elias hoped. He pushed Casper harder and harder until he finally flew away, but there was no flower. Only a winged serpent Casper had been eating on. It was smaller but exactly like the one from Raven Alley and that night on the Whisper. A cold shiver shot through the back of his legs about the time Epekneia and the prince let out another freaky screeching noise and flared their wings full.

Through the dark, mist-filled valley, tiny, golden eyes began floating toward them from all directions, growing brighter as they moved closer. As the wall of serpents closed in, Elias noticed a distinct difference in size from the one Casper had killed. These serpents were as large as Bogan was tall, and their wingspan every bit the size of Enupnion's.

Before anyone could form a plan, Izzy sprinted up the hill towards Elias, and a large serpent quickly dove after her. It caught her around the waste with its long slippery tail and coiled around her. Suddenly it swung its head around to face her, but was instantly stupefied to feel the sharp end of her baton driving through the side of its skull. Its grip loosened and fell limp before it went rolling back down the hill into the valley. She backed Elias up against the rock as two more closed in, and she swiftly dispatched them from the air, sending two more rolling back into the bones below. She had done it so fast, Enupnion couldn't tell if she killed them with her baton or her long curls spinning around like a windmill. The prince was utterly spellbound by her fierce display of brutality in safe-guarding Elias, and something about her dawned on him, but there was no time to consider such things now, for they were under attack.

The bat-winged devils flicked their tongues at the crew, testing the air for fear. Their dripping venom had a pungent aroma that rose from the steamed bones it burned on the valley floor as they danced their hypnotic cadence of death. Bogan smiled and drew his hand cannon from his mod-leg but noticed something around his feet. The same vines that had snagged the Whisper were crawling all over their legs.

"HEY! Look," Bogan pointed at their feet. They all grabbed the vines and began pulling, yanking and jerking at them, but the vines were crafty and shifted away from their grasp, continuing to climb up their legs until they couldn't move. Even the prince and Epekneia were trapped in their clutches as the vines lashed around their wings. Izzy hacked away at them as best she could with her baton, but it was the wrong tool for this job. Soon the serpents wrapped around them all tightly, lifting them off the ground, and the vines that seemed so impossible to remove suddenly set them free.

The winged serpents carried the confused crew back toward the Whisper. It was either the dumbstruck embarrassment of being captured so easily, or the vile medicine smell coming from their captor's breath that prevented anyone from talking. The smell reminded Elias of Abner's Apothecary. Bright lights shining from the Whisper seemed to have an eerie, green glow illuminating below them, but Elias couldn't tell what it was coming from. There also seemed to be visitors standing on the forward deck, but the lights made it near impossible to see who they were. One noticeable item they all were holding over their heads—black umbrellas.

Gideon called out, "WYATT! AVA! Are you okay?" But no one answered.

Without delay, the dark figures ascended over top the Whisper's rails in unison—their feet together, their umbrellas tightly held and their form impeccably perfect. Carried by what seemed to be magical umbrellas, they descended gracefully into the Valley of Vengeance. Their glossy black coats shimmered in the lights of the Whisper, and the cold green glow in the distance behind them left wicked halos around their heads. Elias half expected their feet to touch down on top of the bones, but as they reached the bottom of the valley their feet paused above them, and a puff of black smoke rolled out from beneath the umbrellas.

Other than the flapping of the serpent's wings, their dark visitors were silent. Their golden eyes brightened then dimmed, again and again, as if they were speaking to each other in some sinister code. Then one of them opened their mouth, but no words came out, only smoke and mist forming into a hand that began reaching out toward the prince. The smoky specter took him by the face and turned it left and then right as it carefully studied him, then suddenly stopped. It wisped quickly over to Elias and pulled open his jacket, revealing his heart-mod, then instantly vanished as the dark figure let out a shriek and drew back underneath the Whisper.

Finally, one of them spoke in a ghastly, haunting voice to the serpents, *"Bring them all to the culling floor."*

With haste, their fiendish flight attendants fluttered them back into the valley a short way and turning left stopped at the face a large rock. Off in the distance, two red eyes gave careful consideration to the events taking place. They dawdled a moment, hovering in front of it, and once Wyatt and Ava's serpent captors joined them, the side of the rock opened. A winding entrance leading down into the cold earth had perfectly carved stairs, but they didn't need them tonight. As they floated down, chanting voices rose up towards them, growing louder and louder. Although the words were unintelligible, they had a foul nature about them.

The stairs opened up at the bottom into an enormous, circular room with seats towering all around them. The floor in the center had a platform, and on the far end a large, wooden throne was placed high up, with two round platforms on each side. The seats were all empty as were the thrones, but nine Umbrella Charmers were standing in the center of the platform. Above the platform hung a large glass ball filled with greenish-black liquid that swirled around and illuminated the entire room with a ghoulish green hue. A metal ring encircled the ball, as if it had a greater purpose, and one of the Umbrella Charmers stomped on the platform, commanding twelve wooden beams to shoot up in a circle around them. Their serpent abductors were kind enough to release them just long enough for more vines to quickly wrap their arms and legs around the intricately carved beams. Then the Umbrella Charmer looked up at the giant glass ball and it slowly came down to rest on the beams. Once it settled, the Umbrella Charmers departed.

The cold, dark silence of the stone arena echoed bitter from Wyatt's soft sobbing as tiny droplets of water blipped into a small puddle somewhere in the room. Their faces were illuminated with the ghoulish green glow of the mysteriously captivating orb as it swirled black serpent-like streams in circles. Methodically, in harmony together, as if it was alive.

"What is this place?" Elias asked.

"I don't know," Gideon answered.

"It's the place where dreams die," Wyatt's sobbing words chilled everyone to the bone, causing Bogan and Merlin to jerk at the vines around their arms which only resulted in making the thorns dig deeper into their skin.

Then Wyatt blubbered out, "W-W-We're all going to die."

16

FATHER'S FURY

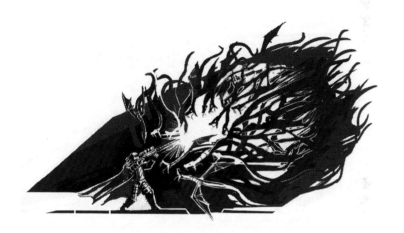

he Weaver's boiler blushed red as Iron Jaw pushed the train harder and faster through the tunnel towards Karl's Labyrinth. Even the wheels on the Weaver had a soft glow of reddish orange as they chugged fiercely on the tracks. No longer did the inside of the train hold the aroma of vanilla from the Jackboot's pipe, or even a gentle floral smell from the bucket of fire berries placed by the mole claw throne. The only aroma Bosarus could sense was that of burning, righteous anger emanating from the Jackboot's presence as he entered the room and walked over to the little bird cage. He placed a fresh dish of water into Flit's cage. The little bird seemed pleased with the reward from his long journey and sipped it vigorously while his tiny heart pumped with joy.

"How long do you think they've been in the valley, sir?" Bosarus asked.

"I doubt very long," the Jackboot answered.

"But, sir, it's an extremely long journey for such a small creature. How can you be sure?" Then the Jackboot took hold of the cage and spun it around to where Bosarus could see the bird's normal eye. Only, it was far from normal, it was now glowing red hot, as if it were on fire.

"When I feed him the berries he flies like a bullet. That's the way it works, Bosarus. That's the way it works." His cold, condescending tone was clear, and Bosarus knew that hardened battle gaze. The Jackboot was preparing his mind for war.

"Come with me, Bosarus."

"Right away, sir."

The Jackboot led Bosarus through the train and into the car with the mounted animal heads. Above a great gray owl was a set of large wings, "Do you see those wings there, Bosarus?"

"Yes indeed, sir. A fine kill that must have been, sir."

"Yes, but those did not come from just any bird, my friend, but a bird-man."

"Sir, those stories are myths. With all due respect, do you take me for a fool?" Bosarus seemed greatly offended by the Jackboot's fantastic mythical story. He stroked his finely groomed white beard as if to remind the Jackboot he wasn't speaking to a child, but a man who deserved some measure of respect. Tall tales were for children and the weak minded, not men who had ruled great cities.

"I don't take you for a fool, Bosarus, but what I say is true. During my war against Angus Grand, I learned he became allies with a winged man. Not merely a man with wings, but more of a bird-man, and this creature was providing him with these flowers. When Angus began using these flower berries in his weapons, it turned the war in his favor. I knew I had to get my hands on them, even at great risk to myself and my dear Izzy. Once I did, I brought them to Thomas Rand."

"Gabriel the Great's grandson, sir?"

"That's correct. He funds the resistance against the harbor. So you now know what only three people know. Keep it that way, Bosarus."

"Of course, sir."

"The other person was Hans Kloppenheimer. You know him better as the Puppet Master and the father of the little glass-brained boy, Merlin. Together we learned to forge mods with these berries. The mods forged in the fire of the berries made great weapons against the Umbrella Charmers that Angus partnered with during the war. For some reason, metal forged with the berries repelled their magic. Hans recently designed three heavily armored war bots to help us take back the harbor, which you will retrieve for me once we're finished in the valley. Our plan is to take back Gabriel's Harbor from the Alchemist and return it to Thomas Rand. Trouble is, I've yet to find out where the Alchemist has been hiding. He's much craftier than imagined."

Then he pointed at the wall. "The wings you see here, Bosarus, are from one of those bird-man creatures. You see this scar down my neck and my missing eye?" the Jackboot unbuttoned his shirt and showed a scar going down his neck all the way to a mass of terrible scaring around his heart. "I fought one of those creatures and he tried to rip out my heart. Thanks to my boots forged in the fire of the berries, I was able to defeat him. Those goodly sized wings you see mounted on this wall belonged to the one Angus Grand called, the Alchemist."

"But I thought the old gray owl was the one who gave you that scar, sir."

"Yes, that's the rumor, isn't it?" the Jackboot grinned as if he was the instigator of his own rumors.

"And the boy's father, sir? You wanted him to help you grow more berries, I take it."

"That was the plan, but my spies messed up and brought the kid. When Flit returned with pictures of the greenhouse, it was crawling with Umbrella Charmers, so I can only imagine what they did to his parents." The Jackboot somberly lowered his head.

"We're coming up on Karl's Labyrinth now, Mr. Jackboot, sir, and you might want to get up here." Iron Jaw's voice clacked from a funnel on the wall.

"Is the suit ready, Bosarus?"

"It is, Mr. Jackboot, sir," Bosarus answered, motioning toward a uniquely crafted silver suit.

"Hans does fine work, doesn't he?"

"Yes he does, sir, but I don't see how such flimsy material could be fire and bullet proof."

"It works, Bosarus. Do you know how I know that?"

"How, sir?"

"I've used it before. Now help me suit up."

"Why don't we just go around Karl's Labyrinth, sir? I don't see how we'll come out of this unscathed."

"It's the fastest way into the valley, and if we go by air they'll see us coming miles away. This is our only option, Bosarus," he said as Bosarus finished latching the buckles and lifting the oversized collar.

Bosarus knew not to question the Jackboot again for fear he would only direct the man's anger towards himself. Best to let him pour it out on the Smoke Charmers.

"And this bucket is the last of the berries?"

"It was the only one in the room, sir."

"Then I'll need them all."

THE PEOPLE OF KARL'S LABYRINTH WERE A SHORT, STOCKY PEOPLE with enormous, bushy beards, and they had crafted an impressive underground city that was possibly the largest of all the underground cities. They were also the most feared underground civilization because they'd dabbled in gene modification and brought terrible man-beasts into the world. Those in the mountain cities, who didn't have access to airships, traveled by underground rail through Karl's Labyrinth, or above ground rail through the Valley of Vengeance if they wanted to trade in the coastal cities. Since no one any longer dared cross through the cursed valley, the tolls became extremely lucrative for Karl's Labyrinth. Money practically fell into their pockets, and if it didn't go the way they liked, they simply stole it. Anyone who passed by without first setting a price or bartering for their toll would be murdered, or worse—made an example of to everyone in the Arena of Heroes.

Today the Jackboot wasn't stopping to barter or cut a deal.

Today there would be no setting a price or begging for passage through the cavernous hole. Today the Jackboot would drive the Weaver's harpoon through their passage at full speed. Today no toll would be paid.

The Jackboot made his way across the top of the train with his magnetic boots humming and clanking all the way. He walked to the top of the engineer's cab where Iron Jaw was operating the Weaver, then across the red glowing boiler toward the bull head. His large rifle was slung across his right shoulder as he climbed on top of the horns, leaning forward ever so slightly, as if he could somehow get there faster by doing so.

He knew he'd miscalculated in placing his spies next to the bird-man in his mine, but he'd hoped the creature would lead them back to his people instead of taking them deeper into enemy territory. When his little bird returned with pictures of them taking the elevator to Harbor III, he knew his plan had back fired. He'd been too hard on Gideon, or maybe Gideon wasn't ready to be captain so soon after Charlie. If he'd only made Izzy captain, they might not be in this mess, but too many questions could have arisen, and she was a much better and safer spy if no one knew who she was. Regrets and second guesses were not fitting the leader of such a great city, but neither was the uncontrollable, furious vengeance of an angry father, or the tear streaming out of his eye. No time for weakness now.

If those wicked monsters dared touch his sweet Isabella with their blades, the whole world would fall into the grips of his righteous indignation. His vengeance would know no boundaries. No rules. He would empty his suffering and agony on them like a whirlwind of brimstone from hell itself. The whole world would hear of what he did to them, and everyone would fear him, great and small alike. All monsters would forever cower in dark places for fear their deeds would be made known to him, and the world would replace their magical charmers for one cruel, heartless ruin of a destroyer. There would be no safe harbor for their wicked deeds. No safe harbor for tricks and schemes. No safe harbor for the mystical lies of smoke. No safe harbor for Gabriel's Harbor.

His back was sweating from the heat of the Weaver's boiler behind him and his body growing hotter from his protective suit, or maybe from his burning anger filling him with rage the more he thought about them cutting his little girl. If there was any sobbing at the front of the Weaver, Iron Jaw never heard it, nor would he dare admit to it. Rather, he would have sworn it was the wind as they neared Karl's Labyrinth.

Those poor souls guarding the entrance to the labyrinth were the first to feel the sting of his fury. The first guard raised his hand in a halting motion, and it disappeared before his very eyes. Two others lifted their rifles but never got a single shot off before their weapons exploded in their hands. Then their heads vanished just as quickly. The last guard was able to fire off a round that ricocheted off the Weaver's harpoon, then the Jackboot swiftly dropped him. Two men began pushing a large iron gate in front of the tracks, but they didn't quite make it in time before the train slammed through the entrance and the Iron Weaver roared on.

The city was still half a mile away, by design, to protect against someone making it past the first gate, and armored guards lined the tunnel walls with heavy artillery. The Jackboot missed the first two guards, but Iron Jaw didn't. Holding a shotgun each out the left and right window, he blasted away, clipping them both. He received no thank you from the Jackboot for doing his job correctly and none was needed. Iron Jaw was a hardened man who'd lost his lower jaw in the war for GFC and didn't concern himself with prissy, emotional formalities like please and thank you, excuse me, I'm sorry or silly tears and hugging. Pat him on the back with an attaboy and you would likely lose your arm. He scoffed at those weaknesses with the clack of his iron jaw. His only fear was disappointing his commander, the Jackboot, and so he pushed the Iron Weaver full steam ahead into madness.

By the time they reached the city, a large iron gate was blocking the entrance, and three Gatling guns were poking out the walls. The Jackboot raised his arm, and Bosarus released the tiny bird right on cue. Flit shot out of the train with an eye of fire and went right for the gate's entrance. He placed a single berry on the gate's lock and disappeared behind the wall. The spray of bullets from the guns felt like hard rain blanketing his suit as he took careful aim at the incoming berry resting on the lock. Too soon and he might miss. Too late and he would be caught in the explosion of the berry. Careful. Only one chance. The rain of hailing ammo was bothersome but not something he hadn't experienced before. He slowly squeezed the trigger and BOOM – then – BA-BOOM and the gate creaked open. Iron Jaw smashed through and the rain of bullets stilled. Several brave men stepped out in front of the Iron Weaver and clipped off shots at the oncoming locomotive. Brave, yes, but now dead at the hands of an angry father, and the Iron Weaver roared on.

Several Ever-Wheels pulled up beside the train and began firing shot after shot, but the Jackboot ignored them as he reached the halfway mark of the city six miles in. It wasn't long before some stocky brutes began hammering away at their own train tracks in a last ditch effort to stop the Weaver, but the Jackboot laid down on the bull's head, and taking careful aim, made short work of those railway rascals. Another mile and they could exit the labyrinth safely.

Stories of how the labyrinth people had delved into darkness were prevalent, but those were mostly stories. They were not something the Jackboot would have considered until today. Until he saw with his own eye what they had been doing in the deep, dark places of the earth. They were not like the Smoke Charmers but more genetic engineers of the human body. Not like Hans the Puppet Master, with metal and science, but more with the flesh and walking out onto the track was one such creature. A giant of a man, with a large gut to compliment his size, and the tales and fables of yore became reality before him. Standing in front of the Iron Weaver was a full grown tunnel troll. Ugly, nasty, gruesome and putrid, wearing less than a large diaper, the creature braced himself to stop the train bare handed. Not wise, either.

The Jackboot clipped two to the left and three more shooters to the right, as well as one not far from the troll, and reloaded his rifle. Even though he'd never seen a tunnel troll, he believed his little girl when she told him she had. Isabella might have been known to tell a few tall tales, but she would never lie to him. For good measure, he raised his signal for Bosarus to have Flit send a small gift to the giant, gelatinous glob of goo standing in his way, and the little guy rocketed out toward the annoying obstacle.

At first the troll was captivated by the little bird darting in and out and around the beast, until it dropped a tiny red berry in his monstrous hand. He sniffed it and then ate it. A most unexpected reaction, but it still had possibilities. The Jackboot popped off a round into the troll's belly and instantly vaporized him into a cloud of fine, red, bloody mist. Not a single bit of evidence remained of what was the great tunnel troll, and the Iron Weaver roared on.

He climbed off the bull horns and back onto the hot boiler as he made his way back toward the train car. He gave pause only when a hail of gunfire from the exit of the labyrinth caught his attention. Forty-seven men, to be precise, were firing directly at him. They were not a problem and he could have left them alone, but they seemed to want a fight. Since his anger was still red hot, he gave them one. Their bullets were mere pebbles pummeling against his suit, and one by one he put an end to their days while the Iron Weaver roared on.

The Iron Weaver had never been pushed as hard as old Iron Jaw was pushing it now, and they surfaced so fast the train practically looked like a giant whale breaching through the earth. The front wheels gave a single spark-filled bounce, fortunately right back onto the tracks, lifting him slightly up inside his magnetic boots. Off in the distance he spotted something he hadn't killed in quite a while. Nasty, wicked bat-winged serpents; hundreds coming right at him. The black mist stung his face as they roared across the tracks towards the vile vermin, and he readied his fearless soul for their unholy game of death. It was going to be a long night.

His rifle barrel blushed red as serpents rained from the sky, screeching and hissing in agony, then instantly silenced by the Weaver's wheels, but it wasn't their screeching and hissing that filled his thoughts. It wasn't even the whistling steam from Weaver's boiler screaming in his ears. Not even the harsh mist-filled wind howling fiercely past him could silence those two words on Bobby's note. Quietly whispering; taunting, pounding in his mind—Isabella knows.

17

WHERE DREAMS DIE

ot dead, but buried beneath the cold, rotten earth nonetheless. Waiting for death to walk through the door and reveal its unholy face to them. The chilled air emanating from the blood-stained platform only intensified their thoughts with the abominable deeds once performed where they now stood. Rich coal deposits covered the walls and ceiling, but the sweet smell of fresh cut pine tickled Elias' nose as he gazed upon the place where dreams die. The swirling, black serpentine liquid snaking around inside the green globe captivated Epekneia as much as Merlin's brain, but no one could shut out the tormented sobs coming from Wyatt's broken heart.

Ava and Bogan tried to console him, but his mind was wrapped inside the reality of his inescapable nightmares. Gideon and Enupnion consolidated their minds to studying the ceiling and walls for possible escape options, or anything that might assist in freeing everyone from the vines. Izzy and Merlin were caught up in a heated argument about something, but Elias was too far away to figure out the details.

The stone seats circled half the room on the left and half on the right, and there were enough to seat several thousand people, from what Elias could tell. The Umbrella Charmers had placed him where the ghastly green globe blocked his view of the throne at the end of the room, with Enupnion on his right and Epekneia on his left. The circular staircase entrance to their backs also prevented a good view of the only exit option they were aware of.

Merlin and Izzy's argument was getting so far out of control that Gideon tried to mediate.

"Can you two cool it? We're trying to find a way out. We don't need more problems," Gideon pleaded.

"There's no escaping this," Wyatt said with a pale glare at the blood-stained platform.

"Just let me tell him, Merlin. It might help him through this," Izzy shouted.

"And it just might be the one thing that makes him snap," Merlin complained.

"We have to work together to figure this out, so can you guys just get along and stop this?" Gideon tried again. But just then, Enupnion spotted something thanks to one of Merlin's blue brain bolts lighting up the room.

"No, don't stop," Enupnion said.

"You know, you're not helping much, prince of wings," Merlin claimed.

"No, I saw something on the ceiling. Something that might help us. Izzy see if you can keep Merlin angry."

"Well, that shouldn't be a problem, I know just the thing." Izzy smirked.

"Now, Izzy, don't do it. Don't go there, Izzy," Bogan warned. "He doesn't need that kind of stress right now."

But it was too late.

"Merlin, where's that puppet brother of yours?" It was harsh, cruel and heartless. It even hurt her own feelings, but she would ask his forgiveness once they were free.

"WHAT! I—but, Isabella, you..." Merlin was cut deeply by her words; words that she promised never to use on him, ever.

"Ah, come on, Merlin, you know it's true. He's not even

human anymore. Your Puppet Master Daddy turned him into a fake boy."

"ISABELLA! WHY ARE YOU DOING THIS? YOU OF ALL PEOPLE," his eyes welled up with tears at her cruel words.

"Stop whining, Merlin. At least he still has a brain even if it is controlled with a rat mod, so he's sort of still human, right?"

"W-WHAT! WHY? I'M NEVER SPEAKING TO YOU AGAIN. EVER! YOU HEAR ME?" A bright blast flashed from his brain, illuminating the entire room for mere seconds, but it was enough.

"Wait, that's it. Right there," Enupnion stopped them. "Right next to that large chunk hanging down. A flower growing out of the coal. It's true. I can't believe it, but it's true."

"Merlin, I'm so sorry. Okay, please, I didn't mean any of it. You have to believe me. You know I love Jimmy. I only did it to get us out of here. — Merlin, please." If Izzy could have dropped to her knees and begged, she would have. She knew how unkind her words were and how she'd promised to never do what others did to Jimmy. Merlin tried to gather himself together, but all he could do was look away from her.

"Merlin," Izzy spoke in a soft, loving voice, "When we get out of here I'm going to hug you. Okay? Really, I didn't mean it at all. Look—I'm hugging you with my mind right now," she closed her eyes to prove her imagined hugging of Merlin, but he ignored her act pf pretense.

"We need a way to get the flower," Enupnion said to the surprise of the clueless crew.

"What good is a flower going to do us now, Prince?" Bogan snapped.

"He's got a point. I don't think it matters what the Jackboot wants with them now," Gideon added.

"It's not for the Jackboot. It's for Elias," he said, turning everyone's gaze directly towards Elias.

"Okay, so what's he going to do with it?" Ava asked.

"If he can eat one of the berries, he might be able to free us," the prince explained.

"Oh, yeah, Wyatt, Ava, meet Elias the Destroyer," Bogan said as a matter of fact.

"What?" Wyatt perked up and looked at Elias as if the new information jolted him with hope again.

"FOR REAL! But how?" Ava hollered.

"I don't mean to make light of our situation here, but, HAVE YOU ALL LOST YOUR MINDS?" Merlin yelled, still tense from Izzy's words.

"Wyatt or Izzy might be able to shoot their mod-hands up there," Gideon considered.

"HA," Izzy laughed, "even if I could, I wouldn't be able to because that ceiling is much too high and my arms are wrapped in – VINES – Gideon, and good luck getting Wyatt to even talk to you right now," she scoffed.

Elias desperately wanted to calm everyone with some words of wisdom, so he blurted out the only thing he could remember. "We have to come up with some kind of plan, or we'll never get out of here. Like my father always said, 'If you don't craft a good plan, eventually you'll end up in someone else's,' and that's where we are right now. So can we stop fighting and figure this out? OUCH!" Everyone stopped for a moment and looked at him.

"What? What's wrong?" Ava asked.

"I-I don't know. Something bit me." Elias reached around the beam, trying to feel for it again, but nothing was there. "Can anyone see behind me?"

"No, it's too dark over there," Merlin said.

"I can't turn my head that far, kid," Bogan scrunched his face for the effort.

"It's too dark," Gideon said.

"OUCH! It bit me again. Right on the thumb," Elias winced.

"Open your hand," Epekneia said, but Elias glared at her confused. "Just open your hand."

When he did he felt something soft and fuzzy with something really hard in the center.

"A BEAK!" Elias shouted. Enupnion quickly clicked his tongue and the bird hopped on the platform.

The whole crew ecstatically shouted, "CASPER!"

"Maybe he can snap off the vines and get one of us free," Gideon said.

"It won't work. The vines will just grow again, faster and bigger than before," Wyatt explained.

"He's right," Ava agreed. "When we cut the Whisper free, they just grew right back."

"We need the flower," Enupnion huffed and then began clicking his tongue, but Casper must have misunderstood and tried to hop on his back. After several tries Enupnion finally got Casper to hop up on top of the glass globe but not up to the flower.

"Well, that's closer than I could have gotten him," Merlin joked as he tried brushing off Izzy's cruelty.

Casper eventually caught on and flew up next to the flower, but did nothing once he got up there. The ceiling was black-coal dark above them, with large rocks hanging down like giant stalactites, which made it difficult see much more than two red eyes glaring down on them. The Petinon's eyesight was much better than the human's, and they could clearly tell that Casper was clutching the rock the flower was growing out of.

"He's right beside it," Epekneia shouted. Her voice was instantly stilled by the sounds of chanting coming from behind the great wooded doors on each side of the throne. Everyone froze. Even the last bit of hope left in them came to a frigid end as one by one the Umbrella Charmers began filing into the great stone auditorium.

THEIR FINE TEAL CLOAKS WITH SILVER STITCHING SHIMMERED gloriously in the light of the great hall. As they reached their places, they stood with the black umbrellas fully open, waiting to take their seats. The chanting words were unintelligible to the captives standing on the platform, but by the looks on their faces the crew sensed the darkness behind the tone. Swirling black streams inside the globe responded to their unholy chanting by spinning faster and glowing brighter as chanting charmers filled each row of seats. Once they had completed their entrance, a single Umbrella Charmer walked into the room and raised his umbrella, closed it and dropped it to his side as the others followed suit. Then two men in long black coats walked into the room holding large curved horns which they sounded for a full minute then stepped near the throne and removed their hats.

"Forsythe! Cillian!" Gideon scowled, but they paid him no attention as they took their places in the great room. Forsythe and Cillian were not much of a surprise to Enupnion, mainly because of how sketchy they'd acted at the harbor.

Councilman Cillian stepped forward and announced the next person entering, "It is my great honor to announce to this gathering of followers, and these sacrifices for his magnificence, the great Alchemist," he paused a moment. "I present to you the Sorceress and Ruler of Gabriel's Harbor."

Then, a strange woman dressed in a dark green robe floated in with her umbrella. The whole of the room bowed down slightly as she entered. Her feet never touched the floor as she rose up to the platform beside the throne but continued to cover her face with her green umbrella.

Then Councilman Forsythe stepped forward and announced the next person, "It is my greatest honor to present to this gathering of faithful – the first Mist Speaker, first Umbrella Charmer and savior of our great ruler." He waved his hand in a silly fashion, bowed completely in half and said, "I present to you the wife of our Great Alchemist." Then the councilwoman from the harbor floated into the room and rose to the next platform beside the throne. Her black umbrella covered her face as she landed softly like she had done so many times before. The whole room bowed down to her until she landed on the platform.

A chant arose from the thousands of Umbrella Charmers as Forsythe and Cillian blasted their horns. This time the chanting turned darker and green smoke began to pour from the mouths of the Umbrella Charmers in the stands. Then the room was hit with a blast of light so bright Elias could even see Casper up on the ceiling, and he hoped they were all too busy with their silly chanting to notice him. Green flashes blasted different areas of the room, and sparks of purple lightning cracked across the beams they were tied to as the globe goo danced a wicked jig and flames exploded from torches lining every wall.

Merlin seemed to like it all and was grinning from one side of his glass brain to the other. After several captivating puffs of green, purple and red smoke, Merlin got the feeling he could do better than these amateurs. So he banged his head against the beam he was tied to and sent a massive blue bolt through the air. It was almost enough to force the wicked vines to relax and free them all, but it was short lived. However, he must have showed them up well enough to end their foolish deeds, because the smoke chanting, horn blowing and all other pomp and circumstance instantly stopped. Merlin giggled and started to smile at Izzy but remembered he was supposed to be mad at her.

Quiet filled the room as a colorfully cloaked and hooded man entered, but with no magnificence about him other than his hooded cloak. He walked with two staffs of the same height, both of them having smaller but similar globes to the one hanging over them. Once the man was inside the doorway, Forsythe spoke, "I present to you the Healer. Conqueror of the creeping mold. Conjurer and ruler of the black mist and future ruler of the earth. I present to you the Supreme Sovereign. I present to you the Great Alchemist."

SERPENT CARCASSES BAKED ON THE SURFACE OF THE BLISTERING hot boiler, which blasted steam a quarter mile high in the sky, so that even the black mist faded from its hot wind as Iron Jaw pushed the train beyond its limits. A strange, gale force wind blew up from nothingness, battering the Jackboot's weary body as if something was trying to hold him back. BOOM! BOOM! His rifle rocked with every blast. A goodly sized serpent came directly at him the moment he was reloading, so he slung the rifle around to his back and grabbed the gnashing beast by the wings, running it through on one of the golden bull horns. Deep inside his mind he punished himself for his mistakes while his heart ached with fear for his dear Isabella.

"FASTER, IRON JAW! FASTER!" the Jackboot cried.

THE ALCHEMIST WALKED UP THE STEPS TO THE THRONE, PLACED his staffs one in each hole on either side of the arms and sat down. The rest of the umbrella crowd followed his example. He sat for a moment, then began whispering something to his wife in the black cloak. The green and black goo swirling around inside the globe distorted Elias' view of them, but they seemed like a loving couple. All be it an evil, sick, demented loving couple, but loving nonetheless. She was still hiding her face with the umbrella as they spoke, but their secret conversation was brought to a halt by Enupnion's mockery of them all.

"Are you afraid of the light, Great Alchemist? Why do you hide your face?"

"Shut up, Hunchy!" Gideon said, drawing a nasty look from Epekneia, but the Alchemist showed no signs of concern for Prince Enupnion's words.

Wyatt had gone completely pale, almost lifeless with fear. He had seen this all before. Four times to be exact. Ava was near hyperventilating at having just learned of Charlie's possible survival only to be captured by an evil mold cult and chopped to pieces. Izzy had her eyes closed as if she were praying, and Bogan looked like he wanted to pull that hand cannon out of his leg and go out in a blaze of glory, but he couldn't reach it with his arms tied down. Elias and Epekneia kept checking the ceiling for signs of hope that maybe a berry would by some chance fall into Elias' mouth and he would suddenly turn into a horrible man eating beast.

The Alchemist leaned over and spoke to the Sorceress, who was obediently standing next to him. Then she uttered something under her breath and black smoke rolled from her mouth. It filled the canopy of her umbrella and she lifted off the platform, floating down in front of Izzy. She closed her umbrella, revealing a short black top hat with a dark red flower sticking through a silver ribbon. Her lips were grayish black and her teeth were not much different. Using the crook of her umbrella, she raised Izzy's head by her chin and stared into her eyes. In a soft, crackling, hollow voice that echoed through the cavernous room, she spoke, "*Issssabeeellllaa.*"

"Vanessa." Izzy replied with a smirk of distaste to the shock of everyone except Merlin, who thought maybe he should at least pretend to be shocked, but it came out all weird.

"OH! What?" Merlin feigned. Izzy rolled her eyes at him, paused for a moment, then looked directly into the Sorceress' eyes as she scrunched her nose.

"Your breath stinks, Vanessa. Have you been eating mold again?" The Sorceress looked down at Izzy's mod arm and sneered, then walked over toward Wyatt.

The chamber was filled with the trembling clatter of Wyatt's mods as the Sorceress approached him. She looked at him in disgust and spoke in her dreaded, ghostly tone, "*Wyatt, darling,*" she cocked her head and squatted down to look him in the eyes. "*I've spoken to him and he has agreed to forgive your betrayal of the sacred smoke and allow you a chance to join us forever.*"

"Really?" Wyatt softly replied, somewhat surprised by her offer.

"*Iiiit's truuuue,*" she said, looking back at the Alchemist.

"No more tests?"

"*No, my sweet little boy. He will give you more power than you will ever have with these metal irons attached to you.*"

"THAT'S IT!" Izzy yelled. "I can't do it, Merlin. She's a monster. Wyatt, I hate to be the one to break it to you, but she's not your mother. She's a liar and a witch!"

"*Curse you, Isabeeelllla—cheatinesst sneak of child!*" the Sorceress instantly screeched at Izzy and floated back over in front of her within a split second. She raised her arm to strike Izzy and a mist hand appeared where a fleshy hand should have been. The mist hand grew large and fierce but was halted by the Alchemist's wife who floated over in front of her. After a brief, tense, silent moment between them, Vanessa returned to Wyatt.

The Alchemist's wife, then sent Forsythe out of the room and gently rose back to her platform.

"*Don't listen to her lies, Wyatt,*" the Sorceress warned.

"They're not lies, Wyatt," Izzy said. "Think about it. It doesn't add up! If she was your mother by the Jackboot, you'd be much younger, but you're 16, same as me. She only wants you for dark magic. It's all she ever wanted from you."

Vanessa's face changed from grayish black to an almost perfectly pliable peach, "I promise you no more tricks, but this is your last chance, Wyatt."

"NO, WYATT! DON'T DO IT!" Izzy and Merlin yelled at him.

"I-I don't know what to do. I-I, Merlin, is it true?" Wyatt desperately searched his friend's faces.

"I thought she was dead. I truly did. I-I didn't think it would matter either way, but she's not your mother." Merlin hung his head in guilt.

"Then who is?" Wyatt pleaded.

"I don't know, but it's not this witch. She's Elias' mother," Izzy claimed, much to Elias amazement.

"Uh—I've never seen this lady before in all my life. Why would you say that? You know the Jackboot killed my parents." Elias was confused and hurt by Izzy's game.

"But Bobby found you on the mountain, where Vanessa was hiding with the Alchemist. I thought you..." Izzy's face froze like stone. Elias disappeared before her as she stared right through him. Her big brown eyes not blinking a wink. Her last hope drowned inside the green globe's methodical light; stealing away her dream of finally finding her father's lost son. Everyone, including Merlin, tried to process her statement, but Izzy was the only one Big Bobby had told about the boy and he'd been wrong—terribly wrong.

Vanessa cocked her head and rolled yellow eyes. "*More lies, Isabella?*"

A wave of the Alchemist's hand and Wyatt's opportunity had vanished.

"*Too late, Wyatt,*" the Sorceress said, "*You had your chance.*" She popped her umbrella and floated over in front of Elias, gazing at him with her gaunt eyes.

She looked him up and down as if she wanted to kill him. *"You killed my apprentice at the harbor. If you were someone else you would be dead already."* Then she howled out a horrible, mist-filled moan and floated back up to her platform.

The prince was about to continue his outrageous insults, but with the wave of the Alchemist's hand the giant doors opened and Prince Enupnion was crushed with silence.

"Not everyone deserted you, Great Prince," the Alchemist said as Forsythe returned carrying Mellontas. Forsythe laid him down on the slab underneath the glass globe then returned to his place by the throne.

Epekneia was horrified and could barely breathe out, "Father?"

"Mellontas," the prince called, but Mellontas was hanging on by single, shallow breaths, unable to move much more than his hand up toward his daughter.

"WHO ARE YOU?" Prince Enupnion cried out at the throne, but he received no response from the Alchemist.

Only the crowd of umbrella lemmings spoke up in unison, "THE GREAT ALCHEMIST!"

BOSARUS MUSTERED HIS GUTS FOR BATTLE AND JOINED THE Jackboot on top of the Weaver. His weapons of choice were two large knives pulled from the Jackboot's personal armory, and he sliced and hacked away at the winged serpents with a fierce fury of his own making. Iron Jaw did his best to clip some through the windows as he burned the iron off the Weaver's wheels. The sounds of scraping metal, chugging gears, whistling steam and a howling train were drowned out by the shrieking and squealing of dying serpents.

"FASTER, IRON JAW! FASTER!" Isabella's father begged.

The Alchemist rose from his throne and descended the steps toward the platform. He moved slowly and almost stumbled once, forcing Forsythe to run to his side and catch him, but the Alchemist pushed him away. He climbed onto the platform with the captives and made his way over towards Prince Enupnion. The black hole deep inside his hooded cloak where a face should be held two faded yellow eyes floating deep in the darkness. His hands disappeared into the oversized sleeves of his cloak as he held them together in front of him. With his back toward Elias he spoke to the prince.

"Of all those in the kingdom you, my prince, have done more to help me than you could ever imagine."

Enupnion was speechless and tried to see into the darkness of the cloak. "Who are you?" he asked again.

"I am the Alchemist."

"Yes, I figured that out, but who is the Alchemist?"

Stepping back away from the prince, the man removed his hood to reveal himself, but Enupnion gazed at an unrecognizable, weathered face. Then, like lighting hitting his eyes, the prince suddenly remembered and in stunned wonder exclaimed, "SUNAGO THE GREAT!"

"I used to be," he answered, dropping the back of his robe to expose a mangled back where glorious wings once honored him, "but the man known as the Jackboot hacked off my glory in battle. If not for the wise enchantress, my wife, I would have surely died that day," the Alchemist boasted.

"To be honest, you look dead already," the prince mocked.

"Our strength is in our wings, as the old books say, and I've been dying ever since he hacked mine off. But thankfully, my wife had been a powerful mold conjuror, and she showed me a different side of the darkness I'd never seen before. She showed me a way to change everything and never worry over the foolishness of replanting again. With her powerful magic and gentle instruction, I became a powerful Alchemist, even greater than she could have imagined, and her student became her master. I taught them all how to fly with smoke and speak its power in their favor, and with it we took control of one of the greatest cities mankind has built since the mold returned."

Elias, could see the pain in Enupnion's troubled eyes as the Alchemist spoke. "You were my hero. I grew up on the stories of your greatness. You planted seeds across the whole world when no one wanted to plant anymore. They even built a statue in your honor when you didn't return, and they called it Sunago the Great,"

The prince's broken heart bled through in his voice, but he continued. "The one prophecy I couldn't figure out was that the child was to have come from a Petinon, so when he said his parents were human I gave up on understanding and just accepted it, but now it's perfectly clear. Although it is most certainly rare for a Petinon to be born without wings, as you and I both know of only one such child and what the Convocation did to it. I am surprised that one such as the "Great Sunago", so strict in our laws, would have let him live. You must have known something. Maybe your sorceress wife was able to figure it out, I don't know, but for you to let such a terrible disgrace live is intriguing to me. You do know wingless Petinon's are prone to insanity and madness? You must have found a way to control those side effects."

The Alchemist seemed to have a greater plan in mind as he completely ignored the prince. "None of those things matter any longer, young Prince. Join me now and I will show you the power of the creeping mold. I will show you things those cowardly fools on the mountain could never dream of."

"How could I follow someone who betrayed his own people, his own great name, for darkness and smoke? When the convocation finds out what you've become, they will come for you and bring you to a terrible end," the prince warned.

"Poor, foolish, Prince. Your father never told you?"

"Never told me what?"

"It was my master plan the convocation put into motion. My plan to end the planting seasons and let the mold grow again so we could force the prophecy into effect. The convocation didn't just approve of the plan, they loved it enough to take credit for it. A grand opportunity, they said, and so I left them to their scheming devices and found something better than fire berries. Black Mist and Smoke Magic!!"

"WHAT? That's not possible."

"Anything is possible with black mist."

Sunago stood to his feet in front of the prince and began speaking foul words that darkened the whole cavern. Even flames held by the torches shrunk back to mere flickers, then Sunago arched his back and wings of smoke formed out of his scars—dark, ominous wings that obeyed the Alchemist's every thought. The Umbrella Charmers cheered their magnificent leader's ability to command the smoke. He rose into the air, landing back on his throne next to his wife, and wrapped his wicked wings around her as they spoke in secret.

Prince Enupnion was awestruck by Sunago's ability to command the darkness, and it saddened him that the once great Petinon was now a conjuror of black mist. He blocked out Sunago's lies of the convocation allowing such a mad plan to ever be put into motion. Sure, many had always talked about such things privately, but the convocation never would have approved of it openly. Especially as long as his father was king.

THE IRON WEAVER'S BLOOD-SOAKED HORNS HAD NOT YET DRANK their fill of the slithering, bat-winged ghouls, but the Jackboot was doing his best to satisfy them. The beasts kept falling through the mist-filled sky like wicked rain, and a foul voice fell with them. Warning him. Commanding him to turn back. The resistance was greater than he could have predicted, but the resolve of an overprotecting father is not so easily conquered.

For Iron Jaw, it would have been better if he'd merely demanded more speed, more results, or cursed his poor performance, but one word nearly broke the man in half. He would rather have torn his iron jaw off and cast it into the fire for more fuel than that single tear his commander caused to slide off his dirty cheek. The echo of a father's heartbreak cracked that hard man's soul as the Jackboot's weary, graveled voice cried out, "IZAABEELLAA!"

AFTER BRIEFLY CONSULTING WITH HER HUSBAND, THE Alchemist's wife reached behind his throne, grabbed a black leather bag, and spoke some foul words of smoke to fill her magic umbrella for the journey to the platform. She levitated about an inch off the platform, her feet firmly together, with toes slightly pointed toward the ground.

She paused in front of Izzy, but never acknowledged her, then moved in front of Merlin, who said, "Cute trick." She ignored him and slowly drifted around the platform, pausing in front of each of them until she stopped in front of Mellontas. Epekneia's eyes streamed rivers of heartbreak, but her father shook his head at her and weakly groaned, *"Be strong."*

The Alchemist's wife sat her bag down near Mellontas, and with a single dark word, a mist-shaped hand opened it and pulled out a needle. She continued to hold her umbrella as she spoke again, and the needle drew blood from Mellontas back where his wings had been cleaved. The hand placed it back into the bag and pulled out another needle, which it laid in her hand. She turned towards Elias and stood in front of him, preparing the needle. The vines holding Elias crawled around his jacket and peeled it opened with their thorny claws.

Merlin gave an audible groan, and everyone present could almost see his heart sink at the realization he should have been checking on his friend more often. Even Wyatt seemed to buck up out of his self-pity after taking notice of Elias' rotted chest and shimmering gold heart beating through the glass. His veins were so damaged it was hard to imagine any blood at all pumping through them. It stole the breath away from his friends, and from the sorrow in their eyes he felt the joy of true friendship. They cared about him, and he'd burned every spare moment he had left for them.

She finished her needle prep and declared in smoke her authority to the crowd, and they responded with a menacing mist-filled chant. An enchanted tune filled her voice as she drove the needle into his chest and withdrew the contaminated blood. Purple lightning crackled across the beams, then into the green swirling globe, and the torches popped greenish black flames at the order of the dark voice. Black mist carried her umbrella into the air above her, revealing the same short top hat as the Sorceress, only with a dark green ribbon. However, her face wasn't gray and ashen like the Sorceress, with rotting teeth and wicked demeanor, but beautifully peach colored with the gentle smile of a mother.

18

THE ALCHEMIST'S WIFE

"MOM! But – how?" Elias' heart nearly skipped through the glass.

"*Momma?*" Izzy said as she melted inside herself.

"WHAT?" Elias jerked his head over towards Izzy. If not for the vines holding everyone else against the beams, they would have fallen to the floor gasping. The Alchemist's wife raised her hand toward Izzy, and the vines lifted her; carried her over to her mother and brother.

"My babies. My children. It's been so long. I've dreamed of this moment for so very long." she hugged them both at the same time, crushing Izzy's face against one cheek and Elias' against the other, but they couldn't speak. They weren't sure if it was her power holding their tongues or their own dumbstruck thoughts as she held them tight.

"W-Why, Momma?" Izzy asked.

"*MOM?*" What do you mean 'YOUR' mom? But how? I don't understand." Elias asked Izzy.

She kissed Izzy on the cheek, "I'm so sorry I had to leave

you, my darling girl, but Sunago needed me. I feared for his safety if your father ever found out about us." She raised her hand and the vines lifted Izzy a few feet into the air and held her there.

"But, Momma we thought you died. Daddy, Momma! H-He was broken. We thought you died. We thought you died. He lost his mind, Momma. W-We thought you died." She wanted to be held by her. To tell her how much they missed her, but the thorny vines pressing against her skin felt more like the embrace of cruel punishment than a mother's remorse. Emptiness filled Isabella's heart.

All Elias could do was gaze at his sister and wonder of all the lost years. What kind of sick joke was this? His mother, who loved and cared for him so many years, could so easily abandon his sister. Indignation filled Elias' heart.

"Your father was never a stable man to begin with, darling. If he'd ever found out about my gifts he would have killed me."

"But that bird man tried to kill Daddy. Why, Momma? Why are you with him?" Izzy's questions were digging too deep, so the witch waved her hand, sending her back to the beam and gently wrapping the vines around her jaw to prevent her from speaking. She turned to Elias and knelt in front of him.

"You are so different from your sister, my dear, sweet boy. Something about your blood was so powerful. I could feel it even before you were born. It was healing Sunago and giving us all power that we had never experienced before you came. Even this powerful globe above you was made with your blood and..."

Elias cut her off. "You used my infected blood to make magic?"

"Kind of; it's hard to explain. We were testing—looking for a way to—certain things to see why you were so different, and I'm so sorry for all those nasty tests, my dear, sweet boy." She brushed her hand over his cheek. "I know they were just terrible; awful, but I had to save Sunago."

"I don't even know who Sunago is, Mom. Where's Dad?"

"Well, darling, Sunago is Dad."

"WHAT!"

"Well, sort of. I mean, he's not your father, but he is the one who raised you."

"THAT'S DAD? I-I don't know what you mean, Mom. That man doesn't even look like Dad."

"I know, dear. I know, but he is. You've just never seen him without his lab clothes and gloves. He was always so busy working in the lab to find a way to make..."

"Why won't he come over here, Mom? Why won't he speak to me?"

"Elias, Sunago is your dad. He is the one who raised you and taught you about plants, but your father is Owen Brock." His mother whispered in his ear so no one else could hear.

"I don't even know who that is, Mom." Elias' strength left his body and he tried to breathe; catch his breath with shallow draws. He must think through this carefully. Surely there was a better explanation for things than what his wonderful, loving, overprotective mother was giving him. His mother kept speaking, but he heard no words. No sounds. All he could hear in his mind were the Jackboot's words he said before casting them into the mine. *"I believe what we need here is a little time of contemplation. Don't you agree?"* Elias accidentally answered the words he was hearing in his head.

"Yes, sir."

"I'm sorry, dear, what was that?"

"Oh—um—I thought, I thought Dad was working every night in his lab to cure me, but all that time he was only using me for smoke magic?"

Her voice rose with great passion as she explained."Well, sort of. You see, darling, Sunago is a great Alchemist, and he needs your blood, and even more so your heart, so he can fulfill his destiny for his people and become the greatest Petinon ruler."

Okay, that was a bit more than what he had expected for an answer, and his response was fitting. "WHAT ABOUT MY LIFE, MOM? WHAT ABOUT MY DREAMS? WAS HE EVER LOOKING FOR SOMETHING TO HELP ME?" Shaking. Sweating. Vision-blurring anger filled Elias.

"Elias that is not a respectful way to speak to me and you know it."

"That night, the storm? Was that you, too?"

"Darling, I was trying to keep them away from you," she pointed at the Whisper crew, "so we could prepare Sunago for your heart. Once he has your heart you'll be one with him and live forever with him. You won't have to worry about dying any longer."

"You were going to give him my infected heart? Why would he want a damaged heart?"

"Sunago is immune to the black mist, and with your heart inside him he would no longer have to keep taking your blood. The heart would heal and he would become the most powerful Alchemist the world has ever known."

"You wanted to give my heart away to Dad—wait— this guy, so he can become the Destroyer? THIS IS ALL ABOUT THAT STUPID PROPHECY?" Elias' sweating intensified with his anger.

"Oh, my dear baby boy, you were dying. We kept you alive as long as possible until the time had come."

"What about that night on the ship when the serpent attacked me?"

"I was calling you back to me, but you weren't ready. You didn't understand the words, so I sent my servant to bring you back to me. He never would have hurt you."

"He tried to choke me to death, Mom," Elias looked at her in disbelief.

"Oh, no. No, never. He would never have done such a thing. He was only going to put you to sleep so you'd be easier for him to carry. I was in complete control of him. I could feel your life in his grip. I promise I never would have let him hurt you."

"So yours was the dark voice on the wind; the one choking me to death," Elias turned cold towards her.

"Now, Elias, don't use that tone with me," she scolded.

"How was I infected, Mom? How did I get mist sickness?"

"When you were three, just like we told you."

"I know, but how did I get it?"

"Your mask came off and you breathed it in. It was a terrible day for us all."

"Really? Something I never understood. How did I get mist

sickness when we lived on the mountain? There was no mist on the mountain."

From the throne, the Alchemist finally spoke, "Elias, that's no way to speak to your mother. Now apologize to her immediately."

Elias ignored him.

"Just what are you saying, Elias? Are you calling me a liar?" his mother asked.

Elias paused and searched his thoughts over the last many days and years, calculating everything he could remember, and even his own heart. "Darkness lies."

In an instant her chest raised, but she controlled herself, rose to her feet and redirected her anger towards Merlin. "Who knows how much damage that monster of metal has done to your precious heart with that infernal gold contraption? No matter, I will punish him for it."

"Leave him alone, Mom," Elias struggled out of his brokenness, but she had already begun speaking dark words, forming a wicked hand of smoke that reached for the top of Merlin's head. The room darkened with a dreadful sound, and the green liquid in the globe bubbled as if it were angry.

"NO, MOM! DON'T HURT HIM," Elias cried.

Her hand of smoke touched down on Merlin's glass brain cap and the room suddenly went dark black, with total loss of vision, even stealing the light from the green globe. Instantly a fierce blue bolt shot out from Merlin's head and struck the ceiling. A massive chunk broke loose and fell into the crowd of Umbrella Charmers, killing about twenty of them and sending the room into chaos.

The Umbrella Charmers became terrified of Merlin, but the Alchemist stood up and spoke his conjured words, bringing the room back under control. "My people, do not be so easily alarmed by simple scientific tricks," the Alchemist ordered.

"Hey, don't blame me," Merlin said, "only my father can remove my cover. That was his idea, not mine. He's weird like that about his kids. Ha! You should see my brother if you..."

"ENOUGH!" Elias' mother demanded.

She stood to her feet and gently caressed Elias' cheek, then placed her cold hand above the heart-mod. "I so wish they hadn't done this, my darling, their act of foolishness has cost us dearly, but I can't stress enough the importance of not letting your heart go to waste. Your death must not be in vain. Your blood will strengthen Sunago until he is ready for your heart. With it, he will be able to save the whole world from the creeping mold and black mist and unite his people under his authority."

A laugh finally broke out from Prince Enupnion, and he offered his advice, "They're lying, Elias. Somehow they've know you're the Destroyer, sent to bring them and their dark power to an end. Even if she is your mother, remember this, she's lied to you for years and so has Sunago." The vines wrapped around him tighter as he spoke, digging the thorns deep into flesh, even drawing blood from his wings, but he fought hard through groans to finish. "If she tried to kill you once, in Gabriel's Harbor, she will try again. Don't—uh—trust—her." He stopped to focus on the pain, and then Elias' mother wrapped the vines around the prince's jaw, preventing him from speaking any longer.

"Vanessa, bring my tools. We need to prep him now, before his heart is beyond repair," she ordered, sending the Sorceress away. She grabbed her umbrella that was still floating above her, let out a deep breath and rose into the air again, floating back to her husband.

"FASTER, IRON JAW! FASTER!" HE ROARED AS THEY approached the Valley of Bones.

ELIAS' MOTHER PREPARED THE GREAT ALCHEMIST FOR THE BLOOD she had taken from Elias' chest by injecting it into both of the globes atop his staffs. Then she connected the globes with tubes and hooked them into his forearms. While she was busy working her craft on him, a simple, yet pleasantly unexpected, event occurred.

Poor Mellontas was still savoring his final moments with his daughter when five berries suddenly fell from the ceiling, landing next to his hands. Two of them splattered on the stone slab, but three of them remained intact. The Whisper crew's eyes nearly popped out of their sockets. The crew was speechless, but not by choice. In their minds they were shouting with hope. Did Casper finally come through for them? Epekneia cocked her head towards Elias. Mellontas wasn't sure what she was getting at until she mumbled, "Feed the boy!"

He was a bit taken aback by her statement and asked plainly, "All?" She shook her head no as best she could through the restriction from the vines, but he didn't get the cue. Even the prince tried to warn him, but he was busy mustering every ounce of energy to get to his feet. Once he did, he shoved all three berries in Elias' mouth and collapsed back on the platform before anyone could stop him. Forsythe quickly notified Elias' mother that something had happened on the platform, and she began floating back over towards them.

Enupnion looked at Elias and tried to warn him with his eyes, but the vines only wrapped around his head harder. Epekneia also tried to warn him. Of course, no one else had a clue what had happened. The prince's words at the tree echoed in his mind, "NEVER, eat a whole, fresh berry!" but they were all out of options. If he exploded into a fire ball of bone-melting flesh, at least maybe it would free his friends from the vines and allow them to escape. For his part, though, Elias considered it a better way to die than being drained of blood by his evil mother to save some wizard. Those were not words he had ever considered using in his mind before this day. If only the Jackboot "had" killed them, maybe everyone would be better for it.

He watched as his mother floated closer and closer, then he bit down on all three berries and swallowed them. Maybe he would take her with him and his friends could escape. Elias looked at them and said, "Thanks for being my friends. I'm sorry for all this." They were clueless to what he meant, but as his eyes began to burn red, fear gripped them all. His mother paused in midair and shrieked.

"WHAT DID YOU DO?" she demanded of Mellontas.

"KILL HIM!" she ordered Forsythe and Cillian, who stepped to the platform and shot Mellontas in the back. The sound of Epekneia's heart shattering would have been the first of many to come that night, but for Elias.

It started with a violent scream deep from within him, even though his mouth had not yet opened. His eyes lit with flames, his hands shook, and from his nostrils red smoke poured like a waterfall. The vines tried to flee from him but caught fire and burned to nothingness, and he collapsed onto the stone platform. Ringing began in his ears so loud it distorted his vision more than the flames in his eyes. Umbrella-charming spectators shrunk back into their seats in fear, and the Alchemist took notice. What kind of DESTROYER was this that his only power was to destroy himself?

Deafening wind rocked his ears; mind shredding, heart piercing, but still no voice calling for him to destroy them, or even a whisper to gently guide him. He accidentally touched Mellontas' body, and much to everyone's horror he instantly set it on fire. Within a moment Mellontas' body had vanished into ashes. Elias looked up at his friends, and pity filled their eyes for him, but not Izzy. Her eyes were closed tightly, and she was saying something under her breath. Even though she was too far away to hear, he somehow felt as if she were saying, "Please hurry." Her mouth was strapped with the vines, and Elias was confused at how he could hear her voice.

The ringing was unbearable, so tormentingly unbearable. He wanted it all to end. It felt as if his heart wanted out. As if it were trying to escape. To be set free. Then, to his horror, the glass on his heart-mod exploded into shards on the floor, and the connection hose burst off, blowing out steam. Momentary relief, but then the pain returned.

Mind shredding pain.

FIRE burning in his bones.

Ringing in his ears.

Heartache. Loss. Anger.

The smell of hot iron searing his mind and burning coal filling his nostrils and—the voice.

THE VOICE!

Loud and clear, but different. Filled with pain and heartache. Terrible heartache, misery and loss. Relentless in its desire to get through to him, unlike anything he'd ever felt before. The pain of holding it in was so great, all he could think of was let it out.

Speak it!

Say the words! Stop the pain!

Say the words! Stop the pain!

Speak them so everyone can hear and maybe the pain would end, and so he did. He spoke them back exactly as he heard them howling through his head, shaking violently until he finally let it out.

"LIGHT IT!" Elias cried out.

The room was utterly baffled by his statement. Even the Whisper crew looked at each other blank faced.

Forsythe stepped onto the platform, "Would you like for me to end him now, your majesty?" he asked the Alchemist's wife.

"No! I want to understand what he is saying. It might be important to Sunago," she explained.

"As you command," Forsythe bowed and stepped back next to Cillian.

The pain quickly returned; burning, aching, searing hot pain, but he was uncertain about the new words filling his mind. Were they coming from him or something else? He held them in for what seemed like forever in terms of pain, but speaking them was such great relief.

Speak it! Say the words! Stop the pain!

"ISABEELLLAA—DADDY'S COOOMIIINNNGGG!" Elias cried.

Izzy's eyes leapt open in astonishment, *"Daddy?"* But the words had come from Elias. She looked over at him as a big red grin slid across his face and she winked back at him. At that moment, it was clear to them both, that they truly were brother and sister.

"KILL THEM ALL!" the Alchemist thundered. Normally

they would have obeyed in an instant, but the roaring sound coming from the circular stairway caught everyone's attention, including Elias'. The pain had mostly left him, so he stood to his feet. His eyes were flames of fire and his skin dark red. His hair had turned solid black, and smoke rolled out of his ears, nose and mouth. He had no more words to say as he watched the staircase like everyone else, in wonder of what was coming.

The stairway grew brighter and brighter as the sounds of roaring increased until a flaming man stepped down out of the entrance. At least it looked like a man, but how could a man be burning and still live? The Umbrella Charmers lurched back in their seats, and some of them got up and ran out of the room. One of them cried out, "HE HAS RETURNED! THE BURNING MAN HAS RETURNED!"

The room was awestruck by the man who walked calmly over toward the Whisper crew and stepped on the stone platform, but Izzy gave it all away.

"DADDY!" she yelled.

The man took hold of the vines and set them on fire. Izzy appeared to want to run to him and hug him, but it was clearly the wrong time for hugging the Jackboot.

Then he spoke in a terrifying voice, mostly due to the protective helmet and voice echo system installed by Hans. "The Iron Weaver is waiting— RUN!" The Whisper crew began bailing off the platform in haste as the Umbrella Charmers were frozen with fear; motionless at the smell of the flames. His great theatrical plan was working perfectly until she called his name.

"OWEN!" The Alchemist's wife removed her hat and lifted her umbrella. Although outwardly he was burning—inwardly his body froze at the sound of her voice. It couldn't be. She was dead. Gone forever. Yet the apparition floating in the air above him looked very much like the love of his life. The most beautiful woman a man like him could ever have wished for—only now a witch. Not just any witch, but the High Sorceress of all black smoke speakers—Queen of the Umbrella Charmers—the Alchemist's wife.

"Cassandra," he melted to his knees on the platform. The Whisper crew was fleeing the room, but Izzy wouldn't leave him and no one could just pick him up and carry him out without burning alive. To make matters worse, Vanessa returned.

"Vanessa?" In his mind he saw this plan going differently. More in his favor, such as the last time he'd burned the wicked valley.

"OOOWWEEENNNNN!" Vanessa called for him, but Wyatt came running instead.

"MOM, I'M SORRY! I change my mind. I change my mind. Please take me back!" Wyatt's metal mods clacked awkwardly across the stone platform to the only mother he'd ever known, and she embraced him.

"NO, WYATT! MY SON!" Something broke inside the Jackboot as he watched his whole life crumbling before his eyes.

Elias ran back to the platform, and Prince Enupnion with him, pleading for him to get out, but he refused to leave without Izzy. Not without his sister. Elias would have preferred to put a pickaxe in the Jackboot's skull, but circumstances being what they were now, he figured on a different course of action. He took hold of the burning man with his bare hands and shook him. "YOU HAVE TO GET OUT OF HERE!" The Jackboot was taken aback by the boy grabbing the flames, and it startled him out of his emotional breakdown.

By this time, the Alchemist's wife had formed a giant hand of black smoke to crush them, but the burning fire berries Iron Jaw had poured on the Jackboot prevented her from grabbing on to them. Her hand kept swiping right through the flames as the three of them stared at her, broken hearted by her betrayal.

Cillian saw this as an opportune moment to strike down the prince and gain position with Sunago. He raised his gun towards Enupnion, but Epekneia crashed down on top of him, and with a slice of her talons, decapitated Cillian. His head rolled off the platform, landing at the foot of the Alchemist's throne.

"FLEE, MY PRINCE," Epekneia warned, and with that they all ran towards the stairway. All except Wyatt.

19

THE LOST CHILD

$\mathcal{R}$ushing up the circular stairs, Gideon burst through the stone door at the top, mashing his face against the barrel of Iron Jaw's gear cooler gun.

"Sorry, fella. Where's Mr. Jackboot?" he clacked.

"He's coming up hot right behind us," Gideon warned.

"Load into the Iron Weaver. We're getting out of here," Iron Jaw ordered.

"WAIT! Where's the Whisper?" Bogan asked, jumping through the doorway.

"Bosarus took it. We're heading back by way of the abandoned harbor tracks," Iron Jaw explained. "Now get into the Weaver." Iron Jaw freaked when the Petinon's exited the stone doorway and fumbled for his sawed-off shotguns strapped to his legs. "WHAT THE DEVIL!"

"No, don't! They're with us," Ava jumped in front of them.

Iron Jaw stammered a bit to regain his faculties but instantly pulled himself together when Izzy leapt through the door, dripping with sweat from the heat.

"They're right behind me!" she shouted.

The Jackboot exhaustedly exited the doorway with Elias holding the burning man up. It was a mind numbing sight for poor Iron Jaw to take in. The boy he'd once declared dead now standing before him holding a man on fire. It shouldn't be possible, but there it was in all its impossibilities. Iron Jaw hesitated until Izzy screamed in his ear, jolting him out of his confusion, and he hit them both with a long blast from the cooler. The fire restarted several times, but he kept at it like the last time they entered the valley many years ago. Once the fire was doused, he grabbed his exhausted commander by the arms and helped him navigate the bony valley to his train.

Elias followed slowly behind them as thoughts of his childhood raced through his mind. Was he so blindly naïve and ignorantly trusting that he couldn't see what his mother and Sunago were doing? Maybe they were just too crafty in their evil deeds that common sense explanations eluded him. However, the green globe lighting their kitchen was an exact match for the globe in the dungeon, as well as all the potion bottles lining her walls like Abner's Apothecary. It only now dawned on him that he'd never seen his father without gloves or a lab clothes. He knew his father's face was strange, but he just chalked it up to all the explosions and burns he'd received in the lab. At least his mother's incessant demands for him to wear that blasted pink ball cap were finally clear to him. They never wanted him to escape.

He was about to board the train of the man he'd wanted to kill for the murder of his parents, but now he didn't know what to believe. He lagged way behind as everyone else started loading into the Iron Weaver, and Wyatt's confusing decision was becoming clearer to him. True, they were evil, but they were the only parents he'd ever known. Even if they did want all his blood to increase their dark magic, at least it made sense if they were trying to destroy the creeping mold. Maybe Sunago really was the Destroyer. He could turn back now and possibly save the world—or enslave it, but at least his life would have some value. If he got on the train with his friends he might live another day, maybe two, then his magical blood and heart, or whatever it was, would never save anyone.

He didn't realize he'd stopped walking and was still standing on the hill. Everyone was waving for him to come, but Izzy and the Jackboot were arguing about something. He felt cold—empty—alone. The heat from the berries was wearing off, and his body temperature was cooling. He didn't like the feeling of it. As indecision filled his mind, so did the wonder of something new. A new life. A different life. He had a sister, and she wasn't anything like his parents. She was strong and caring. His mind began to fit the pieces of the puzzle together. How many times she was there for him, protecting him; her bitter kiss on the Whisper that dulled his pain; her hand of comfort when meeting the Jackboot, her hand of protection during the tower descent and so much more. A whirlwind of Izzy events wove its way through his thoughts. She was always protecting him no matter how simple. Preventing his fall as he walked the streets in the Harbor and even stepping in front of the Petinon's when she thought they were a danger.

Suddenly, Casper swooped directly over top his head, diving down toward the train. He half expected the Jackboot to kill him, but Casper didn't seem afraid of the Jackboot at all. It was a good sign. It was the sign he needed to step forward beyond the lies of his past life. A chance to spend his remaining days with someone that truly cared for him and that someone was his sister, Isabella.

THE TRAIN WAS COVERED IN THE BLOOD OF DEAD SERPENTS, AND several carcasses were impaled on the horns. What once was a beautiful, shiny, black train had now been changed into a terrifying machine of war. The Jackboot was refusing to let Prince Enupnion and Epekneia on the train but was caught off guard by Elias' glowing red eyes as the boy approached, and so he stepped back to take measure of things.

"Daddy, they're not like the old one. He's a prince of his people, and he's helped us," Izzy tried to explain.

"I'm not letting these bird freaks on my train. If they want to return with us to Grand Fortune City, they can fly themselves," he warned. Then Elias stepped up and spoke.

"They're exhausted just like everyone else, including you. Now let them on the train." Elias surprised himself at his courage, but the dying have nothing to fear. The red smoke coming out of his mouth and flames in his eyes helped the Jackboot quickly makes his decision.

"Fine, but I don't want feathers all over the cars, you got it?" The Jackboot had to have some sort of demand to maintain his hard reputation.

"No hard feelings, right?" Prince Enupnion reached out his hand to the Jackboot, who reluctantly shook the claws. Everyone breathed a sigh of relief until the prince spoke again.

"Other than wanting to land a few droppings on your magnificent train after a good washing, eh?" the prince smirked as everyone grimaced.

Some closed their eyes, expecting a full on battle to emerge before them, but the Jackboot let out a single, "HA!" then smacked the prince on the back.

"Sorry, bad bird joke," the prince grinned, and the two old foes boarded the train.

FRIEND OF THE BEAR: STRESSFUL EXHAUSTION BROUGHT everyone collapsing to the floor. They all sat quietly for a while, listening to the Iron Weaver chugging and clanking on the tracks. Blank stares of the dead animals in the trophy car put their hard world into perspective, but Sunago's wings were a terrifying sight for Enupnion and Epekneia. The prince and the Jackboot stared each other down with awkward silence. A stray feather lying beside Enupnion caught the Jackboot's eye, and he gawked at it for a moment, then looked back up at the prince. Enupnion reached over slowly and picked it up, then twisted it in fingers. The Jackboot's thick mustache was matted in the blood of slain serpents, and sweat was sliding down his cheeks, cleaning the blood like war paint. Enupnion's face was grizzled enough that he didn't need war paint as the two foes looked intently at each other.

Suddenly, Izzy couldn't contain her anger any longer and grabbed Vanessa's old umbrella that was hanging on the bull's horn, snapped it in half with her mod-hand, then sat back down next to her father.

The deep red color had left Elias' face leaving him as pale as death while he sat under Sunago's mounted wings. His breathing was more noticeable than anyone else's, and eventually they all looked at his heaving chest as it labored up and down. Their friend was dying. Izzy went over to him and helped remove Charlie's coat, but grabbed him in her arms in horror when she noticed how black his heart had become. The protective glass was gone. Shattered. Left on the Alchemist's platform and all that remained was damaged beyond repair.

Isabella let out a heart-wrenching plea, "HE'S DYING! We have to do something, please!"

"I'm sorry. I don't know what to do," the Jackboot said exhaustedly.

"He's my brother, Daddy! Big Bear told me!" Only her father knew of whom she spoke, for it was her secret nickname for Bobby " the Kitchen" Mahoney since the age of four.

"I know, baby," trying to hold on to the little piece of strength left inside him, he didn't dare tell her Big Bobby was dead. She had just learned her mother was alive, but evil, and her half-brother, finally found, was now dying in her arms.

"My son—my—my wife, I-I have lost my son," the Jackboot said of Wyatt.

"What?" Izzy looked at him, confused and shaking, with irritated eyes, "Wyatt?"

"Yes," he looked down at his iron boots.

"Wyatt wasn't your son, Daddy. He wasn't even Vanessa's child. Bobby thought Elias was, but he didn't know Momma was alive. He didn't know she was a—a—one of those THINGS!" she punched the wall beside Elias with her mod-hand, crushing a dent in it, but the Jackboot didn't care. If he'd had the strength, he would have demolished his whole train with his boots at this point. No son. Dead wife returned to him a witch, ex-wife the same, and his old foe still alive. He hadn't even put a dent in the charmers after burning their whole valley years ago. They'd only grown stronger. The word failure crept into his mind like a rotten river, and he felt that old maddening spirit of vengeance strangling his soul.

"I'm sorry, darling, but Big Bear is dead. Killed by Edgar," he couldn't stop himself. He wanted her to be angry, like him. In pain, like him. Filled with burning fury at her mother, as he was right now, but he didn't consider how hard it would be for her at that moment.

Isabella felt the world stop. Everything in the room became hard. All the edges and corners seemed overly crisp with danger, and the train car felt more like a casket than a place for the living. She sat there next to her dying brother, imagining Big Bear lying alone, deep in the cold, harsh earth, without a last kiss from her to thank him for everything. For being a father when she had none. For teaching her to be brave in a terrifying world. The sound of the Iron Weaver chugging and clacking receded in her ears, and the smell of vanilla returned as her head cleared. Her hand started to shake until Elias took hold of it to steady it. It made her feel small but loved.

"I'm sorry, but who is Big Bear?" Prince Enupnion asked.

"He was my friend. The one who raised my dear Isabella after we lost her mo…" he stopped.

In a most strange and awkward moment, the old hunch-backed prince jumped to his feet with maddening laughter. Everyone thought he'd lost his mind, and Izzy was ready to drive her baton into his skull for the offensive timing of his mental breakdown. The prince picked up the weary Jackboot and lifted him against the wall of his train, knocking a stuffed bird onto the floor. The Jackboot quickly pushed him away in disgust.

Elias had no energy to speak or react to the outlandish behavior and simply sat there blank faced, watching the old hunchback finally crack into madness. Then Elias slumped over on the floor. No one noticed because they were all so captivated by the return of the crazed old hunchback.

"FRIEND OF THE BEAR! FRIEND OF THE BEAR," he cackled, jumping up and down in the car, flinging feathers in the air. "It all makes sense. Prophecy is never what it seems. Never what it seems until it slaps you upside the head! HAHA!" He hit himself in the back of the head, drawing a smirk from Merlin.

Finally Epekneia, filled with embarrassment, stood up and tried to calm the prince, but he knocked her down. Hopping up and down like a chicken before its fed caused a slight grin to emerge on Elias' pale face at his old friend's strange happiness.

The Jackboot mustered some strength and grabbed the crazed prince, slamming him against the wall.

"What your problem, freak?" he asked.

"You're the friend of the bear."

"Huh? So what!"

The prince pointed at Elias, "He's your son."

"Have you gone mad, Hunchy?" Bogan felt the prince needed an insult for acting such a fool.

Izzy stood up fast and hope smashed her in the face. Real hope, not that fake stuff peddled back at the GFC docks. "Why? How? I mean, what do you mean?" she asked.

"Is your father prone to madness and insanity?"

"Look here, you piece of ..." the Jackboot was ready to kill him now.

"Sort of," Izzy said.

"ISABELLA!"

"Yes! Yes he is. Why?" she said as her eyes filled with wonder.

Prince Enupnion grabbed the Jackboot, and with immense force, tore the back of his shirt open in front of everyone, revealing two nasty, fleshy lumps on his back. "I present to you all the lost, wingless child of the Petinon people," the prince declared.

"LIES!" The Jackboot yelled, embarrassed at the strength of the beast he'd chained in his mine.

"Oh, really? Who raised you?"

"My mother and father did, you bird brain, and those are birth marks, nothing more!"

"But Daddy, you were raised by Big Bear's mom. Grandma Cyndelia found you in the mold that day. The stories Daddy, she always told me the stories." Izzy stole his thunder.

"You didn't know your parents, did you?" The prince grinned, "You perch your train out over the mine, sniping your prey from the highest point. My loyal Petinon." The Jackboot was red faced as he removed his torn shirt, and anger filled him.

"See— right there—you're proving me right. You can't control your rage, a common trait among wingless Petinon's," Enupnion said. "And something else. It was something that stood out to me as I watched your daughter protect Elias— your lost child—son of the wingless Petinon and prophesied Destroyer. Her baton she fought with must have been forged in the fire of the berries. The way she wielded it with such skillful accuracy – like it was in the hands of a Petinon warrior. Only a true Petinon can wield a weapon forged in the sacred fires with such miraculous skill. That's why you wanted the flowers. You needed weapons to fight the Umbrella Kooks. If you hadn't panicked, I could have helped you make them, but now I know why you did. You and your daughter had seen one of us before, and I'm guessing those wings on the wall were his."

The Jackboot took a moment to process the maddening dump of information overload then looked looked at Izzy. "He didn't burn when he touched the flames. He didn't burn."

"No he didn't, did he?" Izzy smiled and for a second happiness seemed possible.

"ELIAS," Merlin cried out as he noticed Elias slumped over.

The Jackboot grabbed him, picked him up and looked at the prince, "If it's true, don't let my son die—please."

"But I don't know what to do, I—I," the prince was terrified for Elias as well. It wasn't supposed to be this way. The child wasn't supposed to die. All he could do was stand there dumbstruck. He'd finally figured out one of the greatest prophecies of his people, and it was ending before it started.

"Give him some more of those berries," Merlin said, "That

might help. Seemed to pack a fairly powerful punch back at the wizard's room."

"Yes! Yes! We need a berry. Do you have any more?" Enupnion asked the Jackboot.

"I used everything for the suit," he said dejectedly, holding his dying son in his arms. Silence fell on them all as Elias' labored breathing stung their ears with pain and their minds with emptiness.

Suddenly Iron Jaw pulled on the Iron Weaver's brakes, slowing the train to a crawl and infuriating the already confused and heartbroken father. "Why are we stopping? WHY ARE WE STOPPING? I'll rip that iron jaw off his face and melt it into a lump." The Jackboot was so furious with his conductor he grabbed the com-horn while still holding Elias. "IRON JAW," the car shook from his voice. "WHY ARE WE STOPPING?"

"Mr. Jackboot, sir, I can't go any further on account of this obstacle, sir," he chattered.

"WELL RUN IT DOWN!"

"You might want to take a look-see first, sir." The train came to a halt, and the Jackboot kicked the door open with his iron boot and stepped out without a mask. The blast of pressure from the brakes stole the air from the pressurized cabin, filling it with mist. Merlin, Gideon and Bogan practically freaked out in panic getting their masks on. Epekneia mashed one into Ava's face, but to everyone's shock, Izzy jumped out of the train without one, like her father.

"IZZY!" Bogan cried out.

"I've done it before, Bogan," she claimed. Merlin looked over at Bogan and with an uncomfortable grin, nodded his head yes.

"Is there anything else anyone would like to tell me and Bogan?" Gideon fumed but followed the rest of them out toward the Iron Weaver's obstacle.

IRON JAW WAS STANDING AT THE FRONT WHEN THE JACKBOOT SAW him and started to scold him, but the words never left his mouth. Before them stood an oak tree smack dead in the middle

of the tracks, and from its leafy, green branches were growing
fire berries. Fully ripe, deep red berries ready for picking. Half
the tree was still dead, but the other half was healed and growing. Without second guessing or wondering why or how, Enupnion swooped up to a branch and grabbed a berry. He dove
back to the tracks and placed it in Elias' mouth, then squeezed
the juice of another on his infected heart. It was a near-instant
recovery for the dying boy, who grabbed at his breaths for
several minutes in his father's arms.

It was a strange moment indeed for Elias when he got his
bearings and the Jackboot was cradling him like a child. "You
can put me down," Elias said, but the Jackboot looked at the boy
and kissed his forehead.

"I, uh, I—I don't know if you heard what your winged friend
said," the Jackboot stumbled over his words.

"I don't care what they said, just put me down, please," Elias
demanded, and the man stood his son on his feet. Elias' heart,
still black yet beating, and eyes of fire were hard to take in, but
at least he was standing.

"You're my son," the Jackboot said. Elias looked at Izzy's
beaming face, and his heart visibly jumped.

Prince Enupnion nodded his head in agreement with a nice
smile and a twinkle in his eye. "It's true. Sunago is not your
father."

"First my mom tells me some guy named Owen Brock is my
father, and now you tell me it's the Jackboot. I think I've been
lied to enough," Elias complained.

The Jackboot held out his hand for a handshake. "I'm Owen
Brock, pleased to meet you, son." His hand trembled ever so
slightly as he held it out.

It was a bit awkward to have the Jackboot staring at him
with joy, but if only an hour ago he could learn that Izzy was his
sister and his mother a witch, then anything was possible.
However, it seemed to be even more awkward for Iron Jaw, who
was having a difficult time witnessing such an emotional event
for his commander. He just wasn't geared for this sort of prissy,
emotional showboating of fathers hugging lost sons and sons
reunited with family they'd never known existed. It was all fluff

and stuff to him, and unnecessary softness that rusted the iron in his jaw. But standing there watching them, that iron jaw began to tremble, tingle, clatter and creak.

"There's more," Elias' old hunchback friend said. "Show him your back," the prince demanded of the Jackboot.

The Jackboot turned around and showed Elias the deformed lumps on his back and rolled his eyes at Izzy, who'd always thought the bumps were from a childhood injury.

The Jackboot turned around and looked at his son. "I don't know if I am what they say I am, but if I'd only have known—I —I'm sorry I didn't know you were my boy. I've—we've," he looked at Izzy, "your sister and I have looked for you for so long now, and I can't believe we've finally found you. I don't know how, but we're going to save you. I'll do everything I can to fix your heart, I promise," he knelt down and both he and Izzy embraced Elias.

Iron Jaw was still standing by the Iron Weaver, coming to grips with his emotional constipation. First he punched himself and then he punched the Iron Weaver, which got everyone's attention. Then that jaw started chattering so hard, the Jackboot thought his conductor might crumble in front of them. He'd never had a son to hold or weep for or look for and find, but today it felt like he did, and he didn't know what to do with it all. "I'm happy for you, Mr. Jackboot, sir!" he clacked out with a lump in his throat and ran back to the cabin.

"How did this happen?" Merlin was investigating the whole tree looking for the scientific explanation, but it was eluding him at the moment.

"Elias did this," Epekneia said with a big smile.

"But how?" Merlin asked.

"I don't know," Elias said, "I just threw up on the tree when Hunchy—I'm sorry." He looked at the prince, who was not offended in the least, but seemed to wear his old name with humility. "We were on the way to Mine Five when Prince Enupnion threw me over...revealed who he was. We landed here at this tree and he fed me the berry seeds to see what would happen. He wanted to know if I was the one who would lead his people to replant or the Destroyer or something." Elias looked at his heart, "I guess I'm not much of anything though."

"So you vomited on the tree and it grew the berries?" Merlin asked.

"Yeah, I guess so."

"I've heard of a plant expert with a green thumb, but never one with a vomit mouth," Bogan cracked, and Izzy socked him in the arm. It hurt him, but he smiled at his punishment.

"Iron Jaw!" the Jackboot yelled.

"YES, SIR, MR. JACKBOOT, SIR!"

"Get a container and fill it with the berries," the Jackboot said, then looked at Prince Enupnion. "It's true we forged the mods in fire from the berries when we learned the Umbrella Charmers, or Mist Speakers as you called them, couldn't cast spells on people who wore them. I even forged the Weaver's harpoon with the berries. Even my spies are wearing mods forged with the berries," the Jackboot explained, and then he addressed Gideon out of guilt for not keeping him informed.

"Gideon, the reason I couldn't send you back to get Elias' father was that Flit returned before you did, because of your detour around the storm. He brought back pictures of Umbrella Charmers all over that mountain, so I needed a new plan, and fast. I should have kept you better informed, and maybe the misunderstanding of you thinking I had killed the boy's parents wouldn't have happened. It is clear that you can be trusted with my son's life, even when I didn't know he was my son. As for the rest of you, your mods are special. You might not be able to use them as well as Isabella, but they'll keep…" the Jackboot was in the middle of his explanation when a small light approached them in the distance, coming faster and faster.

JIMMY'S BAD NEWS: MERLIN LOOKED OUT AT IT, "IT'S JIMMY!" Within seconds, a strange little boy arrived. If only you could call him a boy. He was more machine than anything, although he did have human eyes, but his whole body was robotic, and he was flying with booster rockets on his metal boots. There was hardly an indication of anything human left in him, but Merlin loved him anyway and was glad to still have his brother, at least what was left of him.

"JIMMY!" Merlin said excitedly, but the response was less than human.

"Hi, Merlin. I have a report from Father," Jimmy said.

"What is it?"

"Several Umbrella Charmers are attacking Grand Fortune City, and a large train recently passed through Karl's Labyrinth headed our way." Jimmy's words sent chills down the backs of their necks.

"Get that tree off the tracks and fill the containers. Take all the berries," the Jackboot ordered.

"But I've not completed my message, Merlin." Jimmy cocked his head as he floated above them.

"What is it, Jimmy?"

"Bosarus has returned from Mine Five, and the war bots have been destroyed."

"WHAT!" The Jackboot replied in shock. "By who?"

"The Destroyer!" In an instant Jimmy was gone, leaving nothing but a trail of smoke behind him as he rocketed back toward GFC.

NO ONE SPOKE. THE JACKBOOT'S FACE SEEMED TO TWITCH A BIT as he processed the news. Everyone else started slowly backing away, seeking the safety of the Iron Weaver, but stopped instantly when he held up his finger. He didn't want to get angry at his newly found son, but the loss was hard to calculate.

"What was so special about the bots at Mine Five?" Elias nervously asked.

He closed his eyes, trying to think of the right words, and took a deep breath. "They were forged in the fire of the berries for the resistance, so we could take back the harbor for Tom Rand. I sent Bosarus to get them, in case the Umbrella Charmers retaliated against GFC."

"OH! That's why they wanted the bots destroyed. But that would mean the Harbor Council has been..." Merlin grimaced.

The Jackboot noticed Gideon's expression at Merlin. Gideon looked like he wanted to kick himself and maybe his whole crew for swaying his decision in accepting the job. If they'd followed Gideon's gut instincts they probably wouldn't have made such a terrible error. It was a good teachable mistake for Gideon, but a terrible blow to their cause.

"The lead bot still works with my generator. If you can get me there, I'll bring it back," Elias said.

"No, it's too dangerous," the Jackboot said.

"It was my mistake, and I should be the one to fix it." Elias winked at Gideon, who seemed speechless that he was willing to take the blame. The Jackboot smiled at his twelve-year-old son's willingness to accept responsibility for the whole crew. It made him proud, but he didn't like the plan.

"No! We can't afford to lose you again." Izzy said.

"As much as I hate to split up a family reunion, I must agree with Elias. If what you say about the bots being forged in the sacred fire is true, then it makes sense that he was able to operate the bot flawlessly without ever having seen one before. The only way that would be possible is that he truly is of Petinon blood. Let's be honest, you're going to need that bot," Prince Enupnion said.

The Jackboot didn't like the idea of placing so much faith in the Petinon prince, but he'd always wondered how Isabella had become so skilled with her baton without any training. From the moment Hans forged it, she seemed invincible with it in her hands. If the prince was right, it might mean the difference between success and failure for his city.

"You can fly him the eight miles to Mine Five then?" the Jackboot asked.

"Oh—I didn't realize it was that far away. That might take some time." The Prince smirked.

"How far will this thing go?" Elias asked, pointing at the Weaver's harpoon.

"WHAT? No way! Never!" Izzy said. "I didn't take every

precaution on this trip just to launch you into the sky on the Weaver's harpoon."

The Jackboot noticed Gideon glaring straight at her. She turned away, slightly ignoring his facial expression. He'd trained her well, so well that she had kept everyone in the dark just as he had done. She had not only left Gideon and the crew out of every part of her plan, but her father as well. Even to the point of risking everyone's lives to retrieve her lost brother, but she could have told her father something. She'd become fiercely independent and for that he was proud, but maybe a little too untrusting as well.

"It'll travel about a mile," the Jackboot said.

"DADDY!" Izzy was visibly angry that her father would even consider the option. "He can't even stand up without the berries."

"Look at my heart." Elias took Izzy by her hand. "I don't have much time left. At least let me do what I can."

Merlin, who was standing over by the Iron Weaver, seemed to be calculating something in his head, as blue brain bolts were lighting up the area. "Mine Five is three miles south of GFC. If you launch the harpoon from the top of Grand Fortune City, it will get him there in less than one minute. He'll need someone light weight to go with him and help him land, as well as hide him from the charmers, especially if the Alchemist wants his heart," Merlin said looking at Epekneia, who didn't seem to need any convincing.

"I will do it," she answered.

"Wow, girl! That's was a bit fast, don't you think?" Izzy said squinting her eyes, but Epekneia ignored the overprotective sister.

"The Alchemist will need to believe that Elias is still with us," the prince explained. "Someone will need to wear his coat to keep their attention here." He looked at Merlin, who shrugged his shoulders.

"Sure, why not? It'll be fun," Merlin grinned.

"You'll need a fake black heart," Ava said in an epiphany. "I'll draw you something realistic." Then she ran into the train.

It might not have been the best plan, but at least it was something, and something was better than going off halfcocked into war with the Umbrella Charmers. The Jackboot had fought them before, during the war with Angus Grand, but at that time there were only a few and still they were not easily defeated. From what he'd seen in that room, he knew this was going to be a long day.

"This better work, bird-man, or I'll add another set of wings to my wall," the Jackboot grumbled, but the prince was not intimidated in the least bit.

"Iron Jaw!" the Jackboot called out.

"YES, SIR, MR. JACKBOOT!"

"Prep this beast for war!"

Iron Jaw pulled a red lever before they boarded, and the floors of the train cars flipped over, lifting oversized Gatling guns out the windows. Iron plates wrapped around the twelve guns, and cases of ammo lined the floors. The walls lifted into the ceilings, and it was if there was never a room with pictures or trophies of animals or even mounted eyes and tongues. The maniacal monster of iron shook the earth as it roared toward Grand Fortune City, and the flames from its stack licked the sky with angry tongues of fire. Prince Enupnion stood out on the lower cowcatcher, below the bull, and the Jackboot lit his pipe as he took his place on the golden horns, ready to protect his city, his family and his strange new friends. The Iron Weaver was ready for war. Not just any war, but a war of iron and smoke.

IRON AND SMOKE

*B*lack, billowing clouds of Umbrella Charmers approaching from the west stole away the grandeur from Grand Fortune City as the dawn exploded over the horizon behind it. Winged serpents speckled the rainless sky with wriggling tails carrying Charmer apprentices on their backs. The wailing of mothers and fathers haunted the city streets as serpents carried children off to the Valley of Bones. Some to be future Mist Speakers and others just for parts to make their dark magic.

The Iron Weaver dropped down the tunnel entrance and pulled into the mine. Heavy gunfire echoed from the city above as armed citizens sought refuge around every corner, picking off serpents one by one. The miners kept busy beating and stabbing some that fell from the sky. While one miner blasted them with a gear cooler, another would shatter them with his pickaxe. It was great work, but amateur hour at best from the Jackboot's perspective, as they barely made a dent in the slithering beasts.

Iron Jaw rounded the tower entrance about the time the biggest monster train he'd ever seen entered the mine to the left of them. His jaw practically fell off. It was a truly mystifying sight to behold. A large globe, filled with green bioluminescent liquid and black serpentine blood from Elias' heart, made it more of a wizard's lab on wheels than a comfortable means of transportation.

Large iron talons gripped the glass globe as if it were prey. The green beast fumed darkest black smoke crawling with purple lightning from four oversized, jagged stacks on each side that made the smoke look like wings as it rose into the sky. Its oversized wheels looked more like bone than iron, with the skulls of slain tunnel trolls mounted in the center. The cowcatcher at the front was lined with iron talons pointing at the ground, and a large balcony mounted on top of the globe was for the demon-wizard of Black Mist to perch himself.

The Alchemist was standing on the platform, holding both his globe staffs, when Vanessa and Cassandra landed next to him. Cassandra injected something into the globes, plugged them into his arms, and lightning bounced between them and into him. Giant black wings of smoke emerged from the mangled holes in his back, and dark words echoed through the mine, sending workers fleeing in terror.

Prince Enupnion pointed at Vanessa. "So, which one is that?"

The Jackboot took a deep draw from his pipe and let out a fierce roll of smoke. His teeth sounded like iron grinding inside his mouth when he answered.

"That's my ex-wife."

"And the other one?" Enupnion asked in classic, chipper Hunchy fashion.

"That's my dead wife, or...at least I thought she was dead."

"They certainly look angry," his old prisoner replied.

"Indeed they do, bird-man. Indeed they do."

"Going to be a bit of a day then, isn't it?"

"Yeah." The Jackboot breathed out then cracked his neck left to right and loaded a round into his rifle.

The Alchemist's dark wings of smoke crawled with bolts of black lightning as they beat the air, lifting him above the mine. His body, now glowing bright purple, seemed stronger and more powerful with each flap of his smoky wings. Once he was above the mine, he began shocking the earth with green and purple bolts of lightning from his staffs, while chanting the familiar chants of the Umbrella Charmers. The ground around them began to quake, and parts of the mine walls started to crumble.

"Iron Jaw!" the Jackboot yelled.

"Yes, sir!"

"Get us in the tower!"

"Right away, Mr. Jackboot, sir," Iron Jaw released the brakes and filled the mine with the heavy smell of burning coal.

BATTLE IN THE TOWER: BY THE TIME THE IRON WEAVER BEGAN rounding the first circular track at the bottom of the tower, those nasty serpents had already slithered their way in from the city entrance at the top. Councilman Forsythe took over the Alchemist's train while the smoke-winged charmer kept himself busy with his lightning bolt practice. Forsythe quickly followed the Iron Weaver into the tower and ordered his men to inflict some damage on the Jackboot.

"There!" Ava said, pasting her "perfectly black" drawing of a heart on Merlin's chest and squeezing his hat over his green, glowing brain.

"You'll need my coat, too…I mean Charlie's coat, if you're going to play the part," Elias said with a grimace, worried he'd offended Ava.

"It's your coat now, Elias." Ava said with a bubbly smile. "I can't wait for you to meet Charlie. You're going to…well, if he's alive…but I just know he is. I've always known," Ava said and pulled Elias in for a warm hug. Ava was so filled with hope, she'd forgotten Elias' condition was beyond repair. He accepted the hug without destroying her moment with the truth.

"Elias, it's going to be too cold up there without your coat. You need to keep it," Izzy said leaning against the wall, spinning her baton in disgust at the plan. She sounded more like a mom than a sister, but she couldn't help herself. She had dreamed of the day she would find her brother and hated this plan to her very core. She didn't want to lose the city, but more importantly, she didn't want to lose Elias.

"It's okay," Epekneia said, "he'll be warm under my wings while I'm hiding him."

"Ugh! I bet he will!" Izzy scoffed and pointed her baton. "Don't think I haven't noticed your goo-goo eyes at him!"

The room fell silent for a moment until Gideon laid out the plan for the launch to Mine Five. "Once we get to the south side of GFC we'll need a good diversion to get you and Epen— Epenkic—the bird-girl out on the Weaver's harpoon. We can't strap you to it or you might not be able to break free, so you'll just have to hold on like your lives, and ours, depend on it, because they do."

All at once it sounded as if someone was pelting the Iron Weaver with rocks, and Iron Jaw entered the car. "Iron Jaw! Who's operating the train?" Gideon asked.

"Right now she needs gunners. So grab one and let loose your inner dogs," he paused for a moment and looked at Epekneia, "...or birds of war!" He grabbed a gun, and with a pop he gave his iron jaw an adjustment, then got to work.

On the other side of the tower, the Alchemist's train was steaming up the circular tracks quickly and only one track level below them. Winged serpents filled the inside of the tower shaft with an almost formaldehyde-ish stench of venom as their fangs dripped droplets of death. Strange men fired heavy artillery from the Alchemist's beast, with no concern for allied serpents that got in their way. Clank, ting, pinging and ringing sounds covered the Iron Weaver's walls as the enemy pelted them with lead, and the smell of gun powder soon over took the serpent's stench.

Everyone manned a gun except the winged girl, and Iron Jaw was the first to let loose his maniacal madness at them. Here was a man who had seen more war in his life than a hundred life times and should have been broken by it all, but strangely seemed more comfortable behind the guns than in the mines of GFC. His face was etched in battle much like his hard personality, and he let out cries of laughter and joy at his successfully delivered punishment.

"WELCOME TO GFC, YOU SLAGS!" he clacked out, then let loose a barrage of lead at the intruders. Everyone else seemed well-versed in loading and firing the guns, but Elias had never even seen a Gatling gun before. Izzy knelt beside him, excited at the chance to teach her little brother how battle worked. She quickly loaded the ammo band and demonstrated the hand crank by ripping a good line of metal at the Alchemist's train.

"Just spin the crank and point it at anything that moves out there. Don't worry about running out. Daddy always keeps the ammo fully stocked." She winked at him and slapped him on the back. "Now give it a try." Elias popped up the metal sight, peered down the barrel and spun the hand crank, sending rounds flying at the enemy. After several cranks, the satisfaction of exploding serpents grew on him, and he felt like he could play this game all day long. Imagining that night the one choked him only seemed to tickle his trigger finger all the more.

Izzy popped some ear covers on him, and soon every Gatling gun on the train was glowing red with anger as they dropped serpents by the tens and hundreds. White smoke filled the cars, and the addictive smell of gun powder sent Iron Jaw into throws of glorious delight. Elias stopped firing and smiled as he marveled at the old warrior blasting away with glee. Time seemed to slow around Iron Jaw as smoke and flames rolled off his barrel while he embraced his chosen calling. He turned his head and squinted his left eye at Elias as if to smile, then yelled, "WHAT ARE YOU WAITING FOR? LET 'EM HAVE IT!"

Elias was a bit startled by Iron Jaw's encouragement and cranked the handle on the gun so hard it tipped the gun up towards the ceiling. Several rounds shot out and ricocheted around the car until one hit Iron Jaw right in the iron jaw. The two bolts holding the metal mouth in place popped off, sending the food grinder to the floor. Elias was horrified at his mistake, but Iron Jaw picked up the metal prosthesis, hammered it back on and shoved his broken stogie through the new hole. "Watch your aim there, young fella!" he warned, and went right back to his glorious battle.

"STOP THAT MAN!" Izzy suddenly yelled out, pointing at a man holding a large rifle and standing on top of the Alchemist's train. Everyone took aim at him, but it was too late. He fired his strange glowing round at the Iron Weaver, blasting a massive hole in the side of the car. Four winged serpents quickly made their way in, and one hooked Iron Jaw and dropped him to the floor. Izzy instantly jumped into action and practically ran on the side of the car's walls at them. Her baton, spinning in her hand with mesmerizing speed, almost became invisible.

First she drove its point into the one holding Iron Jaw, then a back flip and she grabbed another between her boots and crushed its head in a splattering, bloody mess. She dispatched the other two by simply flinging her baton at the wall of the train car and bouncing it through both of their skulls. Elias thought she'd lost her baton, as it shot right out the gaping hole in the car, but she snapped her mod-fingers together and the baton shot right back inside the car and back into her hand. He had to give it to her, his big sis was pretty awesome.

Black, green and white smoke rose inside the tower as the Jackboot's rifle shook the Iron Weaver on the tracks with every blast. Elias noticed the prince, with eyes of fire, swooping through the center of the tower, taking down large, winged serpents. Prince Enupnion shredded, ripped, gutted and sliced serpents two at a time, as if it were more sport than battle. Elias could see in Epekneia's eyes that she wanted to join the fight. From the look in her eyes, Elias could tell she wanted revenge for her father. She started to jump out the opening, but Izzy stopped her.

"Uh, um, no way, sister! You stay with him and stick to the plan." A serpent instantly wrapped around Izzy's legs, to the shock of Elias and Epekneia, but she flung her baton around her back sideways, through the serpent's body and caught it as it came out the other side. "Stick to the plan," she reminded them.

Bogan pulled out that big hand cannon of his and blasted away as many serpents he could, and even though they were dumb beasts and easy to kill, there were thousands of them. It was a nice change of pace to see Bogan smiling again.

Gideon made good use of his globe blaster, but Merlin and Ava seemed to enjoy the heavy guns for jobs like this. Every now and then Elias could feel the Iron Weaver tilt sideways from the Alchemist's lightning hitting the ground outside the tunnel. Why wasn't the Alchemist engaged in the battle? What odd purpose did it serve to strike the ground? It bothered Elias.

Surprisingly, the serpents backed away from the Iron Weaver as Umbrella Charmers began filling the inside of the tower. They held glass globes filled with that same green biolu-minescent liquid mixed with the swirling blood of Elias inside. Iron Jaw blasted away at some of their umbrellas, sending them perilously down to the earth, but others cast the globes inside the car. The globes exploded and terrifying apparitions of smoke emerged and lunged at the crew. Everyone was mystified at how to fight them, except for Isabella. With every stab, the ghosts of the black mist vanished into thin air. After disinte-grating three of them, she turned around and looked at her crew mates. "It's just smoke magic. Use your mods. The Jack-boot made them for us so we could fight these monsters." A sly grin slid across her face. "That's why he calls you his children."

Ghosts of black mist appeared from everywhere as glass globes shattered against the train amid the sounds of chanting Umbrella Charmers commanding them. Prince Enupnion kept busy darting from one umbrella to the next, ripping them to shreds, and sending them to their doom. The crew adapted quickly to the strange battle, but Elias was growing frustrated that he was unable to assist.

Suddenly, a black hand of smoke slithered through the gaping hole and into the train car. It grabbed hold of Merlin, who at first seemed to chuckle at the attempt. He laughed, "Hey, I guess the disguise worked." His laughter instantly turned to fear when it started to drag him through the car. He just assumed he would pull another shocking stunt and the hand would disappear, until he touched the hand. It had form and function unlike anything he'd imagined; even wicked finger-nails. He grabbed hold of one of the Gatling guns as it pulled him. The laughter and smiles had left him. Only fear and trem-bling gripped him now.

Benumbed by the wicked magic, his mind was bankrupt of scientific explanations and the cold, hard reality had taken hold of him. "IT'S REAL! IT'S REAL!" he cried out. "I CAN FEEL IT! GET IT OFF! GET IT OFF! HELP ME!" Bogan and Ava ran to him and pulled on the hand, but it wouldn't budge. Bogan even kicked it with his mod-leg, and a cry came from outside the train.

Izzy peered out the gunner slot. "IT'S MOMMA!"

Merlin's ghostly pale fingers lost all flow of blood and his grip slipped from the gun. The dark hand of smoke dragged him across the floor toward the opening and Elias, desperate to engage in some part of the battle, grabbed Izzy's baton out of her hand and flung it at the ghastly mist. With shocking accuracy that even surprised Izzy, he nailed it to the floor of the car. A horrible scream echoed through the tower, even drowning out the battling trains, and the hand disappeared. Elias helped the shell-shocked Merlin to his feet and rushed him back into hiding. "It's not easy being me, is it?" he asked his friend. "At least this time I got to play your part." He grinned and mashed Merlin's hat on tighter. The disheveled Merlin gave a tiny chuckle.

THE IRON WEAVER PUSHED HARD UP THE TOWER, AT SPEEDS FAR exceeding the safety of the circular tracks, with the Alchemist's train not far behind. Several times the front wheels hopped ever so slightly as the auto-feed system dumped a new load of coal into the hungry boiler. The winding turns were hard enough, but whatever was shaking the tower outside the city was making things even more edgy. If not for his magnetic boots, the Jackboot would have fallen into the mine many times over from the blasts outside. As his rifle cleaned the tower of serpents and Charmers, he wondered about the Alchemist's strategy for victory and why he was shocking the earth.

Forsythe's gunners were relentless in their task of pummeling the Jackboot's train, and as quickly as their heads disappeared another replacement took the weapon. The Jackboot watched as the bird-man he had chained for nearly a year dispatched serpents and Charmers from the air with enviable skill. Guilt for his mistake in chaining the creature snuck into his mind, but he had to wonder, how was he to know friend or foe? Sunago had stained his view of bird-people, but he was rethinking that now.

It was the right call at the time to protect Izzy, but if the prince could forgive the cruel mistake, a better future seemed possible. He didn't take much stock in what the prince said of the lumps on his back. A simple deformity, no doubt, that might help bring about a peaceful alliance with the bird-prince. Then together they could put an end to these vile charmers of smoke and mist once and for all.

Seemingly out of nowhere, two Umbrella Charmers dropped down in front of the Iron Weaver, sending smoke from their mouths in the form of wicked ropes. One wrapped around his rifle and the other around his body. They gave their magical smoke cables a yank, hoping to pull him to his doom under the wheels of his own train. However, his magnetic boots, forged in the sacred fire, held him tight to the horns. Looks of fear stole the color from their golden eyes as he wrapped his arms around the misty ropes and gave them a hard jerk. Their umbrellas popped backwards as they hurled through the air, each impaled through the horns, one to the left and the other to the right. Foolish Umbrella Charmers.

PRINCE ENUPNION MADE SHORT WORK OF THE LARGE SERPENTS and did a fair share of damage to the Umbrella Charmers as well, until one of them cast a glass ball at him. It exploded a few feet in front of him as he soared above the Iron Weaver. It trapped him inside the deadly globe of mist, sending him plummeting toward the tower floor. Epekneia hadn't taken her eyes off the battle outside the train and screamed when she witnessed her prince in distress. She started to dive after him, but, in keeping with the plan, Izzy grabbed her by the wing and stopped her. However, Elias paused their original plan of saving the city and in the confusion snatched Izzy's baton away, recklessly diving after the prince. Maybe the thought of being a Petinon had sunk in too deep. No doubt the idea was wondrous to him, but wingless Petinon can't fly.

Elias held the baton in front of him and rocketed towards his old friend like a harpoon. He could hear his sister's screams of horror at his foolish act, but he was committed to saving the old hunchback. The baton felt strange in his hands, much like the feeling he'd had back inside the bot at Mine Five. Almost as if he was somehow connected to it, and he understood all the more why Izzy was so skilled with it.

Several hands of mist reached for him as he shot towards his target, but the dark smoke magic was nothing but a failed parlor trick against the sacred metal. He closed in as the prince neared the ground and made his body as tight and small as possible. An Elias bullet, no doubt.

POP! He hit the nasty bubble and grabbed the tumbling prince, who instantly got his bearings and swooped them both into the air just above the tower entrance. With great haste, the prince worked hard at the climb while Elias battled the Charmers on the return trip. Shrieking sounds of pain filled the tower as he drove the baton into their misty mittens of smoke.

The prince dropped Elias in through the large opening in the train car and returned to his place next to the Jackboot as they neared the top of the tower. Elias handed Izzy her baton back expecting a fierce scolding, but instead was given a joyful embrace. He didn't understand how long she and the Jackboot had searched for him or what they'd endured to find him. Her connection to him was deeper than he understood, and he only hoped he would live long enough to understand it better.

BATTLE IN THE STREETS: THE JACKBOOT'S RIFLE ROCKED THE train as they exploded into the warehouse. Serpents feasting on the guards at the doors were a clear indication of how badly the city folk were handling things from their end. The Jackboot quickly cleared their devious minds of brain matter with a few rounds of lead, and the Iron Weaver's cowcatcher scraped their lifeless carcasses from the tracks. Prince Enupnion covered his face as they slammed through the doors into the city streets. They immediately caught sight of the Alchemist, who was now high over top the city, still shocking the earth with his wizard staffs.

"What do you reckon he's doing?" the Jackboot asked the prince as he fired a couple rounds at Sunago. A large green sphere protecting the Alchemist deflected the ammunition back toward the city streets.

"I'm guessing he's waking up those things," the prince replied, pointing down at a giant mole breaching through the earth.

"We need that bot," the Jackboot said, grinding his pipe at the thought of losing his city and even more so at sending his son hurling through the sky.

"I believe he can get it. I mean, he did quite well enough when he dove out of the train and saved me."

"WHAT!" He cleared a few winged snakes out of the roadway as he processed his shock.

"Oh. You didn't see that? He dove out of the train with your daughter's weapon and saved me from one of those mist traps. He is bold—and brave," the prince said, trying to build the Jackboot's confidence.

"He really is my son, isn't he?" the Jackboot said with a gleam in his eye.

The prince smiled. "I do believe he is."

The city streets were filled with thick mustachioed men with stogies battling serpents, still others were dragged off in horror by Umbrella Charmer's smoke traps. One finely dressed lady with a large handbag swatted a serpent out of the air and into a cake shop window. The angry owner blasted it to bits, sending icing splattering all over the side of the Iron Weaver as they passed by. Iron Jaw didn't seem to mind the tasty treat speckled on his face as he continued blasting away. Several people rushed across the tracks, trying to get to the safety of stronger buildings at their own peril. A mother with her baby would not have made it across if not for a man on an Ever-Wheel grabbing them in the nick of time.

High above the city streets, Sunago called forth his giant beasts from the earth, shaking the city tower enough to rock the trains sideways on the tracks. Forsythe was not far behind in his effort to stop them, although he had no inclination of their plans to launch Elias at the south end of the city. His goal was to simply knock them off the tracks so Cassandra could get her boy back. He closed in on the rear of the Iron Weaver enough to get some of his men on the back car about the time the Whisper crew crawled out of the large hole looking to engage them. Forsythe's men did just that, sending a barrage of bullets whizzing by them.

To keep the attention of their enemies on Merlin, Bogan slipped on the Jackboot's bulletproof coat and drew his hand cannon. He walked across the top of the Iron Weaver's car toward Forsythe's men, with Merlin behind him, while Epekneia flew Elias to the front of the train. Iron Jaw returned to his duties at the front of the train, and Izzy and Gideon joined Bogan. However, Ava stayed inside to clear the sky of serpents and Charmers.

Bogan enjoyed the feeling of the bullets bouncing off him as he clipped the men off the back of the Weaver with his gun, but Forsythe hit him with a larger weapon, knocking him off the train. He tumbled through the street but raised his thumb in the air and laughed as the crew continued through the city without him.

They had to keep Merlin visible long enough for Elias and Epekneia to launch, but it was getting harder to provide the illusion that he was Elias now that Bogan was gone. Merlin couldn't be completely exposed, or they would figure him out. His size was a close match to Elias' but his face was not, and his green eyes didn't help either. Gideon moved in front of his crew and his mod-hand spun into a shield. They knelt down behind him and fired away at Forsythe's men.

The ground outside the mine bubbled dirt into mounds as fierce claws slowly emerged, pulling monstrous moles out of the earth. Sunago directed the smaller ones with dark mind-altering chants to attack the base of the city tower, and they slammed their heads fiercely into the side of it, staining the tower red with their blood. Even Forsythe seemed shaken by the Alchemist's attempts to bring down GFC, as he was still chasing the Iron Weaver through the streets. But Sunago only cared about bringing down the city where the Jackboot cleaved his wings. For him it was a vile monument that reminded him of his terrible loss at the Jackboot's hands. Not that he'd forgotten his goal of removing the prophesied child's heart. Soon, very soon.

Dark clouds of mist filled the city streets, and out of the blackest mist Cassandra and Vanessa descended above the Iron Weaver. The prince and the Jackboot were preparing Elias and Epekneia for launch with a large bag of fire berries when Momma Cassandra sensed something strange about her son. He didn't look right. She stopped mid-air and spoke her words of witchery. Elias was the first to hear and feel her words, but almost immediately after, the Jackboot and Izzy looked up at her. They heard it too. She was calling her son, begging him to return to her. She pointed at Merlin.

"IMPOSTER!" she wailed.

"THE JIG IS UP!" Merlin yelled, and they all ran for the front of the train.

Through the city streets, serpents approached from every-where. Hundreds of the bat-winged beasts, small and large, aimed directly for Elias, who had already wrapped his legs around the Weaver's harpoon in preparation for launch. The serpents descended like flies, as he was stuck out in the open like meat on a shish kabob. Epekneia did her best to get to him, but she couldn't break free from the onslaught of the winged, tongue-flicking freaks.

One wrapped around Epekneia's throat and lifted her into the air. Izzy gave a careful assessment and flung her baton at it. The sacred metal slid so close to Epekneia's wing, it slightly cut the top of it before sinking deep into the beast's skull. Epekneia caught herself and swooped onto the Weaver's harpoon, covering Elias with her wings. Prince Enupnion flew over them and kept the serpents busy as the train neared the launch point at the edge of the docks.

Vanessa conjured a large mist-hammer and brought it down on top of Gideon, knocking him off the train and into a light pole. He lay motionless as the Iron Weaver roared on. She raised it for another swing, and Izzy sent the baton like a missile straight at her, but a serpent swooped in front of her, giving the ultimate sacrifice for his master.

"*Misssed Meeee, Issssaabeelllaaa!*" Vanessa mocked. Izzy snapped her fingers, calling back her baton, but Vanessa grabbed her with a giant mist-hand and lifted her into the air, then dropped her toward the city streets.

However, a mother's instinctive nature is not so easily discarded, and much to Vanessa's disgust, Cassandra caught her child about the time the baton returned to her hand. Izzy didn't know what to think. She didn't trust her mother any more than she trusted Vanessa and couldn't understand why the woman had saved her, but she knew at its root there was a sinister motive at work.

"HEY, VANESSA!" Izzy called out, still resting safely in the palm of her mother's dark hand of smoke. Vanessa looked down at her as Isabella flung her baton over the top of Vanessa's head.

"*Misssssed agaaaain, Issssaaabeellllaaa.*" Vanessa's face went blank when Izzy grinned and snapped her mod-fingers, returning her baton through Vanessa's chest and back into her hand. Shrieks of horror filled the city skies as Umbrella Charmers witnessed Vanessa falling, and even Sunago turned his gaze toward the loyal servant's collapse.

Cassandra's hand of smoke disappeared from around Izzy, dropping her on top of the Iron Weaver as she reached for Vanessa. But her smoky hand had not fully formed and Vanessa fell through it and onto the tracks. Forsythe pulled hard on the brakes, but the fast moving beast rolled over Vanessa's body as the Iron Weaver roared on toward the docks.

Iron Jaw stopped the train at the edge of the docks while their enemy was busy mourning Vanessa's mangled body. Ava continued clearing as many oncoming serpents as possible, while everyone else prepped the harpoon for launch. The progress of the attacking moles on the tower was quite clear to them now that the train had stopped and they felt the tower shifting back and forth. Sunago noticed they had stopped and curiously turned his eyes toward them.

"DO IT NOW!" the prince demanded of the Jackboot, who placed his hand on the launch lever. He looked out at Epekneia, covering the son he'd looked for for so long, in fear he would never see him again. Hidden under Epekneia's wings, Elias heard his father call out to him.

"ELIAS!" he yelled. The Jackboot never had a father to tuck him in bed at night or teach him to say things like, "I love you" or "Good job, son." No one to patch a bruised knee after a fall or hug him after someone crushed his feelings. All he could think of was the truth he felt in his bones and that maybe the boy would understand what he meant. "YOU'RE MY SON! YOU HEAR ME! YOU'RE MY SON!"

"DO IT NOW!" Enupnion cried out as Sunago turned his staffs toward them. The Jackboot pulled the lever, and the Weaver's harpoon shot out of the bull's mouth with a blast that knocked Enupnion off the train. They watched the harpoon rocket away from GFC only to be followed by a wicked bolt of purple lightning from the Alchemist's staffs, shocking the harpoon in the sky. Elias felt Epekneia's body go limp, and he held her tight as they soared hopelessly through the sky.

21

IRON ROCKET

*I*f not for the dark battle of iron and smoke taking place behind them, it would have been a beautiful day. The morning had risen above the mine, casting golden rays of light across the bottom of puffy white clouds. Overhead a deep blue sky shouted victory as Elias and Epekneia soared to their doom, their friends back at GFC totally unaware of the tragic outcome of the plan as they spiraled wildly out of control.

Elias held her as tight as he could, but the violent wind crossing over her wings was pulling them apart. At one point the wind caught her wings and lifted the harpoon higher into the sky. He closed his eyes and placed his face next to hers to see if she was breathing. Her face was warm, but no warmth came from her mouth. She was gone. The Alchemist's lightning had stopped her heart. If he couldn't revive her, they would both soon be dead and the battle lost. Maybe, just maybe, he could, if only he could reach a fire berry, but he didn't want to let her go. His anger at Sunago deepened and he hoped to survive, if only long enough to make his false father pay for the ruin of his life and for hurting her. With Mine Five closing in, he had no other options, and so he let her go.

Epekneia fell towards the earth. Elias let go of the harpoon, and fumbled around the bag for a berry. Several flew out before he was able to close it again, but once he had one, he shoved the berry into his mouth and dove after her. In his effort to grab her, he hit her hard in the back, so hard, the impact restarted her heart. He could see by the look of her face she was conscious as they tumbled together toward the earth. Only moments from the ground, he breathed fire berry smoke into her mouth. Her eyes lit up red with flames, and she opened her wings in a landing position. It was enough to slow the impact, but they hit hard on the third bench wall and stopped tumbling right before the edge.

Epekneia lay still, looking into the sky as the fire berry did its work to revive her. She had not eaten, nor had she touched the berries, since her mother and father's failed attempts to force the prophesy on her. She had always worried the next berry she ate might be the death of her, but as she lay there her heart was filled with hope. She felt stronger than she had in years, and the pain and suffering of Gabriel's Harbor disappeared from her thoughts. She felt refreshed and alive.

Elias walked over to her as she lay staring at the sky. "You can't lay here forever," he said. She smiled back at him, catching her breath. He reached out his hand and helped her to her feet. His fiery eyes were unlike anything she'd ever seen among her people during their efforts to force the prophecy. He was different and not at all what her parents had dreamed the prophesied child would be, but she also was not what they'd envisioned. The worst had happened; to be named the most beautiful Petinon child her people had ever seen, only to be disfigured by the flames and marked as a fraud. However, her burned face didn't make him uncomfortable or ashamed. He had no political agenda and his motives were unsoiled by the leaders of the convocation. His only agenda was to live long enough to save his friends, and she was drawn to him all the more for it.

Staring into his flaming eyes, she surprised herself and embraced him. She quickly let go, realizing her overzealous act of affection, but her joy at witnessing the coming of the prophesied child was uncontainable. She stepped back and prepared an apology, but he looked at her and said, "We need to get going or the city is going to fall."

"Of course." She nodded in agreement.

THEY RAN TO THE LEAD BOT, STILL LYING WHERE ELIAS HAD LEFT it, and climbed in. He loaded his generator full with berries and plugged in the bot. He slid his hands into the gloves and his feet into the boots, and he instantly recognized the same feeling he'd felt with Izzy's baton in his hands. Only now he understood better than before. The sacred metal was part of him. Part of the Petinon people, a people he never knew existed, but wished he had.

He only hoped he could right the wrong his mother had wrought on the world by giving power to the Alchemist with his blood. Truth mattered, but darkness had lied to him. It had lied to him his whole life. Those words from the Jackboot's train were more advice than he'd gotten from Sunago in twelve years of lies and torture. Still, his connection to the metal made the idea of being a Petinon easier to accept than the Jackboot being his father. Maybe in time he could learn to accept that as well, even believe it.

A red light began to flash – MANUAL MODE – he waited for the green. When it popped on the gloves and boots vacuumed around his hands and feet, and every light in the bot went mad with excitement. The bot felt as if he was moving in his own flesh as he adjusted the legs and stood up to get his bearings. He lifted the harvesting hammer off the ground and started to leave, but over the wind came a whispering voice. It was very clear and very familiar to him, and it said plainly, "*The Weaver's Rod.*" Elias looked at the bottom of the mine and noticed the Weaver's harpoon driven into the ground, and he remembered what the Jackboot had said about it being forged in the fire with the berries. He engaged the controls for a jump and the bot dropped down beside the harpoon. Twisting his hand in the controls, he maneuvered the bot's arm to grab it.

"Hang on tight!" he warned. Epekneia lit up the biggest smile he'd ever seen, then he mashed his thumb down on the thruster button. The metal bot shook violently as it rose out of the mine, above the mist and into the glorious rays of sun beaming in all directions.

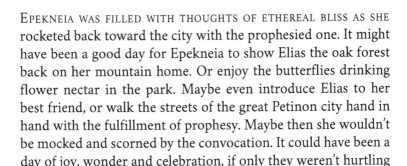

EPEKNEIA WAS FILLED WITH THOUGHTS OF ETHEREAL BLISS AS SHE rocketed back toward the city with the prophesied one. It might have been a good day for Epekneia to show Elias the oak forest back on her mountain home. Or enjoy the butterflies drinking flower nectar in the park. Maybe even introduce Elias to her best friend, or walk the streets of the great Petinon city hand in hand with the fulfillment of prophesy. Maybe then she wouldn't be mocked and scorned by the convocation. It could have been a day of joy, wonder and celebration, if only they weren't hurtling to war inside a furious monster of iron.

THE UMBRELLA CHARMERS WANTED NOTHING TO DO WITH Bogan as he walked the city streets in the Jackboot's coat. He greatly enjoyed his illusion as the Jackboot. Serpents fled from him in terror as he clipped off wings with his hand canon and batted smaller ones across the road. It was a fun game, and he only wished Charlie was there with him. Just the thought of Charlie being alive sharpened his aim all the more. When he ran out of ammo, he walked over to a man blasting away at nothing and stole the gun out of his hands. "Thanks, Mr." He smiled and continued his game of slaughter the street serpents.

The rest of the crew had taken the bullet riddled Iron Weaver back to the Jackboot's perch overlooking the mine and barred the iron doors shut. Although, no one knew what had become of Gideon. The Jackboot was picking off smaller moles with his large rifle while Ava, Merlin, Bosarus and Iron Jaw hammered away on the Gatling guns, doing as much damage as possible. The trouble with the smaller moles was that it took a whole case of ammo to bring one down, and the tower was becoming more unstable by the minute.

Enupnion had taken Izzy to the bottom of the mine to help bring down the moles next to the tower with her baton. Reluctantly, she allowed him to carry her as he swooped over top the moles, and she sent forth her blood-thirsty baton at them. The foundation of GFC had already tilted slightly, and no matter how many moles they killed, more just kept clawing their way out of the earth. Where was Elias? Did he make it? No one knew, and exhaustion was beginning to overcome them. Not to mention they were running dangerously low on ammunition.

Izzy began directing her baton at the moles' eyes, because the hides were so thick it couldn't drive deep enough to stop them. By the time she'd blinded three goodly sized ones that were beating their heads into the tower, her mother arrived with twenty powerful Umbrella Charmers. Evil chanting filled the mine, and men began to flee in terror. Blackest mist rolled from their wicked tongues as they formed giant hammers of mist, and at the command of the Alchemist's wife, they began beating the side of the city tower.

Men and women fled the city in air ships and speeders and some even fled to the tunnels. Izzy flung her baton at her mother, but the powerful sorceress caught it. No matter how hard Izzy tried to snap it back, her mother held tight and wouldn't let it go. Enupnion swooped Izzy into a tunnel away from danger and let her down a good distance away from her mother.

"DID YOU SEE THAT?" Izzy asked the prince.

"Yes."

"HOW DID SHE DO THAT?"

"I don't know, but your father needs to get out of the city. Everyone needs to get out. They're going to bring it down."

"WHERE'S ELIAS? THE CITY IS GOING FALL!" The

sound of battle was still ringing in her ears, and she didn't realize she was repeating the prince. The banging of metal from the Charmer's hammers echoed through mine, only deafening their ears more.

"I don't know where he is. They should have been back a long time ago. Something must have..." Suddenly he closed his eyes and muttered something under his breath.

THE JACKBOOT AND HIS SPIES FOUGHT HARD ABOVE THE MINE, BUT it was clear to him now that he might lose his city. He'd stopped shooting, and now all he could do was gaze at her commanding her evil charmers to bring down everything he'd built. The love of his life and mother of his children had now become his enemy. He dropped his rifle. He couldn't stop looking at her. It had been so long, and he had buried her in his heart and mind many times over. Only in his dreams had he seen her face again, and for a whole year all he wanted to do was resurrect her in his sleep. If he died today, at least he had seen her face one last time before life had ended.

Merlin was yelling behind him as the door to his library garage burst open with an influx of Forsythe's gunners and serpents. They charged the Iron Weaver, and everyone ran for cover. Bullets flew in every direction around the train, but the Jackboot refused to hide. He searched the mine for his dear Isabella, but she was nowhere to be found. He could no longer feel the connection to his lost son. Failure, despair and madness took hold of him as he looked into Cassandra's hollow eyes for some sign of affection. He walked out to the edge of the platform and resolved himself to death. If she still held love in her heart for him, she would catch him. If not, she would let him die.

Much to everyone's shock, something hit the earth and hit it hard. It shook ground. It shook the tower. It shook the moles, and it even shook the Alchemist's attention away from his shocking, mole-raising task. Cassandra and her Umbrella Charmers halted their hammering, and Forsythe's men stopped their assault on the Jackboot. Everyone looked to the south of the tower in wonder.

The Jackboot thought it was just another powerful attack by the Alchemist to bring down his city, and the Alchemist feared the Jackboot had acquired reinforcements. Confused and bewildered, everyone directed their gazes towards a large cloud mushrooming above the black mist just outside the city. The silence of battle was replaced by the groaning iron tower and the slow rumble of earth from the biggest mole yet, about to surface.

About the time the Alchemist decided to return to calling forth his Goliath mole, an ear piercing, brain cringing sound of screeching metal echoed from deep inside the mist. It was so horrible, some of the smaller moles quickly dug themselves back into the earth to escape the spine-raking noise. It was enough to drive a sane and stable-minded person to flee to the safety of the Jackboot's arms. In an instant it stopped. Cassandra looked up at him; he pulled his head back a bit and shrugged his shoulders.

"Don't look at me; I've no idea what it is."

She commanded her Smoke Charmers to raise their hammers and continue their work, but the horrible screeching shot through the mist again. This time it was followed by a thump and a scrape, then a thump and a terribly deep, unintelligible voice spoke through the mist. It was enough to make Sunago envious of its power to strike fear in the hearts of the miners.

Burning moles ran forth from the mist and into the mine, some falling to their doom as the noise grew closer and closer. The voice and screeching became even more maddening and louder than before, and some Charmers began to cover their ears, while others fled in fear. Enupnion flew Izzy up to ground level, and they looked into the mist to see if they could tell what it was. The whole battle field was mystified, waiting for the creature to reveal itself, and they wondered if perhaps the noise of the battle had awakened a terrible beast. As it screeched out its ghastly cries of pain, everyone gripped their weapons tight, anticipating the worst.

ELIAS AND EPEKNEIA HAD LANDED HARD IN A FOREST OF DEAD trees and jagged rocks. Their impact zone was massive, partly due to landing on unstable ground caused by an oil pocket. The oil began to shoot straight into the air. Unfortunately, the impact also popped a steam hose on the bot's arm that was carrying the harpoon. Elias climbed the bot out of the hole, dragging the harpoon behind him and throwing sparks back towards the rising fuel. The explosion was so powerful it leveled the dead trees around them and sent a massive cloud into the sky. Unbeknownst to either of them, the bot was covered in the gooey fuel.

Epekneia worked as fast as she could to fix the popped steam line, but she'd never worked on equipment like this before, and talons didn't help. Elias had no time to waste. They'd have to fix it on the move. He had to get to the mine before the battle was over and the city lost. The bot's loose arm dangled behind them, dragging the harpoon's blade across every sharp rock along the way, making a terrible sound.

"HURRY!" Elias yelled out.

"I'm trying," Epekneia said, soaked by the steam, "But you have to stop for a minute so I can get the line back on." She grabbed a pair of gloves and practically shredded them getting them on, but she was able to push the line back in and the leak stopped.

"Got it!" she smiled and shook the water off her wings, splattering it all over Elias. They shared a laugh for a moment until some wires overhead began to spark and the arm dropped again with a heavy thud.

"UGH!" Epekneia groaned.

"I have to keep going. Do the best you can," Epekneia grabbed the wires and started twisting them together as best she could, but she couldn't find anything to repair them permanently.

"We're close. I can see the top of the city now. Are you done yet?" Elias asked.

Epekneia looked at him with her face covered in grime. "I'm doing the best I can, you know." She raised her gloves, showing him her talons poking through, hoping that would explain her difficulty with the wires.

"I-I'm sorry. Keep trying." Elias gritted his teeth as the mist began to clear around them the closer they got to the opening of GFC's mine.

"Do you smell that?" Elias asked.

"EXCUSE ME?" Epekneia thought he was accusing her of smelling bad, but unbeknownst to both of them, the outside of the bot had ignited and was covered in flames. They were also unaware of the damage to the external communication system. Everything they were saying was being broadcast everywhere in some garbled mess of infernal madness enough to send Charmers fleeing for their lives.

"GOT IT!" Epekneia hollered and the bot's arm lifted the harpoon off the ground. Elias filled his generator hopper with berries and mashed down on the lid. He didn't want to run out now. He knew he was beginning to feel the exhaustion from his damaged heart, and for good measure he had Epekneia give him three berries. He warned her to take cover, in case he exploded all over the inside of the bot, but she refused to leave him. He popped the berries into his mouth and walked through the mist toward the city.

"I hope we're not too late," Elias said.

CLOUDS OF MIST ROLLED AWAY, AS IF THE MIST ITSELF WERE BEING forced to flee some terrible nightmare. Battle weary, good and wicked both stood watching the coming of something truly terrifying. Something they had never witnessed before. It was burning bright as the sun and lit the ground around it with flames as it walked ever closer. Black smoke poured from its head, and it carried some kind of flaming weapon in its hand. It stopped just outside the mist and looked over the battlefield, then spoke the most horrible, terrifying shrieks that echoed into the mine below. Strong men, battle hardened men, froze in their tracks.

"Why aren't they coming after me? I'm right here!" Elias asked Epekneia.

"I don't know? Maybe it's over."

"Did we win?" Elias asked. He beat the harpoon twice on the ground and motioned with his other hand for them to come at him, but no one moved or spoke. The flames were so bright and fierce, no one could tell it was a bot. All they saw were gigantic flames speaking. They were terrified. However, the Jackboot was impressed by the fiery beast's efforts to steal his title of burning man.

An enormous mole emerged from the ground directly in front of Elias. It was twice the size of the flaming steam bot, with claws to match its powerful body. It should never have gotten in his way. He raised the harpoon, and with one swipe he cleaved off its left claw, then ran the harpoon straight through its head. The beast slumped over and fell back into its hole.

"Ugh! I can't stand moles," he told Epekneia. "One time in the greenhouse I killed at least thirty in a single day. They ruin everything you plant."

However, those outside heard a more sinister voice filled with anger and vengeance. Then one man dropped his weapon and cried out in terror as he fled the battlefield, "THE DESTROYER COMES!"

22

THE DESTROYER'S HEART

"*E*LIAS!*"* Izzy shouted. The Jackboot heard Izzy's voice and spotted her standing next to the prince. That alone would have been enough hope for him, but to hear her call out Elias' name, strengthened him all the more. He sensed the battle was turning in their favor.

"My son. My boy." he said to himself in admiration as he watched the fiery bot cut down the giant beast. "MY SON HAS RETURNED!"

The magnificent morning sky had been swallowed up in the darkest black clouds, striking green and purple bolts of lightning all around the Alchemist. Sunago's complexion was now a darkish purple, and his wings of smoke had their own electrifying bolts crawling, climbing and sneaking their way out, like feathers breaking free in the wind.

An Umbrella Charmer rose up next to him and injected more dark liquid into his powerful globes, and once again the Alchemist lit the sky with lightning. A stray bolt came out from his staffs and hit the Umbrella Charmer fleeing away from him, who was instantly vaporized into a cloud of gray ash. The ground began to shake, and moles poured forth like water from the earth; giant moles, angry green ones, terrifying and deformed.

The hour of destruction had finally come upon Grand Fortune City, but who and what was to be destroyed was yet to be determined. Not even the Destroyer knew who or what he was to destroy, or if he would be the one doing the destroying at all. Elias only knew he needed to save his friends and their city and was battle ready to do so. Some of the Jackboot's men fled in horror at Elias' arrival, while others stood bewildered and confused at his joy and wondered if he'd had formed an alliance with the Destroyer.

Cassandra took advantage of the Jackboot's distraction and immediately smashed her dark hammer of smoke into the tower, knocking him off the edge and sending him plummeting toward the mine floor. If not for Enupnion, he surely would have died that day, but the Petinon had looked his way when he cried out and dove after his old captor. Enupnion caught him at the halfway mark as he swooped back into the air, but the Jackboot was too heavy and they both spiraled to the ground. It was a hard hit, but nothing either of them hadn't experience before.

They adjusted their sore bones from the impact and got to their feet. The Jackboot was clearly embarrassed by his old prisoner saving him and did his best to hide it. He gave the prince a slap on the chest for a thank you and hopped a speeder back up to his tower. Prince Enupnion darted back to Izzy and they both agreed to return to the Iron Weaver to help their friends fight off Forsythe's attack.

HIGH ABOVE THE CITY, SUNAGO CALLED FORTH HORRIBLY disfigured moles to stop Elias before he gained any momentum. He sent them charging; biting, scratching, clawing with nasty madness at Elias. Some had claws coming out of their backs, and others had claws coming out of their claws. Some had multiple, tiny greenish eyes and others were utterly blind. Elias beat them, sliced them and hacked them into a bloody mess as their heads rose from the ground.

Once they were above the ground, they moved with surprising speed, snorting dirt and creeping mold out their nostrils as they shook the earth. Heavy grunting sounds came from deep inside their empty bellies as they leapt into the air above the flaming bot. The Iron Weaver's harpoon finding its mark just under their fatty bellies made quick work of the gruesome creatures.

Elias spun the Weaver's harpoon in the bot's hand, slicing moles to the left and the right. Their thick, meaty hides were no match for the harpoon's sacred metal, and it cut through them with ease. As the dead moles began to pile high around him, he made an effort to stay above the fray, but they just kept coming, until finally he was buried beneath their bodies. While more piled on, Elias jabbed the harpoon through the dead ones, stabbing as many as he could until the loose ground beneath his feet crumbled. It was weak and thin from the digging moles, and his bot collapsed through into a large mole cavern. The dead ones piled high on top of him, filling the hole and blocking his exit back to the top.

"HANG ON!" he told Epekneia and he mashed down on the thruster button. Unfortunately, he didn't know what direction the bot was pointed, and they launched straight through the tunnel and blew out through the mine wall. By now the flames on the bot were extinguished, and it was clear to everyone the Destroyer might just be a simple harvesting bot gone mad.

Two enormous moles, beating their heads against the tower, were hit with a bolt from Sunago's staffs, and they turned around and went straight for Elias. One of them crushed the bot's left arm, sending sparks all over Elias and Epekneia. The heavy blow made him drop his harpoon and the other monster jumped on top of them. Elias wrestled with the beast as best he could, but he couldn't get it off. They rolled and smashed into walls and mining equipment until the beast pinned Elias to the side of the tower.

The one that had smashed his bot's arm joined back in battle and tried rooting around to get in under the other one. It had a deformed claw that seemed to poke straight at the one on top of him, and Elias seized the opportunity by grabbing the claw and stabbing it into the head of its fellow dirt digger. It let out a horrible groaning sound, reared up and fell over backward, wriggling all over the ground.

The other beast was caught off guard by the strike, so Elias reached over and tore off the rest of his bot's arm and began to beat the beast with it. It was a furious spanking from the Destroyer, and Elias shamed the beast so badly it ran back into the mine tunnel. What felt like a good victory to Elias, quickly vaporized when the mine began filling with smaller moles. They were so numerous he could barely get his footing with the bot as they covered the ground like rats on a feeding frenzy. No matter how many he killed, more just kept coming, and now that the bot's fire was out, the Umbrella Charmers were more emboldened to attack.

It wasn't a matter of skill that concerned Elias, for he was doing extremely well beating the smaller moles with his broken arm, but the problem was quantity not quality. They needed more than just one sacred metal bot with a prophesied Destroyer to handle this many moles. They needed a hundred bots, each with their own Destroyer.

At Cassandra's command, the Umbrella Charmer's stopped smashing their smoky hammers on the side of the tower and turned them on Elias. With haste, he blocked the first hammer using the bot's broken arm and then flung it at the Charmers, knocking them out of the sky. Spotting his harpoon, he rolled over top the moles like rushing water and reaching down into the mess he grabbed it. Several hits from the Charmer's hammers pushed him deeper into the mess of moles until he finally pulled his way out.

From the mouth of a dark, green-toothed Charmer a spear of smoke emerged. It was instantly hurled at Elias, but it missed him by just a pinch and instead sliced through several moles splattering slimy guts all over his bot. Then several other Charmers joined in with spears of their own, sending them soaring down into the bot's chest. Much to their shock, the spears left not a single mark on the bot, and fear crawled across the Charmers' faces.

More Umbrella Charmers deserted the battle for fear the

prophecies of the Destroyer were about to come true, but they never made it past Sunago and Cassandra, for their masters did not tolerate deserters. The Alchemist stuck down some, and his wife formed a bow and killed the others with her black misty arrows. That ended the desertion of Umbrella Charmers, and from that point on their obedience was secured.

In a surprising change of course, the moles began digging back into the ground. It cleared the ground for better battle, but confused Elias. He suffered major blows from the Umbrella Charmers' hammers as he tried to figure out the changing battlefield. The moles seemed to be trying a new attack strategy to bring down the tower.

"I think they're trying to dig out the foundation!" Elias said to Epekneia. Then suddenly the whispering voice came to him.

"Do you hear that?" he asked her.

"Hear what?"

"The voice, can you hear the voice?"

"No. What does it sound like?"

"It's a whisper, or well, it was a whisper, but now it's loud. It's never been this loud before. I thought maybe you could hear it too." Elias blocked swinging hammers as he continued talking.

"But I'm not the Destroyer. Why would you think I could hear his voice?"

"His voice? Whose voice?"

"Prince Enupnion's."

"Why would I hear his voice?"

"Only the prophesied one can hear his voice. He was told of the prophecy as a child, and ever since he has always tried to find the prophesied one by whispering. Among our people he is called the Whispering Prince. You didn't know this?"

"NO! How could I know? I don't know anything about the prophecies."

"What's he saying?"

"DESTROY THE ALCHEMIST!"

"THEN DO IT!" Epekneia yelled.

It was the clear direction he needed. A target to strike and a way to win. Elias set his sights on Sunago, the Alchemist, that false father. He hit the thruster button and launched into the air. He was instantly hit with two smoke hammers, sending him crashing right back into the mine, but he got his bearings and launched the bot again. He blocked the next attack and struck the Charmers with the harpoon.

It was messy work, but they were evil and he needed to save the city. The fight went full force in the air, and he could feel his strength leaving his body as the berries began to wear off. He crushed and sliced at the Umbrella Charmers, making his way toward the Alchemist. They tried hard to stop him, and even Mother Cassandra fought against him. Their efforts were futile, mostly due to the sacred fire the bot was forged in. It confused them, and they fell under the blade of his harpoon, ten Charmers at a time, as he swung it like a windmill.

"Epekneia! I-I can't see! I'm blacking out!" The winged girl grabbed three more berries and put them in his mouth, but it didn't work. Elias' heart was growing too weak even for the berries to help him. The damage was so bad the berries were no longer healing his heart but destroying it.

"MORE!"

"WHAT? NO!"

"I-I'm not going to make it. We have to stop him. Just—just do it." Elias felt his body weaken. Epekneia put four more berries in his mouth and took cover inside a storage container.

His sight returned, but the world around him turned completely red. He could only see the glowing shadows of the Umbrella Charmers around him, but at least he could see something. He sliced the harpoon, clearing away a wall of Charmers, and went straight for the Alchemist. Nothing could stand in his way as he crushed their flimsy umbrellas like feathers in a steam bot blender. Slithering serpents tried their best to protect their master, but Elias spun his harpoon like a whirlwind, sending wings and tails scattering, flopping; flecking blood through the sky.

By now Elias was hovering over the city circle. He was close. Close enough to hurl his harpoon and strike down Sunago. He drew back the harpoon like a javelin, took careful aim and sent it soaring through the sky at the dark-winged Alchemist. The harpoon struck Sunago's green force field, sending it flipping out of control and down toward the city streets. The Alchemist turned his sights on Elias, and dark words echoed through the sky. Bolts of lightning and crashing thunder vibrated the air around him, and then everything went dark. All Elias could see was a faint glow of something where the Alchemist had been flying.

In a flash, lightning burst forth from the Alchemist's staffs and struck Elias. The electrical systems on the bot instantly shut down and the thrusters flamed out. The bot fell from the sky and bounced off of Isabella's monument, crashing down on the streets of the city circle. The world around him faded to blackest darkness.

ELIAS OPENED HIS EYES TO THE DANCING CURTAINS IN HIS TOWER bedroom. The gentle breeze pushed fresh clean air into the room, with a hint of pine at the finish. He turned his head toward his mother sitting beside him, and she dabbed the sweat from his forehead with a cloth. She smiled the most beautifully joyous smile he'd seen in years as his father entered the room with a fresh cup of coffee and handed it to her. The sun shot glorious rays of light into his bedroom as the curtains gently pushed back and forth and up and down from the soft, hypnotic breeze.

"Mom? Dad?" Elias asked. He tried to process what had happened to him. "I thought..."

"It's okay, my dear sweet boy. Everything is okay. We thought we'd lost you for a moment."

"But I..."

"It's okay, son. You blacked out, but I was able to bring you back. I think I'm really on to something here, son. I think I might have found something that could cure you. I'm so excited. It's a very promising find. As soon as you gain some strength, we can give it a try." His father seemed happy, and his smile was filled with such promise, Elias felt like maybe there might be hope for him after all.

"I-I guess I must have had a terrible nightmare."

"It's okay, darling just rest your eyes for now."

"Mom, you wouldn't believe the things I dreamed. It was…"

"You never mind those silly old nightmares. You need your rest so you can get your strength back and Father can try the new treatment."

"Dad, I'm serious. It was crazy. The things I saw were so amazing."

"Listen to your mom, okay, son? Rest is very important to the healing process right now."

"I guess my chest does hurt some." Elias said with a grimace.

"And it will soon feel much better after you've had some rest. So just close your eyes, and I'll hum you a sweet lullaby to help you forget the pain," his mother offered.

"Mom, my heart is really starting to hurt. Is everything okay? I don't feel so good all of a sudden."

"Let me take a look-see, son." His father walked over and pulled back the covers.

"WHAT! WHAT HAPPENED TO MY CHEST?" Elias screamed at the sight of a large hole cut in his chest. His beating heart was completely exposed and black as night. "AND WHAT'S WRONG WITH MY HEART? WHY IS IT ALL BLACK?" Elias cried out in terror, wondering if he'd somehow injured his heart.

"Now calm down, son. Let me take a look at it." His father reached his hand inside Elias' chest and took hold of his heart. A horribly sharp pain sent chills through his body and stole his breath away as his father's hand gripped his heart tight.

"D-D-Dad w-what's wrong with me? Mom, I thought you said it was a nightmare!" Elias was shaken with fear at what was taking place.

"Everything's going to be alright, son. It's going to be just fine. Now don't you worry," his father assured him.

Elias' mother smiled and began humming her enchanted tune as his father's hand seemed to do more harm than help. Elias didn't want to seem rude, but whatever the man was doing hurt like mad, and he just wanted it to stop. Back and forth, up and down, the curtains danced to his mother's tune as the lights in the room grew darker.

Landing just inside the window, a small, strange bird caught his eye.

"MOM! DAD! Look at that bird," Elias said. The weird creature was so captivating while it hopped up and down on the window sill as if it had gone insane with excitement. Suddenly it had the face of a man. A freakish man with strange eyes, and he was saying something.

"MOM! Look at it," Elias cried out, but she seemed embarrassed by the little creature hopping all around.

"Just ignore it, dear. Concentrate on your healing, okay?"

The little bird was incessantly persistent in its efforts to keep Elias' attention, but his mother and father seemed more annoyed than fascinated by it.

"Well, if this isn't the most unruly bird I've ever seen," his mother complained.

"But, Mom, it has a man's face. Aren't you shocked by that?" Elias was dumbstruck that his parents weren't surprised in the least by the strange bird-man. He closed his eyes and blocked out the pain in his heart so he could concentrate on the creature's whispers. Finally, he was able to make out its words.

"Darkness lies," it said over and over again as it hopped up and down in crazed madness.

Elias looked at his mother and asked, "Do you hear it, Mom? It's saying, "Darkness lies" over and over again. Is that weird?"

"I've never heard such a thing in all my life," she said, but Elias noticed how embarrassed she was at the tiny creature. Something felt different. Something was off. The pain in his chest was so sharp he felt as if he might die.

"Can you hear him, Dad? Why is he saying that? What's happening, Dad?"

"I'm afraid I don't understand, son."

The smell of coal filled his nostrils, and his father's eyes had turned bright as gold. Something in his mother's hand caught a glimmer of light from one of the sun's rays, and Elias noticed she was holding a sharp-pointed baton. Indeed, it was very strange, but he almost felt like it wanted to come to him. Almost as if the baton sensed his need for it. That it wanted him to take it, but how was that possible? How could he be connected to something made of iron?

"Can I see that, Mom?" he asked her.

"Oh, darling, you don't want that nasty old thing."

"This is all a lie, isn't it, Mother?"

"What? Don't be silly, Elias."

"You can't hear the bird, can you? But I can. Do you know why?"

"Why, darling?"

"Because only the Destroyer of the creeping mold can hear the voice of the Whispering Prince."

"Elias, stop that crazy talk. Here, I'll take care of that annoying little bird for you," his mother said, raising the sharp-pointed baton into the air. To Elias' horror, she hurled it at the little bird to kill it.

Instantly the powerful charm broke with a violent shake, and Elias awakened in the sky above the city circle, face to face with the Alchemist. Unimaginable pain struck his heart as Sunago's hand squeezed it tightly. Izzy's baton was hurling toward Prince Enupnion, who was swooping around them and shouting,

"DARKNESS LIES! DARKNESS LIES!"

Below, the crew of the Whisper had gathered, watching helplessly as the Alchemist had worked his magic on Elias for some time. By now the city was surrounded by a thousand or more moles, and was so unstable, several buildings had collapsed from the shaking.

Elias stretched out his hand toward the sky. He could feel the metal in the baton as it hurtled towards his friend. He closed his eyes and concentrated on his connection to it. Suddenly, the baton veered off course, away from his friend, and he felt it arrive in his hand. He turned toward Sunago and drove the weapon deep into his chest, like a needle searching for a cure.

Sunago was so stunned he was at a loss for words, or maybe the sharp baton stuck in his heart made it difficult to speak.

"I loved you like you were my real father," Elias said, looking into his dimming eyes. He pulled the weapon from the Sunago's chest, then smashed both globes on his staffs. Lightning spattered everywhere, and Umbrella Charmers floated in dreadful despair at the devastating blow Elias had delivered to their master. In an instant, the moles stopped and seemed at a loss over their original task to bring down the city, and they wandered in confusion for a moment, then scuttled quickly back into their tunnels.

"SUNAGO!" Cassandra cried out. Her horrified shrieks filled the clearing skies above GFC as beams of sunlight blasted through Sunago's fading wings of smoke. Then the great Alchemist and the Destroyer fell from the sky toward the city. Prince Enupnion caught Elias mid-air, but in her anger, Cassandra formed a wicked spear of black mist and launched it at them. She sliced off one of his wings, sending them both spiraling out of control. Then Cassandra caught her alchemist lover with a black hand of smoke and fled into the sky, howling with grief.

23

WHERE THE LIVING GO

*T*he crew was appalled by Cassandra's strike on the prince, and they watched him and Elias plunged toward the city. The Jackboot quickly reversed the polarity on his magnetic boots, launched himself into the sky and caught his falling son. Epekneia shot into the sky behind him to catch Enupnion, but he was covered in so much blood he slipped out of her hands and landed hard on the circle platform. Epekneia landed next to him and tried to stop the bleeding as best she could until Ava and Merlin made it over to her.

As the Jackboot lowered himself and Elias back to the platform, he called out, "BOSARUS! My personal physician. Quickly." At Elias' request, his father laid him next to Prince Enupnion while everyone worked hard to save him.

It wasn't long before Bosarus returned with the Jackboot's physician, who had been just around the corner working on Gideon. Bogan was with them, and helped Gideon, who had suffered a broken leg and several fractured ribs when he hit the light pole.

Epekneia held the leaking wound as tight as she could, but nothing could stop the leaking tears from her eyes. The physician knelt down beside Enupnion and inspected the wound. The strange Petinon was something he'd never seen nor heard of before, and he seemed at a loss for solutions. He looked up at the crew, and his eyes did most of the talking while he frowned and shook his head no.

"You're going to save him, right?" Elias asked.

"He's lost too much blood, and I believe his back is broken," the physician answered.

"You can save him, right, Merlin?" Elias asked, looking to Merlin for a small bit of hope. "Look what you did for me. You can fix anything, right?"

"I-I don't…" Merlin's voice cracked.

"There has to be something we can do," Elias demanded.

"Please. I wish to speak with Epekneia alone," The weak prince muttered softly. "Please?" he asked again. The Jackboot and the crew carried Elias as they backed away to give the Petinon's time to speak privately. At first she grew angry with him, but after a brief moment of comfort Epekneia calmed down and walked over to the crew. She looked directly at Elias and spoke.

"He wants you to have his heart."

"WHAT? NO! We have to save him. Somehow, please!" Elias begged the Jackboot.

"It's what he wants for you." she continued.

"No, I won't do it."

"Elias," Enupnion called and they returned to the platform. "Please. You must live. Besides, it's prophecy that you would have the heart of a prince. I didn't understand it at first, but I do now. Do me this honor, and don't forget your responsibility to the prophecy. You must replant."

"But I-I don't want to lose you. Y-You're the best friend I've ever had."

"Your heart is ruined, Elias. If you don't take mine, you'll die." The prince barely got through his words.

Elias paused for a moment, and through weeping he answered, "That's what they keep telling me." They both shared a small laugh at the memory of their first words together.

"You can do this, right?" the Jackboot asked his physician.

"The boy already has a hole in his chest, so it should be fairly easy as long as the hearts match up well. Rebuilding the chest won't be easy, though, and we need to do this quickly. This fellow is dying, and we can't let the heart go bad."

"WAIT! Wait—I have to—put me down, put me down," Elias demanded of his father. By now the streets around the circle began to fill with the battle-weary men and women of Grand Fortune City, and Iron Jaw did his best to keep them at bay. It wasn't every day you see mythical bird-people flying around your city and their curiosity couldn't be helped.

The Jackboot let him down next to Enupnion, and Elias embraced his old hunchback friend with weeping. It was there, during the embrace of Prince Enupnion, that Elias first laid eyes on the city monument titled "Isabella's Light". He gazed at the title plate and looked back at his sister. She smiled at him with tear-stained cheeks, and he knew at that moment he wanted to know her better and maybe even the Jackboot too. Looking back at his friend, he forced his answer through the heavy lump in his throat, "Okay."

The Jackboot's physician looked to Bosarus, "Send word to my staff—ready my operating room, and someone find me a good blade. We need to take the heart as soon as he's gone."

Everyone instantly turned to Bogan, who suddenly went pale as a ghost. "No. No. I-I can't. I... Not my knife. Any blade but mine," Bogan stammered out.

"Bogan I'm sick and tired of dealing with your attitude. I can't understand why you insist on treating him so poorly? Now hand over your blade," an exhausted and pained Gideon barked out with his last bit of strength.

"But you don't understand, Gid. Please. Anyone's knife but mine," Bogan said persistently, refusing Gideon's order.

"Give the man your blade." The Jackboot stepped in to solve the dispute with a firm tone.

"But I told him I would cut out his heart and feed it to the birds, and...and...well, he's a bird and..." Bogan said with tears rushing down his face. "I'm so sorry, mate. I-I didn't mean it. I-I never really would have done it. I was just trying to be hard with you. You know?"

Through heavy gasps, old Hunchy spoke, "Only the blade of a friend will do."

Izzy looked over at the Jackboot with a wonky eye as a tear rolled down his cheek. The Jackboot noticed her watching and tried to hide his emotion through praise, "He always keeps a sharp blade." Reluctantly, Bogan handed his blade to the physician as the whole crew gather around their dying friend.

Shuffling sounds of people filling the streets and miners already hard at work to stabilize the city tower disappeared from Elias' ears. All that remained were the shallow breaths and last words of Enupnion.

"I'll always be with you now."

The dirty hunchback—Hunchy they called him—who wasn't their enemy at all, but a prince and not just any prince, but the Whispering Prince of the Petinon people. He took his last breath under Isabella's Light, with the prophesied child he'd searched for his whole life next to him in the end.

With shocking speed, the Jackboot's physician stepped in and forced them out of the way. He made his cuts swiftly, and within moments Enupnion's heart was placed into a bag and sealed up. "Let's get moving," he said. The rest of the crew rushed Elias to surgery while Bogan remained behind with the body.

Iron Jaw called for some men to come help remove the prince, but Bogan stopped them. "NO! No one touches him!" Bogan said, kneeling down. "No one." He gently picked up the body of Enupnion and faced the crowd of people. "HE'S MY FRIEND, YOU HEAR? HE'S MY FRIEND!"

Bogan stepped off the platform and carried the prince through the crowd. The fascinated people barely moved out of the way as they gawked at the body of the winged man, so Iron Jaw scolded them. "OUT OF THE WAY! OUT OF THE WAY! HE'S CARRYING HIS FRIEND, HERE! HE'S CARRYING HIS FRIEND!"

By the time they reached the operating room, it was prepped for Elias, but there was no time for small talk or best wishes. They swiftly placed him on the table, and within seconds of an injection, darkness closed around his eyes. His last view was that of Izzy planting a big, wet kiss on his forehead, her curls soaring through the air as they pulled her away.

PUFFY, WHITE CLOUDS EXPLODED AROUND HIM AS HE SOARED through them like a missile. If this was death, then it was more exciting than he could have ever imagined. He'd never seen the sky so blue or smelled air so fresh and clean. He'd also never been told that you could fly after death. The warm air rolled over his head as he looked down at Grand Fortune City below him. As far as he could see, there wasn't a single spot of black mist floating anywhere on the horizon. He couldn't tell if he was alive or dead, but whatever it was, it felt real to him, and why complain when you can fly?

Suddenly Prince Enupnion shot through the clouds next to him, and they flew beside each other for a moment. Elias was filled with joy at the sight of his friend. "HUNCHY!" he cried out by mistake, but the prince just smiled at him.

"ELIAS! WHAT ARE YOU DOING UP HERE?" he asked.

"I'M FLYING! CAN YOU BELIEVE IT?"

"BUT YOU CAN'T FLY, ELIAS!"

"WHY NOT?"

"YOU DON'T HAVE ANY WINGS!"

Elias looked at his back and then at Enupnion with surprise in his eyes.

"GOODBYE, ELIAS!" the prince said. Instantly, he fell from the sky toward the city like a harpoon shot from the Iron Weaver, and with a terrible jolt he awoke in a room surrounded by the Whisper crew.

"HEY, SLEEPY HEAD." IZZY SAID. "GLAD YOU COULD JOIN US. You've been asleep for five days." She smiled and ruffled up his hair.

"How do you feel, kid?" Merlin asked.

"I-I think I was dreaming," Elias said, looking down at his

chest. The dark veins crawling towards his heart were now just fading memories of a terrible nightmare. A large scar traveled down the middle of his chest, and behind it beat the heart of a prince.

"Well, I hope it was a good dream," the Jackboot said with a grin.

"I think it was."

"It wasn't about her, was it?" Izzy asked, looking at Epekneia. "I'm just kidding. She's super nice. You've missed a lot in five days, right, Daddy?"

"Yes, he has, but I'll let the Petinon explain." The Jackboot said.

She stepped over to his bedside. Her wings folded so snug behind her, you could barely tell she was a Petinon, if not for the slight, feathery hump.

"I'm glad you're doing better."

"Thanks. What are they talking about?"

"I'm returning Prince Enupnion's body to his father so he can be buried among his people."

"WHAT! No, you can't go."

"Calm down, kid. Hear her out for a minute, will you," the Jackboot said.

"We're returning the prince to his father and they've all—your friends are going with me. As soon as you feel well enough, we'll be leaving," Epekneia explained.

"Daddy agreed it was a good plan. Well—not at first, but I helped him understand. Didn't I?" Izzy said with a raised eyebrow.

"Yes, you did."

"The Jackboot—I mean—your father, believes an alliance between our people will be good for everyone, and with you along they might be more willing to agree. Some won't, but maybe you can convince them," Epekneia said, cracking half a grin.

"So, when are we leaving?"

"You have to get well enough to travel first, but we're hoping soon. It will be a long journey though."

Gideon adjusted his crutches under his arms, then cleared

his throat. "Merlin's father has placed the prince's body in a cooling chamber for the journey. It looks like it may take a month to get there. We also need to make a few repairs to the Whisper before we leave, and Merlin's brother, Jimmy, will be our new pilot since we—well, since Wyatt's gone."

Bogan was leaning against the wall with his hands stuffed deep into his pockets. His usual practice of blade sharpening seemed out of place now. In fact, Elias couldn't even see the blade anywhere on his belt. He was staring at his boots and seemed alone in a room filled with friends. "You alright, Bogan?" Elias asked.

Bogan left his head down and spoke. "Out of all of us, I treated him the worst. All the cruel words and mockery, all I accused him of, he still called me friend. Why?"

"I guess he could have cursed you and made you a prisoner to your words, but it's not who he was. He just wanted to get the cure to as many as he could. Maybe you could honor him by doing the same." Elias' words brightened his face, but not as much as Ava's, who reminded Bogan that Charlie might still be alive. At which point, the room erupted into confusion, mostly since the Jackboot was unaware of Charlie's possible survival.

AFTER A FEW WEEKS OF HEALING FOR ELIAS, THE WHISPER CREW finally met out on the docks of Grand Fortune City in preparation for their journey. Street vendors had made good use of the abundance of free snake meat after the battle, but the smell of welding fumes mixed poorly with them now that reconstruction was fully underway. The miners working furiously below the city drowned out the noise of the bustling docks, and the repairs to the airships were even louder.

The crew stood waiting for the Jackboot's send off, but there was no sign of the Iron Weaver's smoke stack rising through the streets. Gideon was growing impatient, as he hoped for an early morning start, when no small commotion momentarily brought the docks to a near standstill. Horrible black smoke rolled through the crowded streets as a monstrous tank of an Ever-

Wheel stopped next to the Whisper. It let out a loud bang and a black cloud when the driver shut it off, and several battle weary people ducked for cover.

The Jackboot climbed off, dressed in his finest suit. It was firmly pressed and tailored to fit his large iron boots that glimmered in the morning sunshine. He squeezed a nice leather top hat onto his head and adjusted his lapel, then walked over toward them. He might not have known how to be a father yet, but he wasn't about to send his newly found son off with a bad impression. As he approached, Flit darted through the crowd, flashing along the way, and landed on top of his hat. Someone had to chronicle this moment. Elias and Izzy walked out to him while the citizens of GFC gazed in wonder.

"I worked on a speech all night, but it wasn't any good so—anyway—I want you two to take care of each other." He held up his hand to stop Izzy from responding. He knew when her hands popped up on her hips he was about to be scolded. "I know you've both had your share of battles, and I'm sure you can handle anything, but I have to say it. I'm sending Flit with you. When you arrive and feel safe, send him back to me, and I'll join you as soon as the city is stable. It's best I'm not there at first anyway."

With heavy clunks of his iron boots, he knelt down front of his children. "Elias—I know it's hard to believe, but I've spent years searching for you. Isabella did as well, and we just knew—somehow—we knew we would find you—and we did. I know that—that monster..."

"Daddy." Izzy stayed his anger.

"I didn't get a fair chance to be your father, and I-I just hope that one day you might give me that." He paused for a moment to swallow a lump in his throat. "Do you think you can give me..." Elias' arms exploded around him, squeezing him, before he could finish his words. Izzy couldn't contain herself and wrapped her arms around them both. Cheers erupted from the docks, and men fired off their guns in jubilation for the lost child of Owen Brock had been found, and even more so, the little girl they loved so much had finally found her brother.

After a longer than expected goodbye, Gideon was happy to finally pull the Whisper out of the dock.

The Jackboot stood at the very edge and lit his pipe as they eased out into the morning skies.

Jimmy was at the helm and practically needed no instruction for piloting the Whisper. He took them high above the clouds into the bright sunlight. Ava was bubbling with so much joy she didn't know what to do, so she sat down and started drawing everything that had happened. Bogan, Gideon and Merlin were in the command room looking over the route Epekneia gave to them, in hopes they could make better time than expected.

Elias, Epekneia and Izzy walked out onto the forward deck as they sailed into blue skies far above the creeping mold and black mist to return their friend home. The fresh, clean air filled Elias' lungs and his new heart seemed overjoyed by it. Things seemed brighter, cleaner, and fresher than ever before, as if life was just beginning. He felt new and alive—reborn.

Elias would never forget his friend. How could he? He would always carry that old hunchback with him where ever he went, even more than he could possibly imagine. From this moment on, anything in life was possible. He clicked his tongue and Casper hopped up next to him on the railing and rubbed his feathered head on Elias' chest.

It wasn't at all how he'd expected to live.

AFTERWORD

Thank you, good reader, for joining this adventure. If you enjoyed Elias Reborn, an honest review on Amazon would be greatly appreciated.

The adventure continues in Book 2: The Four Miraculous Deeds of Isabella Brock. Book 2 is a prequel that follows young Isabella through the world of Iron and Smoke and reveals how some of the Whisper Crew first met. For more information goto Joseph A Truitt: Tales of Iron and Smoke on Facebook or visit talesofironandsmoke.com for more information on this series.

Made in the USA
Lexington, KY
03 August 2019